MURDER AT THE OPERA

MURDER AT THE OPERA

AN ATLAS CATESBY MYSTERY

D. M. Quincy

CROOKED
LANE

NEW YORK

Published in the United States by Crooked Lane Books, an imprint of The Quick Brown Fox & Company LLC.

Crooked Lane Books and its logo are trademarks of The Quick Brown Fox & Company LLC.

Library of Congress Catalog-in-Publication data available upon request.

ISBN (hardcover): 978-1-64385-235-5
ISBN (ePub): 978-1-64385-236-2

Cover design by Mimi Bark
Book design by Jennifer Canzone

Printed in the United States.

www.crookedlanebooks.com

Crooked Lane Books
34 West 27th St., 10th Floor
New York, NY 10001

First Edition: December 2019

10 9 8 7 6 5 4 3 2 1

For Sameer, who possesses Atlas's finest attributes

CHAPTER 1

They emerged from the Covent Garden theater just as the black sky erupted again, spewing cold rain onto the mud-slogged streets like a frigid volcano.

Atlas Catesby had neglected to button his overcoat and regretted the oversight the moment the icy dampness sliced through him. It felt as though it had been raining for a year.

Hunching against the elements, he hoisted his black umbrella high above Lady Lilliana Sterling Warwick's hooded form to shield her from the downpour. Fat rivulets of rain clung precariously to the umbrella's edge before dripping onto the rim of Atlas's black beaver top hat, dangling momentarily and then plopping onto his cheeks and racing down to his chin as he hastened Lilliana to the waiting carriage.

Around them, hundreds of fellow theatergoers poured out of the building. Figures with bowed heads scurried toward waiting carriages and hackneys cramming the street. Other patrons streamed away on foot, an army of black umbrellas moving with the urgency and purpose of soldiers rushing toward a battle.

There was far more jostling among the throngs at the public entrances than at the exits set aside for wealthy patrons. A recent enlargement at the entrance vestibule for the well-to-do assured that he and Lilliana could depart in relative comfort after enjoying the luxurious hospitality of the Duke of Somerville's private box.

The ducal accommodation located to the side of the stage had provided an excellent view of that evening's performance. The star, the acclaimed singer Juliet Jennings, was Covent Garden's shining light. She was also a woman with whom Atlas had once been rather well acquainted.

But that felt like another life to him now.

When they reached the Earl of Charlton's rain-glistened town coach, a handsome vehicle pulled by matching grays, Atlas quickly handed Lilliana up himself rather than pausing to allow the waiting footman to do it. She settled into the forward-facing seat while he climbed in to sit opposite her on the matching tufted velvet bench. He took care to keep his long legs from crowding her.

Her face was a glimmer in the shadows of the carriage. Family obligations had contrived to keep them out of each other's company for several months—until this evening. He'd been eager to have this moment alone with her.

Her red silk evening gown contrasted favorably with her dark hair and pearl-like skin. In the theater, he'd noticed how the shade of the fabric highlighted the unique copper tinge of her magnificent eyes.

She shivered. "Will it ever stop raining?"

"This autumn has been unusually wet and cold. Windy as well," he replied, wondering when their interactions had been reduced to idle comments about the weather.

She gazed out the window into the storm. "I cannot imagine why Somerville and Charlton would care to stay out on an evening such as this." The duke and the Earl of Charlton had been among their party earlier that evening, but the two men had gone off after the performance in Somerville's coach, bound for St. James Street.

"Gentleman's clubs hold a great allure for many." Atlas had declined to join the other men, much preferring to see Lilliana home in Charlton's conveyance.

She looked away from the window. "But not for you?"

He held her gaze. "What is most alluring to me cannot be found in a gentlemen's club."

Her eyes softened. "Is that so?"

He found it difficult to hear her through the unrelenting rat-tat-tat of the rain striking the metal carriage roof. At first, he assumed the sonorous bang that cut through the clatter on the roof was thunder. But then the screaming started.

The hairs on the back of Atlas's neck rose. He couldn't immediately make sense of the spine-tingling cries, but after a moment the panicked utterings took the form of a word he could discern only too well. And there was no mistaking its meaning.

"Murder! Help! Murder!"

★ ★ ★

Atlas threw open the carriage door and leaped into the street, his feet splash-landing in a puddle, the icy dampness immediately soaking through his leather dress slippers.

"Atlas!" Lilliana's concerned voice called out from behind him. "Have a care!"

Slamming the carriage door hard behind him, he battled his way through the swirl of people and weaved through the snarled traffic. The carriageway was clogged with conveyances parked close to the theater, awaiting the return of their employers.

He moved toward a crowd gathered near the portico, where cries of distress could still be heard, pushing through the crush of elegant ladies and fashionable men, soldiers on furlough, and fruit women carrying baskets laden with oranges.

When he reached the front, Atlas peered down at the prone figure sprawled on the ground before him. The rain pouring off the rim of his top hat impeded his view while the crude oil lamps suspended from the arches overhead provided minimal light.

It was a woman. He could tell that much from her fine evening clothes. Silk and of the latest fashion. Expensive. He could not see what she looked like. In the rainy darkness, her face was lost in black shadows.

"She's been shot!" one of the soldiers exclaimed.

Shock stamped the face of a middle-aged gentleman kneeling next to the woman. He suddenly scooped her up and staggered to his feet carrying his burden. The woman's arm dangled lifelessly at her side. "Make way! Make way!" he commanded.

"I saw the one that done it." A woman's excited cry distracted Atlas from the grim scene before him. "I seen it all. The man was kneelin' beside 'er with a pistol in 'is 'and."

Atlas turned toward the voice, a fruit vendor carrying oranges in a sling around her neck. "Did you get a good look at him?"

"I saw 'im, the one that done it, wearin' black 'e is." Damp, silver-streaked hair framed a narrow, lived-in face, and she was even more rain soaked than he felt. "Almost as tall as yer lordship, but skinnier than a Seven Dials beggar compared ta ye." She pointed toward Hart Street. "'e ran that way."

Atlas scanned the crowd. It wasn't much to go on. Singling out the killer in this throng of people would be nearly impossible. But few men possessed Atlas's stature, and that was something at least.

He started in the direction of Hart Street, nudging his way through the crowd, continually searching for a tall, thin figure clad in black. The darkness, umbrellas, and relentless rain contrived to make his task all the more difficult. After about fifteen minutes of searching, by which time he was completely soaked to the skin, Atlas conceded defeat.

He made his way back to the scene of the crime, but there was little left to see. The body was gone, as were the spectators who'd swarmed around the poor woman's corpse. Atlas stood there, hands planted on his hips, still stunned by what had just occurred, considering what to do next.

"The gentry cove took 'er away." The speaker emerged from the building's shadows. Despite the rain, Atlas could discern the fruit vendor who claimed to have witnessed the murder. Something glinted in her hand. "But 'e left this behind."

Under the cloudy lighting from the oil lamps overhead, he could just make out the outline of a slender stock and a silver-encased barrel. "A pistol? Where did you find that?"

"The cull who done 'er in dropped it."

"The killer?" He stepped closer for a better look.

She retreated. "'Tis mine now, if ye take my meanin'."

He drew a few silver tokens from his pocket, enough to buy her a hot meal on this wet evening—and a few more besides that—and dropped them into her open palm. The money disappeared somewhere in her clothing before she handed her prize over.

The pistol was cold against Atlas's skin, and a chill rippled through him, knowing it had recently been used to take a life. "What is your name?"

"Mary White."

Shoving the pistol into his pocket to shield it from the rain, he raised his eyes to meet the fruit woman's gaze. "Tell me, Mary, the gentleman who carried the lady away—did you see where he took her?"

"Ta the tavern on the corner. Said 'e was goin' ta call for the doctor."

Atlas exhaled. Summoning medical help would be a pointless exercise. The poor woman had in all likelihood been dead before she'd fallen to the ground. Earlier, when the man had gathered the victim in his arms, Atlas had realized why he'd initially been unable to see most of her face.

It was no longer there.

★   ★   ★

Unsurprisingly, Lilliana was full of questions when Atlas returned to Charlton's coach to accompany her home.

He promised to call upon her on the morrow to fully apprise her of what had occurred outside the theater. But at the moment he was anxious to return to the Covent Garden tavern, where the body had been taken.

When he entered the Blue Star Tavern some thirty minutes later, he found the Westminster coroner in the taproom, busily gathering a jury for the inquest. The air smelled of roasting meat and spirits. Spotting a familiar rumpled figure in conversation near the entrance to one of the private rooms, Atlas waded through the assembled jurors who were milling about awaiting the start of the official proceeding.

"Endicott." He greeted the man.

"Mr. Catesby." Interest glimmered in the portly Bow Street runner's narrow eyes. "Do not tell me you are caught up in this murder as well."

"Unfortunately," Atlas answered grimly, still shaken by what he'd witnessed. He pulled the pistol from his pocket. In the light, he could see the weapon more clearly. It was trim and light, polished walnut with silver inlay. Not a poor man's weapon. The particularly distinctive barrel was sheathed in silver. "I was in attendance at the opera this evening."

Ambrose Endicott's bemused expression traveled from the pistol to Atlas's face. "Are you confessing to the crime?"

"I recovered this from a fruit woman on the piazza. She says the killer dropped it before he escaped. I gave chase, but to no avail."

The Bow Street runner took the pistol from Atlas, turning it over in his fleshy hands as he examined it. A disheveled appearance and distracted air made it tempting to underestimate the man, but Atlas had learned that beneath that unassuming demeanor lay a keen observer with a perceptive mind.

"This fruit woman claims to have witnessed the crime?" the runner asked.

"She does. She described the man as being about my height but very slender."

"Did you happen to catch her name?"

"She called herself Mary White. I imagine she can be found in Covent Garden most evenings." He went on to describe the woman in greater detail.

"If she is a witness, this Mary White should be present for the inquest." Endicott turned to his companion, a junior runner from the looks of it, given his youth and eager countenance, and instructed him to find the fruit vendor and return with her posthaste.

"I gather the inquest shall be held this evening?" Atlas asked after the boy had been dispatched.

Endicott nodded. "The surgeons have just completed their examination of the corpse. I expect we'll begin shortly."

Corpse. The ghastliness of it burrowed deep inside Atlas's gut. Just an hour ago, she'd been a vibrant woman enjoying an evening at the theater. And now she was no more. "Have you identified her yet?"

"Oh, yes. Yes, we have. The victim is Mrs. Wendela Pike."

"She was married then. Has her husband been notified?"

Endicott stared at him with small black eyes that appeared even more meager among the beefy folds of his face. "Surely you have heard of Wendela Pike."

"Should I have?" Atlas passed more time away from London than he actually spent in the metropolis. He seized every opportunity to leap aboard any accommodating vessel bound for a foreign land. His most recent adventure, last year, had taken him to Jamaica, and before that he'd explored Constantinople.

"Wendela Pike was no innocent. She was the queen of London's demimonde."

An unrespectable woman then. More than likely the mistress of a wealthy nobleman. "Who was her protector?"

A hush descended upon the tavern, the air tightening with expectation. Endicott looked past Atlas. "There is Mrs. Pike's protector now."

Atlas turned and stared across the taproom into the grief-ravaged face of the person he despised most in the world.

"Where is she?" Ashen-faced, Malcolm Lennox, Marquess of Vessey, stumbled into the taproom like a lost little boy. "Where is Mrs. Pike?"

The air left Atlas's lungs. He hadn't seen Vessey in more than twenty years. This wild-eyed, windblown man in a rain-splattered greatcoat bore no resemblance to the fearsome monster imprinted upon Atlas's mind, a memory stored by a frightened and distraught young boy.

With his shock of white hair and grooved face, the marquess must be past sixty now. The last time they'd met, he'd towered over the boy Atlas had been, but now the two men were of a height.

Endicott stepped toward the marquess. "My lord, we have laid Mrs. Pike out in a private room."

Every gaze in the suddenly silent tavern fixed on Vessey. Perhaps mindful of this, the man seemed to pause for a moment to gather himself before assuming command of the situation. "Take me to her this instant."

Endicott led him to the parlor. "This way, my lord."

As Vessey followed, the fascinated spectators stepped out of his way like the Red Sea parting for Moses. To be in company with a peer of the realm was rare indeed for the likes of them. Many would dine out on the tales they would tell after witnessing this dramatic spectacle.

Endicott paused before a closed door and gestured to the marquess. Vessey stepped forward and pushed it open. From his vantage point, Atlas could see a sliver of the private chamber and the lifeless figure laid out on the table. When Vessey reached his mistress's side, he crumpled. Shoulders hunched, his tall form collapsed over the body.

"Oh, Wendy," he choked out in a voice laden with emotion. "What has he done to you?" A harsh, feral sob escaped the marquess before he bent over the body and wept.

CHAPTER 2

It was almost dawn before Atlas returned to his bachelor's lodgings above a tobacconist shop on Bond Street.

Drenched and weary, he peeled off his rain-saturated vestments, dropping them to the floor as soon as he stepped into the front hall. Divested of the wet outer garments and soaked leather slippers, he continued barefoot into his sitting room and sank with great relief into his favorite stuffed chair. The lively blaze crackling in the hearth enveloped him in cozy warmth. Jamie, his young manservant, must already be about somewhere.

He inhaled the pleasant scent of the burning firewood, surprised at the comfort these lodgings brought him. It had been many years since any place had felt like home. A never-ending restlessness had plagued Atlas since his sister Phoebe's death. As soon as he'd been old enough, Atlas had begun his travels, going from country to country, exploring new lands and cultures, never settling anywhere for long.

He'd been forced to take these apartments two years ago while recovering from a carriage accident and had grown partial to the slightly shabby surroundings since then, despite often being away from Town. His friend the Earl of Charlton often lamented the garish decoration that came with the apartments—bright orange wallpaper, crimson carpets, and blue chintz furnishings—but it had all begun to have the feel of home to Atlas.

Prior to securing these accommodations, Atlas had not kept lodgings in London. He lived modestly on a limited annual income derived from a piece of property his father had bequeathed to him, while a moderate sum of money inherited from a favored bachelor uncle remained untouched.

Soaking up the fire's nourishing heat, he closed his eyes and rested his head back against the chair, his mind still absorbing the shocking events of the past several hours. He'd sat through the inquest and all of its grim details about Wendela Pike's final moments.

The bullet had practically sliced her brain in half before exiting approximately an inch behind her right ear. Several witnesses spoke, including the fruit woman, Mary White. Vessey had not stayed for the inquest. About twenty minutes after arriving at the tavern, he'd departed, leaving a footman behind to watch over the body.

Although Atlas still felt mostly numb, anger began to percolate in his gut. Vessey hadn't shed a single tear after killing Atlas's sister all those years ago, and yet the violent murder of his mistress had left the man bereft. Vessey's verbal lament the moment he laid eyes on the body clung to Atlas's memory.

"Oh, Wendy. What has he done to you?"

★ ★ ★

"Sir? I am sorry to wake you, sir." The voice of his young valet pierced Atlas's consciousness, dragging him reluctantly from a deep slumber.

Atlas's eyelids fluttered open, and he found himself staring into Jamie Sutton's large brown eyes and wide, boyish face. Through his sluggishness, Atlas tried to recall what day it was and where he was. And then he remembered. The opera. The murder. Wendela Pike. *Vessey.*

"I must have fallen asleep." The words were croaky and muffled. He cleared his throat. "What time is it?"

"Eleven o'clock, sir."

Atlas straightened in his chair, and pain shot up his neck. "Damnation." He kneaded the offending muscle. Everything ached, most especially his left foot.

He'd broken several bones in his foot in a blasted accident involving a drunken hackney driver who'd become insensible while manning the vehicle, forcing Atlas to jump to safety from the runaway carriage. That was two years past, and although doctors assured him his foot would completely heal, Atlas sometimes wondered. The injury still pained him on occasion, particularly when it was damp outside, and he remained reluctant to put his full weight on his left foot.

"I am for my bed." He rose heavily from his chair. "Do not disturb me unless the building is on fire."

"Begging your pardon, sir, but you have a visitor."

Atlas yawned. "Who is it?"

"He calls himself Samuel Brown."

"I am not acquainted with anyone of that name." He trudged toward the bedchamber, eager to bury himself under the warm blankets and pass the remainder of the day in slumberous oblivion. "Send him away."

"But—" Jamie's face reddened. "He is a man of God, sir! How am I to send him away?"

Atlas paused. "What is a clergyman doing here?"

"He said it is something to do with a murder."

Atlas instantly became more awake. "I suppose sleep shall have to wait." Mindful of his state of dishabille, he continued on to his bedchamber. "Show him in while I endeavor to make myself presentable. Then dash out and get us some coffee and something to eat."

After a quick splash of water to his face and a comb through his dark, wavy hair, Atlas donned a burgundy silk banyan and pushed his feet into worn black leather house slippers. He returned to the sitting room to find a tall, handsome young man in his twenties clad in the dark attire of a clergyman standing by the window.

"Mr. Brown," he greeted his visitor, "I am Atlas Catesby."

"I know who you are." Dark circles ringed the young man's eyes, and Atlas sensed his agitation. "I am hoping you will help me discover who killed my betrothed."

Atlas fell silent, momentarily confused. He'd naturally assumed the clergyman had sought him out in connection with the previous evening's murder. "I am sorry for your loss, Mr. Brown, but I am not certain how I can be of any help."

"I am given to understand that you found the murder weapon." Mr. Brown's words were full of urgent feeling. "Now I implore you to assist me in bringing the blackguard who killed my Wendela to justice."

Atlas thought he'd misheard. The man standing before him was easily a full decade younger than the dead woman he had seen on the piazza.

"You were betrothed to Mrs. Pike?"

"Yes, she was going to leave her sinful past behind to become my wife." The clergyman's voice broke, and he fell silent, pressing his lips together, taking a moment to compose himself. Finally, he said, "She was dearer to me than my own life."

"Please." Atlas gestured for Brown to take a seat and then did the same. "Mrs. Pike was . . . er . . . a bit older than you."

"Age was not something a man considered once he had enjoyed the pleasure of Mrs. Pikes's company. She was a shining light with a sweet and cheerful countenance." He drew a snowy kerchief from his pocket and dabbed his eyes. "Lord Vessey killed her. I am certain of it. He could not bear to lose her."

Altas's hands clenched on the armrests at the mention of Vessey. "Are you suggesting the marquess was aware that Mrs. Pike intended to leave him?"

"Mrs. Pike had promised to inform his lordship that she had transferred her affections to me and that we were intent on marrying. She had grown tired of his faithlessness."

"Meaning?"

"His lordship lives a sinner's life. Wendela feared he would afflict her with disease because of his continual pursuit of carnal pleasures outside their arrangement."

"I see." Atlas could readily see Vessey as a faithless man. But he did not know what to make of the young man before him, a clergyman who seemed on the verge of hysteria, or of his unlikely love story. "How long were you acquainted with Mrs. Pike?"

"For almost two years."

It was difficult to fathom this clergyman consorting with the queen of London's demimonde, a woman who also happened to be far older than he. "And you engaged in a liaison during all of that time?"

"Certainly not!" Brown flushed. "Despite her unfortunate circumstances, Mrs. Pike was a woman of virtue. Lord Vessey corrupted her when she was scarcely more than a girl. Fortunately, she came to see the error of her ways."

"You are suggesting that Mrs. Pike intended to leave Vessey to become a clergyman's wife?" Atlas had no idea what kind of living a minister made, but it was safe to assume he wouldn't be able to keep a woman like Wendela Pike in the same comfort as a marquess. "Had she informed Vessey of her decision?"

"That is just it. I cannot say." He wrung the white kerchief between his hands. "She had promised that she would. I have been presented a living on the East Anglian coast and intended to depart for there as soon as Wendela and I were wed."

"May I ask how you came to be acquainted with Mrs. Pike?"

"We met at Stonebrook, the marquess's country estate in Huntingdonshire."

Atlas was familiar with Stonebrook. It was where Phoebe had fallen down the stairs and broken her neck. He'd never been able to erase the sight of his sister's mangled body lying at the bottom of Vessey's massive white marble staircase.

"I quitted the army on Mrs. Pike's advice," Brown continued, "and am now wedded to the church."

"You were a soldier," Atlas said with some surprise.

"Indeed. My uncle purchased a commission for me in the Sixty-eighth regiment."

The front door squeaked open and then shut. Jamie appeared with two coffees and a tray of meat pies.

Brown waved Jamie's offering away. "My thanks, but I have been unable to eat or drink since I heard the terrible news. I may as well have perished alongside my love."

Atlas gratefully accepted the coffee. Inhaling the scent of the freshly brewed libation, he took a long, fortifying draught. Jamie withdrew with the coffee Brown had declined, which he would undoubtedly enjoy with a meat pie the boy would have kept aside for himself.

"Well?" The clergyman regarded Atlas expectantly. "Will you look into the matter?

"Bow Street is investigating." From personal experience, Atlas knew Endicott to be a thorough and competent investigator.

"Not if Lord Vessey killed her," Brown spoke bitterly. "A peer of the realm shall never be made to pay for the murder of his mistress."

The truth of Brown's words caused the coffee to turn acrid on Atlas's tongue. Vessey had already gotten away with killing Phoebe, a marchioness. Society would certainly never hold him to account for the death of an unrespectable woman like Wendela Pike.

"Very well," Atlas said. "I shall make some inquiries."

★　★　★

Having reluctantly relinquished any immediate hopes of Morphean bliss, Atlas decided to call upon Lilliana as he'd promised he would the previous evening.

Leaving his apartments, he trotted down the stairs and onto Bond Street. Last night's deluge had eased into a dreary drizzle, leaving carriages to trudge through mud-slogged streets. As Atlas stepped onto the stone pavement that protected pedestrians from the boggy road, he spotted his friend, the Earl of Charlton, alighting from a familiar shiny carriage in front of the tobacco shop below Atlas's apartments. The earl's vibrant emerald tailcoat provided a flash of color on an otherwise gray day.

"Atlas," Charlton called out in greeting as he stepped onto the pavement. A tall, well-built footman hoisted an umbrella high above the nobleman's precisely ruffled golden hair to shelter him from the rain. "I hear you had quite a bit of excitement after Somerville and I took our leave last evening."

"Unfortunately." Atlas followed Charlton into the shop. "It is a grim affair."

Charlton's focus went to the petite proprietor behind the long, wooden counter that ran almost the full length of the narrow shop. Jars filled with varieties of hand-blended tobaccos lined the shelves behind her. "Good day, Mrs. Disher."

Olivia Disher's eyes twinkled. "My lord." The young widow had taken control of her husband's shop after his unexpected death the previous year and was now engaged in a liaison with Charlton. "Will you be having the nargileh this afternoon?"

"No, not the hookah today." He removed his hat. "I believe I shall try that new blend you have been raving about."

She appeared pleased. "Very good, my lord."

Charlton continued on toward the wood-and-glass-fronted smoking room at the rear of the shop. Since commencing his affair with Mrs. Disher, the earl had made a very public show of frequenting her establishment. The exposure seemed to have achieved its purpose. Atlas noticed that patrons now roamed the shop floor at all hours. A half-dozen men currently indulged their habit in the smoking room and seemed to be surreptitiously watching them.

"Are they awaiting your arrival?" Atlas asked.

"To be sure. I have made it known that I can be found in Mrs. Disher's smoking room on Wednesdays."

"And I suppose those who aspire to be fashionable present themselves at those times."

"Naturally." Charlton spoke as if adulation was his due, given his gilded good looks, wealth, and noble title.

Atlas shook his head with a smile. "Naturally." He marveled that he and his closest friend could be so dissimilar. Theirs was an unlikely friendship that had begun at university, where Charlton had sought Atlas out precisely because he was one of the few students who'd neglected to fawn over the young heir to a wealthy earldom.

Charlton paused outside the smoking room while the gentlemen within made a show of pretending not to watch him. "About this nasty business at Covent Garden—did you see the cur who killed Mrs. Pike?"

Atlas shook his head. "No, but I heard the shots. By the time I reached her, there was nothing that could be done. She died where she fell."

"Ghastly."

"Were you acquainted with Mrs. Pike?"

Charlton paused before replying. "I did . . . have the pleasure," he said with some awkwardness.

Atlas studied his friend. Surely Charlton and Mrs. Pike hadn't engaged in a dalliance. "You and she were not—"

"Certainly not," Charlton interjected before Atlas could complete the sentence. "As I understand it, Mrs. Pike was not free with her favors."

"I have heard the same could not be said of Vessey."

Charlton dipped his chin. "The marquess is known to enjoy the company of various women."

One of the smokers inside the glassed room ran out of patience and opened the door, bringing the smell of burning tobacco with him. "Good afternoon, my lord."

"Ah, Seaton," the earl drawled. "Have you come to partake in Mrs. Disher's fine blended tobaccos?"

"Indeed, my lord. Will you not join us?"

"I should de delighted." Charlton turned to Atlas with what seemed like relief in his vibrant blue eyes. "Duty calls," he murmured, stepping into the hazy chamber and firmly pushing the door shut behind him.

CHAPTER 3

"I cannot believe the victim is Wendela Pike," Lilliana said to Atlas.

"You are familiar with the name?"

"Of course. I expect most of London is."

"Apparently I am the sole person in the entire country who had no idea who Mrs. Pike was."

"She was quite notorious." Lilliana scooted to the edge of the stuffed peach sofa to pour the tea. She wore a becoming white muslin morning dress with lace at the high neckline and dangling from the cuffs.

She'd received him in her private upstairs sitting room, a sunny chamber she'd refurbished to her own tastes once she'd reunited with her brother after a decade apart.

"What do you know about Mrs. Pike?" he asked.

"Gentlemen are said to have found her most appealing. You will have heard that she was the Marquess of Vessey's special friend." She spoke cautiously, supremely aware that the subject of his former brother-in-law was a sensitive one for Atlas.

"Yes, Endicott, the Bow Street runner, informed me as much. He was at the inquest." Tea in hand, he took a seat opposite her.

Atlas belatedly realized he'd settled in a new chair, one large enough to comfortably accommodate his brawny form. The last time he'd visited, he'd worried the spindly legs of a dainty cream silk bergère would collapse under his weight. He noticed now that the bergère had been set aside in a corner.

"And then Vessey himself came in to view the body," he said.

"The marquess went to the tavern?" Interest lit her beautiful autumn-hued eyes. It dawned on him how deeply he had missed Lilliana in the months they'd been apart. "Did you speak with him there?"

"No, I doubt that he took any notice of my presence. His focus was solely on Mrs. Pike." He crossed one knee over the other. "Vessey seemed truly distraught when he laid eyes on what was left of her. But he is not the only admirer left devastated by Mrs. Pike's demise."

Lilliana paused in the act of bringing the teacup to her lips. "How do you mean?"

Atlas relayed the events of that morning, telling her about his morning visitor's claims that Mrs. Pike had intended to leave her protector. "And so," he said in conclusion, "the question is whether Mrs. Pike told Vessey she intended to leave him and whether that revelation drove him to violence. I imagine it would have been an intolerable shock for Vessey to be jilted for an impecunious clergyman."

"I think all of society would have been stunned," Lilliana remarked. "I have heard they lived together practically as man and wife. She presided as mistress of Stonebrook whenever his heir was not in residence."

"How do you know so much about Vessey?"

An appealing blush deepened against her creamy skin. "Naturally, once I realized your connection to him, I made some inquiries. Out of curiosity, you understand."

"He killed my sister. I would not be surprised if he did the same to his mistress."

"But why have her murdered in Covent Garden of all places? Why in such a public arena, where it was bound to draw attention?"

"I do not know." He pondered that. Lilliana had a valid point. The last thing a peer such as Vessey would care to do is purposefully draw attention to himself in such a sordid manner.

Lilliana sipped her tea. "The man who carried Mrs. Pike to the tavern after she was injured—did he see anything?"

"Very little. He spoke at the inquest." Atlas helped himself to a bread-and-butter sandwich. "The man is a banker by the name of Walter Drummond. He claims to have had only a passing acquaintance with Mrs. Pike. He encountered her just moments before the shooting and offered to escort her to her carriage."

"Where was Mrs. Pike's escort for the evening?"

"I have no idea. Mr. Drummond said he exchanged the briefest of pleasantries with Mrs. Pike after spotting her outside the theater. When she first fell to the ground, he assumed Mrs. Pike had fainted and knelt to assist her. It was only then that he realized she was mortally wounded."

Lilliana shuddered. "How terrible." She paused and he could see her thinking. "Who then was Mrs. Pike's escort or companion? No woman attends the theater alone."

"I had not thought to wonder about her escort for the evening. I suppose that is as good a place as any to begin my inquiry." He reached for a biscuit. Atlas was a great admirer of the Somerville cook's culinary skills. The food was always sublime. "Did your boys enjoy the country?"

"Very much. Somerville acquired an Arabian for each of them." Lilliana had two young sons, Peter and Robin. "They were loath to return to Town until he allowed them to bring their mounts with them." She shook her head, but Atlas could see that she was pleased. "Somerville spoils them terribly."

He marveled at the thought of Peter and Robin piercing the duke's glacial exterior. "I should like to see them ride one day."

"They would enjoy that." She paused. "And your brother? How does he fare?"

"Apollo is much improved. The doctor anticipates a full recovery." His brother's riding accident was the reason Atlas had not been in Lilliana's company since the summer. He'd been forced to quit Town rather suddenly in order to attend to Apollo at the family home in Berkshire. "You received my note, I trust, explaining why I departed for Langston Park without properly taking my leave of you?"

She nodded. "Yes, of course. Your brother had need of you. I understood completely."

He'd been with Lilliana in the garden of Somerville's palatial townhouse when he'd received news of Apollo's accident. A disagreement between the two of them had just concluded in a most delightfully unexpected way when they'd been interrupted.

"Did you pass the entire summer in Berkshire?" she inquired.

"No, I remained there about six weeks, until I was assured of Apollo's recovery." And then he'd hastened back to Town only to discover, to his regret, that Lilliana had already left for the country with her children and the duke.

"You must have been most disappointed to miss your voyage to India." She shifted to pour him more tea, and he admired the grace of her actions. "You had already booked your passage."

Easing forward to take the tea, Atlas looked into her eyes. "Apollo's accident is not the reason I decided not to go abroad."

"Oh?"

"I stayed because we left matters between us unsettled."

"Yes." She leaned ever so slightly toward him. An air of expectation swirled between them. "We certainly did."

"And I should like to speak honestly about what occurred."

She regarded him expectantly. "Yes?"

They were interrupted by a discreet tap on the door, followed by the appearance of the butler.

Hastings clasped his hands behind his back. "I beg your pardon, my lady, but His Grace requests that Mr. Catesby attend him in the library."

Lilliana did not hide her surprise. "Whatever for?"

"His Grace mentioned something about being in possession of information that might be of interest to Mr. Catesby."

Atlas wondered what Somerville might know. "Perhaps I should go in now," he said to Lilliana.

"Indeed." She glided to her feet. "I shall accompany you."

"Lead on, my lady."

The duke was awaiting their arrival. Atlas had visited Somerville's library once before, but that previous experience did not keep him from once again being struck by its grandiosity. Soft blues and vivid golds swathed the massive two-story chamber. Books seemed to line the walls as far as Atlas could see, the soaring book stacks almost reaching the ornate gilded plasterwork on the ceiling.

"Ah, Catesby, there you are." The duke's precise tones echoed off the high walls of the cavernous room. Impeccably attired as always, the young duke's slender form was ensconced in one of the chamber's two facing deep velvet sofas, where the afternoon light slanted across Somerville's coffee-colored eyes, strong cheekbones, and soft jaw.

"Your Grace," Atlas bowed. "I confess that you have piqued my interest."

"And mine." Lilliana perched on the armrest of the sofa, opposite her brother. "So I decided to come along to hear what you have to say."

Somerville did not appear surprised to see her. "Naturally, I would expect no less of you, Roslyn." At times, it still took Atlas aback to hear anyone refer to Lilliana as Roslyn, even though that was her given name. When Atlas had first met the duke's sister, she'd gone by Lilliana, her middle name, and was known simply as Mrs. Warwick, a tradesman's widow.

Somerville gestured for Atlas to take a seat on the sofa. Although he exhibited the confidence and self-possession of someone twice his age, the duke was a young man, somewhere in his mid-twenties. He'd taken up his responsibilities early, before his twentieth birthday, just a few short years after his and Lilliana's parents had perished in a carriage accident, orphaning the young heir and his two sisters. "I understand you found the weapon used in last evening's unfortunate incident in Covent Garden. "

"Yes, that is true." Atlas wondered why the duke had summoned him. Somerville wasn't the sort to take a prurient interest in the gruesome murder of a fallen woman.

"Will you be investigating the matter?"

"As it turns out, yes, I shall be. A young clergyman who claims he was Mrs. Pike's betrothed has asked me to look into her death."

The duke wore a look of pure astonishment. "Mrs. Pike was betrothed to another?"

"I have no way of knowing if the man speaks the truth, but that is what he claims."

"I certainly have not heard that. What is this clergyman's name?"

"Samuel Brown."

The duke's forehead puckered. "I would find such a connection very difficult to believe. Mrs. Pike appeared to be completely devoted to Vessey."

"You were acquainted with her?"

"I met Mrs. Pike when I attended Vessey's famous oratorios."

"Vessey hosts oratorios?"

"Yes, twice a year. They are quite elaborate, with an orchestra, a choir and soloists, costumes—all of it."

Hosting such musical entertainments seemed entirely too civilized for the brute who'd wed Atlas's sister more than twenty years ago.

"The marquess holds one at Christmastime and another in the summer," Somerville continued. "Some of the finest professional performers in the country are often invited to perform at Stonebrook."

"And Mrs. Pike was present?" It surprised Atlas that Vessey's mistress would have kept company with Vessey's noble guests, particularly someone as exalted and as bound by propriety as the duke.

"Not only was she present, she was arguably the shining light of the proceedings." Somerville draped a pale manicured hand over the high armrest. "She played the harpsichord and possessed a beautiful singing voice."

Atlas rarely mixed with society's highest-born denizens, but it struck him as deuced odd that an unrespectable woman like Mrs. Pike would mingle freely among the marquess's guests. "And gentlewomen were in attendance?"

"Yes, some, although I did not see Mrs. Pike converse with any of them."

Lilliana puffed a surprised breath. "I thought men hid their mistresses away in some sort of love nest. I have certainly never met a disreputable woman at a social event."

Somerville fixed a chilly dark gaze on his sister. "This conversation should not be held in the presence of a gently born lady, which is why," he said pointedly, "you were not asked to join us."

Lilliana looked skyward. "Pray do not be ridiculous." Atlas watched the interaction between Lilliana and her brother with some amusement. Lilliana was probably the only person in London who was completely uncowed by the considerable force of Somerville's glacial displeasure. "In the ten years we were apart, my dear brother, I was wed and most certainly exposed to the more unsavory aspects of life."

Somerville looked pained. "There is no need for us to revisit that unfortunate time, nor to continue your miseducation."

Lilliana did not budge. "If you have information that will help Mr. Catesby learn who murdered Mrs. Pike, pray do not let my delicate ears prohibit you from sharing it."

"Very well." The duke gave an almost imperceptible shake of his head that prompted Atlas to suppress a smile. Somerville was clearly unused to being disobeyed or challenged. He ably presided over an immense and lucrative duchy and had entry to all of London's finest abodes, even those of the royal princes, yet His Grace seemed to be at a loss as to how to manage his own sister.

Somerville addressed Atlas. "Mrs. Pike resided with Vessey for more than two decades."

"I see." Atlas felt lightheaded. *Twenty years.* That meant Vessey had taken up with Wendela Pike immediately after Phoebe died. "It was a serious affair then."

"Precisely. Mrs. Pike presided over Vessey's table and managed his household."

Atlas suppressed a curse. The whoreson had wasted no time moving his mistress into his sister's place at Stonebrook. He had not expected Vessey to mourn Phoebe, but this blatant disrespect for her memory stirred his emotions—and added more fuel to his simmering hatred for the man.

Atlas clasped his hands behind his back to keep from clenching them into fists. "Mrs. Pike was a demi-rep, then." The realization that Vessey might be capable of tender feeling but had spared none of that affection for Phoebe roused his temper. "Are there children?"

"Yes. Two, I believe. Both quite young, under the age of twelve as I understand it."

"A demi-rep?" Lilliana interjected. "What is that?"

Atlas clamped his mouth shut. He certainly was not going to be the one to enlighten her, particularly not in the presence of her brother.

Somerville sighed his resignation. "A demi-rep," he explained with obvious reluctance, "is a woman of dubious moral character. A woman who is more than a man's casual mistress but also, obviously, far less than a respectable wife."

Atlas's mind reeled from the realization that Nicholas, Phoebe's son with Vessey, had half sisters. "Are the girls Vessey fathered with Mrs. Pike being raised alongside his heir?"

"As I understand it, Vessey keeps all of that away from Beaumont," the duke replied. "He preferred for his prized heir not to be tainted by any association with Mrs. Pike and her children."

Beaumont. Atlas had forgotten that Nicholas held the courtesy title of Viscount Beaumont. An infant at the time of his mother's death, Nicholas was now a young man of one-and-twenty, but Atlas knew almost nothing about the boy. Vessey had cut off all contact between Nicholas and the Catesbys after Phoebe's funeral.

The whoreson had deprived Atlas's family of both Phoebe and her son. When Atlas had finally met the young man by chance last spring, the encounter had been extraordinarily awkward.

"Is this why you summoned me?" Atlas asked the duke, still unsure as to the purpose of this meeting. "To discuss the murder?"

"I found Mrs. Pike to be quite charming and extraordinarily talented. I liked her very much."

Lilliana stared at her brother. "Surely you and Mrs. Pike were not—" Her voice trailed off.

Somerville flushed. "Certainly not," he said cuttingly. "I merely found her to be quite amiable, and I should like to see her killer brought to justice."

Atlas had no doubt that Somerville had never been intimately acquainted with Mrs. Pike. He was in a position to know that the duke had a secret working-class lover, a person who happened to be of similar birth to the late Mrs. Pike. But that was not the reason society would find the liaison shocking—scandalous even—were it ever to be made public.

Atlas addressed the duke. "I gather you and Vessey are very well acquainted."

"Not especially. I have attended a handful of his oratorios over the years. And since her return home, Lilliana has insisted we decline all invitations from Stonebrook."

Atlas's surprised gaze flew to Lilliana, but she was studying her brother. "Was Mrs. Pike friendly with other gentlemen?"

Somerville grimaced. "You might very well be comfortable discussing life's more unsavory topics, but I do not care to entertain these conversations in your presence."

Lilliana made a sound of frustration, the chill between the siblings so glacial Atlas suppressed the urge to shiver. It was like two ice statues confronting each other.

Atlas turned to the duke. "Is there anything else you can tell me about Mrs. Pike that might be helpful to the investigation?"

"As I said, I was not well acquainted with Mrs. Pike. However, you might care to ask Charlton."

"Charlton?" Atlas blinked. "Why would I ask him?"

"He attends the marquess's oratorios," the duke answered, "and is a frequent guest at Stonebrook."

CHAPTER 4

Atlas paused outside the imposing building on Charing Cross that housed Drummond's Bank.

He'd decided to commence his inquiry with Walter Drummond, the man who'd encountered Wendela Pike outside the theater and shared her final moments.

Eager to take advantage of a brief lull in the rain, Atlas had walked to his destination by way of Pall Mall. He relished the opportunity to at last stretch his legs, which the soggy weather had denied him for far too long. The exertion always helped to clear his mind. He'd forced aside the lingering shock and deep sense of betrayal after discovering that Charlton, his dearest friend, had consorted with his greatest enemy. He would deal with Charlton later.

A few discreet inquiries had revealed that Drummond, a descendant of the bank's founder, was a prosperous banker with a number of diverse holdings. He was a man of wealth but only limited social standing given his status as a merchant.

Atlas wondered whether Drummond might have been the victim's escort for the evening. And if so, might the banker hesitate to admit that he'd accompanied Mrs. Pike to the theater for fear of incurring the wrath of Vessey, a powerful peer?

Atlas entered the bank lobby and made his way past soaring white columns to speak with one of the clerks at work behind the dark paneled counter. Drummond agreed to see Atlas immediately.

"Do come in." He ushered Atlas into a sleek office furnished with polished woods. "Benton," Drummond called out into the lobby after Atlas entered the office, "bring us some tea."

The banker invited Atlas to take a seat. "It was a dreadful, dreadful business. I thought she had swooned."

"You did not hear the shot?"

The banker sat opposite Atlas. "It was terribly noisy, with the storm and crush of people, the clatter of the carriages. I suppose I thought it was thunder at first. Until I realized Mrs. Pike had been shot. I understand you found the murder weapon."

"A fruit vendor did. I recovered it from her."

Drummond regarded him with great interest. "The Marquess of Vessey is said to be inconsolable."

As ever, the mention of his former brother-in-law sliced through Atlas like a bitter winter gale. "Did you speak with Mrs. Pike at all before the unfortunate incident?"

"Just as I said at the inquest, we exchanged niceties. I was not very well acquainted with the woman. How is Vessey faring?"

The question threw Atlas off. "I have no idea."

"But the two of you are family, are you not?" Drummond pressed. "After all, your nephew is Vessey's heir."

The reason Drummond had instantly agreed to see him dawned on Atlas. The banker was eager to engage in gossip regarding Mrs. Pike's death.

"My sister passed more than twenty years ago," Atlas said. "My family's connection to Vessey ended at that time."

"But surely you see your nephew?"

Atlas attempted not to show his irritation. "So you were not Mrs. Pike's escort?"

"No, decidedly not. I do not believe she had an escort. She said the marquess was meant to accompany her but that he had gone to his club instead. I myself met a friend, and we sat in the gallery. As you can imagine, a woman like Mrs. Pike would hardly sit in the gallery. Surely she was accustomed to the comforts of Vessey's box."

They quieted momentarily when the clerk came in with the tea, which Atlas found to be surprisingly good, strong and aromatic.

"Did you see Mrs. Pike in the marquess's box during the performance?" he asked when they were alone again. Atlas himself had not. But then again, he had no idea which box belonged to Vessey.

"I did not." Drummond bit into a biscuit. "The marquess's box remained unoccupied for the entire evening."

"You are familiar with the location of Vessey's box?"

"I make a point of being aware of such things. I am a man of business. People such as the marquess are, of course, my patrons. I myself am not an admirer of the theater, you understand. However my patrons, as well as future customers whom I wish to cultivate, often are."

Atlas glanced around the high-ceilinged chamber and wondered whether Vessey's considerable fortune was deposited in this bank. Drummond would not divulge his customer list, which most banks kept confidential. But a financial association with Vessey would be incentive enough for Drummond to hide any illicit relationship he might have enjoyed with Mrs. Pike.

Atlas leaned forward and lowered his voice. "Anything you tell me about your acquaintance with Mrs. Pike shall be held in complete confidence."

Drummond burst out laughing so suddenly that tea spurted out of his mouth. "I do beg your pardon." He wiped his mouth with a kerchief produced from his pocket. "If you are suggesting that I had a liaison with Mrs. Pike—"

"I am not suggesting anything," Atlas said. "It just strikes me as rather odd that any woman would attend the theater alone."

"Yes, I thought so too."

"Perhaps you could walk me through the evening, beginning with when you first encountered Mrs. Pike at the theater."

"Certainly." He settled back in the chair with his tea in hand, as though preparing for a long and friendly chat. "I did not see Mrs. Pike until after the performance. I noticed she was outside alone, unescorted, and so I went to her. We chatted briefly while she waited for her carriage. We could see that her driver was caught in traffic, so I left her and went to see if I could help direct her coach to where she stood waiting."

"And then the shot rang out."

"I suppose, although I really did not realize it was a gunshot. I supposed it was thunder. But then the commotion started just as her coach finally arrived. I had turned back to go and escort her to the carriage. People began crowding around the area where I had left Mrs. Pike."

"When did you realize she had been injured?"

"Not until I fought my way through the crowd and finally reached her. My first thought was to pick the poor woman up and see if I could get her to a doctor. I realize now that it was a futile endeavor, but at the time, in my shock, I thought perhaps there might be some way to save her."

"Did you see her assailant?"

"No. As I told you, by the time I turned around, all I saw was the crowd surrounding Mrs. Pike. At that time, I didn't even realize she'd been shot, so it would not have occurred to me to look for her killer."

Atlas drank more tea. If the banker hadn't been Mrs. Pike's escort, then where had Mrs. Pike sat during the show? "No one seems to have seen her in the theater during the performance."

"She told me she watched from the wings."

"From the wings?"

"Backstage." Drummond set his tea down and reached for another biscuit. "When I encountered her outside the theater, I mentioned to Mrs. Pike that I had not seen her in the marquess's box, and she replied that she had watched the performance from backstage."

"Was she acquainted with the performers?"

"I have no idea."

Perhaps Mrs. Pike had befriended the Covent Garden performers who had performed at Vessey's famed oratorios. As he pondered the possibilities, Atlas bit into a biscuit. It was dry and stale, a disappointment, especially in comparison to the incomparable biscuits he'd recently consumed at Somerville House.

"May I ask what your interest is in Mrs. Pike?" Drummond inquired.

"I have been asked to look into her death."

"Ah, I see." Curiosity lingered in the banker's eyes, and Atlas feared he'd whetted the man's natural interest in the affairs of others. "The marquess no doubt has turned to you because you were once family."

"Not exactly." Atlas came to his feet, even though he would have liked to finish his tea. But he had no inclination to feed the banker's desire for idle talk. "I shan't take up any more of your time. You have been most helpful."

He could feel Drummond's disappointed gaze following him as he departed.

★   ★   ★

"Atlas, there you are." Thea Palmer looked up as her brother entered the crowded dining room of her home on Great Russell Street. "I thought you'd forgotten."

"As if you would allow that." He greeted the assembled guests around the long table. "My apologies for being late."

Consumed with the investigation, Atlas *had* almost forgotten that evening's engagement but dared not confess the failing to his exacting sibling.

His mood lifted when his gaze met Lilliana's. He hadn't known she'd be in attendance, though he was not surprised. Thea had once provided shelter for Lilliana when the duke's sister had had nowhere else to go. The two women had been great friends since.

Charlton was also present, as were two of Thea's mathematician friends, a couple named Ernest and Hester Gulliver. Atlas and Thea's elder brother, Hermes, rounded out their group.

Atlas tread over the old parquet floors to take the empty seat next to Charlton. The battered mahogany chair groaned under his full weight.

"I thought my chair would collapse when I sat in it," Charlton murmured to him. The earl was turned out in his customary bright colors. He adjusted a snowy, frilled cravat, which was paired with a paisley waistcoat and matching solid puce tailcoat. "Your sister will likely seat us on the floor once these ancient seats finally give way."

Thea was not a spendthrift—quite the opposite. She did not believe in unnecessary luxury and waste. As long as an item remained somewhat serviceable, Thea refused to replace it. Mr. Palmer had had his eye on a residence off fashionable Cavendish Square in Mayfair, but Thea had insisted on remaining in their mellow brick mansion on Great Russell Street. She preferred the shabby splendor of middle-class Bloomsbury, with its doctors, artists, writers, and politicians, to snobbish Mayfair.

"I trust Mr. Palmer is well," Mrs. Gulliver said to Thea.

Thea gestured for the attending footman to fill Atlas's wine glass. "Oh yes, busy as ever with his lands in the country."

"Which no doubt keep Farmer Palmer hearty and hale," Charlton remarked. "All of that country air can be so tiresomely bracing."

It was not unusual for Mr. Palmer to be absent. Although the couple appeared devoted to each other, Charles and Thea Palmer had spent most of their long marriage apart, with Thea in the metropolis, surrounded by her mathematician friends, and Palmer tending to their vast farm in the country. Atlas had always suspected that Palmer would prefer to spend more time in his wife's company, but Thea appeared content with the unusual arrangement.

"I hear you have undertaken a new investigation," Thea said to her brother.

"Yes." Atlas reached for his wine. "It is a dreadful business."

The footmen came in and arranged a variety of dishes in a precise symmetrical arrangement on the table, bathing the dining room in the mouth-watering scents of basted pork leg, haricot mutton, and freshly cooked pastries. Since Thea did not stand on ceremony, her guests mostly served themselves from the meat and fish dishes, along with a variety of puddings, sweet pies, and tarts. The foods were laid out under the wobbly direction of Thea's ancient butler, another old thing she refused to get rid of.

Thea leaned forward to carve the meat for her guests, serving Lilliana first. On the opposite end of the table, Herm was obliged to do the same for the guests nearest to him.

Thea placed a slice of lamb on Atlas's plate. "Do you think Vessey did it?" she asked quietly. "Where was he when it happened?"

"At a gentleman's club with plenty of witnesses."

"How convenient."

"Isn't it? But he could easily have engaged someone to do away with Mrs. Pike."

A roar of laughter sounded at the opposite end of the table, where Herm regaled the Gullivers with the story of an outrageous bet he'd recently won. Herm's primary vocation in life was maintaining a fashionable appearance, including artfully unruly hair, which was painstakingly achieved by infrequent washing and the careful application of hair wax.

Atlas sipped his wine. "Perhaps we should ask Charlton if he thinks his friend is capable of killing not one, but two women."

Charlton blinked. "My friend?"

"Vessey." As Atlas spoke, a decided chill descended on their side of the table. "I understand you socialize with him quite frequently."

Thea stared at Charlton. "Is that true?"

Charlton flushed. "Where did you hear that?"

Atlas took another draught of wine. "Certainly not from you," he said, resentment edging the words.

"Somerville mentioned that you attend Vessey's oratorios," Lilliana explained to Charlton.

"That is true." Charlton cleared his throat. "I have gone on occasion. The affairs are not intimate in nature. There were many others in attendance."

Atlas's curiosity trumped his vexation with his friend. "I presume that you met Mrs. Pike?" he could not resist asking.

"I did. In fact, she is the sole reason I attended."

Charlton's revelation provoked another outburst from Thea. "You were one of Mrs. Pike's admirers?"

"Solely on the basis of her talent." At Thea's raised eyebrow, Charlton hastened to clarify. "She possessed the voice of an angel, the most beautiful singing voice I have ever had the pleasure to hear."

Lilliana nodded. "I have heard that. Somerville said as much."

"What was she like?" Thea asked.

"Very lively and engaging." Charlton set his fork down. "But I did not envy Mrs. Pike her place in Vessey's household."

"Why ever not?" Atlas said coolly. "As I understand it, she presided over his table and ran his household." *As Phoebe once had and should still.*

"Because he never allowed Mrs. Pike to forget her place."

"How so?" Lilliana inquired of Charlton. "Somerville says Vessey often appeared with Mrs. Pike in public, at concerts and such."

"Yes, but at Stonebrook he required that she behave in a much more circumspect manner. Supper invitations to Stonebrook did not extend to ladies due to Mrs. Pike's presence. And when a lady of rank attempted to speak with Mrs. Pike at one of the oratorios, Vessey immediately cautioned the lady that there were certain lines he did not wish to see crossed in his home. That included having a lady of quality acknowledge Mrs. Pike in any way."

"What a horrible man!" Thea exclaimed. "To flaunt his association with Mrs. Pike in public but then also to feel the need to humiliate her before his guests."

"I confess I did feel badly for Mrs. Pike." Charlton dabbed the corners of his mouth with his linen serviette. "She was clearly terribly embarrassed and promptly excused herself. Vessey's cruelty greatly dampened my enjoyment of the evening."

Atlas gestured for the footman to refill his glass. "Yet it did not keep you from continuing to avail yourself of the marquess's hospitality."

"Why are you all so serious?" Herm's gay voice cut into the tension at their end of the table. "Thea, this pudding is delicious." He helped himself to another serving.

Mr. Gulliver directed his conversation in their direction. "Mr. Catesby, did I hear that you are investigating the murder at Covent Garden?"

Atlas cut into the quickly cooling lamb on his plate. "I am making some inquiries."

Mrs. Gulliver leaned forward. "Have you heard anything new as of yet?"

"Yes." Atlas cut a glance in Charlton's direction. "I have learned one or two most surprising things."

CHAPTER 5

The following afternoon, two days after Mrs. Pike's unfortunate demise, Atlas hoisted his black umbrella high above his head to shelter himself from the drizzling rain as he set out for Covent Garden.

If Mrs. Pike had indeed watched the performances from backstage on the evening of her death, the theater manager, a man Atlas learned was named Simon Cooke, would likely be in a position to know who had made those arrangements for her.

Atlas entered through the Bow Street entrance, purposely avoiding the Covent Garden door and its proximity to where Wendela Pike had taken her last breath. The building retained a sense of newness, having been rebuilt just a few years back after a fire had gutted the theater. Atlas passed white-veined marble walls and a wide, grand stone staircase, which led to the boxes where Atlas had watched the performance with the Duke of Somerville's party two evenings ago.

A worker in the front lobby directed him to the spacious pit, the viewing area with the least expensive seats in the venue. Simon Cooke stood near the stage, directing a boy of about twelve on the removal of stains from seats covered in light blue cloth and edged in scarlet.

As it turned out, the man was not unfamiliar to Atlas. He realized he'd seen Cooke the previous evening, although Atlas hadn't known who he was. The Covent Garden manager had wandered the corridor outside the boxes frequented by nobles, stopping here and there to inquire if all was well. His manner had been polite, engaging, and appropriately respectful as he'd interacted with patrons who were among London's highest born.

"Some of last evening's patrons imbibed too much gin and cast their accounts," Cooke explained once Atlas introduced himself. "It must be cleaned before the spots become permanent."

Cooke, a former actor, held himself like a person who knew his worth. A man of middle years, with graying hair at the temples, Cooke possessed a distinguished air and still retained his good looks despite a slight thickness around the waist. It was not difficult to envision this man commanding the stage in his younger years.

"I have come to inquire about Mrs. Pike," Atlas said.

"What is your interest in her?" Cooke pressed a hand against watery red eyes.

"I would like to find her killer and make certain he faces justice."

Cooke sniffed, bringing a kerchief to his nose. "I do beg your pardon. I have been feeling poorly for more than a week now." He blew his nose. "But the theater goes on and so must I."

Last evening the theater manager had given every appearance of energetic good health. Atlas marveled at the man's acting ability; he'd certainly hidden his ailment well.

Atlas propped his closed umbrella against an end seat. "I understand that on the evening of her death, Mrs. Pike watched the performance from the back of the stage rather than from her usual seat in the Marquess of Vessey's box." Atlas's gaze wandered up to the cream, pink, and gold-fronted boxes supported by gold fluted columns. "Do you know who invited her to watch the show from there?"

"Yes, I do." Cooke gave a light cough. "I invited her."

"And why was that?"

"I was trying to convince her to come and sing for me here at the theater."

Atlas recalled Charlton saying Mrs. Pike possessed the voice of an angel. "You are suggesting Mrs. Pike was talented enough to sing professionally?"

"Absolutely. Unlike other demi-reps, Mrs. Pike had true talent outside the bedchamber." Cooke's voice grew wistful. "She possessed the finest singing voice I have ever had the pleasure to hear."

"And you were prepared to engage her."

"Yes, indeed. I was of the opinion that her voice would do very well for the stage, and I told her so. I would have paid her more than Juliet Jennings."

Atlas blinked. "But I was under the impression that Mrs. Jennings is the toast of London."

"She is at the moment. However, Mrs. Pike possessed the superior voice. She had a wider range and could hit higher notes than even our fair Mrs. Jennings."

Atlas knew enough about the stage—and Juliet Jennings, for that matter—to comprehend London's most acclaimed performer would not appreciate being upstaged by a newly discovered talent. "Did Mrs. Jennings know you were interested in replacing her with Mrs. Pike?"

Cooke shrugged. "Very possibly. She was well aware of Mrs. Pike's talent. Vessey employed Juliet to give Mrs. Pike singing lessons, but it was not long before the student surpassed the teacher."

"So the two ladies were rather well acquainted? Did they get on well?"

"I have no idea. Anyhow, I was prepared to pay Mrs. Pike upwards of a thousand pounds per annum."

Atlas resisted the urge to whistle. "She could have looked after herself quite nicely with that much money." He studied the red-nosed man and wondered if perhaps there was another reason he'd been prepared to pay handsomely for the demi-rep's services. "Exactly how well acquainted were you with Mrs. Pike?"

Cooke shook his head. "I know what you are implying, and you could not be more mistaken. Mrs. Pike was not free with her favors. She did not invite advances from men."

"Maybe you were a little taken with her? It seems that many men were."

"I admired her talents, and I was not alone. Reuben Elkins, the manager at Drury Lane, also attempted to entice her to perform at his theater."

"Was she seriously entertaining either of the offers?"

"She was more than entertaining them. Mrs. Pike had accepted my offer. She'd decided to leave Vessey for a life on the stage."

"She was going to leave him?" It took a moment for the revelation, and its accompanying implications, to sink in. The Vessey Atlas knew would not take kindly to being abandoned to the theater or a man of the church. "Was the marquess aware that she intended to embark on a new life without him?"

"What do you think?" Cooke's voice trembled. He looked like a man resisting the urge to punch something. Or someone. "If you are asking me if I think Vessey might have killed

Mrs. Pike in a fit of jealousy to keep her from leaving him, my answer is a resounding yes."

Atlas studied the man's rigid posture and flushed face. "You seem extraordinarily upset for a man who says he did not know Mrs. Pike particularly well."

Cooke visibly took a deep breath before speaking in a calmer voice. "Mrs. Pike was a decent person who did not deserve what happened to her. Moreover, she could have made this theater a great deal of profit. Perhaps you are not aware that I am also a part owner of this theater."

"I was not aware."

"I thought not." Cooke heaved a heavy sigh as he wiped his nose. "We are still paying off the costs of reconstructing this building after the fire in 1808. Putting Mrs. Pike on the stage could have assisted in that endeavor. Our debts are great, and now they shall continue to be so due to her unfortunate end."

"I see." So Atlas's initial instinct had been correct in at least one way. Cooke had had a serious interest in Mrs. Pike, just not one of a romantic nature.

"Vessey may act lordly, but that whoreson is as cold as they come." Cooke practically spat the words out. "I have no doubt in my mind that man is capable of murder."

★　★　★

Atlas would have liked to speak with Juliet Jennings immedi-after his conversation with Simon Cooke, but Covent Garden's leading lady had yet to arrive at the theater. She would not be taking to the stage for several hours yet. While he waited for Juliet to make her appearance, Atlas decided to walk over to the Drury Lane theater, which was just down the block from

Covent Garden. He crossed the intersection of Bow and Russell Streets and walked over to Catherine Street.

The Drury Lane theater was even newer than Covent Garden. It too had been devastated by fire a few years prior, and the new structure was just three years old. The seats in the the ater formed a semi-circle in colors of gold and green, although the boxes were done up in crimson.

He found Reuben Elkins, the theater manager, in the painting room, where sets were being constructed or mended for the current production. A round-faced, slim man of average height, Elkins had a no-nonsense demeanor and struck a business-like tone when speaking of Mrs. Pike.

"I regret not being able to tempt her to perform here, but she had her heart set on Covent Garden."

"You agreed with Mr. Cooke that Mrs. Pike was talented enough to sing professionally?"

"To be sure. Be careful with that!" he barked at two young workers edging past them, carrying a wall of painted mountain scenery. He directed his attention back to Atlas. "Not that she wasn't talented, you understand, but Mrs. Pike's notoriety would have also brought in the crowds." Elkins's eyes gleamed. "I would have paid her eleven hundred pounds per annum. Average folk would have been most curious to see the long-time mistress of one of the highest lords in the land."

"No doubt." Atlas found it curious that two of the metropolis's premier theaters had been anxious to engage Mrs. Pike for so high a price. "Had she performed in public before?"

Elkins shook his head. "She said his lordship wouldn't allow it. Vessey preferred to keep Mrs. Pike all to himself, a beautiful little songbird that he allowed out of her cage to perform for his friends from time to time. But he was loath to share her with the world."

Atlas could certainly understand why Mrs. Pike would have wanted to leave Vessey and, from what he'd learned today, she'd had the means to do so. "I wonder why Mrs. Pike chose Covent Garden rather than accept your more generous offer."

Elkin frowned. "Cooke was going to pay her less? I naturally presumed he'd offered her more generous compensation."

Atlas thanked the man for his time and headed back to Convent Garden, hoping to find that Juliet had arrived. As he opened his umbrella to shelter himself from the incessant rain, Atlas contemplated why Mrs. Pike would have decided to perform at Covent Garden when she could have earned one hundred pounds more per annum at Drury Lane. And if she had indeed accepted Cooke's offer, then that meant Samuel Brown was lying about his secret betrothal to Mrs. Pike. Either that, or Mrs. Pike had lied to the clergyman about her future intentions.

★ ★ ★

"Atlas Catesby!" Juliet Jennings's radiant blue eyes shone as she regarded him in the reflection of her dressing table mirror. "What a lovely surprise."

The toast of London sat at a table littered with small bottles, perfumes, and pots of rouge. Scarves and necklaces hung from the edge of the mirror. A tattered red velvet settee left little room to maneuver in the cozy space. The floral scent of the singer's perfume filled the air.

"Juliet." He smiled. "It has been a long time."

She swiveled in her seat to face him, her azure silk robe catching the light. Juliet always wore a shade of blue because it enhanced her stunning eyes. Her golden hair was pulled up, and her open robe revealed her stays, which showcased a generous bosom and slim waist.

"It has been far too long." She took her time appraising him, her jewel gaze wandering from his face down his body and back up again to meet his eyes. "How many years is it since we last met?"

Atlas felt his face heat. Juliet had always been bold. "About eight and I see you haven't changed much during that time."

Her slim fingers toyed with the sapphire necklace dangling low into her décolletage. "Being shy is for ladies." She favored him with a naughty smile that, in times past, had had the power to do things to his body. "And we both know I am no lady."

He barked a laugh. Conversation between them had always been playful as well as frank. There was a time when neither of them had been shy about what they wanted. Few men could resist Juliet. She was a beautiful woman and at one point he'd been completely infatuated with her. But even back then his wanderlust had been stronger than his considerable desire for Juliet or any other woman.

"I am readying for my performance this evening," she said. "But perhaps we could meet for a late dinner."

He knew she offered more than a meal. "Unfortunately, this is not a social call between two old friends."

"Simon tells me you are investigating Wendy Pike's death." Her eyes sparkled. "Do tell. Am I a suspect?" She lifted her arms in supplication. "You are most welcome to search me."

"I do not think that shall be necessary."

"A pity." She turned back to face the mirror and reached for a tube on her cluttered dressing table. "What would you like to know?"

"What did you think of Mrs. Pike?"

"She was amiable enough. Very pleasant to talk to. There was a certain freshness to her countenance."

"You liked her?"

"Certainly. I considered her a friend. I think most people who were acquainted with Wendy thought very highly of her."

"I understand Vessey engaged you to give Mrs. Pike voice lessons."

"He did." She peered into the mirror as she applied a black paste to her eyebrows. "And we became very friendly."

"Did Mrs. Pike have talent?"

She caught his gaze in the mirror. "Come now, Atlas. I know you have spoken to Simon, a man who thought Wendy had the most magnificent voice he has ever heard."

"Did you know he intended to engage her services?"

"Yes, and it mattered little to me, if you must know." She applied a little sooty paste to her eyelashes. "A woman like me does not rise from nothing to become the toast of London without being resilient as well as resourceful."

He watched her darken her eyelashes. "Most women in your position would see Mrs. Pike as a threat."

"I am not 'most women.'"

"And well I know it." They exchanged a warm glance in the mirror's reflection.

"Wendy knew very little of the world. Vessey took her to his bed when she was but fifteen. She never learned to how to survive alone, as I was forced to do." She used her finger to mix a small amount of pomade with a touch of bright red powder. "I have never relied on any man, and that includes Simon Cooke. As you can imagine, I have had repeated offers from both Drury Lane and Haymarket to perform on their stages. I would not have starved had Wendy taken to the stage here. "

"You said the two of you were friends." Atlas leaned against the doorjamb and crossed his arms. "Did Mrs. Pike ever mention a man named Samuel Brown to you?"

"She did." She gave a derisive laugh. "He was a clergyman who was infatuated with her."

"Did Mrs. Pike return his affections?"

"She was fond of him. It was flattering to have a young man fawning over her. She said they had many agreeable conversations, and she appreciated that he showed an interest in her children."

"Was she fond enough of Mr. Brown to perhaps run away with him?"

"Even if she had loved her clergyman, which I am quite convinced she did not, I can assure you with complete confidence that Wendy would never leave Vessey for a poor man."

"Did you speak with Mrs. Pike on the evening of her death?"

"No." She brushed color onto her cheeks with a brush. "I had a performance."

"She watched from the back of the stage."

"Did she? I never saw her, but it is not as though I was looking for her."

"Can you think of anyone who would have hated Mrs. Pike enough to kill her?"

"No." She rubbed some color onto her lips. "As I said, everybody found Wendy to be most agreeable."

"Do you know if she has any family beyond her children with Vessey?"

"She mentioned a sister in Southwark. Wendy was very fond of her and often visited."

"Do you recall her name?"

Juliet paused in the application of her lip color to consider the question. "No, but she makes hats. I remember because I complimented one of Wendy's bonnets once, and she said her sister had trimmed it. She's a milliner. Or maybe she's married to a hatmaker. I honestly do not recall." She rose and discarded her robe, baring a wide expanse of smooth female skin on her arms and shoulders. "I must dress. You are welcome to stay and watch."

"My thanks, but I shall leave you to it."

"Truly?" She gave him a quizzical look. "Is there a Mrs. Catesby?"

"There is not."

"Not a wife, then. But some woman has captured your heart?"

"I am as unattached as ever." He placed his hat on his head. "Good afternoon."

"So you say." Juliet's knowing laughter followed him as he left her.

Making his way home, umbrella perched above his head while trying to avoid the worst of the mud, Atlas began to feel a certain empathy for the late Mrs. Pike, who'd been coveted by men—both powerful and not—for different reasons and all for their own purposes.

He wondered if she'd truly been prepared to strike out on her own and whether that decision to at last follow her own passions and desires—as was her right as an unmarried woman who by law belonged to no man—had led to her violent end.

★ ★ ★

Atlas paused outside Number 10 New Bond Street, the address of Grierson's gun shop, located just a few doors down from Atlas's own accommodations on the same street.

The murder weapon had likely been purchased from this shop, according to Ambrose Endicott, who had informed Atlas that Charles Grierson, the proprietor, had been less than forth-coming with the runners, pointedly refusing to identify the buyer.

The reticence of Grierson, who proudly boasted of his status as gunmaker to the royal family, did not surprise Atlas. Grierson's clients included the highest lords of the land. Revealing who had purchased the weapon was tantamount to pointing a damning finger at one of his noble patrons, a stance that would not endear a merchant to the very people he depended upon for his livelihood.

Atlas entered the shop and strolled along red-velvet-lined dark cabinetry that showcased the gunmaker's handiwork. Pistols and rifles were also laid out on mahogany tables.

"Good afternoon, sir." An older man, clad in black except for a snowy cravat, approached Atlas. "How may I be of service?"

"My name is Atlas Catesby. I should like to speak with Mr. Grierson."

"I am Charles Grierson." The man tipped his head in a respectful manner. "Are you perchance any relation to the late Baron Catesby, the great author and poet?"

"I am." The question was a familiar one that Atlas had been answering practically his entire life. "He was my father."

The gunmaker's gray eyes lit up. "It is an honor. I am a great admirer of your late father's work."

"That is very kind." Atlas was accustomed to hearing strangers praise his father. Silas Catesby was among England's great modern writers and poets, so widely admired that he'd been awarded a baronage some twenty years earlier. The unexpected elevation had suddenly catapulted the Catesby family onto the fringes of high-society London.

"How may I assist you this afternoon, Mr. Catesby?" Grierson swept a hand out, signaling that the contents of the shop were at Atlas's disposal. "Perhaps I can interest you in one of our finest pistols."

"As a matter of fact, I should like to know about a pistol that you have already sold."

"Which weapon is that? Do you wish to purchase a similar one?"

"Not exactly. I am inquiring about a specific piece, a flint-lock pistol, carved walnut stock." Atlas searched his memory, trying to recall details about the gun he'd recovered from the Covent Garden fruit seller. "It is inlaid with silver, and its barrel is particularly distinctive because it is also sheathed in silver."

The gunmaker's expression grew more wary, as if an open window welcoming a pleasant spring breeze had suddenly slammed shut. "What is your interest in such a weapon?"

Atlas opted to speak plainly. "One like it was used to murder the Marquess of Vessey's . . . *chère amie*." He used the most polite term he could think of. Leave it to nobles to attach an elegant phrase to the basest of transactions: money for sex provided by impoverished women and girls with few alternatives. "The pistol came from this shop. Your name is engraved on the barrel."

"I have sold a number of pistols such as the one to which you refer."

"I do not suppose you could provide me with a list of the people who purchased one."

"Decidedly not. As I told Bow Street, my client list is private."

Atlas suppressed his impatience. "I appreciate your discretion, but a woman died, and I am attempting to bring her killer to justice."

Grierson remained intractable. "I am not without sympathy. What happened to Mrs. Pike is a terrible tragedy, but nothing can be done to help her now."

"Her killer should be punished for his crime."

"I cannot risk my entire business concern for a dead woman." Grierson held his hands out, palms upward. "Giving you that list would anger all of my customers. A man lives and dies by his reputation."

The bell above the door rang, and two young bucks entered.

"Good afternoon, gentlemen," Grierson greeted them. "I shall be with you momentarily."

He turned back to Atlas, speaking quietly. "I cannot and shall not risk my business concern for a woman who is already beyond saving. You must appreciate my position in this matter."

Seeing that pursuing the matter any further at the moment was futile, Atlas bade the gunmaker farewell and departed, leaving the man to attend to his customers.

CHAPTER 6

Atlas's young manservant greeted him in the front hall upon his arrival home.

So eager was Jamie to assist his master that the youth practically tugged one of Atlas's arms out of its socket while helping to relieve him of his damp great coat.

A year into his service as Atlas's valet, the whelp remained as anxious to please as ever. He knelt the instant Atlas lowered himself onto the carved bench in the front hall to shed his muddy boots. Atlas soaked up the welcome warmth from the fire as Jamie tugged them off.

"Perhaps I should not have walked," Atlas said apologetically when he registered the young valet's dismay at the sorry state of his boots. "But I could not bear the thought of being confined indoors for yet another day without taking at least some exercise."

"Yes, sir." Jamie's tone lacked all enthusiasm. "I shall clean them right away." Atlas could very well polish his own boots. He remained unaccustomed to being looked after, but he'd felt obliged to engage the boy last year as a favor to Lilliana.

"Good man. And after that, run out and get us some supper. Whatever you like."

Jamie's eyes brightened. "Very good, sir." Nothing cheered the boy quite so much as the prospect of filling his belly. "Oh, and Lord Charlton is here, sir."

Atlas smothered a groan. He was in no mood to see Charlton, but there was no avoiding the earl now. Leaving Jamie to attend to his muddy boots, Atlas stepped into his slippers and ventured into the sitting room. He found Charlton in his usual perch, the most comfortable seat in the room, staring at a wooden object in the palm of his hand.

"What the devil is this?" he asked when he spotted Atlas.

"Good evening to you too." Atlas dropped into his seat opposite the earl. "It is a burr puzzle."

"You say that as if I am supposed to comprehend what in Hades a *burr* is."

"Interlocking pieces of notched wood that you take apart and see if you can put back together."

"Why in God's name would anyone of sane mind want to do that?"

"For amusement." Atlas was partial to all puzzles, physical or otherwise. Even as a boy, he'd felt driven to understand what made a clock tick or why dough rose. And he enjoyed puzzling out what made people behave the way they did. Putting everything into order in his mind, reasoning it all out, calmed him immensely. "People, myself included, do it for the challenge."

"For the headache, you mean to say." Charlton set the puzzle on the table between him and Atlas. "I am beginning to suspect your overly serious nature is due to the frustration that comes with trying to work out these infernal puzzles."

Atlas reached for the three-dimensional cross. "Quite the contrary, they relax me."

"How anything specifically designed to confuse and confound can be appealing to anyone is beyond my understanding."

Atlas took the puzzle apart, setting each of the six individual burrs on the table. "I presume there's a reason for your visit."

Charlton sighed. "You are the only person of my acquaintance who makes a habit of forgetting whenever we have a dinner engagement."

"It had slipped my mind." Atlas hooked two of the pieces together to his satisfaction. "And I have just sent Jamie to bring me some supper."

"It is fortunate the boy has appetite enough to eat both of your portions." Charlton would be in a position to know. The earl took Jamie into his employ whenever Atlas was away on one of his extended journeys. "We are engaged to go to the Voyager's Club this evening."

Atlas added a third piece to the contraption in his hand. "I have been traipsing out in the rain all afternoon. I have no desire to brave the elements any further this evening."

"It is called a carriage. Fortunately for the both of us, I have one. Who in their correct mind walks in this weather?"

"A bedlamite like me, I suppose." He slid the fourth knobbed wooden piece into place. The fifth and sixth quickly followed, and he held up the completed three-dimensional cross for his friend's inspection.

Charlton barely glanced at it. "Now that you've finished playing with your toy, perhaps you would care to dress for dinner, before I starve. I shall wait."

"Do not bother. As I said, I have no interest in accompanying you this evening."

Charlton's normally smooth forehead wrinkled. "I say, is all well with you?"

He held his friend's gaze. "Whatever could be wrong?"

Charlton blinked. "Supper on the morrow then?" he asked lightly.

Atlas rested his head against the cushioned chair, suddenly feeling extraordinarily fatigued. "If agreeing is the only way I can persuade you to go away, I suppose I have no choice but to accept your invitation."

"Excellent." Charlton came to his feet with alacrity. "I shall see you on the morrow."

★ ★ ★

The following evening, Atlas and Charlton were dining at the Voyager's Club when the Marquess of Vessey entered the eating room, accompanied by his son, Nicholas, Viscount Beaumont.

The new arrivals were seated just a few tables away, by a wall of floor-to-ceiling windows, which afforded Atlas an excellent view of both men. Vessey's haggard appearance stunned him; his cheeks were hollowed and the reddened eyes devoid of their customary sharpness. Every one of the marquess's movements seemed weighted down by an unseen burden.

Nicholas leaned toward his father as he spoke, his warm hazel eyes lit with obvious concern, but Vessey seemed only marginally aware of his son. It was impossible for Atlas to reconcile this hunched old man with the soulless monster who'd inhabited his memory for his entire adult life.

"It is a surprise to see Vessey out and about," Charlton remarked as he sliced a neat piece of roasted beef in his porcelain plate. "I have heard that he has not left his bedchamber since Mrs. Pike's tragic demise."

Atlas did not bother to hide his rancor. "I suppose you are privy to such private information given your intimate acquaintance with the man."

Charlton's hands stilled. "I attended his oratorios and that is all," he said evenly. "We are not now, nor have we ever been, friends."

Atlas's focus shifted back to Vessey and Nicholas. "Your definition of friendship obviously differs from mine." He watched Nicholas rise, murmur something to his father, and leave the eating room.

"He is alone," Charlton observed. "Now is your chance."

"My chance for what?"

"Vessey is obviously a suspect in his paramour's death. Surely you wish to speak with him."

"I would much prefer to kill him," Atlas mumbled, setting down his wine, "but I suppose I shall have to settle for having a word with the bastard."

He rose, his heart beating hard, his muscles tight. Atlas hated Vessey intensely, but somewhere deep within him, a boy's fear of the man who'd murdered his sister also lingered. It was a distress born out of Atlas's conviction that Vessey had briefly considered shoving Atlas down the stairs along with Phoebe.

He would never forget the paralyzing terror that had engulfed him as he stood at the top of the wide marble staircase at Stonebrook, staring down at his sister's mangled body. For as long as he lived, he would always remember the sensation of his sister's murderer looming behind him.

Later, he'd wondered if he'd exaggerated it all in his memory; perhaps he'd only imagined Vessey hovering impossibly, threateningly close before finally stepping away.

Now Atlas forced himself to approach the marquess's table. "Vessey."

The older man looked up, his face blank. "Yes?"

Atlas's ears pounded. For two decades he'd imagined the moment he'd confront the man who'd killed his sister. "You do not recognize me."

Vessey blinked. "Should I?"

Atlas's hands tightened on the back of Nicholas's empty chair. "Atlas Catesby at your service."

The marquess's rheumy gaze considered him now with only slightly more interest. "Ah, come to take your revenge? I had heard that you are asking questions about Mrs. Pike's death." His voice thinned at the mention of his late mistress's name.

"Is that a confession?" Atlas kept his voice cool while he resisted the urge to tear the man's head off. "We both know I would have good reason to seek revenge."

"You want to avenge your sister's death." Vessey regarded Atlas with open contempt. "Due to some outlandish boyish fantasy that you have harbored all of these years that I purposely did away with my own wife."

"It is no fantasy." Atlas resisted the urge to wipe his dampened palms on his trousers. "You can lie to the world, but you and I? We both know what you did."

"Filthy lies." Vessey's hands curled into fists on the table. "I suppose you now intend to convince society that I have done away with another woman who shared my life."

"Have you?"

"No." Vessey's face momentarily crumpled before he took hold of himself, but red-rimmed eyes and a gaunt face betrayed his apparent inner turmoil. "Unlike with your sister, who was a bit of a nuisance, I cared a great deal for Mrs. Pike."

"You had an interesting way of demonstrating your affection."

"What the devil is that supposed to mean?

"Did you care for Mrs. Pike so deeply that you preferred to see her dead rather than with another man?"

"There was no other man." The statement was definitive, spoken without an inkling of doubt, in the same manner one would declare that the sky is blue. "Mrs. Pike was completely and utterly devoted to me."

"I have recently become acquainted with a clergyman who claims Mrs. Pike had every intention of leaving you and wedding him."

Vessey guffawed. "Are you speaking of Samuel Brown? The man is touched in the head. He was obsessed with Mrs. Pike and would not leave her alone."

"Are you certain she wanted to be left alone?"

"Absolutely. Mrs. Pike even suggested that Brown become a clergyman. He used to be a soldier. She hoped his ardor might cool once he moved closer to God and found a calling in the church." Vessey paused to indulge in a leisurely draught of his wine. "It was a source of great amusement between us. Mrs. Pike anticipated that Brown would be given a living somewhere far away so that she could be free of the nuisance he presented."

"Brown believes you killed Mrs. Pike because she intended to leave you."

"I have heard that you are a man with keen insight. This absurd line of questioning suggests that those reports have been greatly exaggerated." He peered at Atlas with actual interest for the first time since the start of their conversation. "Did you truly recently solve the murder of someone connected to the Duke of Somerville's household?"

Atlas remained silent. He had no desire to converse with Vessey about anything unrelated to Mrs. Pike.

Vessey continued. "I do hope your misplaced desire to avenge your sister's death shall not blind you to the truth in this case. There is no one on earth who is more desperate to know why Mrs. Pike was murdered. That woman was at the center of my life for twenty-five years."

Twenty-five years. Yet Phoebe had been dead for twenty-two. Vessey had taken up with Mrs. Pike well before his marriage to Phoebe.

Atlas could not resist asking. "Why did you bother to wed my sister? It was obvious from the start that you never cared for her."

"Your father was a favorite of King George; he'd just been styled a baron. It was a worthy alliance. You understand this was well before the king became a bedlamite." His mouth curled. "However, as my marchioness, Phoebe was far too quiet, always away in some corner with her sketchpad."

"Was my sister aware of your arrangement with Mrs. Pike?"

Vessey shrugged. "I could not say. Your sister was quite sheltered and far too naïve for her own good."

"Unlike Mrs. Pike I suppose."

"Mrs. Pike was engaging and most agreeable. Inquire of anyone who was acquainted with her. No one, man or woman, failed to be charmed by her. She was beloved by all she met."

"As was Phoebe, except by you, her wedded husband, the man who should have looked after her."

"Instead of shoving her down the stairs?" Vessey asked derisively. "That is what you believe, is it not? You might have grown up, but you are still nothing but a boy."

Atlas imagined the immense satisfaction he'd feel snapping the man's neck in half. "I am putting you on notice."

"Is that so?" Vessey did not appear to be the least bit concerned. "Dare I ask what sort of notice?"

"I am no longer that frightened child who stood by while you got away with murder." Atlas leaned in, hands palm down on the table. "If you killed Mrs. Pike, I shall make it my life's mission to prove it. And nothing and no one will stop me from seeing that you hang for the crime."

★　★　★

Atlas tried to ignore the banging at his front door.

Unfortunately, his unwelcome visitor's determination to disturb him appeared greater than Atlas's current inclination to shut out everything and everyone beyond the walls to his apartments.

"Atlas!" The heavy door did little to muffle Thea's demanding voice. "I know you are in there and I am not leaving until you let me in."

With an exasperated sigh, Atlas set down the hookah hose and rose from his sitting room chair. He hadn't seen anyone in two days. Following his encounter with Vessey, he'd sent Jamie away and secluded himself in his rooms.

He opened the old door to find not only Thea but also his brother Hermes, standing on the landing at the top of the stairs.

"See there?" Hermes gestured toward Atlas. "I told you he is perfectly fine. There was no need for you to drag me over here."

Thea sailed past Atlas, with Hermes trailing. "You look like the devil," she said to Atlas.

"I was not expecting uninvited visitors." He followed his siblings into the sitting room.

"Your hair is a mess." Thea coughed and waved the smoke away. "It looks as if you have not taken a comb to it in days."

He hadn't. Not that it was any of his overbearing older sister's affair. "Have you looked at Herm's hair of late?"

"I beg your pardon!" Hermes made the pretense of acting affronted. He patted his wildly unruly hair with a gingerly hand so as not to disturb the fashionable coiffure currently favored by London's dandies.

"For some reason, which completely escapes me, Herm purposefully makes a squirrel's nest of his hair," Thea pointed out. "You, however, do not."

"May I ask to what I owe the pleasure of this unexpected visit?"

Thea frowned at the shuttered windows. "Why is it so dark in here?"

"Because I prefer it that way at the moment."

"This chamber needs some air." She marched over to the window by the game table, threw the heavy velvet curtains open, then bent to battle with the window sash until it opened. Her gaze dropped to the puzzle pieces scattered across the game table. "You have not worked on your puzzle."

Atlas dropped into his stuffed chair with a yawn. "You say that as if it is a cause for alarm."

"You've been shut up in here alone for two days, and you have not touched your puzzle? Putting these infernal things together is what settles your mind."

Atlas reached for the nargileh. "Why do you assume that my mind needs settling?" He drew on the water pipe. A fruity tobacco taste filled his mouth as the sound of percolating bubbles filled the momentary silence.

"I spoke with Charlton," she said meaningfully.

"And?" Atlas knew he was behaving in the manner of a recalcitrant schoolboy, but Thea had the power to provoke the worst in him.

"He says you encountered Vessey just before you went into self-imposed exile."

Resting his head back against his chair, Atlas exhaled long and slow, watching the silvery streaks until they dissipated in a smoky miasma. "I fail to see how that distasteful exchange is related to your barging into my home."

"You neglected to come to the door when Charlton called yesterday, and he informs me that your valet is in his household until you summon the boy back, which means you have been quite solitary these past two days." Thea ticked her verbal list off on her fingers. "And according to Lilliana, a note she sent around yesterday morning went unanswered."

"I have not had a chance to look at it as of yet." At some point, he had noticed that a note had been slipped under his front door, but he hadn't bothered to read it. "Is a man not entitled to some peace of mind when he needs it?"

"You saw Vessey?" Hermes slipped into the chair opposite Atlas, the seat Charlton favored when he visited, and stretched his long legs out in front of him, crossing them at the ankles. Hermes was tall like Atlas, but far more slender, and they shared the same deep gray eyes. However, the similarities between the brothers ended there. A Bond Street lounger if there ever was one, Hermes's greatest desire in life was to parade about town modeling the latest fashions. "What did the bastard say?" Hermes asked.

"Nothing worth repeating."

Thea moved to the next window. "And yet the encounter resulted in you shutting yourself up in your apartments for two days." She threw open the curtains. The sun streamed in, its rays cutting across the old parquet floors.

"I prefer to be alone from time to time." Atlas squinted against his first glimpse of daylight in two days. He realized it had stopped raining. "My travels usually allow for that. Unfortunately, it has been almost a year since my last voyage."

"You have been present a great deal more of late," Hermes acknowledged. He reached for the burr puzzle on the marble table between them. "I suppose that's because Apollo's accident kept you from journeying to India."

Being in the presence of his brother and sister made him think of the sibling who would never join them again. An image of Phoebe sketching by the lake came to him. Even then, before Vessey, she'd seemed far too gentle for this world. She had never been any match for the heartless bastard. "If I had made him pay for killing Phoebe, then perhaps Mrs. Pike would still be alive."

"Made who pay? Vessey?" Hermes looked up from the burr puzzle. "That is rather ridiculous. You were barely out of apron strings when Phoebe died. What do you think you could have done? Thrown a tantrum? Or called Vessey out on a field of honor with your pretend pistol?"

Thea turned from the window, a dark silhouette outlined by the glare of the sun behind her. "Surely, you cannot blame yourself for Phoebe's death."

He drew on the hookah. "Our parents did."

She crossed over to stand behind Hermes's chair. "Did they tell you that?"

"What was there to discuss?" Sorrow crept in uninvited, burrowing deep into his bones. "Phoebe was dead. They knew it was my fault. Their silence spoke volumes."

"I have always thought they blamed themselves." Hermes pulled the burr puzzle apart, and the notched wood pieces came loose, scattering onto the faded carpet. "I heard them talking shortly after the funeral about how they should never have allowed Phoebe to wed Vessey."

"Precisely," Thea agreed, "but Papa had just been ennobled, and they felt they had no choice in the matter because His Majesty favored the match."

Atlas had never known that his parents blamed themselves for his sister's death nor that royal pressure had influenced their decision to allow the union with Vessey. But it was of no account. Atlas was the sole family member who'd been there when Phoebe died. He alone had been in a position to save his sister. But he hadn't even tried. Instead, when Vessey and Phoebe had begun to argue, he'd locked himself away in a guest bedchamber.

"This explains a great deal," Thea remarked.

"It does?" Hermes scooted forward in his chair and bent to retrieve the puzzle pieces. "How so?"

"This sense of guilt is why Atlas has never settled down. Why he is always dashing off to parts unknown. And it is why he has locked himself away here now."

Atlas groaned. "Not this rubbish again." His sister had spewed this sort of nonsense on previous occasions, and he had no patience for it. "If I promise to make myself presentable and go out this afternoon, will you go away posthaste and leave me in peace?"

"Excellent." Hermes practically leapt to his feet. "Do let us depart, Thea." He threw the pieces of the burr puzzle onto the table. "Leave the man in peace."

Thea reluctantly allowed Hermes to shepherd her out. "And respond to Lilliana's note," she instructed Atlas as she moved into the front hall.

He raised a hand in surrender. "I shall do so." Anything to get her to leave.

He waited to hear the door close behind them. Then he set down the nargileh hose and reached over to gather the puzzle pieces. As he absently put the pieces together to form the three-dimensional cross, Atlas wondered how his siblings were able to continue on with their lives when Phoebe had not lived to see her twenty-second year. She'd been robbed of raising her own child and would never know that, despite his father, her son had grown into a worthy young man, one who was, by all accounts, kind and generous.

Setting the completed burr puzzle down, he heaved himself out of his chair. He might not be able to find justice for Phoebe, but it wasn't too late for Mrs. Pike.

If Atlas could prove that Vessey had killed his mistress, then perhaps justice for Mrs. Pike would also mean justice at last for his sister.

CHAPTER 7

Jamie returned by the time Atlas emerged from his confining hip bath an hour later.

"What are you doing here?" Atlas asked, pulling on his dressing gown.

"Mrs. Palmer called at the Earl of Charlton's and directed me to return to my post at once."

Atlas resisted the urge to roll his eyes. Leave it to Thea to send Jamie home to ensure that Atlas kept his word about going out.

Jamie's gaze went to the wood and porcelain tub. "You just bathed?"

"Indeed." Atlas rubbed his damp hair with a linen towel, feeling clean and refreshed, the lemon and bergamot scent of his shaving soap filling his nostrils. "I was in need of a bath."

"And you prepared the water?"

"Obviously. The hip bath did not fill itself." The small tub barely accommodated Atlas's brawny frame, but it was quicker and easier to fill than a full bath. Besides, now that Atlas had decided to resume his investigation, he was impatient to get on with it.

"It is my place to prepare your bath." Jamie's face reddened. "A gentleman should not prepare his own bath. That is for his valet to do."

"It is your place to do what I ask of you." Atlas threw the towel onto the bed and reached for his comb. Jamie had always been overly eager to please, but he was even more tiresome now that he'd received valeting instructions from Charlton's man. "And I am perfectly capable of preparing my own bath."

"It is as if you do not even care to engage a valet." Jamie's voice was an octave higher than usual, and for a moment Atlas feared the boy might burst into tears.

"Nonsense." He set his comb down and turned to face Jamie. "Anyone can prepare a bath, but I have tasks far more important for you to attend to. Ones that require a resourceful young man with a quick mind."

"Oh." Jamie brightened. "What do you need me to do?"

"Are you up to a bit of sleuthing?"

"Absolutely, sir." The boy straightened to his full height, which was considerable. In the past year, Jamie had grown even taller than Atlas. But his height seemed incongruous with his coltish form, wide eyes, and full cheeks; he was like a boy on stilts who hadn't quite mastered how to walk in them. "What is it that you require of me?"

"Firstly, I would like for you to locate Mrs. Pike's sister. I do not know her name. However, either she or her husband is a hatmaker in Southwark."

"Very good, sir. Shall I go to Southwark as soon as you are properly dressed?"

"Certainly." He didn't have the heart to send Jamie away before giving him the satisfaction of putting his valeting lessons to good use. "Also, after that, please look into Vessey's private life."

Jamie blinked. "His private life, sir?"

"Yes, I want to know about the women in his life."

"But I thought Mrs. Pike was his . . . companion."

"Some men have more than one companion, and Mr. Brown, the clergyman who claims he was betrothed to Mrs. Pike, says Vessey had a number of them."

"Oh. I see." Jamie's ears flushed a bright red. "Very good, sir."

Atlas felt a tinge of regret for his role in denting the country lamb's innocence, but Jamie had proven to be an intrepid investigator thus far. His boyish earnestness tended to win people over, prompting them to lower their guard and speak more freely. Besides, Jamie could move among the servant class in a way that Atlas could not. And servants were an excellent source of information.

"And finally, Jamie."

"Yes, sir?"

"Vessey has two young daughters with Mrs. Pike. I should like to confirm their ages as well as where they go to school."

Jamie's chest puffed out. "You can depend upon me, sir."

"I would not have asked if I had any doubt about that." Atlas finished dressing and had just gotten into his Hessian boots with Jamie's help when a knock sounded at his front door.

"Another visitor?" Atlas murmured while Jamie went to see who it was. Looking into the mirror, he straightened his cravat. "I can only hope Thea has not returned to harangue me."

The sounds of the door opening were followed by faint feminine tones. So it was Thea. He walked into his sitting room, calling out to her only half in jest. "What must I do to entice you to stop badgering me?"

"You might try responding to my notes." Lilliana's acerbic voice reached him a moment before she appeared in his sitting room, looking like a duchess in a sea-green ensemble ornamented with gold buttons and tassels. A matching hat and ethereal veil shrouded her aristocratic profile in a touch of mystery.

Her unexpected appearance brought a smile to his face. "Lady Lilliana."

"I thought perhaps you had finally made your escape to India."

"No, indeed," he responded with a bow.

She did not seem impressed. "So courtly and yet you could not find the courtesy to respond to my note."

His smile broadened. He'd missed her sharp tongue. "Do forgive me. I have been unaccountably rude."

"So true." She lifted her veil to reveal flushed cheekbones. "A lady should not have to come to a gentleman."

He acknowledged her well-taken point with an incline of his chin. "How can I be of service, my lady?"

"It is I who can be of service to you." Her eyes gleamed. "I have learned something intriguing about the case."

He offered her a seat before directing his attention to Jamie, who hovered in the entranceway. "Run and fetch some refreshment for Lady Lilliana."

"That shall not be necessary," Lilliana interjected. "Somerville's cook has sent you a basket."

"Has he?" Atlas's mouth watered. He couldn't recall when he'd last eaten. "You are both spoiling me terribly."

"Somerville's cook is a *she*. It seems Mrs. Pitt has learned how much you appreciate her efforts and now seems determined to keep you well fed."

"How amiable of her. I can see no disadvantage to being in Mrs. Pitt's good graces."

Jamie came in with the straw basket. "Where shall I lay it out, sir?"

The considerable size of the basket suggested the need for a generous surface area. "The game table should do."

The boy didn't hide his surprise. "But your puzzle, sir."

"I have not yet begun the puzzle. You may gather up the pieces and set them aside for now."

Jamie did as he was asked. Atlas watched with great interest as the boy revealed the basket's culinary treasures— buttered apple tarts, ratafia cakes, and other assorted cakes and puddings. The scent of the freshly baked sweet foods made his mouth water. Jamie arranged foods on the rosewood table's square leather surface, the bounty reaching the table's gold trim edging. Somerville's cook had even sent lemonade.

Lilliana came to stand beside Atlas. "I can see there will be no discussing the case with you until you have had your fill. When did you last eat?"

"I honestly cannot remember." Once they took their seats, he immediately helped himself to a ratafia cake. "Now, what is it that you have learned?"

"I heard something of great interest about Mrs. Juliet Jennings. You will recall she is the singer whose performance we attended the evening of Mrs. Pike's murder."

"Yes, of course. Go on." He washed the cake down with a gulp of delicious lemonade, prepared with just the right balance of sweet and tart.

"It seems that the theater manager was considering engaging Mrs. Pike to perform at Covent Garden."

"I have heard that. The manager informed me as much when I visited him at the theater to inquire about Mrs. Pike."

"Did he also tell you that Mrs. Jennings attended one of Mrs. Pike's private performances?"

"No. However, Vessey had previously engaged Mrs. Jennings to give his mistress voice lessons." He reached for an apple tart. "It would be natural for Mrs. Jennings to attend a performance given by one of her students."

"The two women engaged in a very nasty row after the performance."

"Is that so?" Atlas paused. "Now *that* is something I had not heard."

Lilliana's satisfied expression lifted his spirits. She had a crooked smile that seemed rather like a smirk, and he had grown to appreciate how worthwhile it was to elicit one from her. "I suppose that means I have learned something of interest that you had not discovered yet," she said.

"Yes, you certainly have. No one I have interviewed mentioned anything about an altercation between the two women." Least of all Juliet herself. "Did someone witness this row?"

She sipped her lemonade. "The melee occurred in the ladies' retiring room at Stonebrook, with only a single maid in attendance. The girl had been assigned to the retiring room for the evening."

He bit down on a biscuit, enjoying its distinctive, nutty taste. "What occurred exactly?"

"It was apparently a very physical encounter. Mrs. Jennings tore Mrs. Pike's dress beyond repair, so much so that Mrs. Pike was required to change into another gown before rejoining Vessey's guests."

Atlas found it hard to envision a woman as contained as Juliet losing all self-control. But if she had, it did not surprise him that she'd neglected to mention the encounter. Juliet would be reluctant to share a less than flattering story about herself.

Especially after her fellow combatant turned up dead. "I suppose few people have heard of this encounter because neither woman cared for it to be known."

"Imagine how angry Mrs. Jennings must have been to physically attack another woman," Lilliana said. "Perhaps even furious enough to engage someone to kill Mrs. Pike. It makes perfect sense, does it not?"

He shook his head. "Juliet has a temper, but I cannot imagine her actually killing anyone."

"How can you possibly reach that kind of conclusion solely by seeing someone on the stage?" Lilliana stilled. "Oh. You called her Juliet."

Heat scorched his cheeks. "She is a friend."

"I see." She looked at him as if waiting for him to elaborate. Which he had no intention of doing. When it became clear he wasn't going to speak further on the subject, she added, "I suppose you are very well acquainted with Mrs. Jennings."

He knew what she asked and, again, had no intention of sharing any details of his past liaison with Juliet. "We are not well acquainted . . . at present."

"At present. I see." A pause. The icy disdain coating each word made him want to reach for his greatcoat. "Are you currently *well enough acquainted* with Mrs. Jennings to assess whether she is capable of killing another woman?"

"That would surprise me very much."

"Even if her livelihood depended upon it?"

"Anything is possible. People will do almost anything if their very survival is at stake. And Juliet is definitely a survivor."

"As you are undoubtedly in a position to know." She came to her feet, as did he. "I shan't intrude upon you any longer."

He followed her out of the sitting room, sorry to have chased her away with his indelicate revelation about Juliet. "You could never intrude."

"Hmm." She paused in the foyer. Jamie had made himself scarce, so they were alone. "Intruding can become quite tedious. One eventually tires of it." She reached for the doorknob to let herself out.

"Lily." She'd once asked him to call her that when they were in private. He rarely had. "I have no interest in Juliet."

She paused with her back to him, and he could feel the warmth from her body. His eyes were drawn to the sliver of pale skin where the nape of her neck, and the soft wisps of hair there, disappeared into the green fabric of her spencer. After a moment, she opened the door and went out.

He watched from the landing as she descended the stairs, elegant and straight spined, without once looking back.

★　★　★

While Jamie went to Southwark in search of Wendela Pike's sister, Atlas made his way to Covent Garden to speak with Juliet Jennings about the violent disagreement she'd had with the dead woman.

Atlas was glad he'd decided to walk. The sun shone brightly for the first time in days, adding a golden crispness to the pleasant autumn day.

He found the performers rehearsing when he arrived. Slipping into a chair in the pit, he waited until they paused for a break, and managed to catch Juliet's attention.

She came over immediately. "This is an unexpected pleasure." Juliet had not yet dressed for the evening's performance and wore a silk dressing gown belted at the waist. The violet color somehow managed to bring out streaks of lavender in her vibrant blue eyes.

"It is always good to see you, Juliet."

She took a chair next to him, shifting her body so that she faced him. She laid a hand over the back of his chair. "Is this a social call?"

"Regrettably not."

"I thought as much. What can I do for you? Is this about Wendy?"

"It is."

She waited expectantly. "And?"

"You said the two of you were friends."

She nodded, her posture remained relaxed. "We were."

"Two friends who engaged in a physical fight that was so violent that you ripped Mrs. Pike's gown, forcing her to change before rejoining Vessey's guests?"

"My goodness." Her magnificent eyes twinkled. Not the reaction he expected. "Surely you know me well enough to comprehend that I have no need to resort to murder in order to vanquish my enemies."

"And was Mrs. Pike your enemy? You neglected to mention your disagreement with her the last time we spoke."

"Because it is an embarrassment. I paid that little snitch of a maid very handsomely to hold her tongue about what she witnessed in the ladies' retiring room at Stonebrook. But I obviously wasted my money."

"What did you argue about?"

Juliet's cheeks reddened. He'd never seen her embarrassed. Flushed with passion, yes, but he'd never seen her blush purely due to chagrin. "I would rather not say."

"Juliet. This is an important matter."

"It was beneath us both. I do not care to remember that unfortunate event. And it has nothing to do with how she died."

"You cannot know that for certain."

"I most certainly can. I know I had nothing to do with my friend's death. And you know me well enough to know when I speak the truth."

Atlas did find it difficult to imagine Juliet killing anyone. At her core, she was a pure-hearted person. "I do not believe you murdered Mrs. Pike. But the reason you argued could have some bearing on her death in a way that you are unaware of."

She huffed an exasperated breath. It sent one of the loose tendrils of her hair blowing like streamers in the wind. "Oh very well! But you must give me your word that you will not share the regrettable details with anyone."

"Very well. I give you my word."

"It was a fight over a man. I felt Wendy was being too forward with him."

"A man you were interested in?"

"A man I felt I had a claim to. Wendy denied having any interest in him. She insisted she was merely being hospitable as mistress of Stonebrook."

"Who was this man?"

"An acquaintance of Vessey's who was just passing through. The man is no longer in England."

"You believe Mrs. Pike was unfaithful to Vessey?"

"I acted foolishly," she admitted. "It was folly to believe Wendy would look at any other man. As far as I knew, she had never been with anyone but Vessey."

"When did this man you fought over leave the country?"

"Months before Wendy was killed."

"I need his name."

She looked heavenward. "Aleksey Witte. He was a diplomat from the royal Russian court and has long since returned home."

"And I presume you had a flirtation with Witte?"

"A liaison, yes." Juliet had a tendency to speak plainly. "But I do not believe that Wendy did. Believe me when I tell you that it was a silly fight fueled by too much drink on my part."

Atlas couldn't help smiling. "I am in a position to know that imbibing brings out your belligerent side." He recalled that was the reason Juliet rarely took a drink. "You are a woman who likes to remain in control of herself at all times."

"That is correct." She reached over and pressed her lips firmly against his. Pulling back, she said, "Now go away before I climb into your lap and have my way with you."

CHAPTER 8

The following day, nearly a week after Mrs. Pike's murder, Atlas hailed a hackney to Southwark to meet the dead woman's sister.

Jamie had proven to be as resourceful as Atlas had hoped. The boy traced Mrs. Rose Booth to a hat shop on Fish Hill Street. He'd also confirmed that Vessey's two young daughters attended a boarding school in Berkshire and received brief monthly visits from their parents.

Once the hackney dropped Atlas in Southwark, he trod along the wet pavements in a light drizzle, umbrella in hand, but not open. The fortifying appearance of the sun the previous day now seemed like a beautiful long-ago dream.

The sloping street was lined with shops bustling with respectable middle-class shoppers, professionals, and merchants. Up ahead, as Atlas approached the Thames, the aging London Bridge rose into view like a giant emerging from the fog. The span had been damaged during the previous year's Frost Fair, and construction on a new span was slated to begin soon.

Atlas paused outside the emerald-green, Rococo-style storefront that Jamie had described. The name "Booth & Co. Hatters," was emblazoned in gold above the shop's bow windows, surrounded by fanciful architectural curves and ornamentation.

He entered to find a long, narrow space with numerous men's hats on display, the scent of clean, new fabrics and wares filling the space. A neat-looking, pleasantly plump woman in bifocals busily arranged the wares—top hats with narrow, curved brims, of varying colors and fabrics, made of both beaver and silk.

"Good afternoon." She greeted him cheerily. "May I interest you in a hat?"

"No, thank you." Atlas introduced himself. "Are you perchance Mrs. Rose Booth?"

"I am."

He set his umbrella down, leaning it against the wall in the nearest shop corner. "You are the sister of the late Mrs. Wendela Pike?"

Her face darkened. "If you are from one of those scandal sheets—"

"I am not," he hastened to reassure her. "I am looking into Mrs. Pike's death and am determined to see to it that her killer is held to account for his crime."

She regarded him suspiciously from behind wire-rimmed spectacles. "The Quality do not usually concern themselves with common folks like Wendy, unless they have a use for her. Like her fancy lord did." Her gaze traveled over him. He supposed she saw a man in well-tailored clothing, albeit not of the absolute highest quality. "Is that who sent you?" she asked. "The Marquess of Vessey?"

"No, indeed," he said. "As a matter of fact, if Vessey had anything to do with Mrs. Pike's demise, I should like to see him face justice."

She gave a derisive laugh, absent of any mirth, and returned to her task, moving to another display table. "No one takes the

Fancy to account." She adjusted a tricorn hat, a style made popular by the military. "I do not expect you shall be the first."

He understood her skepticism. "My sister was wed to Vessey."

She paused, tricorn in hand. "I do not pretend to understand the peculiar ways of the Quality, but why would you care to find the person who killed your brother-in-law's mistress?"

"My sister is deceased," he clarified. "And if the man who killed my sister and the person behind Mrs. Pike's murder are one and the same, then he is going to pay for what he has done."

Her eyes opened wider. "You believe Lord Vessey killed them both?"

"I was eleven years old when my sister fell down the stairs at Stonebrook and broke her neck. I was not in a position to properly look into the matter then. I am now."

All at once, sorrow lined Mrs. Booth's face, as if she'd drawn back the curtain to reveal her true emotions. She suddenly seemed much older. "My sister's name was Esther Gillray. Gillray is our family name."

"My sister was Phoebe."

Sympathy blossomed in her eyes. "That is a lovely name." She set the hat down. "Mrs. Pike was a name my sister adopted after she went to live with her lord. It was not her true name." She drew a breath and her steady gaze met his. "Her middle name was Wendela, but she preferred to be called Wendy. That is what you should call her. Wendy. "

"It would be my honor."

"What is it you would like to know about Wendy?"

"I wondered if she was content in her life with Vessey."

"You could say so. She lived like a grand lady, after all. She was fond of Lord Vessey, but she did not love him."

"Did she ever tell you that she planned to leave him?"

"Heard that, did you? Yes, it is true." She absentmindedly reached out to straighten a selection of round hats, the kind worn by sailors. "The last time I saw Wendy, she told me that she was leaving the sinful life and intended to be wed."

This was the first confirmation that Wendy had intended to leave Vessey to wed the clergyman. "When did she tell you this?"

"About a fortnight before she died. Despite everything, Wendy still craved respectability." Bitterness tinged the words. "Lord Vessey robbed her of that by taking her to his bed when she was but fifteen."

Atlas didn't know exactly what kind of woman he'd expected to find when he came looking for Wendy's sister, but the dignified woman before him was a surprise—although perhaps that should not have been the case. She and Wendy were sisters, and everyone who'd met Wendy seemed to have been enchanted by her.

"Your parents approved of the arrangement with Vessey?"

"My mother died of fever when we were young. It was our father who forced her to accept Lord Vessey's offer. The marquess came into my father's hat shop one day and saw Wendy there."

"Was Wendy reluctant to accept?"

"She took a realistic view. Ma was gone and Da insisted he could not afford to keep feeding Wendy for much longer."

"So she accepted Vessey's offer."

"Yes, but she was smart about it. She negotiated with Lord Vessey before she agreed to go with him. He was tight-fisted, but she managed to get most of what she wanted."

"Did she come to regret their arrangement?"

Mrs. Booth shrugged. "He was mostly kind to her, and Wendy appreciated the deference she enjoyed as his mistress. But of late, she had become restless. My sister was frustrated with Lord Vessey because he was not free with his money. They argued a great deal over her spending."

"Did your sister spend freely?"

"What is the point of living in sin with a wealthy nobleman if you cannot spend his money?"

Atlas saw her point. "Did Wendy mention that she had been offered a great deal of money to perform at Covent Garden?"

"Had she?" Mrs. Booth's brows drew together. "She was certainly partial to singing, but my sister never mentioned any intention of taking to the stage. The money would certainly have appealed to her. Lord Vessey refused to settle a sum on Wendy and the children to ensure a comfortable life once his lordship tired of her or upon his death. They fought about it for months."

Atlas wondered why Vessey had been so reluctant to secure Wendy's future. It was common enough for noblemen to bestow annuities on their long-time lovers to ensure that they would always be looked after. "Did Vessey tell your sister why he refused to make any such provision for her or their children?"

"No, she was truly vexed about it. Wendy had a friend, a mistress of an important lord, who received a very generous annuity. Her name was Mrs. Walker and her marquess even attempted to persuade Lord Vessey to provide an annuity for Wendy and her children, but Vessey refused to be persuaded."

"Do you know the name of this lord? Mrs. Walker's protector, the man who spoke to Vessey on Wendy's behalf?"

She considered for a moment. "I believe she said it was something such as Roxford or Roxman."

He stilled. Could it be? "Not Roxbury?"

She pointed a finger at him. "Yes, that is it! Roxbury."

Surprise filtered through him. "The Marquess of Roxbury?"

"Yes, the marquess. Are you acquainted with his lordship?"

"Somewhat." Not so long ago, the Marquess of Roxbury had been determined to make Lilliana his wife.

Mrs. Booth sighed. "As I said, despite the Marquess of Roxbury's urging, Lord Vessey refused to settle any funds on Wendy. It was after that, about a fortnight before her death, that Wendy told me she had made a decision about her future."

"She told you that she intended to wed. What did she say about the man she was going to wed?"

"Only that she had finally fallen in love with a man who worshipped her and was desperate to make her his wife."

That certainly seemed to fit the rather hysterical romantic picture the clergyman had painted about his association with Wendy. But why would a woman who enjoyed luxury place her fate and future in the hands of an impoverished clergyman? Had Wendy valued respectability over financial security? Perhaps she'd intended to marry her clergyman while also accepting the offer to perform at Covent Garden. "Did she tell you the name of her betrothed? Or anything else about the man who had won her heart?"

"No, she planned to tell me everything the next time we met." She gave a sad smile. "Of course, there never shall be a next time. I must be content, I suppose, to know you intend to bring her murderer to justice."

"I give you my word that I shall do my best." He paused. Brown had said that he'd planned to take Wendy away from London. "Did Wendy perchance say anything about possibly leaving London for good?"

"No, but it would have surprised me if she had. Wendy did not enjoy the quiet life. She appreciated the liveliness of the metropolis."

Atlas thanked Wendy's sister for her time and departed just as an ominous roar sounded from the sky. Glancing up at the brooding clouds hanging low in the sky, Atlas hurried along Fish Hill Street and managed to hail a hackney just as the rain started.

Settling back against the timeworn leather seat, Atlas thought about Mrs. Booth's confirmation that her sister had intended to leave Vessey for another man. At the very least, Wendy's abandonment would have been a public humiliation. If Vessey had actually cared for her, losing Wendy to another man could have also been emotionally devastating.

The threat of abandonment, coupled with public humiliation, gave Vessey a strong motive for murder. God knows he'd killed Phoebe for far less.

CHAPTER 9

When the hackney arrived at New Bond Street, Atlas quickly alighted in the pouring rain and dashed inside to take shelter.

As he passed the tobacco shop beneath his apartments, he caught sight of Charlton leaning up against the long counter, chatting with Mrs. Disher. Shaking off the rain, he went up the stairs to find a bright-eyed Jamie eagerly awaiting his return.

"Why do you look as if you have just won the lottery?" he asked, shedding his greatcoat.

"I inquired about Lord Vessey's . . . er . . . private life."

"And what did you learn?"

"I went to a coffee house Vessey's servants often frequent in their off hours."

"And?"

"It seems their master was . . . is . . . very, very well acquainted with many different women."

"I see." Confirmation of Vessey's faithlessness did not come as a surprise. "Did he set any of them up in their own house?"

"Not that they know of. "

Atlas handed his topcoat to Jamie. "It makes one wonder whether Vessey has a younger, fresher mistress waiting in the wings to take Mrs. Pike's place."

Jamie looked puzzled. "Would he have to kill Mrs. Pike to take a new mistress?"

"No, not necessarily." Noblemen often exchanged their long-time mistresses for someone younger and fresher. Perhaps Wendy's concern that Vessey might grow tired of her was why she'd prevailed upon Vessey to make a settlement on her.

A thought came to him. "Jamie, run and find Mr. Brown."

"The clergyman, sir?"

"Yes, he gave me his direction." He strode into his bed-chamber and pulled open a drawer. Atlas handed the calling card bearing Mr. Brown's information to his manservant. "Please ask him to call upon me at his earliest convenience. This afternoon, if possible."

"Very good, sir."

Atlas followed Jamie out the door, but while the boy went out into the deluge, Atlas proceeded only as far as the tobacco shop. He greeted Mrs. Disher as he passed the counter, and continued back to the smoking room, where Charlton held court with several other men.

"Atlas." Charlton greeted him cheerily while taking a languid puff on a hookah that Atlas had secured for Mrs. Disher after she'd shown an interest in offering the experience to her smoking-room patrons.

"Do you have a moment," Atlas asked, "for a private word?"

Charlton took a last draw before removing a mouthpiece from the pipe hose. The earl was a fastidious man who insisted upon his own personal mouthpiece. The men gathered around him seemed to be sharing one mouthpiece among them. "If you will excuse me, gentlemen."

They stepped out of the smoke-filled, glass-enclosed room. "This way," Charlton directed. "We can have some privacy back here."

Atlas was hesitant to enter Olivia Disher's private accommodation behind the shop, but Charlton appeared to have no such qualms. Atlas knew the earl spent some evenings here with Olivia. He'd seen the earl departing in the early morning hours on more than one occasion. They entered to find a snug space with modest yet comfortable-looking furnishings.

"It is gratifying to see you have not decided to give me the cut direct on account of my practically nonexistent friendship with your former brother-in-law," Charlton remarked. "I called the day before yesterday, and no one came to the door, not even that boy servant of yours."

Atlas vaguely recalled someone pounding at his door during his brief, self-imposed exile from the world. "I believe Jamie was at your residence."

"Was he? My valet made no mention of it. Why? Were you away?"

"You could say that."

"What is so important that you have decided to seek me out despite your displeasure?" Charlton asked. "Do not tell me your sister's hearty husband has met with a tragic accident and Mrs. Palmer is now a widow."

Charlton's caustic remark took Atlas by surprise. It was hardly a secret that Charlton had once held a *tendre* for Atlas's very married sister. But Atlas assumed his friend had since transferred his affections to Mrs. Disher.

"I am sorry to disappoint," he said, "but Palmer is heartier than you or I, and Thea remains very much Mrs. Palmer."

Charlton scowled. "Very well then. What is it that you would like to know?"

"I am interested to learn more about Vessey's liaisons with other women."

"What exactly are you asking?"

"Was there a particular woman who engaged his interest? Perhaps a younger woman he wanted to move into Mrs. Pike's place?"

"I cannot say."

"Surely you can tell me how I would go about finding out. Before Olivia, you were certainly a man about town."

"If that is your polite way of saying I frequented brothels, that is true."

"Where would a man like Vessey find other women to cavort with?"

Atlas knew there were plenty of carnal enticements available to aristocratic men in London. One could find prostitutes anywhere, from St. James Park, down the Strand, and into Covent Garden. There were even discreet sporting hotels just outside these doors, on New Bond Street, that catered to wealthy noblemen. The London sex industry was so vast that Atlas had no idea where to begin.

"There is a house in Soho Square that I believe Vessey prefers to use."

"Is it a house he keeps specifically to engage in liaisons with women other than Mrs. Pike?"

"No, it is not a private house. It is a bagnio called Tom's that is well known for its discretion."

"Does Vessey engage the women who work there? Is there a particular one he prefers?"

"No, no. Tom's is not that sort of bagnio."

"I was not aware that there are brothels without women on the premises."

"That is because you are practically a saint," Charlton said.

"I may not frequent brothels, but I am familiar enough with the concept to comprehend that the point of visiting one is to engage in carnal relations with a woman, which is where, as I understand it, Vessey's tastes lie."

"Just so. Tom's keeps a book where women of an obliging sort write down their name and their direction. They are sent for when needed and pay the proprietor five shillings for each use of a room. They are independent operators of a sort."

Atlas had never heard of that sort of business arrangement. "One has to admire their industriousness." At least these women kept what they earned. In a proper brothel, the proprietor helped himself to most of the profits.

"If you are trying to ascertain whether there is a woman, aside from Mrs. Pike, that Vessey retains a particular interest in, Tom's would be an excellent place to start."

★ ★ ★

From the outside, Tom's bagnio gave every appearance of being an aristocratic townhome. Inside was much the same, boasting luxurious furnishings with gleaming surfaces, the air tinged with notes of lemon and beeswax.

The butler who answered the door escorted Atlas to a well-appointed drawing room with plush furnishings and original artwork gracing the walls. Atlas, who had never been inside a brothel before, had expected something far less decorous. Running a bagnio was obviously a profitable enterprise.

"Mr. Catesby." A well-dressed man, who would not have looked out of place in any of Mayfair's finest gentleman's clubs, hurried into the room, with Atlas's calling card in hand. He was about Atlas's age, with smiling eyes and a few extra pounds around the middle. "I am Tom. Welcome! I do hope you have not been kept waiting for overlong."

"Not at all. I was just admiring your paintings."

"I am gratified that you find them pleasing. Might I offer you a brandy?"

"No, thank you."

"Perhaps you prefer whiskey?"

"Nothing at the moment, thank you."

"I see." A knowing look came over Tom's face. "Perhaps you would like a look at the book?"

Atlas presumed Tom referred to the ledger containing the names of accommodating women. "Yes, I believe I would like to see your book."

Tom produced a surprisingly small notebook from his pocket. "I presume you are interested in nothing but the finest we have to offer."

Atlas held out his hand. "May I?"

Tom handed the book over and stood silently as Atlas flipped through the pages. The handwriting was neat and contained. All of the names appeared to have been written by the same hand. He turned one page and then another. He recognized none of the names, not that there was any reason that he should.

"Do you see anything of interest?" Tom inquired. "We offer something to all tastes."

"Hmm. There is such variety." Atlas regretted not asking Charlton to accompany him. He had no idea how to conduct himself when it came to transactions of the flesh.

"Perhaps you could tell me what you are looking for." Tom pointed to names on the list. "Miss Jones is a strong, plump girl, very eager to please. I am told that Mrs. Baker is very lusty, a very agreeable congress." He paused. "Perhaps you prefer a virginal beauty. A young girl fresh from the country?"

Atlas cut the man off. "No, that shall not be necessary." His cheeks burned as if he'd spent the day basking in the intense Mediterranean sun. "My brother-in-law, the Marquess of Vessey, recommended a particular woman that he . . . er . . . very much enjoyed. But I fear I have forgotten her name."

Tom nodded knowingly. "You would be speaking of Edith Hayes. His lordship has enjoyed sharing Mrs. Hayes and her wide array of talents with other members of his family in the past."

"He has?" Atlas's stomach churned at the thought of that sort of familial bonding.

"Shall I send for Mrs. Hayes? She resides nearby."

Atlas thumbed through the book, looking for her name. He soon came upon it, but as with the others, there was no direction for her. The only way to expediently find Mrs. Hayes was through Tom's.

"Yes, please do call for her." He puffed out his cheeks and exhaled. "And while I wait, does that offer of a whiskey still stand?"

★ ★ ★

Within the hour, Atlas found himself alone with Edith Hayes in a sumptuous above-stairs chamber.

She was at least a decade younger than Wendela Pike and could not be described as beautiful, but her skin was smooth and her brown gaze clear and bright, and the intensity with which she stared straight into Atlas's eyes made him feel as if he was the only person in the world. "I understand that Lord Vessey sent you."

"Not exactly." He swallowed the last of his whiskey and set the glass down a bit more forcefully then intended.

"It does not matter who sent you." She gave him a look of pure sensual desire, her musky perfume permeating the air. "Let us begin, shall we?" She drew off her cape, revealing an expensive-looking silk grown that showcased pale shoulders and other admirable womanly assets. "What would you like? You will find that I can be very accommodating."

He gestured toward the bed. "Not that." He was eager to stop her practiced seduction. Atlas could see why this woman might appeal to Vessey. She had a way of making a man feel seen, as if he were the most appealing person she'd ever met. "I am here for information, and I am prepared to pay your usual fee in order to obtain it."

"Is that so?" She eyed him speculatively. "What sort of information?"

"I am looking into the death of Mrs. Wendela Pike."

She dropped any pretense of wanting to bed him in much the same manner as she'd dropped her cape. The chemistry she'd created between them fizzled like a brilliant candelabra doused with a bucket of water. "I will take double my usual fee, and you may ask anything you like," she said matter-of-factly, all business now. "However, to be frank, I doubt I will be of much assistance. I never met Mrs. Pike."

"But Vessey does visit you here regularly?"

"He does."

"How long have you been . . . associated . . . with the marquess?"

"I suppose he has been coming to see me weekly for about eight years now." She smiled with supreme confidence. "I am very good at what I do."

Atlas believed her. "Did he ever speak of becoming your protector?"

She pondered the question. "Are you thinking that Lord Vessey killed Mrs. Pike in order to create a place for me in that grand house of his?"

"I am wondering about that possibility, yes."

She laughed and made herself comfortable, lounging on the bed, propping her curvaceous form up on one elbow. "No, he never talked of an exclusive arrangement, but even if he had, I would never have agreed."

"Why ever not?"

"I enjoy having control over my own affairs. I would only take on a protector who could guarantee my future."

"In the form of an annuity."

"Exactly. And Lord Vessey was well known to be rather frugal with Mrs. Pike."

"Do you believe him capable of violence?"

"Against Mrs. Pike?" She shrugged her snowy shoulders. "I believe he was truly fond of her, but one never knows. If you would care to know about his amorous abilities and his sexual preferences, I can be of much more assistance. Now if you inquire about that son of his—"

Atlas could not have been more surprised. "You are acquainted with Vessey's son?"

"I am. And of late, he is in possession of enough coin to visit me regularly."

"I see." A wave of disgust washed over him. "You regularly service both father and son?"

"Yes—not together of course. At least not after that first time."

He felt ill. "The first time?"

"Vessey brought his son here for his first initiation into carnal delights. He desired that I make a man of the boy."

Atlas was aghast. That bastard had brought Phoebe's son to a prostitute. "How old was the boy when this occurred?"

"I believe he was fourteen. Such a lovely boy. And he has grown into a most considerate lover."

Atlas grimaced at this violation of Nicholas's privacy. "You continue to see Vessey's son?"

"He began visiting again recently. He apparently came into a great deal of money."

"Did Nicholas tell you where the money came from?"

Her forehead wrinkled. "Nicholas who?"

"Vessey's son." At the confused expression on her face, he added, "Perhaps you know him as Beaumont—Viscount Beaumont."

"Oh no." Her eyes crinkled. "I am not referring to the heir. Lord Vessey brought his oldest son to me."

"The heir, Beaumont, is his oldest son. His only son."

"No, he has an older boy, by two years. His name is Francis. He is another of Vessey's by-blows."

Atlas's mouth fell open. "Are you certain?"

"I am more than certain," she said crisply. "After all, I have bedded Francis on a number of occasions. Often enough to hear him sing his father's praises. I am not surprised that you have not heard of him. Vessey kept the young man's existence a secret until quite recently."

"Why would Vessey keep this Francis a secret? After all, he has two young daughters with Mrs. Pike that everyone seems to know about."

She shrugged. "You will have to ask his lordship."

Atlas digested this new information. "Do you happen to know who Francis's mother is?"

Edith looked at him as if he were a simpleton. "Why, it was Mrs. Pike, of course."

CHAPTER 10

Atlas directed the hackney driver to drop him several blocks from his Bond Street quarters so that he might complete the remainder the journey on foot.

He needed to settle his mind and arrange his thoughts into some semblance of order. They were both a jumbled mess after Edith Hayes's shocking revelation.

Vessey had another son. A young man older than Nicholas. Had his sister known about her husband's bastard? It was not uncommon for married aristocrats to keep a *chère-amie*, but the ways of the ton would have been alien to his innocent sister. At times, being among the aristocracy was as stupefying as trying to decipher one of Thea's infernal mathematical calculations.

He crossed Brook Street, attempting to sidestep the worst of the mire. Gulping in a lungful of air did little to ease the tightness in his chest. Thinking of his late sister was always painful. Still. After all of these years. As he turned onto New Bond Street, a voice called out from behind.

"Mr. Catesby!"

Atlas turned to find Samuel Brown in his dark clergy clothing rushing toward him with an umbrella hoisted above his head. That's when Atlas realized his own hair was damp. He'd been so consumed with his thoughts that he'd taken no notice of the light rain.

"Good day to you, sir," the clergyman said as he drew near.

Atlas tipped his hat. "Mr. Brown."

"I was just on my way to your apartments. Your manservant asked that I call. Dare I hope you have found proof of Vessey's guilt?"

"Not as of yet." He belatedly opened his umbrella to shield himself from the elements. "I am hoping you will clarify a few matters for me."

"Of course." The younger man fell in step beside Atlas, who imagined they made an interesting sight—two men of approximate height, in dark clothing, walking side by side with matching black umbrellas over their heads. "What is it you would like to know?"

"Mrs. Pike's sister confirms your story."

The clergyman lifted his brows. "She does?"

"You seem surprised."

"I thought our betrothal was our own private secret. I was not aware that Wendela had shared our happy news with anyone."

"Except Vessey."

"I beg your pardon?"

"You said you believed Vessey knew. That he had Mrs. Pike killed because she told him she was leaving him for you."

"Exactly right. And I hope you will soon prove that to be the case."

"You mentioned that you had been presented with a living that would take you away from Town."

"Indeed. In East Anglia. Wendela was going to accompany me there after we wed."

This was the part of Brown's story that puzzled Atlas the most. It diverged significantly from what others had told him of Wendy's plans for her future. "I have it on good authority that Mrs. Pike intended to take up a singing career."

Brown stiffened. "Where did you hear that horrendous lie?"

"From the manager at Covent Garden. He said Mrs. Pike was extraordinarily talented and that he was prepared to pay her handsomely to perform at his venue."

Brown halted and faced Atlas, his expression partially obscured by the rain dripping from the edge of his umbrella. "Simon Cooke is a liar. He wanted Wendela for himself."

Atlas wondered if that was true. Or whether Brown assumed all men found Wendy to be as enchanting as Brown himself had. "It sounds as if there are plenty of men who felt the same."

"Despite her association with Vessey, Wendela was a respectable woman," Brown said stiffly. "Taking to the stage is not a respectable vocation for a woman. She would never have countenanced it."

"Are you certain about that?"

"Absolutely." He firmed his mouth. "I would stake my very life on it."

"I confess there is something else that has been puzzling me. Mrs. Pike was known to be a devoted mother. Why would she leave her children?"

"The two young girls are away at school, so Wendela saw little of them."

Atlas knew that much was true given that Jamie had looked into the matter. "What of the oldest? The boy called Francis."

Brown's eyes widened. "Ah, so you know about the young man."

"Is he a secret?"

"For most of his life, yes, he has been."

"Why? Vessey has not been discreet about the young daughters he had by Mrs. Pike."

"Vessey initially viewed Francis's birth as a mistake, an embarrassment to his name. At the time, Vessey expected his arrangement with Wendela to end after a year or so, once he tired of her."

"Which"—heat flared in the back of Atlas's neck—"he apparently never did."

"Precisely. And then, several years after his wife died, once it became clear to Vessey that he would never remarry, he gave in to Wendela's desire to have more children."

"That certainly explains why the daughters are so young despite the fact that their parents had conducted a liaison for many years before they were born."

Brown nodded. "Up until then, Francis had been mostly hidden away at private boarding schools, perfectly respectable establishments, you understand, but certainly not up to the standard of Eton or Harrow. Vessey did not care to risk the ton finding out about his by-blow."

"Did he allow Francis to come home to visit?"

"Vessey took a house near Francis's school, which is where he and Wendela would spend time with the boy on school holidays."

"And now?"

"After the daughters were born, Wendela convinced Vessey to allow Francis to come home to Stonebrook on holidays. For the most part, Vessey has remained discreet about Francis's existence. Although he did eventually move the boy to Eton. However, the boy was directed to be circumspect about who his father was. And just recently Vessey allowed the boy to come to London and move about in society."

"How recently?"

"Within the last year or so."

"What is Francis Pike like? Are you acquainted with him?"

"Oh yes, I met him at Stonebrook. A most amiable young man, even if he is overly concerned with his consequence. He can be a bit prideful, but who among us is perfect?"

"What do you know of Francis Pike's relationship with his mother?"

"Francis was very protective of Wendela and her reputation. And it is a mutual admiration society between Francis and Vessey. According to Wendela, Vessey used to say it was a shame that Francis was not his heir because the young man is clever enough and strong enough to do what needs to be done."

Atlas bristled at this affront to his nephew. "What of Nicholas, his actual heir?"

"Vessey's fond of the boy, of course, but says Beaumont is soft, a quality Vessey used to say came from the mother's side of the family."

Atlas hoped that much was true, that Nicholas did indeed take after his mother and not his whoreson of a father. "Do you have any idea where I might find Francis Pike?"

"At the moment? I cannot say. However, on Monday evenings you are very likely to find young Francis at The Rising Sun in Knightsbridge."

"And what sort of establishment is that?"

"A tavern. But more importantly, it is where lottery members meet."

"Francis Pike belongs to the Lottery Club?"

"Wendela often lamented about her eldest son's fondness for gaming. Francis has a taste for the finer things in life, but unfortunately for him, Vessey is as tightfisted as they come. Wendela said Francis was determined to gain a sizable lottery prize in order to live in the high style to which he would very much like to become accustomed."

Atlas thanked the clergyman for taking the time to come to see him. "I suppose I am for The Rising Sun come Monday."

★ ★ ★

Atlas entered the tea garden the following afternoon, scanning the arbors and flowered walkways for any sign of Lilliana.

By some miracle, the sun had appeared that morning, allowing Atlas to walk to Somerville House and then to the tea garden in search of Lilliana and the boys. He proceeded through the spacious gardens until he reached the bowling green, where he found Lilliana seated under the shade of a fruit tree.

"Mr. Catesby!" Peter, the older of the two boys, came running over from the bowling green the moment he spotted Atlas. "Look who is here, Mama!"

"Hello, Atlas." Lilliana greeted him from her seat at the table. She was a welcome sight in her lemon-colored dress with billowing sleeves and a matching hat topped by a feathery flourish. "This is a surprise."

"I do hope I am not intruding." He bowed to her. "I called at Somerville House and Hastings informed me that I would find you here."

"Will you come and bowl with us?" Peter asked. "Our rink is just over there." He was dark-haired and slimly built, like his mother, while seven-year-old Robin possessed his late father's lighter coloring and sturdy body.

Robin ran up behind his brother and slipped his small hand into Atlas's. The boys wore matching gray outfits, jackets and trousers designed in a military style. Their clothing was slightly askew from their play, and they smelled of exertion. "Do you bowl on the green as well as you bowl hoops?" Robin asked. Atlas had taught the boys how to bowl hoops when they'd first met.

"Yes, do tell," Lilliana said. "Do you play at bowls, Mr. Catesby?"

"One cannot grow up in a household with three older brothers without becoming at least somewhat proficient in sport."

Robin tugged on Atlas's hand. "Come and play with us."

"Perhaps for just a few minutes." Atlas found it difficult to deny Lilliana's boys.

"Just until the tea arrives," Lilliana instructed her children. "After that, you must play on your own while Mr. Catesby and I have our visit."

The boys were already dragging him away before their mother finished speaking. Atlas and the boys took their positions on their rink to begin their game. Around them were several other parties bowling on the green, each playing on its own divided portion.

Atlas and the children took turns launching a series of heavy balls toward a smaller ball called the jack. They played for about twenty minutes, with Atlas stopping each boy at intervals to help correct his form.

Lilliana watched from the shade, applauding enthusiastically when either of the boys threw well. Atlas always marveled at the marked change in Lilliana whenever she was in the presence of her children. Her natural reserve fell away, and she laughed more easily, her deep maternal affection for her sons apparent in every look she gave them.

She signaled to Atlas once the refreshments arrived, and he left the boys playing on the green to rejoin their mother in the shade of the fruit tree.

"You ordered lemonade," he noted gratefully when he took his seat.

"I thought you might be in need of fortification."

Flushed from his exertions, he drank and took a moment to appreciate the rare beautiful day and the pleasure of being in Lilliana's company. It was one of those singular moments in life, brief and unanticipated, that is unexpectedly perfect.

"How goes the investigation?" she asked.

He told her what he'd learned from Wendy's sister.

"That suggests the clergyman is telling the truth about Mrs. Pike's intention to leave Lord Vessey."

"So it appears."

"Which gives Vessey a motive," she noted. "The jealousy and humiliation of being jilted in favor of a penniless, untitled nobody might very well drive a gentleman such as Lord Vessey to murder."

He reached for a small mince pie. "It is certainly one of many avenues to explore—I scarcely know where to begin."

"I gather you've spoken with your friend, Mrs. Jennings."

"I did." He did not miss the acidity in her tone at the mention of Juliet. "She says she and Mrs. Pike fought over a man, a Russian diplomat who left the country and returned home months ago."

"Do you believe her?"

"I plan to check her story." He bit into the pie, appreciating the mix of flavors—meat, fruit, sugar, cloves, and other spices, with an added dash of brandy. "The man's name is Mr. Aleksey Witte."

"I have become acquainted with some Russian diplomats here in London," Lilliana said. "But I do not recall meeting a Mr. Witte. Shall I inquire into it?"

"That would be most helpful. In the meantime, I shall explore some other possibilities that have recently opened up."

"Such as?"

"I intend to speak with Vessey's oldest son that he had by Mrs. Pike."

"I thought all of Mrs. Pike's children quite young and away at school."

"Not the eldest, who happens to be two years older than Nicholas. Vessey apparently kept the boy a secret from society, but now Francis Pike is grown and has come to London."

"Oh. I see." She studied his expression. "That must have come as a shock."

"It rather was. The existence of young Francis confirms that the ties between Vessey and Mrs. Pike both before and during his marriage to my sister were even stronger than I previously thought."

"They shared a child. There are few bonds more consequential than that." Something tender touched her fine eyes. "This must be painful for you."

"It certainly revives certain memories that I would prefer not to revisit. But it also provides me with an opportunity to right a wrong that was done twenty years ago."

"I understand your desire to bring Lord Vessey to justice, but what if he is not guilty?"

"Given what Mrs. Pike's sister said, it is beginning to appear rather likely that Vessey is the guilty party. But I will continue to pursue all possibilities. "

"What other possibilities are there?"

Atlas took another bite of mince pie, chewing slowly to give himself time to formulate a sufficiently discreet answer. "Mrs. Pike was friendly with the companion of another peer here in town, a Mrs. Walker. This woman's protector appealed to Vessey to settle an annuity on Mrs. Pike."

"That was rather decent of him." She spoke over the rim of her teacup. "Who is this lord?"

He hesitated before deciding to be completely truthful with her. He knew she would expect nothing less. Besides, the baser part of him took pleasure in bringing Lilliana's former admirer down a notch or two in her esteem. "Lord Roxbury."

Her eyes rounded. "Are you jesting?"

"I am not."

She appeared to ponder the revelation. "Well," she said after a moment, "that certainly confirms what I have always believed about Roxbury's character."

"Is that why you broke with him?" It surprised Atlas to hear she might have suspected Roxbury of less than honorable behavior. "You detected he was not as respectable as he appeared?"

"Quite the contrary." She looked at Atlas as if he'd spoken to her in Turkish. "I have always believed Roxbury to be a good man. The sole reason I rejected his offer of marriage is because I did not feel the sort of warmth for him that a woman should have for her husband."

"A *good* man?" Perhaps Lilliana expected a husband to keep a mistress. Maybe her own father had. "Are you referring to Roxbury?"

"Naturally."

He wrinkled his nose. "The man kept a . . . special companion . . . while he pursued you to be his wife."

"Yes, but more importantly, Roxbury spoke to Lord Vessey on Mrs. Pike's behalf even though he had nothing to gain from it. He came to the assistance of a helpless woman of questionable reputation. He acted with honor."

Atlas swallowed the last of his pie, which gave him an excuse to say nothing.

She gave him a wondering look. "My goodness. It is almost as if you are jealous." He registered her delight at the realization.

"Nonsense," he lied, busying himself with selecting a small, round egg custard artfully garnished with lemon zest.

"No?" She sat back in her chair, a satisfied smile wreathing her face. "Then you will not mind if I invite Roxbury to join me at the theater this evening."

"Perhaps I will join you as well." He bit into the cheesecake but could not properly appreciate the sweet creamy symphony of lemon, orange, and almonds. "I do so enjoy Mrs. Jenning's performances at Covent Garden."

Her expression soured. "By all means, do as you like," she said coldly, reaching for an egg custard, even though they both knew she did not care for sweets.

He intercepted her pale, fine-boned hand mid-air and brought it to his lips. "And so I shall. Do as I like."

"Will you?" Challenge sparked in her beautiful eyes, and neither of them was thinking of Roxbury or Juliet. She made no attempt to slide her gloved hand from his grasp. "I suppose we shall see about that."

Chapter 11

The Rising Sun in Knightsbridge, where Francis Pike apparently hoped to find his fortune, was a century-old red brick building with carved and paneled rooms where Atlas was forced to battle his way through the boisterous crowd. The air was thick with smoke and the smells of ale and perspiration.

A man leapt onto a tabletop and cupped his mouth with both hands to address the crush. "We are closing the book." He shouted to be heard above the din. "We will use the entire fund to purchase lottery tickets."

A cheer went up. All around Atlas people argued and debated, the overconsumption of spirits no doubt adding to the rabble. After making a few inquiries, Atlas was directed to a well-dressed young man sitting at a back table with another man.

"That is another fifty pounds," remarked the buck Atlas presumed was Francis Pike.

His companion scoffed. "I would say all of our debts are settled."

"Previous debts, perhaps." Pike regarded his companion with tolerant amusement. "But not the ones you have incurred in the last week."

"All of my debts should be erased, past and future," his table-mate said as he tossed what appeared to be a comfit into his mouth. "Have I not already proven myself?"

"Francis Pike?" Atlas asked, raising his voice to be heard.

Vessey's son looked up, providing Atlas with his first proper view of him. Francis Pike's hair was very blond, almost white, and he might have been handsome except for the long, sharp nose that dominated his face. It was as if fate had conspired to announce this man's common birth by stamping a blatant imper-fection at the center of his otherwise flawless aristocratic features.

"I am he." The young man spoke in a precise accent that sounded a bit too studied to be completely natural. Atlas recalled the clergyman's remark that Mrs. Pike's son was very aware of his consequence. "And who, might I ask, are you?"

"My name is Atlas Catesby. I would like to speak with you about your mother."

Pike visibly stiffened. "My mother is no longer with us. And I shall not hear a negative word about her. She was an honorable woman, and I do not intend to have her name besmirched by anyone."

Pike's spirited defense of his late mother impressed Atlas. Most in society would find Mrs. Pike unworthy of respect, particularly this straight-spined young man, who seemed very conscious of his societal standing.

"I have heard as much from everyone I have spoken to," Atlas said gently. It was true. No one he'd encountered had uttered a single unkind word about Wendy.

"Catesby?" Pike's companion interjected, speaking around the confection in his mouth. He was slight and disheveled, his expensive clothing wrinkled, his cravat undone. "You are the one who is investigating Mrs. Pike's death." He nudged Pike with his elbow. "Catesby here wants to find your mother's killer."

"Is that so?" Pike regarded Atlas with increased interest. "Why?"

"She was an innocent woman who was murdered. Is that not reason enough?"

Vessey's bastard regarded Atlas warily. "There are some who would not call her innocent."

"She was killed. The person who murdered your mother should not be allowed to get away with it."

"I agree." Pike's guarded expression relaxed a fraction. "Please do forgive my bad manners." He gestured toward his companion. "This is my friend Jasper Balfour."

His friend gave an easy laugh. "Mr. Catesby is not interested in me. He is here to meet you." Balfour came unsteadily to his feet. "I will be on my way now that the books are closed. Good evening." He sauntered into the crowd and disappeared from view.

Atlas took the liberty of slipping into the high-backed wooden bench Balfour had just abandoned. "I was hoping you could answer some questions for me."

Pike gave Atlas an intent look. "Do you truly believe you can find my mother's killer?"

"It is my intention to try."

"I rather expected you to have accused my father by now."

The comment took Atlas by surprise. "Why is that? Do you think Vessey killed your mother?"

"Of course not. But I know who you are. Your sister was married to my father."

"Yes." Atlas maintained a placid exterior. "My sister was wed to Vessey. She was his marchioness and the mother of his heir."

"Thank you for stating the obvious." Francis seemed amused. "I am very well aware of who my father's heir is."

"What kind of relationship do you have with Nicholas?" Atlas asked, more out of curiosity than anything else.

"I cannot see how my relations with my half brother can possibly be relevant to my mother's murder."

"It never hurts to have a complete picture of all of the aspects of a victim's life."

"Beaumont was not in my mother's life. My father preferred not to cross certain lines of propriety."

"Surely she met the boy."

"She did not and neither have I," Pike said courteously. "My half brother and I do not have a relationship. And before you assume that I am consumed with hatred and jealousy, allow me to assure you that the sole reason we have no relationship is because Nicholas is not aware of my existence."

Atlas stared at him. "Still? Even now with you residing in town?"

Pike nodded. "It is as my father wishes."

"Why? Is it because Vessey does not care for Nicholas to learn his father kept a mistress at the same time he was married to Nicholas's mother?"

"Perhaps. My father has mentioned that Beaumont is something of a Puritan. There is no reason to upset the boy."

"But the two of you are now in London at the same time. Nicholas is bound to learn of your existence soon, if he hasn't already."

Pike lifted one shoulder, as if the matter barely concerned him. "I do as my father pleases. He wishes to orchestrate our meeting at a time of his choosing."

Atlas tipped his head to the side. "Do you always do as your father asks?"

"I try. There is no man in the world that I admire more than the marquess."

Atlas managed not to grimace at the complimentary words. "Did your mother have any enemies that you know of? Did she by chance mention anyone who frightened her or made her uncomfortable?"

Pike thought for a moment. "There was a clergyman who was infatuated with her."

"Samuel Brown."

"I see you have heard about him." His expression darkened. "In the last month or so, she became more uncomfortable in Brown's presence. The intensity of his unrequited affection unsettled her."

Atlas was not at all convinced that Brown's love for Wendy was unrequited. Everything he'd learned thus far suggested otherwise. "Did your mother ever argue with your father?"

"Of course. They were together for many years. They were bound to have disagreements."

"Did they argue about anything in particular?"

"My mother enjoyed buying nice things, and there were a number of disagreements about her spending habits. However, mostly they argued about my father awarding my mother an annuity."

"Which he refused to do, as I understand it."

The edges of Pike's mouth turned downward. "He thought it was crass of Mother to ask. Lord Vessey had always taken care of her and, I am quite sure, would have continued to do so had she lived."

Atlas wasn't so certain. It seemed to him that Vessey had used money as a tether to keep Wendy tied to him. But why had he felt the need? Was it simply the frugality for which the marquess was well known, or had he felt Wendy slipping away?

"My father had nothing to do with my mother's death," Pike told him. "My mother and father were not married, but we are his family, my mother, my sisters, and I. He would never hurt Mama. He adored her."

"How old are your sisters?"

"They are just girls. Helen is eleven and Caroline is nine. Vessey would never deprive them of their mother."

After asking a few more questions, which yielded little useful information, Atlas rose and thanked Pike for his time.

"You may reach me at the Albany should you have any further questions," Pike told Atlas as the two men exchanged goodbyes. "I will do everything in my power to help you find my mother's killer."

The mention of the Albany did not go unnoticed by Atlas. Fashionable young bachelors about town coveted the prestigious Mayfair address. Residing in the apartments off Piccadilly might confer some of the consequence that Pike's illegitimate birth denied him.

As Atlas made his way out of The Rising Sun, he wondered what Wendy had been playing at toward the end of her life. She'd apparently agreed to wed Brown, yet had told her family that the clergyman made her uncomfortable. She'd also told Brown she would move to Anglia with him, while also apparently consenting to perform at Covent Garden. Everywhere Atlas turned, he encountered another contradiction about the dead woman's intentions for her future.

Despite all of the many facts he had gathered about Wendela Pike's final days, Atlas somehow felt further than ever from finding her killer.

CHAPTER 12

"Catesby." Jonathan Bradford, the Marquess of Roxbury, greeted Atlas from the comfortable surroundings of his study, a well-appointed chamber that spoke of the man's immense wealth. "This is a most unexpected visit."

"I must confess it is for me as well," Atlas said with a bow.

"And yet here you are." Roxbury sat in a comfortable leather armchair, with one knee crossed over the other. Smoke from the lit cheroot clasped between his thumb and forefinger engulfed him in a silvery haze. Atlas had been in the marquess's darkened study once before. When the man had summoned him to warn him off of Lilliana.

"I am investigating the death of Wendela Pike."

"It is a very tragic affair." The pale light from the window illuminated Roxbury's face. Although he was not an overtly handsome man, Roxbury possessed even features and a generally agreeable manner. "However, I fail to see how Mrs. Pike's unfortunate end has any bearing on me."

"Allow me to come straight to the point."

"Please do."

"I understand you spoke with Vessey on Mrs. Pike's behalf, regarding her desire for an annuity or a settlement of some kind."

Roxbury's cheeks hollowed as drew on his cheroot. "What of it?"

"May I ask what prompted you to intercede?"

"I spoke to Vessey because Mrs. Pike's desire for financial security was not unreasonable." He exhaled through both his mouth and nostrils as he spoke. "I was very sorry he declined to settle a sum on Mrs. Pike after all of the years she had devoted to him. She resided with Vessey for the better part of twenty years and presented him with robust children of whom he seems quite fond."

"Perhaps he suspected her of being unfaithful."

"That would surprise me very much." Roxbury exhaled a long stream of diaphanous smoke. "From all I observed of her conduct, and in my conversation with her, Mrs. Pike never once hinted of an attachment to another man. Indeed, I am convinced she had bedded no other man."

"I understand that Mrs. Pike turned to you because you are very generous to your own mistress."

Roxbury examined his cheroot and did not respond.

Atlas persisted. "I am interested in speaking with your . . . with Mrs. Walker."

"Whatever for?"

"I understand she and Mrs. Pike were friends. I am hopeful Mrs. Walker will be able to shed some light on Mrs. Pike's state of mind before her death."

"What possible difference could that make now?"

"I shall not know until I speak with Mrs. Walker. Could you provide me with her direction?"

"There is no need for that." Roxbury rose, moving with purpose and precision, to pull the bell ring. A butler appeared immediately.

"Summon Mrs. Walker, if you please," Roxbury directed.

"She is here?" Atlas asked.

"Indeed." Now Roxbury seemed slightly amused. "I am nothing if not accommodating."

Before long, Mrs. Walker presented herself. She was in her mid-thirties, about the same age as the late Mrs. Pike, trim and neat in a severe dark gown that was in no way designed to entice or seduce. The large ring of keys attached to a band at her waist explained the morose gown. Mrs. Walker wasn't just Roxbury's ladybird; she was also his housekeeper.

Indignation burned in Atlas's belly. This woman's presence in the mausoleum where Lilliana might very well have presided as mistress appalled him. Lilliana had already suffered through one intolerable husband. Atlas had thought Roxbury was different.

"Ah, there you are, Mrs. Walker," Roxbury said when the housekeeper came in. "Catesby here has some questions for you about Mrs. Pike. He is attempting to discover who killed her."

She shot a questioning gaze at her lover. In return, Roxbury gave a reassuring incline of his chin. "I am not sure I can be of any help." She spoke in a clear, contained voice.

"I understand you were friendly with Mrs. Pike," Atlas said.

"Yes, sir, I was." She stood with quiet dignity, shoulders back, with her hands lightly clasped before her waist. "Mrs. Pike was a fine person. Very agreeable. I cannot imagine who would want to harm her."

"Do you know if she intended to leave Vessey for another man?"

Her hand went to her breastbone. "No, indeed."

"She never mentioned an attachment to another man?"

"She did not, and it would surprise me very much if Mrs. Pike were to leave his lordship."

"Even though he refused to assure her financial future?"

"She maintained hope that his lordship would eventually provide an annuity for her and the children."

"Did she ever mention performing in public, specifically at Covent Garden?"

"She did. She had the voice of an angel." Mrs. Walker smiled at the memory. "But his lordship would not allow it."

"Do you think Mrs. Pike would have performed at Covent Garden despite Vessey's disapproval?"

"I do not believe that she would have. Although they were not wed, Mrs. Pike viewed herself as bound to the marquess for life. She was not a licentious woman."

"Did she ever mention a man named Samuel Brown to you?"

"The clergyman? Yes, she did. He was infatuated with her. But Wendy . . . Mrs. Pike . . . had no interest in him."

"Yet Mrs. Pike told her sister that she had fallen in love with a man and intended to leave Lord Vessey to be with this man."

The housekeeper's perfect composure fissured when her mouth fell open. "I can assure you that Mrs. Pike never told me any such thing. If anything, Mr. Brown had begun to make Wendy feel uneasy."

"In what way?"

"He seemed to have become fixated with her. The cooler and more distant Wendy was with him, the more intense his ardor for her seemed to grow."

"So as far as you are aware, Mrs. Pike remained devoted to Vessey all the way up until her unfortunate demise and never seriously entertained the notion of taking to the stage."

"Yes, sir. She was a good woman. Her only vice was that she spent a bit too freely, but we are all flawed in some way. She did not deserve to be killed in such a manner."

"Few people do," Atlas remarked.

Mrs. Walker turned to Roxbury. "If that is all, my lord, I should like to return to my duties."

Roxbury looked to Atlas, who gave his assent with a dip of his chin.

"Thank you, Mrs. Walker," Roxbury said to her. "You may leave us."

When she was gone, the marquess turned an inquiring look in Atlas's direction. "Did you learn anything of interest?"

"You intended to bring Lady Lilliana into this house?" Atlas could no longer disguise his contempt. "With your ladybird cozily available just below stairs?"

Roxbury's nostrils flared. "Watch yourself, Catesby."

"I thought you would treat her honorably. That is the only reason I agreed to step aside."

"We both know that is not entirely true." Roxbury spoke with derision. "You stepped aside not because of some noble sacrifice, but because you know what everybody else in London is well aware of—that you are beneath the lady's touch."

Atlas's face warmed. "From what I have seen here today, neither of us is worthy of her."

"Not that it is any of your concern," Roxbury spoke through clenched teeth, "but I settled a generous annuity, the one that so impressed Mrs. Pike, on Mrs. Walker in anticipation of wedding Lady Lilliana. Once our betrothal was official, I intended to engage a new housekeeper."

Atlas curled his lip. "One wonders whether you would have required the same services of your new housekeeper."

A muscle twitched in Roxbury's cheek. "You go too far, Catesby. We are done here." He reached for the bell pull. "My butler will see you out."

"Do not bother." Atlas headed for the door. "I can see myself out."

Roxbury spoke to Atlas's retreating form. "You are not fooling anyone with that insufferable honor that you wear like an open wound on your chest for all to admire. The true reason you are not courting the lady is quite obvious."

Atlas could not resist taking the bait. "And what is that reason?"

"It is simple cowardice. You are afraid to make a claim on her."

Atlas went out and slammed the door hard behind him.

★　★　★

"You actually went up to one of Tom's bedchambers with a strumpet?" Charlton couldn't stop laughing. "What were you thinking?"

Atlas puffed on his hookah. "There was no other way to proceed."

"It does seem like a rather shabby plan on your part." The two men had assumed their usual positions in Atlas's sitting room.

He handed the nargileh hose to Charlton, who took a moment to wipe the mouthpiece with his kerchief before taking a draw on the water pipe. "You are the one who sent me there under the misassumption that the woman's direction would be written down in the book."

"It used to be so." Charlton chuckled. "But it has been a while since I have visited a bagnio."

"What else would you have had me do?" Atlas asked. "I could not ask Tom to provide Edith Hayes's direction. The man makes his living by bringing girls to customers, not by sending patrons away to the women."

"What I would give to see that." Charlton's brilliant blue eyes twinkled. "Vicar Atlas Catesby in a bordello."

"The bagnio incident is the least of my concerns at this point." Atlas exhaled twin columns of smoke through his nostrils, enjoying the accompanying sense of peace and calm that gently flowed through him. "Everyone I have spoken with suggests Mrs. Pike had absolutely no romantic interest in the clergyman. And yet her sister says Mrs. Pike was in love and ready to run away."

"Perhaps she kept her feelings for the clergyman a secret to protect him from Vessey."

"I suppose that is possible. And then there is Francis Pike, Vessey's eldest by-blow."

"The boy who won the lottery?"

Atlas returned the hose to Charlton. "Pike won the lottery?"

"Yes, it was quite the talk of the town when it occurred."

"When was that?"

"Not long ago. Perhaps three months past. Vessey is known to be tight with his purse, and Pike lived in very modest lodgings before he came into his lottery money."

"That explains how he can afford to live at the Albany."

"Indeed. And he now frequents only the finest establishments and tradesmen. I understand he even uses the same tailor as Somerville."

"Kirby Nash on Pall Mall."

Charlton pointed at Atlas with the mouthpiece end of the hookah pipe. "Yes, that's the one."

"I wonder how much the lottery prize was."

"They say it was twenty-thousand pounds."

Atlas whistled low. "That is quite a sum."

"Francis Pike might not be the heir, but he is using his small fortune to give himself some consequence."

"And possibly to make a name for himself about town, which is clearly very important to the boy, after being kept hidden by his father for most of his life."

"Well, yes, he is well aware of propriety. Vessey is said to be very fond of young Pike. He saw to it that the boy was educated at the finest schools."

"Just not the same ones as Nicholas, apparently. According to Pike, Nicholas is unaware of his elder brother's existence. But with Nicholas down from university now, it is only a matter of time before the half brothers meet."

"That is quite a secret for Vessey to keep."

Atlas exhaled long and slow. "It makes one wonder what other secrets Vessey is keeping."

"Whatever they are, Francis might kill to keep them secret."

"Are you suggesting the boy is violent?"

"Not exactly. However, I am saying he is not a man to be trifled with, especially when it comes to his adored parents. He challenged some young blood, a relation of Merton's, to a duel after the man insulted Mrs. Pike."

Atlas leaned forward. "When did that occur?"

Charlton thought about it. "Perhaps a year past."

"What was the insult that made Pike call out this relation of Merton's?"

"He made some reference to Mrs. Pike being a whore."

"The man clearly deserved to be called out. Do you know his name?"

"Harry Dean, I believe it is." Charlton yawned. Atlas could relate. Indulging in the nargileh could sometimes prove entirely too relaxing. "As I said, he is some relation, distant relation, to Viscount Merton. Son of his cousin or something of that manner."

"Did a duel take place?"

"It certainly did." Charlton gave a lazy stretch, reaching his hands high above his head as if straining to touch the ceiling "I attended."

Atlas blinked. Given his friend's blithe manner, he couldn't be certain he'd heard correctly. "You did?"

"Yes, I had enjoyed a late evening at the gaming hell. It was near dawn when I set out for home. But everyone was talking about a duel that was to take place shortly between Vessey's son and a distant cousin of Merton's."

"And you decided to go? For what purpose? Entertainment?" Atlas was appalled at the notion his friend would attend a duel solely for its entertainment value, to witness foolish men, often young ones, putting their lives at risk.

Charlton held up a well-manicured hand, palm facing Atlas. "Please spare me the usual tirade about the uselessness of the nobility. The reason I attended is because I thought they might be referring to young Nicholas. I presumed you would call me out yourself if I allowed anything to happen to your nephew, so I went along with some friends."

"I see." He paused to consider that. "What would you have done if it had been Nicholas?"

"I had not thought that far in advance. Imagine my relief when I found out it was Vessey's by-blow and not his heir."

"What happened with the duel?"

"Pike got off the first shot and was very gentlemanly about it. He made certain the bullet barely grazed Dean's arm."

"And Dean, did he return the shot?"

Charlton shook his head as his eyes drifted closed. "Francis Pike is no fool. He made certain to injure Dean's shooting arm."

Charlton's soft snores soon filled the room. Atlas inhaled deeply as he drew on the hookah and thought about Francis Pike. Again, he had to admire the young man for defending his mother's honor.

Charlton's eyes popped open. "I just recalled something." He was instantly awake and alert again. "I do not know how I could have forgotten it. At the time, I just assumed Dean's words to be the toothless ranting of a boy whose dignity had been injured."

"What did he say?"

"Dean was furious. I suspect he was foxed as well, which did nothing to temper his anger. People around him were laughing and teasing him for allowing himself to be defeated by a bastard."

"I imagine he did not react well to that."

"No, indeed. Dean said matters between them were not settled. He vowed to make Pike pay for humiliating him."

Atlas studied his friend's patrician face. "You think it is possible Harry Dean killed Mrs. Pike?"

"Who knows?" Charlton's eyes fluttered shut again. "The boy is not normally known to be hot tempered, but—" He finished the sentence with a shrug.

Atlas mulled over the possibilities. "And what better way to make Pike pay than by killing his mother in a spectacularly public manner? The scandal would be especially damaging to a young man who wants nothing more than to be respectable in the eyes of society."

Charlton's eyes remained shut. "The publicity surrounding Mrs. Pike's death, and the papers reminding all and sundry that she was the Marquess of Vessey's mistress, would have only added to the pain of losing his mother."

Atlas was silent for a moment. "Charlton."

"Hmm?"

"Thank you."

"Whatever for?"

"For looking out for Nicholas."

Charlton's only response was heavy rhythmic breathing followed by soft snores.

Chapter 13

Atlas sent a note around to Viscount Merton the following morning, inquiring as to where his young relation Harry Dean, Pike's hot-tempered dueling partner, could be found.

Atlas felt fairly confident the viscount would respond favorably to his inquiry. Not because the two men were friends—they were not—but because Atlas had shown the utmost discretion several months prior, after discovering Merton's reckless young daughter engaging in scandalous conduct. Public disclosure of the girl's unseemly behavior could have devastated her marital prospects. Naturally, her father the viscount remained appreciative of Atlas's continued circumspection.

As expected, Merton did prove to be forthcoming. He provided Atlas with Dean's address. However, when Atlas called there, Dean's servant directed Atlas to the Three Swans Inn on Albemarle Street. As it turned out, Dean was an avid reader, and his love of books took him to Albemarle Street most Mondays for a meeting of his book society.

When Atlas arrived at the Three Swans, a barmaid pointed Dean out. A nondescript young man with sandy brown hair and ordinary features, Dean sat at a table with about a dozen other men of all ages. Several books were strewn across the table as the reading society members engaged in animated conversation.

Atlas took a table nearby and ordered some claret. Observing his quarry, it occurred to Atlas that a man of such unremarkable looks could easily disappear into a crowd, especially the crush that spilled into Convent Garden following a performance. Dean might well be able to walk up to a woman, shoot her, and blend right back into the masses. Any witness might be hard pressed to describe him beyond sharing the man's height or the color of his hair. Harry Dean's was not a face you'd remember.

After an hour or so, the book society meeting finally came to an end. Suppressing a yawn, Atlas downed the last of his claret, set the earthenware tankard down on the scarred table in front of him, and made his way toward Dean.

"Mr. Dean," he called out as he approached.

Still seated, Dean was gathering his books. "Yes, that is correct. And you are . . .?"

"Atlas Catesby."

"Catesby?" He studied Atlas for a moment. "Would you by chance be any relation to Silas Catesby?"

Atlas dipped his chin. "He was my father."

"Truly?" Excitement lit the other man's eyes. "He was a remarkable talent."

"Yes, he was." Atlas saw no reason to feign modesty where his father was concerned. Few in England would expect him to.

"Our Book Society recently read one of his earlier titles, *Another Land*." Dean's plain face glowed. "It was transformative, truly."

"He was proud of that work."

"Are you interested in joining our society? Is that why you are here? You would be most welcome. Please do have a seat."

Atlas slipped into the chair opposite Dean. "That is very kind, but no. The truth is that I am here on a rather unpleasant business."

"Oh?" he inquired politely. "And what is that?"

"I am looking into the death of Wendela Pike."

Dean looked on expectantly, as if waiting for Atlas to say more. But Atlas remained quiet. He'd learned that people often felt compelled to fill the silence, and what they said, or how they said it, could prove illuminating.

"I see," Dean finally replied. "But what has that to do with me?"

"I understand that you participated in a duel with her son, Francis Pike."

Dean blanched. "I am not proud of what occurred in Hampstead Heath. Nor of the events leading up to it."

Atlas wondered whether being bested by Francis Pike had anything to do with Dean's deep regret. "Would you mind telling me what happened?"

"I would rather not." Dean seemed to visibly shrink back in his chair, like a sensitive plant closing in on itself when touched by humans. "I prefer to forget that evening, and the most regrettable morning that followed."

"There were people who witnessed the duel who recall that you made certain threats against Francis Pike."

Dean's face blanked. "What sort of threats?"

"You said that matters between the two of you were not settled. You vowed to make him pay for humiliating you."

Dean's head drooped. "I cannot say I fully recall the events you describe."

"Do you deny making those threats?"

"No, to be frank, I simply do not remember that day very well. My friend Jasper Balfour had invited me to come out with him and his friends."

"Are you well acquainted with Mr. Balfour?"

"Yes, we were at university together. But I was not at all acquainted with Mr. Pike before that evening. I did not realize his connection to Mrs. Pike until it was too late."

"Until after you had insulted her."

"Precisely. I had consumed entirely too much brandy and whiskey when someone raised the subject of Vessey and his oratorios. I believe I remarked that Vessey's whore was a talented singer."

Atlas studied the man sitting opposite him. "Are you suggesting that although you recall insulting Mrs. Pike, you have no recollection of threatening her son a few hours later?"

Dean nodded. "I was out of sorts because of the impending duel, as nervous as a virgin bride on her wedding night. I am an average shot at best. My interest is in books and poems, not pistols. I vaguely remember someone giving me something to calm my nerves. Whatever it was, I obviously did not react well to it."

"What did you take?"

"I honestly have no idea."

"Who gave it to you?"

"I do not remember that either. I was panicked about the duel, and people all around me were taking bets that that evening would be my last on this earth. I was not at all in my right mind. Consequently, when someone offered something to calm my nerves, I very happily took it."

"Could you have taken this substance and killed Mrs. Pike without remembering?"

Dean drew a sharp breath. "I do not make a habit of ingesting strange substances. I have not ingested any dubious substances since that evening. I do not even know what it was!" He reached for a book and gripped it with both hands. "Nor do I kill innocent women exiting the theater. In any case, if you speak to Pike, you will see that we have made amends."

Atlas's eyes widened. "I had not heard that."

"Nonetheless, it is true," Dean said stiffly.

"How did you settle matters between you?"

"I apologized for my offensive remark. I would never have uttered such a thing had I known Pike's identity and what his relation to Mrs. Pike was." He stacked the books one atop the other. "And furthermore, it was ungentlemanly, and I should not have spoken in such a manner even if Pike had not been there to defend his mother's name."

"Am I to gather that you and Pike are friends now?"

"I would not go so far as that." Dean came to his feet and picked up the pile of books. "Now, if you will excuse me, I am in dire need of fresh air."

As Atlas watched Dean weave his way around the tables and patrons toward the exit, he realized something he'd missed due to Dean's having been seated the entire evening.

Mrs. Pike's assassin had been described as being almost as tall as Atlas. And though Atlas had not stood next to Dean, he was fairly certain that the young man making his exit, with books clutched to his chest, would barely reach his shoulder.

★ ★ ★

Atlas sat at his game table by the window with his latest puzzle.

He'd started working on it just after breakfast and was now astonished to see the mid-afternoon sun casting a long, narrow triangle of light across the faded, threadbare carpet. He had not realized how long he'd been focused on the puzzle.

He pushed a piece into place. It was bright, crimson and gold, part of a woman's gown. Cocooned from the outside world, Atlas savored these moments of absolute concentration. He'd completed the frame relatively quickly. The edges were brown, straight, and not particularly complicated, unlike the rest of the puzzle.

As with all of his puzzles, Atlas had commissioned this artistic recreation of a *Danse Macabre*. The usual available puzzles were far too rudimentary for his taste. Making his own puzzle required commissioning an artist to produce an original piece of art or, as in this instance, to recreate a famous painting. He then took the art to a mapmaker on Regent Street, who pasted it to a piece of wood to be cut into small irregular segments. This habit of customizing his own puzzles made for an expensive hobby, especially for a man such as Atlas, who was far from wealthy.

He reached for another piece of the crimson gown, considered it for a moment, and then set it aside, unable for the moment to determine where it belonged. Atlas enjoyed the chaos of beginning with hundreds of disparate pieces and then painstakingly arranging them into perfect order. Alone, a single puzzle piece was insignificant and of no use. Yet every single piece was vital to the bigger picture. A puzzle was wholly incomplete if it was missing even one small segment. Everything had its place for the greater purpose. Atlas appreciated the symmetry in that.

"What are you working on now?" It took a moment for Lilliana's voice to cut through his reverie, and a bit longer still for him to register her presence.

"Lady Lilliana."

"Atlas," she said, acknowledging him with a haughty nod that he now found endearing. "I hope you do not mind. I told Jamie I would announce myself."

"Mind?" He stood, straightening his cravat. "On the contrary, I am delighted to see you."

She crossed over, her attention on his game table while his admiring gaze remained solely on the lady. She wore deep purple velvet, the slim silhouette of her gown flattering the gentle curves of her lithe figure.

"I see you have begun working on a new puzzle," she remarked. "What is it this time?"

Delicate notes of jasmine and cloves, Lilliana's scent, flushed the air. "It is a recreation of a *Danse Macabre*."

Her vibrant gaze went from the game table to Atlas's face. "The *Dance of Death*?"

"It is a sort of art—" he began to explain.

"I am familiar with what it is," she said, cutting him off, her chin held high. "It is an old artistic genre devoted to death. Rather morbid, don't you think?"

"Not especially. It speaks to the universality of death no matter what one's station—king, nobleman, or Seven Dials beggar. It makes no difference how far apart the division of the classes drives us in this life, because, in the end, we are the same. Death unites us all."

She stared down at the puzzle sections Atlas had grouped according to color. "How long will something like this take you to complete?"

"That depends."

"On what?"

"How much time I have to work on it. Completing a puzzle can take a fortnight or two for the simpler ones."

"And for complicated ones such as this?" She gestured toward the game table.

"Anywhere from six weeks to a couple of months. This one might take longer because I do not know which *Danse Macabre* the artist chose to paint."

"You have no idea what the original picture looked like before this puzzle was cut up?" she asked, incredulous.

"No, I wanted it to be a surprise. It is more of challenge that way. Which is why it could take more than two months to finish."

"That seems like a great deal of time to spend in company with death."

He smiled, acknowledging her point. "Maybe I should look into something a bit more cheery next time."

She strolled away from him, stopping momentarily to look down at the burr puzzle on the marble table between the two stuffed chairs. "I have come to inform you that you will want to escort me to Countess Lieven's party on Tuesday next."

Atlas noted the emphasis she placed on the hostess's name. "I suppose I am meant to know who this Countess Lieven is."

"Really, Atlas." Lilliana sighed. "I know you take a perverse sort of pride in knowing nothing about London society, but Dorothea Lieven is a woman of whom even you should take notice."

He wanted to tell her that she was the only woman he took notice of these days, but instead asked, "And why is that?"

"Because not only is she the wife of the Russian ambassador, but Countess Lieven is a woman to be reckoned with in her own right. She is a prominent social hostess and has the ear of many powerful men in England and across Europe. She is even one of the patronesses at Almack's, the only foreigner ever to have been so honored."

He suppressed a groan. "Pray do not tell me we are attending a ball at Almack's." Atlas knew very little about the exclusive, invitation-only assembly rooms on King Street other than that they were frequented by London's highest born and known for their weekly balls—tedious affairs where the marriage-minded hunted for suitable matches.

"No, indeed. The duke and I, and now you, have been invited to the Lieven's country home in Richmond."

"I see." He had no doubt that Somerville and Lilliana were the reason for his inclusion in what was undoubtedly an exclusive affair. "And while we are there, I suppose we will inquire about her countryman Aleksey Witte, who recently departed for the motherland."

"Precisely." She reached for the burr puzzle and turned it over in her gloved hands, examining how the wooden pieces fit together. "And then we shall see if his acquaintance with the late Mrs. Pike has anything to do with her murder."

"Her sister says that Mrs. Pike did intend to leave Vessey for another man, and Brown professes to be that man."

She looked up. "Do you believe, then, that the clergyman was telling the truth?"

"Mrs. Booth, the sister, did not know the name of Mrs. Pike's betrothed, but what is the likelihood she would have betrothed herself to two different men? And Roxbury describes Wendy Pike as a faithful woman. He believes she'd been with no other man apart from Vessey."

"You spoke with Roxbury? How did that go?"

"Well enough. We managed to refrain from coming to blows."

A slight smile dangled at the corner of her lips. "I see. So what do you make of it all?"

"I am not certain what to think. Everyone I have spoken to appears convinced Samuel Brown's ardor made Mrs. Pike uncomfortable and that she had taken to avoiding the man whenever possible." He watched Lilliana pull the burr puzzle apart. "However, it is entirely possible that she behaved in that manner so that Vessey would not suspect her of having any attachment to Brown."

"There is another possibility." She perched on the edge of a stuffed chair, spine straight, her attention on the notched pieces of wood as she worked at putting them back together in one connected whole.

He settled in the seat opposite her. "Such as?"

"That Mrs. Pike really did have a dislike of Mr. Brown."

"That would make the clergyman completely delusional."

"Is that so difficult to imagine?"

Atlas considered her question. "No," he said finally. "I suppose it is possible that Brown lives in a world of his mind's own making."

"He could be the sort of man who is unwilling to accept rejection." She worked on the two remaining puzzle pieces, her tapered fingers moving with self-assuredness. "Perhaps he was Mrs. Pike's harasser rather than her lover. Maybe the man she intended to leave Vessey for is someone else entirely."

He had an inkling of where she was going with this line of thinking. "Such as?"

She looked up from her task with a knowing gleam in her eye. "Aleksey Witte."

They both spoke the Russian's name in unison. Both smiled at that and momentarily locked eyes.

"Please do continue." He sat back in his chair, resting both hands on the armrests, enjoying puzzling out the case with someone with as keen a mind as Lilliana's. "Surely there is more to your theory."

"Are you certain you wish to hear it?" she responded tartly. "It involves your opera singer."

"Juliet is not my anything. She is a friend, nothing more. Now please enlighten me as to what you are thinking."

"What if Mrs. Pike intended to run away with Mr. Witte?"

It was an interesting thought. "If that were the case, why would she not have gone with him when he departed England?"

"Maybe something here delayed her. She did have children." Lilliana slipped the last piece of wood into place, completing the burr puzzle.

"Bravo." Atlas was thoroughly impressed. "Few people can complete a burr puzzle so easily."

"Truly?" She seemed surprised to hear that. Setting the puzzle aside, she continued. "It is possible that your friend Mrs. Jennings wanted Mr. Witte for herself. We already know she and Mrs. Pike came to blows over the man. And if Mrs. Pike had truly decided to take to the stage—"

"Then she would have been stealing not only Juliet's starring role at Covent Garden, but also the man that Juliet had set her sights on." Atlas finished the thought for her. "An interesting theory."

One of her brows lifted to form a pointed upside-down V. "But Romeo does not believe his Juliet is capable of killing a romantic rival?"

He laughed. "Mrs. Jennings in not my Juliet. You have confused your stories. In your scenario, Aleksey Witte is Mrs. Jenning's Romeo."

She sniffed, but he could see she was pleased with his disavowal. He paused before continuing. "We have never discussed the intimacy that occurred between us in Somerville's garden last summer."

Her gaze sharpened on him. "We are constantly being interrupted by the most dramatic happenings. Your brother's accident, then Mrs. Pike's murder."

"As I was saying, Mrs. Jennings is not my Juliet."

"Are you suggesting there is a Juliet to your Romeo?"

He rose and towered over her chair, placing his hands on both armrests, somewhat caging her in. "What do you think?"

She sat erect in the chair, not giving an inch, her gaze holding his. "Perhaps you should enlighten me."

He came closer, close enough to inhale her appealing scent and to glimpse the sparkles of copper in her dark eyes. "Perhaps I should."

She lifted her lips to meet his, as bold as you please, which appealed to him very much. He gratefully accepted the offering, taking care to keep his kiss gentle and unhurried; suspecting that these sorts of intimacies did not come easily to Lilliana after the loathsome way her late husband had treated her.

To his delight, she showed no hesitation. Her mouth was warm and sweet and welcoming. Eager even. He lost himself in the sublime sensations of kissing her, until he remembered that his valet must be about somewhere nearby.

"Jamie," he murmured after regretfully ending the contact.

"Was leaving when I arrived." Her breath was humid, her cheeks flushed. "He said something about retrieving your clean clothing from Charlton's."

"Is that so?" The earl's staff tended to Atlas's laundry, which Jamie delivered and retrieved. Atlas brushed his lips against hers again. "So we find ourselves quite alone."

"Yes," she said against his mouth, "but Somerville's coachman awaits below to return me to the boys. They will have completed their lessons by now."

He straightened immediately and stepped back, watching as she came to her feet. Looking down, she smoothed any creases in the skirt of her gown.

"I hope I have not offended," he said.

"Of course not." Despite her words, Lilliana seemed flustered and avoided meeting his gaze.

His alarm rose. Had he overstepped? Perhaps even misinterpreted Lilliana's interest in him? "It was not my intention to cause you discomfort."

"And you have not." She appeared to have regained complete command of herself.

"You are certain?"

She met his worried gaze with a reassuring smile. "Absolutely."

He returned her smile. "Then I suppose I shall see you on Tuesday."

"Tuesday? Ah yes, Countess Lieven's rout."

"I shall look forward to it."

She smiled softly. "As will I."

Beyond them, in the front hall, the door opened, and Jamie's voice reached them. "If you could wait for a moment, my lord, I will see if Mr. Catesby is at home to callers."

"Who is it?" Atlas asked when Jamie appeared in the sitting room.

"A young man who says it's rather urgent." The valet presented a white calling card to Atlas.

"Did he give a name?" Atlas felt the blood rush from his face as he stared at the cream-colored card with bold black lettering.

"Yes, sir," Jamie replied. "He says he is Lord Nicholas Lennox."

"Vessey's son?" Lilliana asked.

Atlas looked up from the card. "And my nephew." He turned to Jamie. "Send him in."

CHAPTER 14

Atlas tried not to stare at the young man who joined them. He had interacted with his dead sister's son just twice in the past twenty years; both meetings had been fairly recent and decidedly brief. On the first occasion, Atlas had not even recognized his own nephew.

Nicholas bowed immediately, his posture impeccable. "Good afternoon."

"Nicholas," Atlas greeted him. "This is Lady Roslyn."

Only the flush in the young man's cheeks betrayed any discomfort. "I do beg your pardon for this regrettable intrusion."

"Not at all," Atlas said.

Lilliana spoke kindly to the boy. "I believe you are styled Viscount Beaumont, is that not correct? Heir to the Marquess of Vessey."

"Yes, my lady, at your service." Although Phoebe's son wore the finest tailored clothing, there was no sign of flamboyance in his sartorial choices. His golden-brown hair was neatly combed. "Are you acquainted with my father?"

"Only by reputation," she said mildly.

They lapsed into a momentary silence. Atlas's heart felt too large for his chest. This appealing young man with warm hazel eyes was his last link to his sister, the last vestiges of Phoebe that remained on this earth.

Perhaps sensing the charge in the air, Jamie had not retreated as usual. He hovered on the threshold of the sitting room rather than withdrawing as he should.

Atlas's throat felt constricted. "It is good to see you, Nicholas."

Propriety dictated that he should address the boy by his courtesy title, but to Hades with that. Nicholas was his own blood. Atlas would be damned if he'd allow pretty manners to put any more distance between himself and Phoebe's child than Vessey already had.

Nicholas stared at his hands. "This is somewhat difficult."

"You are among friends," Atlas said in a gentle and encouraging manner.

Nicholas darted a look at Lilliana. "It is just that . . ."

Registering the boy's obvious discomfort, Lilliana assumed control of the situation. "Perhaps Beaumont would care to take a seat," she said briskly. "Jamie will fetch some refreshment, and then Beaumont here can enlighten Mr. Catesby as to the reason for his visit."

She reached for her reticule. "And I must take my leave. Good day, gentlemen." On her way out, she paused by Atlas's valet, who had not stirred. "The tea, Jamie?"

"Yes, my lady." He reluctantly dragged his eyes from Atlas and Nicholas and turned to follow her.

Nicholas did not meet his uncle's eye as he took the seat Atlas indicated. The boy was clearly uncomfortable, and yet he'd sought Atlas out. The thought cheered Atlas even as it roused his curiosity.

Nicholas stared at the floor. "I barely know where to begin."

Atlas sat opposite the boy, shifting in his chair to face him more fully. "At the beginning, perhaps? And do take your time."

"My father's . . . companion . . . was killed recently at Covent Garden."

"Yes, I have heard."

The boy looked Atlas fully in the face for the first time. "I understand that you were present, that you witnessed the crime."

"I reached Mrs. Pike directly after she was mortally injured. I did not see the shooting."

Nicholas took a breath. "I am aware of whispers, reprehensible gossip really, that my father is responsible."

"Such talk is to be expected," Atlas said carefully. "It is not surprising that the murder of a nobleman's mistress would inspire gossip."

"Do you believe he did it?"

The directness of Nicholas's question took Atlas by surprise. "I cannot see how what I think has any bearing on the matter."

"But it does." The boy's gentle and agreeable manner was so like his mother's that it made Atlas's chest ache. "I am given to understand that you are investigating Mrs. Pike's murder."

"Yes, I am. But it is an informal inquiry."

"I comprehend that you do not care for my father, but I implore you to find Mrs. Pike's true killer in order to clear my father's name." Nicholas licked his lips. "I know it is a great deal to ask, especially as you and I are barely acquainted."

"Has your father told you why that is?" Atlas struggled to contain his bitterness. "Did Vessey ever mention the reason you do not know your mother's family?"

"He said relations between the two families became most uncomfortable after my mother's unfortunate death and that he judged it prudent to shield me from that unpleasantness."

"I see." Atlas had to admire Vessey's approach. The marquess hadn't told his son any untruths. He'd simply withheld the most pertinent reason for the divide—that the Catesbys believed Vessey murdered the boy's mother by pushing her down the stairs, causing her neck to break.

"I must be honest with you, Nicholas," Atlas finally said. "If my investigation shows that the Marquess of Vessey is responsible for Mrs. Pike's death, I shall not and cannot hide the truth."

"I would never ask that of you," Nicholas stammered. "All I request is that you do not accuse my father based upon your dislike of him. I have already lost my mother. Please do not deprive me of my father as well."

Watching the boy, it became clear to Atlas that if he had a hand in condemning Vessey to the gallows, he would lose Phoebe's son all over again.

He exhaled heavily. "I give you my word that I will follow all possibilities. I have not and shall not make any assumptions."

That seemed to satisfy Nicholas. "I have heard that you are a man of honor."

The sound of the front door opening reached them. Jamie had returned with the tea.

"Are there any others?" Nicholas asked.

"I beg your pardon?"

"You said you are following all possibilities." Nicholas edged forward in his seat. "Are there others? Have you identified any potential suspects?"

Jamie came in and set the tea on the table between them. The valet straightened and handed a note to Atlas. "It is from Ambrose Endicott at Bow Street. The messenger said it was rather urgent."

"Bow Street?" Nicholas asked as Atlas read the missive. "Is it about the murder?"

"Yes." Atlas raised his gaze to meet Nicholas's. "It appears that a very strong potential suspect has just revealed himself."

★   ★   ★

Atlas set out for Bow Street directly after receiving the note from Ambrose Endicott. Although the rain held off for the moment, a ghostly gray mist hung over the streets, obscuring buildings that seemed to suddenly rear into view as he passed them.

He spotted the runner emerging from the fog at the corner of Hart and Bow Streets, near the Covent Garden theater and just down the way from the Bow Street offices.

"This is a surprise," he said to Endicott.

"My office *is* just down the street," the runner returned. "I gather you are coming to see me about the clergyman."

"Your note said he shot someone. Have you arrested Mr. Brown in connection with Mrs. Pike's murder?"

"No, this is not about Mrs. Pike's murder. You will have to walk with me." He turned to continue walking down Hart Street. "I am running late for a meeting near Leicester Square."

Atlas fell in step beside the much shorter, rotund man. "Who did Samuel Brown shoot?"

"The manager at Covent Garden."

"Simon Cooke?" Shock rippled through Atlas. "Is he dead?"

"No. Fortunately for Mr. Cooke, the clergyman is a poor shot, which is ironic when one considers the man used to be a solider."

They turned into a narrow lane that led to Long Acre, treading with care over the slick cobblestones. "Brown's bullet missed Cooke?"

"Oh, he hit him all right. But just grazed the man's shoulder. Cooke had the flesh wound bandaged and returned to work, preparing for this evening's performance."

"He is nothing if not devoted."

"The man has significant debts to consider, the cost of rebuilding after the fire."

"Why did Brown shoot him?"

"That is what I should like to know and why I sent you that note. Mr. Brown demanded to see you. He insists you are the only person he will speak with."

Atlas's curiosity piqued. "And Mr. Cooke? Did he say what transpired between the two men that could have provoked Mr. Brown to violence?"

"He claims to have no idea why Brown would want to shoot him." The two men paused when they reached Long Acre, a busy thoroughfare cluttered with carriages, riders on horseback, and carts, all of which looked like they were moving among the clouds.

"When can I see Mr. Brown?"

"I should return within the hour, and you can see him then."

"Very good. Perhaps I will call upon Mr. Cooke in the meantime."

★ ★ ★

After parting ways with Endicott, Atlas retraced his steps back to the Covent Garden theater.

He found Simon Cooke sitting behind a tattered desk, pouring whiskey down his throat in a cramped, poorly lit room.

"Catesby." Cooke released an exhausted sigh once he registered his visitor's identity. "I have already had the day from Hades and am in no mood to be tormented any further."

"Rest assured that I am not here to harass you." Atlas stepped carefully among the fabric samples, opulent costumes, and wigs cluttering the tight space. He saw no physical evidence of the man's injury, but the strain showed plainly on Cooke's drawn and haggard face. "Should you not be at home resting? I understand you were shot today."

"What concern is it of yours?" Cooke scowled. "The last time I checked, you were not my keeper."

This foul-tempered man was a far cry from the brusque but generally agreeable man Atlas had met shortly after Wendy's murder. Not that Atlas could blame Cooke for his lack of courtesy given what the man had just endured. "Perhaps I should return another day, once you have recuperated." He turned to go.

"Brown killed Mrs. Pike, you know," Cooke muttered from behind him.

Atlas turned around. "Did he tell you that?"

The man rolled his bloodshot eyes. "No, but it is bloody obvious to anyone who has ever had the misfortune to encounter that bedlamite."

"Why did he shoot you?"

Cooke poured himself more whiskey. "He apparently learned fairly recently that I had convinced Wendy to take to the stage."

Atlas stilled. He'd been the one to inform Brown that Wendela Pike had intended to perform at Covent Garden. "He said that?"

"Said many other choice words as well." He tossed the entire glass of whiskey down his throat. "The man does not talk like any other clergyman I have ever met."

"He used to be a soldier."

"Ah yes, that makes much more sense." Cooke set his glass down with a clank. Atlas noticed the man kept his left hand completely immobile. "He accused me of ruining Wendy's reputation, with her being a respectable woman and all."

A demi-rep hardly had a reputation to lose. But Atlas was beginning to comprehend that Brown saw things as he wanted them to be, rather than how they truly were. "Brown claims he was betrothed to Mrs. Pike and that it was her intention to go away with him."

"Bollocks." Cooke glared at Atlas. "The man's brain is flawed. He became obsessed with Wendy simply because she was kind to him, as she was to everyone."

The manner in which Cooke spoke about Wendy suggested the man had been a bit more familiar with her than Atlas had initially believed. "How well did you know Mrs. Pike?"

Cooke shrugged his left shoulder and froze midway, wincing. "The devil! That's my injured side." He paused as if waiting for the pain to subside before continuing. "Mrs. Pike came by every now and again, whenever she could, and often watched the performances from backstage. She admired the theater greatly and was anxious to join our ranks."

"Why do you think Brown would react so violently to Mrs. Pike's taking to the stage if they were not betrothed? If he had no claim on her, it would be none of his concern."

"Because the man's head is full of delusions," Cooke spat out. "He truly believed Mrs. Pike belonged to him when the truth of the matter is that she wanted nothing whatsoever to do with him."

"She told you that herself?"

He nodded. "Ask anyone who was even remotely associated with Wendy, and they will tell you the same."

"I have heard from others that the clergyman was a source of unease," Atlas acknowledged, "but that does not prove that he killed Mrs. Pike."

"I have proof." Cooke's words had begun to slur together due to the copious amounts of whiskey he'd consumed. "One of our fruit sellers recognized Brown when he came here today. She says he was there the night Wendy was killed. She saw him bending over Mrs. Pike directly after she'd been shot."

If true, this was news indeed. Brown had certainly never mentioned being at the theater the evening Wendy Pike died. "What is this fruit woman's name?"

"Mary White."

The same woman who had found the murder weapon and testified at the inquest. "Do you know where I can find this Mary White?"

"She is probably out on the piazza somewhere, staking her claim before the theater crush descends upon us for this evening's show."

"What are you doing here?" An indignant smoky female voice called out from behind Atlas.

Atlas turned to find Juliet Jennings glaring at him. "Hello, Juliet."

"Simon is in no condition to receive callers."

Cooke smiled goofily. "You are such a dear, dear, girl to look after me so." The warbled words made Cooke sound as if his mouth was filled with loose marbles. "Esther has come to rescue me."

"Who is Esther? I am Juliet." She removed the whiskey and set it beyond the theater manager's reach. "And you are foxed."

"Indeed. I am at that." Cooke leaned back in his chair, his body so loose that he seemed in danger of sliding out of the seat.

Juliet wore a deep blue dressing gown that complimented her eyes and other womanly assets. Most men would find her incredibly alluring, but Cooke seemed to take little notice of his star.

She turned to Atlas with flashing eyes. "You should go. Can you not see that the man is not himself? He is recovering from the shock of being shot."

"You certainly are protective of Mr. Cooke," Atlas noted as he watched Juliet fuss over the man who employed her.

"As would you be were you in my position, if your livelihood depended upon it." She ushered Atlas out of Cooke's tiny office. "If Simon were to die, where would that leave me?"

"Are you suggesting this show of concern is motivated purely by self-interest?"

"Everything I do is in the interest of my own survival." She gave him the kind of stare one might bestow upon a simpleton. "You of all people should comprehend that."

CHAPTER 15

After leaving Simon Cooke in Juliet's protective hands, Atlas wandered the piazza in search of Mary White.

If the fruit vendor confirmed that she had seen the clergyman near Wendy's body on the evening of the murder, some of the more disparate pieces of Atlas's investigation would finally fall into place. Brown as a rejected suitor rather than a clandestine lover struck Atlas as a far more likely situation than the desperately romantic picture the clergyman had painted. But why then would Brown insist that Atlas investigate the murder?

The mist from earlier had developed into a light drizzle, and the late afternoon was headed toward the gloaming, making it more difficult to locate his quarry. Atlas finally spotted the fruit vendor near the portico of St. Paul's Church, the house of worship frequented by performers from Covent Garden and nearby Drury Lane.

"Mary White," he called out to her.

The older woman focused on Atlas as if trying to place him. She adjusted the load of oranges she carried in a generous fabric sling around her neck. "Yer the cove from the other night, from when the marquess's ladybird was killed."

"Yes, I am Atlas Catesby. How are you, Mary?"

"Fine enough to know ye ain't 'ere to ask me 'ow I fare." She shifted her burden, which seemed much too heavy for her slight frame. "Yer 'ere cuz ye be wantin' ta know about the shootin' that happened this very mornin'."

"True enough." Mary White was no one's fool. "Mr. Cooke says you recognized his attacker. I would like to ask you about that."

"I am a busy woman." She grinned and he saw that most of her teeth were missing. "Ain't me time worth a shillin' or two?"

"It certainly is." He reached into his pocket and drew out a few shillings.

"The cove 'oo shot the Covent Garden manager is the same one that done it ta Mrs. Pike," she said immediately.

"Are you certain?" He dropped the money into her open palm. "Did you see him shoot her?"

"No, I ain't seen nothin' like that. But I did see the preacher kneelin' next ta Mrs. Pike's body after 'e shot 'er. Then 'e jumped up like a scared rabbit and ran away. That was the last I seen of 'im 'til today, when the same cove tried to crash that cull."

Atlas had been among sailors often enough to understand her meaning. "You are saying that the same man you saw kneeling by Mrs. Pike tried to shoot the theater manager today?"

"'Tis wut I said, ain't it?"

"Indeed. Could you tell me exactly what you saw today?"

"The Covent Garden manager come in late this mornin' and 'e was going in ta the theater when the preacher popped 'im."

"And you are certain Mr. Brown, the clergyman, is the same person you saw kneeling next to Mrs. Pike that night?"

"I never forget a face." She cradled her sling of oranges like a baby, lifting the weight to relieve the pressure on her shoulder.

"Did you see the clergyman holding a gun the night Mrs. Pike died? Or dropping it, perhaps, as he ran away?"

She guffawed. "It ain't like I could see 'is hands when it was so crowded."

The vendor had a point. There were few crushes worse than the one that occurred once the theaters released a mass of humanity after a performance.

"Now, guv," she said, "is there anything else I can do for ye?"

"Yes, there is." He reached into his pocket again. "How much are the oranges?"

Brightening, she grinned, baring the formidable gap between her teeth. "How many would you like, guv?"

"I will take them all."

★   ★   ★

Samuel Brown was locked up in the gaol yard, which is where Atlas spoke with him after meeting Endicott at the Bow Street offices, as they'd arranged. Surrounded by a high brick wall, the yard formed a neat square measuring about thirty feet across.

"Mr. Catesby!" In shirtsleeves, with his hair wildly disheveled, the clergyman's face lit up when Atlas stepped into the yard. "I knew you would come."

"Did you kill Mrs. Pike?" Atlas dispensed with any sort of greeting. He held nothing but contempt for a man who had shot and injured one person and likely murdered another.

"No! I swear it on our Lord." He pressed his hand flat against his chest. "I could never do such a thing."

"You are obviously capable of shooting Mr. Cooke."

"He deserved it." Brown showed no remorse. "As he is well aware."

"And why is that?" Atlas raised his voice to make himself heard amid the shouts, jeers, and protestations of innocence from the other prisoners in the surrounding yard cells.

"He knows why. He tempted a goodly woman into disgrace. He encouraged her to take to the stage."

"Mr. Cooke offered Mrs. Pike a means to support herself and her children that did not require whoring herself out."

Brown's hands clutched the bars to his cell. "I did not ask you to come in order to discuss Mr. Cooke."

"Then why am I here? I presumed it was to hear your confession."

"I shot Mr. Cooke. I can only regret that I did not kill him. I will happily go to the gallows because without Mrs. Pike my life is not worth living."

"Please spare me the dramatics." Atlas was fast losing his limited patience. "I am not interested in hearing your over-wrought declarations of devotion. I cannot help but wonder whether you were ever truly betrothed to Mrs. Pike."

"Of course I was. I swear it."

"People who were well acquainted with Mrs. Pike say you were an unwelcome admirer who made Mrs. Pike uncomfortable."

Brown's mouth fell open. "Is that what she told them? It must have been so that they would not suspect the truth about us. I am not a man given to subterfuge. I fear my deep regard for Mrs. Pike was obvious for all to see." He looked pleadingly at Atlas. "I did not shoot Mrs. Pike. You must believe me."

"No, I really mustn't," Atlas replied in an acid tone. "As a matter of fact, I believe now more than ever that you did kill the poor lady. A Covent Garden fruit vendor saw you there the night Mrs. Pike was murdered."

"I was there. I do confess that much. But I went to admire her from afar, not to harm her. I could never hurt her. Killing Mrs. Pike would be like killing myself."

"You admit you were the tall man in black who knelt beside Mrs. Pike after she fell."

"I was." His eyes filled with tears. "I lost sight of her for just a moment—there was such a crush that night—and then I realized I could not see my beloved because she had fallen. I rushed to her side, and when I saw the pistol I reached for it."

"Why would you reach for the weapon?"

"I was not in my right mind. I thought maybe the killer was still there and that he might pick up the gun and shoot her again."

"But then you ran away." Atlas crossed his arms over his chest. "That is hardly the reaction of an innocent man."

"I panicked." Brown hung his head. "I am not proud of it. I did run away, and when I realized that the pistol was still in my hand, I dropped it as I made my escape."

"Made your escape? That is an interesting choice of words. An innocent man would feel no need to escape."

"I feared people would presume that I had accompanied Mrs. Pike to the theater. Gossip can be most unkind. I did not want to besmirch my beloved's reputation. Even in death. You must believe me."

"No, I mustn't believe you," Atlas said cuttingly.

"You are a man of reason. Why would I prevail upon you to investigate Wendela's murder if I had been the one to kill her?'

"Why indeed?" The man might be completely unhinged. But another possibility also occurred to Atlas. "Maybe you knew that my late sister was once married to Vessey and that my family holds Vessey responsible for her untimely death. Perhaps you believed you would find a natural ally in me—that I would be very pleased to see Vessey accused of murder."

"No, that is not true! If you take me for a liar then Mrs. Pike's true killer will escape punishment." Brown reached through the bars to grab Atlas's arm. "What if Vessey is responsible? Will you stand aside and let him go free? Do you wish for that to be on your conscience?"

Atlas jerked away. "Perhaps you should leave it to me to worry about my conscience while you take what time you have left on this earth to examine yours."

★ ★ ★

"Do you credit Mr. Brown's claims of innocence?" Lilliana handed Atlas a plate laden with the Somerville cook's latest culinary masterpieces. "Or do you think he killed Mrs. Pike?"

"It is difficult to say." His attention went to the sponge cake, an unassuming plain little square that gave no hint of its feather-like consistency and divine buttery sweetness.

He had immediately accepted Lilliana's invitation to tea the day after his encounters with both Nicholas and the clergyman, and was now contently settled into the new, larger chair Lilliana had recently added to her sunny sitting room.

However, Lilliana's manner was more slightly constrained, which troubled him. He could not help but wonder if her current aloofness related to the intimacy they'd shared in his apartments.

"Can the pistol be linked back to Mr. Brown?" she was asking. "Was he known to carry a weapon?"

"We are fairly certain the pistol came from Grierson's gun shop on Bond Street." He bit into the sponge cake, the rich, full flavors of almonds and vanilla bursting on his tongue. "Your

cook is going to kill me. I am liable to die of pleasure from con-
suming her food."

"Death by cake." She smirked as she nibbled on a biscuit.
"Imagine what people might say."

"That I died happy." He drank some tea. "I will never
understand how you, or anyone, can possibly dislike sweets."

She made a moue of distaste. "Sugar hurts my teeth."

"Perhaps you need to see a dentist." He chewed the final bite
of cake slowly, rolling it over his tongue to make it last longer in
order to fully appreciate how close it brought him to heaven.

"I have already visited one, and my teeth are perfectly fine,"
she retorted. "He has seen other patients with healthy teeth who
also cannot tolerate sweets."

He reached for another cake. "How dull their lives must be."

"If you are done expounding upon the virtues of sweet-
meats, perhaps we could discuss the case?"

He smiled. "As I was saying, we believe the pistol came from
Grierson's."

"I presume you visited Grierson to see who purchased it. Or
does he not keep a list of such transactions?"

"Oh, he keeps a list." He bit into a savory biscuit—flat,
round, crisp, and perfectly symmetrical—that paired beautifully
with a square of Somerset cheddar. "He just refuses to share it
with me."

"But why? Surely he cannot like the idea of a murderer running loose through the metropolis."

"He said something about not being able to do anything for
Mrs. Pike, given that she is already deceased."

"How heartwarming."

"Indeed. Any perceived lack of discretion on his part could
anger his patrons. I imagine they would be none too happy to find

me on their doorstep inquiring as to whether the murder weapon belongs to them." He reached for a slice of plum cake. "I will have to pursue other avenues in regards to the ownership of the pistol."

She made a skeptical humming sound in her throat as she sipped her tea. "We shall see about that. Now, what of young Beaumont?" she asked carefully. "Or is your nephew a subject you prefer to keep private?"

"Not at all." He set down his plate. "Truth be told, the subject of Nicholas has been weighing on me." He relayed the particulars of his conversation with his nephew. She listened attentively, her eyes fixed on his face.

"It is not as though you intend to blame his father for a crime he did not commit," she said when he was done. "But if Vessey is guilty, you can hardly allow him to escape unscathed."

"I told the boy as much."

"And now you fear losing Nicholas should you prove his father guilty of this crime."

"I do." The thought of it made Atlas feel as though someone had dropped an enormous rock on his chest.

"How then will you proceed?"

"As I always do. I will seek the truth, no matter where it leads me." And in both of his previous investigations, it had led to the darkest chambers of the human soul, baring truths he'd rather have no knowledge of, that even the best of mankind could be driven to violent murder. That a drowning man might cling to the nearest person, not for succor, but to use his dying breath to drag an innocent into hell with him.

"I suspect you could not live with yourself if you were to do otherwise," she remarked.

"Even if he is guilty, Vessey could very well escape justice. It is not as though he will face a trial. His peers in the House of

Lords are unlikely to condemn him for the death of an unre-spectable woman."

"But Mrs. Pike was very well liked." She nibbled on a piece of Stilton cheese. "And it is widely accepted that she was inti-mately acquainted with no man other than Vessey. She was virtuous in that way."

Atlas picked up the direction of her thoughts and gave voice to them. "Mrs. Pike was also kind and well liked. She charmed people at Vessey's oratorios. Even Roxbury came to her defense, as you know."

"And he could very well be inclined to do so again if Vessey were to be tried in the House of Lords."

"Which would not be a positive outcome where my nephew is concerned."

"The possibility remains that Vessey is not at all involved in Mrs. Pike's demise."

Atlas stilled, trying to grasp a memory just out of reach. And then, like a piano player who has forgotten a song that suddenly comes back to him, he remembered. "I feel certain Vessey knows more about Mrs. Pike's death than he is sharing with me or with Bow Street."

"Are you certain that is not wishful thinking on your part?" she asked, her voice gentle.

He thought back, trying to recall Vessey's exact words. "When he first saw the body laid out in the tavern, the first thing Vessey said was, 'Oh, Wendy. What has he done to you?'"

"What has *he* done to you." Lilliana repeated the words. Looking past him, she gazed unseeing into the distance, slightly narrowing one eye as was her habit when she concentrated. "He could have been referring to Brown. After all, he has told you that he believes the clergyman killed Mrs. Pike."

"That makes perfect sense, of course. However, it was something about the way he said it that struck me as odd. It was with complete anguish, perhaps even horror."

"That seems like a natural reaction."

"Yes, but the words were completely absent of any sort of anger or fury. There was something more there. It was almost as if he was not surprised."

"What do you make of that?"

"I am not certain yet. But I will put all of the pieces together eventually."

"Of that I have no doubt. Now do finish indulging yourself." Her gaze fell to his plate. "We have an errand to run."

"Do we?"

"Yes, we are going to Grierson's."

"Why? Are you in need of a weapon?"

"I might be." Her mouth curved into a coy smile. "You will just have to wait and see."

CHAPTER 16

When Atlas escorted Lilliana into Grierson's on Bond Street, the proprietor rushed forward to greet them. However, his demeanor changed when he recognized Atlas.

"Mr. Catesby," he said, "unless you are here to make a purchase, we have no business between us. I have nothing further to say on the"—his glance darted to Lilliana—"matter we discussed earlier."

Lilliana lifted her chin. "I presume you are Mr. Grierson?" She was at her imperial best, her voice condescending, her glacial manner threatening to freeze the man where he stood. If her countenance did not do enough to convey her high societal status, her apparel surely would. Her burgundy silk gown, exquisitely designed and tailored, easily cost a year's worth of Atlas's living expenses. And the elaborate high-standing plumage of her matching bonnet tempted even Atlas to cower in her charismatic presence.

It all had the desired effect. Grierson immediately became conciliatory. "At your service, my lady," he said while executing possibly the deepest bow Atlas had ever witnessed.

Atlas suppressed a smile. Only a fool would be unable to discern Lilliana's superior birth and breeding, and the prosperous gunmaker was clearly no idiot.

Rather than acknowledging the gunmaker's abrupt volte-face, Lilliana glided past him toward the red velvet–lined dark cabinetry that showcased Grierson's handiwork. She paused and then turned to peruse the pistols and rifles laid out on mahogany tables.

Grierson hurried to her side. "How may I be of service, my lady?"

"I am considering purchasing a gift for my brother, the Duke of Somerville."

Grierson's face lit up at the mention of one of England's most prosperous and powerful peers, clearly a highly coveted prospective patron. "It would be my greatest pleasure to provide a pistol for His Grace."

"Perhaps you could recommend a design worthy of his superior status," she said. "I know little about guns."

Grierson immediately selected a pistol from a nearby shelf. It was made of walnut and beautifully crafted with finials, silver fittings, and intricate silver inlays. Atlas would wager his mount, had he owned one, that the pistol was among the most expensive in the shop.

Lilliana studied the gun. "What is your opinion, Mr. Catesby?"

Atlas suppressed the urge to inquire about the cost. "It is a fine piece."

"Then I shall take it," Lilliana said to Grierson. "Please have it delivered to Somerville House."

"Yes, my lady." Grierson brimmed with barely restrained delight. "I shall see to it immediately."

"Please do." She paused. "I also hope you will grant me a small favor."

Atlas observed quietly, marveling at Lilliana's wily methods. She was certainly a woman to be reckoned with.

"Anything at all, my lady." Grierson could not seem to stop bowing. "I am always happy to be of assistance to personages as exalted as the Duke of Somerville and his relations."

"I understand Mr. Catesby has inquired about a certain flint-lock pistol. One with a barrel that is quite distinctive because it is sheathed in silver. I should like to know who purchased it."

Grierson blanched at the dilemma facing him; to deny Lilliana's request was to risk the wrath of the Duke of Somerville. To acquiesce could anger long-standing patrons. "My lady, if word were to spread that I have behaved indiscreetly, most of my patrons would take their custom elsewhere. Surely you can appreciate my predicament."

Her wintry, close-mouthed smile sent a chill down Atlas's back. He almost pitied Grierson. "And surely you can understand that one of your patrons possibly cut down an innocent woman in the street with a weapon that you yourself might well have crafted." Each word cut the air with the precision of a scalpel.

Grierson swallowed, appearing pained, his Adam's apple visibly moving in his throat.

"Surely the custom of the Duke of Somerville will protect your business," she prodded.

Grierson considered for a moment and then exhaled. "Unfortunately, discretion prevents me from sharing a list of the gun shop's patrons." He spoke in measured tones. "However, it is curious that Mr. Jasper Balfour called recently, inquiring about the same exact pistol."

Atlas's pulse quickened at the mention of Jasper Balfour, but he forced himself to remain outwardly dispassionate.

"Did he now?" Lilliana asked. "And when did Mr. Balfour make this inquiry?"

"Two days after Mrs. Pike's unfortunate demise."

She exchanged a look with Atlas before addressing Grierson again. "Did he mention why he was looking for that particular style of pistol?"

"He wanted to replace one that belonged to his father that had been lost."

"I see." She dimpled, and this time her delightfully crooked smile held some warmth. "My thanks, Mr. Grierson. You have been most helpful."

"It is my pleasure to serve you, my lady." The obviously relieved gunmaker performed yet another deep bow.

Atlas and Lilliana took their leave, stepping out onto the stone pavement along Bond Street. "Have you heard of this Mr. Balfour?" she inquired when they reached her waiting carriage.

"Indeed, I have. He is a particular friend of Francis Pike's."

A footman clad in smart black and gold livery hastened forward to pull down the carriage step. Atlas waved the young man away and saw to it himself.

Lilliana paused before the open carriage door. "I suppose you will now go and speak with Mr. Balfour."

"Yes, that is what I intend." He looked at her, all admiration, as he assisted her into the carriage. This was an important step forward in his inquiry. And he had Lilliana's cleverness to thank for it.

"We shall drop you at your apartments, if you would like."

"There is no need. My lodgings are just down the street. A walk will do me good."

"As you like." She studied him. "You were awfully quiet in the gun shop."

"You had matters well in hand."

"I thought you might at least attempt to assist."

"You did not require any help." He propped a booted foot on the carriage step, leaning into the chaise. "You were master-ful in your handling of that man. You are a marvel."

Lilliana's radiant, off-kilter smile momentarily caused him to forget to breathe. "It is far past time that you noticed." He sensed no discomfort on her part. Perhaps he'd misread the unease he thought he'd discerned earlier.

He took the liberty of reaching for her gloved hand, which seemed too delicate in his clumsy paw. "A man would have to be dead or blind not to." He pressed his lips against the delicate bare skin on the inside of her wrist. "And I assure you that I am neither."

★　★　★

The following day, after making a few inquiries, Atlas ran Jasper Balfour to ground at Manton's shooting gallery on Davies Street in Berkeley Square.

He stood in the shadows, watching Jasper practice with a renowned Manton, a pistol produced by London's premier gun-maker. Manton's pistols were objects of beauty, admired for being trim, light, and impeccably finished. Even Grierson had once been in Joseph Manton's employ.

Jasper took careful aim at the row of paper wafers hanging from a circular iron frame at the opposite end of the shooting gallery. He squeezed the trigger and hit his mark. The bullet shredded the paper target, coating the air with the acrid odor of burnt gunpowder.

"Excellent shot," Atlas said from behind him. "I would certainly consider carefully before challenging you to a duel."

Jasper turned, narrowing his eyes in Atlas's direction.

"My name is Atlas Catesby," he said. "We met at the Lottery Club when you were accompanied by Francis Pike."

"Yes, I know who you are." The young man tossed some sort of confection into his mouth and then opened his palm to offer one to Atlas. "Care for a comfit? It is almond."

Atlas glanced down at the almonds wrapped in a sugary paste. "No, but it is kind of you to offer."

Jasper sucked on his sweet confection. "Are you here to practice your shot?"

"No, I came looking for you."

"Did you?" The man shifted his weight from one foot to the other. "Whatever for?"

"I am interested to know why you would want to purchase a certain a flintlock pistol with a barrel sheathed in silver."

Jasper crossed one ankle behind the other. "My father has one like it that was either lost or stolen. He would like to replace it."

"When did you, or your father, notice that the pistol was missing?"

He sucked on his sweet as he appeared to consider the question. "I would say about a fortnight ago."

"That would be shortly after Francis Pike's mother was killed."

Jasper uncrossed his ankles. "How does that signify?"

"I believe your father's pistol was used to shoot Mrs. Pike."

Jasper's mouth fell open, revealing the half-eaten comfit on his tongue. He snapped his lips shut. "The devil you say!"

"If I were to ask your father, Lord Balfour, would he confirm what you have just told me? That the pistol was stolen?"

Jasper looked beyond Atlas. "Why do you not ask him?"

Atlas turned to find himself looking at an older, plumper version of Jasper Balfour.

"This is my father, Lord Balfour," Jasper said. "Father, this is Atlas Catesby."

The older man scrutinized Atlas. "Silas Catesby's son?"

Here then, was another of his late father's many fans. "One of them, yes."

"I knew your father quite well. He was a good man."

This was an unexpected development. "You were acquainted with my father?"

"Yes, and I remain a great admirer of his work. Whenever the baron visited the metropolis, he would call on me, and we would share a drink."

"I had no idea." His father's acquaintance with the elder Balfour, the younger son of a viscount, came as something of a jolt to Atlas. Despite being awarded a title, Baron Catesby had had little use for the peerage. If he had taken to calling on Lord Balfour, it would have been solely because Silas Catesby had enjoyed their meetings. Atlas's father had rarely done anything that did not please him.

"I remember he anguished over whether to send you to Eton or Harrow," Lord Balfour continued. "Silas said you were having some troubles. I seem to recall that he decided on Harrow. Was it the right choice?"

Atlas was momentarily stunned into silence. It shocked him to discover that Silas had discussed a matter as personal as his unruly fourth son with this nobleman.

"It was as good a choice as any," Atlas replied after a lengthy pause, "given my state of mind at the time."

He preferred not to recall the dark period following Phoebe's death, when he'd spiraled into a sort of madness. His bewildered parents, uncertain of how to manage him and submerged in their own grief, had packed him off to boarding school at the age of eleven, three years earlier than his brothers.

"Mr Catesby wants to know about your missing pistol," Jasper informed his father. "He says it may have been used to kill Vessey's lightskirt."

Atlas noted with distaste the disparaging manner in which Jasper referred to his friend's mother. It also prompted him to wonder just how close a friendship existed between Jasper Balfour and the dead woman's son.

Lord Balfour jerked his head from his son to Atlas. "Is that true? Was my pistol used to kill that poor woman?"

"Unfortunately," Atlas responded. "Jasper tells me the gun went missing and was possibly stolen."

"Yes." The older man nodded. "That is the truth of it."

"When did you notice the pistol was gone?"

"November fifth."

Three days after Wendy's murder. "You recall the precise date?"

"Yes, because we had hosted a salon at my home off Grosvenor Square on the previous evening, on the fourth. Lady Balfour and I enjoy entertaining in that manner. We hold salons on the second and last Wednesday of each month when we are in town. We much prefer to facilitate diverting discussions about the arts and politics. We have decided we are too old to be hosting balls, which we do not enjoy."

"I see. Would you mind telling me where you kept the pistol in question?"

"Not at all. That piece is a particular favorite of mine. I purchased it from Grierson a few years ago. I keep it—kept it, rather—in my bottom desk drawer in my study. The day following the salon, I wanted to show the pistol to a friend, but when I went to retrieve the piece, it was nowhere to be found."

"Are you certain it vanished during your salon? Could it have been taken before then?"

"Possibly. I cannot be certain when exactly the pistol went missing. I had not checked on it in weeks. The last time I can recall seeing the pistol in the drawer was probably in late September, when we returned from our summer in the country."

Lord Balfour's recollection meant that the pistol could have been taken anytime in the month leading up to Wendy's murder. "You say that you and Lady Balfour host your salons twice a month?"

"That is correct. On every other Wednesday."

"And do the same guests attend each time?"

"Not at all. Some of the guests are the same, but about half are not."

"How large are these salons?"

"Between thirty and forty people attend." Lord Balfour crossed one arm over his chest while resting his chin on the fist of his opposite arm. "We do prefer to keep the gatherings somewhat intimate."

A few dozen guests did not strike Atlas as a particularly intimate group, but he'd recently learned that the peerage saw such matters through very different eyes.

"I see," Atlas said. With that number of guests, not to mention servants, having access to the weapon, it would be extraordinarily difficult to isolate who had absconded with Lord Balfour's weapon.

"Thank you for your time, my lord," Atlas said. "I shall not keep you from your shooting practice any longer."

"Not at all," Lord Balfour responded warmly. "I am pleased to have met you. Your father always said you possessed the keenest mind of all of his sons. He had the highest of hopes for you."

As Atlas walked home in a cold light rain, he reflected on Lord Balfour's revelations about his father. Silas Catesby had rarely complimented his sons. That his father might have admired his intellect buoyed Atlas. It seemed a man was never too old to crave his father's praise.

He found it difficult to envision his father discussing his children with Lord Balfour or anyone else. Silas Catesby had been too wrapped up in his life's work, his writing, as well as his passionate love for Atlas's mother, for either of them to bestow an abundance of attention on any of their six children.

Not that Atlas's childhood had been any hardship. The children had been fed, clothed, and educated in comfort. The six siblings had kept one another company while their father and mother had indulged in their secret society for two that no outsider could ever hope to breach. Phoebe, twelve years Atlas's senior, had been more like a mother to Atlas than their own mother had been.

The arrangement had never struck any of the children as abnormal. Atlas certainly held no ill will toward either of his parents. Quite the contrary. He'd always held them in high, albeit somewhat distant, esteem.

As he crossed through Berkeley Square, Atlas tried to ignore the growing ache in his left foot. Not for the first time, he silently cursed the drunken idiot hackney driver responsible for his accident and the lingering pain in his left foot. He passed colorless grass and bare trees that had surrendered most of their leaves to the late autumn frost. He had the square all to himself, the foul weather having driven most people away.

It was dusk, and the damp cold had seeped into his bones by the time he reached home. He trudged up the stairs, pain now radiating through his left foot. He was eager to divest himself of his sodden garments, warm up with a brandy, and settle in to work on his puzzle.

He caught sight of a huddled figure sitting on the landing outside his apartments. As he came up the stairs, he realized it was Nicholas.

His nephew's stricken expression made Atlas's heart momentarily lose its rhythm. "What is it?" he asked. "What has happened?"

"Did you know?" Emotion strained his nephew's voice. "Did everyone know except me?"

"I am not sure what you are asking."

"Did you know that I have a half brother?"

CHAPTER 17

"You had better come inside."

Pale-faced, the boy came to his feet. "You did know."

Atlas set a light hand on his nephew's shoulder to usher him into the welcoming warmth of his sitting room, where Jamie had lit a fire. He then excused himself just long enough to change out of his wet clothes before rejoining his nephew and pouring them both a drink.

"Yes, I knew." Atlas handed the boy a brandy. "But I have not known for long. I only recently became aware of Francis Pike's existence."

Nicholas held the crystal with both hands and took a long, deep swallow.

"Go easy." Atlas settled into his chair, filling the soft grooves his body had imprinted onto the cushions. "Are you accustomed to imbibing?"

"My father was with Mrs. Pike well before he married." Nicholas's eyes glistened. "He consorted with that woman while he was wed to my mother, and then he moved his doxy into our house after my mother died. It is as if he cared nothing for my mother."

"How did you find out?" Atlas spoke in a gentle manner. "Did you run into Francis?"

He shook his head. "My father told me. I have never met this man who is supposedly my brother."

"Your half brother."

Pain clouded Nicholas face. "I am not my father's eldest son."

"What does that matter? You are his sole legitimate son and his heir. You will be the Marquess of Vessey one day. Not Francis Pike."

"I inherit the title and Francis receives our father." Nicholas bottomed out his glass. "Hardly a fair bargain."

Atlas frowned. "What do you mean about Francis getting your father?"

"I have never had a family. Not really. Father did not want me to be tainted by his mistress and her children. I have long known that I have two half sisters. But I have never seen them."

Atlas had no interest in protecting Vessey, but at the same time he did not care to witness his nephew's suffering. "It is not unusual for a man to keep his by-blows away from his legitimate heirs."

"That is just it. I was the one who was kept away. Mrs. Pike and her children lived with my father at Stonebrook while I was sent away to live at school. I rarely saw my father, and I had no other family."

You could have had us, Atlas wanted to scream, but he did not because the last thing Nicholas needed at the moment was to feel the weight of Atlas's long-simmering resentment toward Vessey.

"But the worst part of it all was how my father showed such disregard for my mother. To keep a mistress before, during, and after their marriage. First Mrs. Pike came between my mother and father, and then she came between my father and me. That woman ruined both of our lives. And my father allowed it."

Atlas took a long draw on his brandy and forced himself to he consider his words carefully. "Many noblemen have a mistress, even if they are wed."

"Would you keep such a loose commitment to your wedding vows?" Nicholas asked sharply. "Will you engage a mistress after you wed Lady Roslyn?"

Surprise rippled through Atlas. "What makes you think I intend to wed Lady Roslyn?"

"Everyone in society speaks of it."

"They do?" He'd had no inkling that society had made certain assumptions about his acquaintanceship with the duke's sister.

"You are her only escort aside from her brother."

Atlas knew London society watched Lilliana with open curiosity. The duke's sister was something of an enigma to the ton. She'd vanished from society as a girl of sixteen and returned ten years later as the widow of a murdered merchant.

Only Somerville's exalted title and powerful position in society had spared Lilliana's reputation any hint of scandal. That and, Atlas believed, Lilliana's own innate patrician manner, which commanded respect and deference in its own right.

"It is well known that she rejects all other potential suitors," Nicholas continued. "Do you deny you are courting her?"

Atlas paused for a moment. "No." It was the first time he had admitted the truth to anyone, including himself. "I do not deny it."

He had wanted to make Lilliana his almost from the first, when he'd thought her to be a merchant's widow, before he'd learned she was the daughter and sister of a duke. Given the wide social chasm between them—he was the lowly, untitled, unmoneyed fourth son of a newly anointed baron—he had relinquished any hopes of wedding her. Now Atlas had to admit that he'd never given up on Lilliana and never would.

"And, in answer to your question, no, I would never keep a mistress," Atlas continued, buoyed by a new sense of surety. "If I am so fortunate as to wed Lady Roslyn, I would keep faith with her. When I give my word, I keep it."

Nicholas flushed. "Yet you excuse my father for behavior you could never countenance for yourself."

"I have never excused your father's behavior."

"Is this why you hate Vessey?" Nicholas studied Atlas's face. "Is it because he humiliated my mother by keeping a mistress?"

"No," Atlas answered truthfully, if not fully, "I only recently learned of Mrs. Pike's relationship to your father."

"Then what is it?" Nicholas demanded. "I want to know about my mother. My father never speaks of her."

"You are a great deal like her," Atlas answered, taking pains to sidestep Nicholas's question about why Atlas detested Vessey. He'd been given the perfect opening to tell the boy the truth, had in fact dreamed of doing so for years, but now, looking into his nephew's ravaged face, Atlas knew he could not add to the boy's anguish. "I loved your mother very much."

"What was she like?" Nicholas all but whispered the words. He sat forward, eager to resurrect his mother's memory from its early grave, where it had been prematurely consigned along with her body. His earnest green-brown gaze was so like Phoebe's that a piercing nameless sensation that had been dormant since his sister's death quietly unfurled inside Atlas's chest.

"She was very loving and gentle, too gentle for this world, as it turned out. She was twelve years my senior, the eldest of six.

I was the youngest." Strong emotion pressed on his vocal chords, constraining his voice. "She mothered me, coddled me." He smiled, remembering their bond. "She helped me hide a frog in my bedchamber once. I had captured the creature as a tadpole in the creek near our country home. Once it transformed into a frog, Phoebe convinced me to release it. She said all living things were meant to be free."

"Please do continue," Nicholas implored. His face was pale, as if he'd seen a ghost, and Atlas supposed that in a way he had. "Tell me more. I want to know everything."

And so Atlas did. He went on and on, speaking openly about his lost sister for the first time in more than twenty years, wandering from story to story, traveling from one memory to inhabit another. He shared Phoebe with the boy who should have known her but who would never remember his mother's touch or her scent or her particular way of covering her mouth with her fingers when she giggled. Nicholas would never know Phoebe's sense of fun and mischief.

Atlas told Nicholas of his mother's love of drawing—Phoebe was rarely without a sketchbook—and how her siblings were often her subjects. It is almost impossible to convey all of the qualities that make a person uniquely him- or herself, but Atlas tried for his sister's sake and for that of her beautiful son.

As he shared his sister with her son, Atlas experienced a strong visceral sensation he had never felt before—one that would compel him to always look after his sister's child. He would envelop Nicholas in a shield of love and devotion, as Phoebe had done for Atlas while she'd lived. Atlas would do whatever was required to protect the boy from harm. He hadn't been able to save Phoebe from Vessey, but here at last was something he could finally do for his sister. A way for him to make amends. And this time he would not fail her.

The fire was low in the grate by the time Atlas stopped speaking, and the sun had long since gone down. Sometime during their conversation, Jamie had slipped in to light the candles and lanterns, bathing the sitting room in soft, glowing light, but Atlas could not recall his valet doing so.

He did take note when Jamie entered carrying a food basket. Atlas realized he must have spent well over two hours introducing Phoebe to her son, answering the interested questions the boy interjected at intervals during their conversation. They'd laughed together at some of the memories and grown somber at others.

"I do beg your pardon for interrupting, sir," Jamie said tentatively. His gaze darted between his master and Nicholas, "but the Duke of Somerville's cook has sent over some food."

"From the Duke of Somerville's household?" Nicholas grinned at his uncle, a knowing look on his young face. "Interesting, that. I suppose we do not have to wonder who sent it."

Atlas grinned back, delighting in this sudden unexpected camaraderie with the nephew he had longed to know, and be known by, for so many years.

He gestured for Jamie to come forward. "That was very kind of Lady Roslyn to think of me. Let us have it then," he said heartily. "My nephew will be joining me for supper."

★　★　★

"You must bring Nicholas around for supper one evening soon." Thea sipped her coffee from a chipped porcelain cup made of the finest of china but worn by years, perhaps decades, of use. "I will invite Jason and Hermes as well."

Atlas grimaced. "Let us try not to scare the boy away. Too many Catesbys in one room is a great deal to cope with all at once." He reached for another slice of plum cake. "Perhaps gradual introductions would be more the thing."

He and Charlton were having breakfast at Thea's after their early morning hack through Hyde Park. Charlton provided the horseflesh for their twice-weekly outings. Atlas did not keep a mount. He found it difficult to justify the costs of stabling his own animal when he spent months at a time traveling abroad, far from London. Besides, Charlton kept only the finest horseflesh, far better than Atlas would ever be able to afford. Stopping by Thea's for breakfast after these outings had become their custom in recent months.

"Your cup is chipped." Charlton surveyed the table and the plates full of warm buns and plum cake. "In fact, several of these dishes are damaged. Why does your butler not replace them?"

"Why ever should he?" Thea shot the earl a scornful look. "They are still perfectly serviceable." Charlton was well aware that Thea found a use for almost everything until it was completely in tatters.

Thea and the earl could not have been more different in that respect. Charlton favored tailored clothes, expensive horseflesh, shiny carriages, and a well-appointed home. Thea's Spartan-like philosophy was difficult to comprehend by a man who surrounded himself with every luxury.

"Nicholas really is so like Phoebe." Atlas brought the conversation back to their nephew. He'd been particularly eager to see his sister today in order to share the details of his encounter with the boy. "I told Nicholas all about his mother. I cannot wait for you to become acquainted with him. He is a fine young man."

Thea moved a hot roll onto her plate. Faint cracks spread across the porcelain surface, branching out like veins. "I do hope you were not terribly morose about it."

Atlas swallowed the last of his plum cake. "What does that mean?"

"It is just that you are always so glum when you speak of Phoebe. It can be tiresome."

"At least I remember that she existed," Atlas snapped. "You do not even think about her. It is as if you do not even care that she is not here."

"Yes, we all know how much Atlas has suffered because Phoebe died young. And we are aware of your distress because you never allow us forget it."

"Go to the devil." He flung his linen napkin on the table. "I barely mention Phoebe."

Charlton uttered an exclamation of disapproval. "Now, there is no need for coarse talk in the presence of a lady." Charlton's wary gaze bounced from Atlas to Thea and back again. "Surely we can all be civil."

Thea ignored him. "You do not need to mention her name because Phoebe is that big heavy weight on your shoulder that prevents you from having a family of your own. She is in the ships in the wharf that carry you away from us for months at a time."

Atlas rubbed his temples. "Please do spare me your prattling." No one had the capability to irritate Atlas more than Thea. They were almost of an age, with Thea barely a year his senior, yet that proximity did little to curb her desire to manage him.

"Has it ever occurred to you," Atlas said, "that I travel because certain members of my family can be insufferable?"

"No, it has not." She spoke matter-of-factly, striking the same tone she might use to explain one of her complicated mathematics equations. "You have been unmoored since Phoebe died. Do you not think it is rather past time you moved on from that unfortunate episode?"

"Unfortunate incident?" Atlas's temper flared. "That is how you refer to the murder of your sister? You truly are a heartless shrew."

"Enough now, Atlas." A pained expression stamped Charlton's aristocratic face. "Thea might not be one to show emotion, but that is no reason to insult her. After all, she did look after you after your carriage accident when—"

Thea didn't even look at Charlton when she interrupted him to respond to Atlas. "Do you think Phoebe would want you always to be sad when you think of her? I choose to remember the good in Phoebe, to remember the happy times."

"Are you implying that I do not recall how wonderful Phoebe was?"

"Not at all." She tore her bread roll in half. "You have made her a proverbial saint in your mind. Which she most certainly was not. Phoebe was lovely, but she was far from perfect."

"I know she was a real person. I was there when she died."

"You do Phoebe a disservice by making everything about how she died." She spread butter on her roll, methodically covering the entire surface. "Perhaps you should focus on how she lived. You have made her this tragic figure, almost a symbol, and hardly even a person."

Atlas rubbed his chest. It felt like a hot iron rod was wedged inside it. "Forgive me for not being a heartless bastard."

"Really, you two, this is hardly appropriate conversation for mealtime," Charlton interjected before muttering, "or ever."

Atlas glared at his sister. "It is really no wonder that your husband stays as far away from you as he can most of the time."

"Atlas!" This time, the earl's tone was sharp in its defense of Thea. "You go too far."

Thea flushed, her usual equanimity no longer in evidence. "Do you think you are the only one who suffered a tremendous loss?" She tossed her buttered roll onto her plate. "I lost my sister. *My only sister.* Nothing and no one can replace that. You still have one sister. I do not. As the lone female in a sea of brothers, do you imagine that I have not felt rather lonely in this family?"

"Thea," Charlton said, laying a gentle hand on her forearm, "please do not upset yourself."

Thea shrugged his touch away. "I am particularly alone, as you have so kindly pointed out, because my husband can rarely be bothered to come and visit me."

Shocked, Atlas slumped back in his chair. Thea had never given any indication of dissatisfaction with the state of affairs in her marriage, with a husband who'd elected to remain in the country for most of their wedded life. "Why do you not go to him in the country?"

She shook her head, her fury and frustration apparent. "Do you not think I would if that were possible?"

Surprise lit Charlton's face. "You would?"

"Why is it not possible?" Atlas asked her gently, genuinely curious. "I had no idea that you have felt neglected by Palmer all of this time."

His conciliatory manner seemed to further agitate Thea. She shot to her feet. "Perhaps you have not noticed anyone else's troubles because you are too busy wallowing in your own." Both men stood as soon as Thea did, but she had little use for either of them. "You two can see yourselves out."

Without sparing either of them another moment of her attention, she stormed out of the room, slamming the door behind her.

Atlas stared after Thea, stunned not only by this rare outburst from his sister but also by her surprising distress over her husband's continued absence.

"You owe your sister an apology," Charlton said tightly.

"I do. And she will have one. Once she is in a more agreeable state of mind." Thea rarely showed anger, but when she did, it was like a hurricane passing through. A wise person took shelter until it was safe to emerge to clean up the mess. "What was that all about?"

Charlton's nostrils flared. "I have no idea." He was as furious as Atlas had ever seen him. "All I know is that Palmer is an idiot who deserves to be strung up for the way he has neglected your sister."

CHAPTER 18

"She is extraordinary," Lilliana said as she and Atlas listened to Dorothea Lieven expertly play the pianoforte for her guests, the instrument's crisp, colorful notes swirling through the room.

Atlas concurred. "The countess is certainly a gifted musician."

"She is far more than that." Lilliana was radiant in a simple cream silk gown with a square-cut bodice and magnificent double strand of pearls that fell almost to her waist. "She is a woman to be reckoned with in her own right."

"You admire her," Atlas noted with some surprise.

"Most certainly."

Atlas shifted to study the object of Lilliana's high regard. He was curious to know what sort of person drew the appreciation of someone as discerning as Lilliana.

Dorothea Lieven was tall and slim, with impeccable posture. Although no one would mistake her for a beauty, the distinguished countess's lively manner and magnetic presence drew all eyes.

Her husband, Count Christopher Lieven, stood by the piano, watching the performance. At least a decade older than his wife, the Russian ambassador to the Court of St. James possessed a trim athletic form, deep blue eyes, and a dimpled chin. He was not unhandsome, but his extraordinarily charismatic countess completely eclipsed him.

Atlas had traveled to the ambassador's party with Lilliana and the Duke of Somerville. Although the ambassador maintained a lavish primary residence in town, the Lievens also rented this elegant Richmond home, where marble floors met richly carved wainscoting, and costly paintings ornamented the silk-covered walls.

"The countess is a woman who lives life on her own terms," Lilliana explained. Atlas detected a touch of envy in her voice. "She does not hide her ambition."

"What more does she aspire to?" he inquired. "Did you not say that she is already a leader of fashion as well as a celebrated hostess?"

"The countess cultivates relationships with powerful men. Although her husband is the ambassador, she is a political force in her own right."

"To what end?"

Lilliana's gloved fingers toyed with the pearls around her neck. "It is said she has the tsar's ear and that he appreciates her intellect . . . as well as the information she provides about England and the people who rule it."

The music came to an end, and Countess Lieven rose from the pianoforte. She engaged a small group of her guests in animated conversation. Large, dark eyes sparkled with such vitality that one hardly noticed the lady's pointed nose and large ears. "She and her husband appear to be quite the team," Atlas said.

Lilliana lifted an elegant shoulder. "It would hardly matter if they were not. It is clear the countess does as she pleases."

"Unlike English women?" He wondered whether Lilliana thought of her own marriage, when she had chafed under the complete control of the bastard she'd wed as a desperate girl of just sixteen. "Do Russian husbands not have complete authority over their wives just as men in England do?"

"They do, of course, except that in Russia women control their own property."

"Ah, yes. I can see how that would make a difference." In England, a woman lost everything when she wed. All of her riches became the property of her husband.

"Countess Lieven has the power to dispose of her own wealth," Lilliana said. "And with money comes power and ownership of one's future."

They both grew quiet as the subject of their conversation approached.

Dorothea Lieven smiled once she reached them, and Atlas greeted her with a courtly bow. "And how do you like our Russian vodka, Mr. Catesby?"

"It is excellent," he answered truthfully, finishing the last of his glass as if to emphasize his point.

The countess raised a hand, signaling for a footman to appear with more vodka. "We must drink together," she said jovially as they all accepted a glass of the amber liquid. "In Russia, we believe vodka adds to our *bonhomie*. In my language, this is called *dusha–dushe*."

Atlas contemplated the phrase. He had a love of both words and languages. His mind searched for an appropriate translation. "Soul to soul?" he said to her.

Surprised delight lit her gaze. "You speak Russian?"

"Only a bit. And I must confess that most of it relates to vodka."

She threw her head back with a smile. "And how did you learn the language of vodka?"

"I traveled once with a Russian gentleman. It was a long voyage, and over those few months he was kind enough to teach me a bit of your beautiful language while also sharing his supply of excellent vodka."

The countess tapped her throat with two gloved fingers.

Atlas laughed and bowed again. "How could I refuse?" He clinked his glass against Countess Lieven's, and then Lilliana's, before he and the countess both poured a considerable amount of vodka down their throats.

Lilliana sipped hers more delicately, her questioning gaze traveling between the countess and Atlas.

"Do forgive us, Lady Roslyn," Countess Lieven said with a friendly smile. "In Russia, when one taps their throat, it is an invitation of friendship forged in the drinking of vodka together. It is always pleasant when one is reminded of home."

"Do you miss Russia?" Lilliana asked. "I understand St. Petersburg is very beautiful. I should like to see it one day."

Atlas's brows shot up. He had not known Lilliana harbored a desire to see other parts of the world.

"Oh, heavens no, I do not miss Russia." The countess addressed them as if they were long-time friends that she had taken into her confidence. Atlas understood the lady's appeal. Countess Lieven most definitely had a way of making a person feel special.

"I am enjoying the best time of my life here in England," the countess said. "Do not mistake me. I love my country and am completed devoted to Russia, and St. Petersburg is indeed lovely, but I do not miss the harsh weather, the snow and the cold."

"I also dislike winter." Lilliana sipped more of her vodka. "I suppose I should make certain to visit during the Russian summer."

"You must come as my guest when you do visit," the countess said warmly, "and I shall introduce you to everyone at court."

"That is very kind of you." Lilliana paused. "Is it a very long journey? I wonder whether Aleksey Witte has already reached St. Petersburg."

"Are you acquainted with Aleksey?" the countess asked.

"Not exactly. However, a friend was recently speaking about Mr. Witte and his return to his mother country. She said his absence from the capital will be sorely felt in England."

"Aleksey is most agreeable. He was invited almost everywhere when he was here."

"Is he traveling with his wife and children?"

"Aleksey has no wife. The gentleman enjoys his freedom. He did say he would miss a certain opera singer that he had been keeping company with."

Atlas exchanged a look with Lilliana. The countess appeared to be confirming Juliet's claims.

The Duke of Somerville chose that moment to join them. "Am I intruding?" He was attired in superfine navy. Somerville made a habit of dressing in the most understated manner yet always managed to be the most elegant man at any gathering.

"Not at all," said the countess. "We were just speaking of Aleksey Witte."

"Lilliana," Somerville said to his sister, "the Lievens have sons about the same age as Robin and Peter. I have just met them. Fine young men."

"You have sons?" Countess Lieven said to Lilliana.

"Yes, indeed." Lilliana's eyes shone as she spoke of her children. "Peter has just turned nine, and Robin is almost seven."

"I can see you are a devoted mother," the countess said. "I also adore my children. Would you like to come and meet them? They are in the nursery."

After Lilliana went off with the countess to meet the Lieven children, the duke turned to Atlas.

"You mentioned Witte," Somerville said. "Is he part of your investigation?"

"He is."

"Surely you do not think Witte had anything to do with Mrs. Pike's death?"

"No, nothing of that sort," Atlas assured him. "However, I do wonder whether he could have been at the center of a love triangle involving Mrs. Pike and another woman."

"No, he could not," the duke said firmly. "I advise you not to waste your time and effort looking in that direction."

Surprised, Atlas stared at Somerville. "Were you well acquainted with Mr. Witte?"

"No, I hardly knew the man. However," he said meaningfully, "I am in a position to know about these matters, as you are aware."

Atlas's forehead wrinkled. "What matters?"

"Whether a man such as Witte could be seriously involved with Mrs. Pike . . . or *any* woman for that matter, if you take my meaning."

Comprehension struck Atlas like a gale force wind. The duke's subtle reference to his own private predilections caused Atlas's cheeks to burn as if with fever. "And you are certain?"

"Absolutely. Without a doubt," the duke said with a firm nod. "Aleksey Witte was not the sort of man to pursue a liaison with a member of the fair sex."

"But what about the opera singer? He was known to have had a liaison with Juliet Jennings."

"What of the artist that I keep in Kensington?" Somerville gave him a look. "Everyone presumes her to be my mistress." Marian Smith was an artist Somerville admired. When he'd become her patron, many in society had made erroneous assumptions about their relationship.

"I see." The duke's disclosure about Witte led to another revelation. Atlas's old friend Juliet Jennings was a liar.

It remained to be seen whether she was also a killer.

★ ★ ★

The following evening, Atlas burst into Juliet's dressing room without bothering to knock.

She turned from her dressing table. "Atlas, this is a surprise."

"Is it?" He dispensed with any greeting. "Did you truly think I would not discover the truth about Aleksey Witte?"

She shifted back to face the mirror, but her reflection carefully watched him. "What truth is that?"

"That neither you nor Mrs. Pike had an affair with the man."

"You could not be more mistaken." She powdered her face. "Ask anyone. Aleksey and I were hardly discreet."

"Oh, you were entirely discreet. The liaison never happened. I would wager that it was a clever masquerade to keep people from guessing the truth about your Russian."

"What truth is that?"

"That Aleksey preferred men."

She froze, set down the cosmetic, and slowly turned to face him. "That is ridiculous. I can assure you that Alek was very virile. If you would like to hear the details—"

"Spare your lies for someone who will believe them," he interrupted. "If Alek was virile, it certainly was not with you."

Her delicate eyebrows lifted. "I am shocked to hear you speak of such matters. The Atlas I kept company with just a few years ago certainly never would have."

"I am not as young, nor as innocent, as I once was."

"I can see that your travels have certainly made you more worldly." She leaned forward on her stool. "Even so, Alek's preferences are not the sort of thing a man like you would learn of firsthand. Someone enlightened you. Who was it?"

He flushed. "Certainly not you. Do you admit there was no affair between you and the Russian?"

She shrugged. "Alek paid me handsomely to pretend there was. Being in his company was no hardship. He was engaging and took me to interesting parties."

"If the disagreement you had with Wendela Pike was not about a man, then what was the cause of it?"

She remained silent, and he could see her calculating what to say next.

"The truth this time," he demanded. At her continued silence, he prodded her again. "Juliet? One could take your silence as an admission of guilt."

"I did not kill Wendy."

"Then tell me what you were fighting about. You have already confessed that it was not over a man."

"It was over a man. Just not Alek."

"Then who?"

She shook her head. "It is not my place to say."

He took in her posture. Juliet was tense. Stress seemed to roll off her in waves. She seemed almost afraid. But of what? "Why would you hide his name?"

"Because his identity is of no consequence. I was foolish to fight with Wendy. She had already won this man's heart. I just had not realized it at that point."

"Yet, you lied and gave me Aleksey Witte's name, even though this man—whoever he is—was devoted to Wendy. Why do you protect him still?"

"Because Wendy is dead, and I am not. And neither is he." Her blue gaze met his. "There is always hope."

"Did you kill Wendy so that you could have this man all to yourself?"

"If I did, do you think I would admit it?" When he did not answer, she continued. "I did not kill Wendy, nor did I hire a cutthroat to do it in my stead."

Atlas's first instinct was to believe her. The Juliet he knew was not a murderess. But he had been wrong before.

He went still and quiet, filtering through everything he had learned up until that moment. Remembered emotions, words, or gestures that had seemed out of place at the time he had witnessed them all began to fall into some semblance of order. It was rather like one of his puzzles coming together. His mind shuffled through the fragments, moving them around until they formed a comprehensible picture. Not the entire picture, but enough to know what Juliet was hiding.

"You need not say anything further," he assured her. "I know who the man is."

★ ★ ★

"Why did you lie about your relationship with Wendela Pike?" Atlas demanded of the man who, he now knew, had been conducting a liaison with Wendy at the time of her death.

Simon Cooke blanched. "I beg your pardon?"

"It all makes sense now. The reason no one saw Wendy backstage the evening she died is because she was with you."

"That is absurd."

"No, the idea that she would have even contemplated going off with the clergyman is what could be considered farcical. But you are another matter entirely."

Cooke lifted his chin. "An interesting theory, but it is far from the truth."

"The first time we met, directly after Mrs. Pike was killed, you claimed to be ill. You blamed a cold for your red, runny eyes. But that was not it at all. You were in mourning for the woman you loved."

Cooke scoffed. "That is quite a leap you are taking."

"And the second time we met, after you had been shot, you referred to somebody named Esther coming to save you."

"As if that is proof of anything. I was foxed."

"It proves that a certain familiarity existed between you and Wendela Pike, as few people were aware that her true given name was Esther Gillray. And even fewer people of her acquaintance referred to her as such. Your liaison also explains why she turned down a more lucrative offer to perform at Drury Lane."

Cooke adjusted his cuffs while avoiding Atlas's gaze. "I am sure Mrs. Pike had her reasons for making that decision, just as I am certain it had absolutely nothing to do with me."

"Mrs. Pike was in love. She told her sister as much, and she was very excited about her future with this man." Atlas was convinced he had uncovered the truth. "But Wendy was not in love with the clergyman. It was you that she loved. She accepted an offer to perform here so she could be with you, her lover."

"Not her lover," Simon burst out, his eyes glistening. "Her husband. I was wed to Wendela Pike. She was my wife."

CHAPTER 19

Atlas gaped at the theater manager. "You were married to Wendela Pike?"

"Her name was Esther Wendela Cooke, and she was my wife."

"Do you have proof of this?"

Cooke went behind his desk and used a key to unlock the center drawer. He drew out a piece of paper and handed it to Atlas.

He stared down at the document, a common license that could be acquired for a few shillings. "This proves nothing. There are no names on it."

"We wed a week after I obtained that license. Our marriage is recorded in the church register."

"Where did you marry?"

"At St. Paul's." Atlas knew the place. It was the church just across the way, frequented by performers from Covent Garden and nearby Drury Lane.

"Did Vessey know?"

Cooke shook his head. "We wed in secret. Wendy worried the marquess would try to stop us."

"What was the plan? For your new bride to go on living with another man?"

Cooke flushed. "She intended to tell Vessey the truth once our marriage could not be undone. She feared what Vessey might do."

"She thought him capable of violence?"

"Possibly. Vessey seemed all powerful to Wendy. She had been under his control practically since girlhood and had never truly stepped out on her own."

"You elected to keep the marriage a secret after Wendy died." Atlas had a fairly good idea of why.

"I lied to you about our association because there was no reason to reveal the truth. I wanted to protect Wendy's reputation. Imagine the scandal if word of our marriage had come to light."

"And why incur Vessey's wrath?"

"Precisely. At least if I had Wendy by my side, challenging a powerful peer would have been worth the risk. But without her, there was no point."

Atlas saw the theater owner in a new light. Cooke must have loved Wendy very much to risk antagonizing someone like Vessey, a powerful noble with the capacity to ruin him. Cooke was already deeply in debt with rebuilding costs. Making an enemy out of Vessey could only have worsened matters.

"Does Juliet know?"

"Know what?"

"That you and Wendy were wed."

He shook his head. "No one knew except the clergyman who married us. And his wife, who witnessed our wedding."

"If it is in the public register, how ever did you keep your marriage a secret? Wendy was a well-known woman."

"Because it is the name Esther Gillray that appears in the church register. Not Wendela Pike."

"Did you not worry the church rector would tell someone?"

"Rector Gilmore is a man of honor and discretion. We have been well acquainted for many years. St. Paul's is known as the actors' church for good reason. We here in the theater community are the rector's parishioners. I knew he could be entrusted with our secret."

"I have taken up enough of your time." Atlas rose to go. "I am sorry for your loss."

Cooke stopped him from leaving by placing a hand on Atlas's arm. "You should know that Wendy was a good woman, a virtuous woman. If that father of hers had not practically sold her to Vessey, she would have lived a respectable life. We did not even share a bed until after we wed."

As Atlas went out, he reflected on Wendy's daring secret marriage. Although he had never met her, he did feel as if he'd become acquainted with her during the course of his investigation. It heartened him to know that before she'd died, Esther Gillray had found a way to escape the man who'd violated her as a child and disrespected her as a woman. At least in Cooke she'd found a worthy man who had been willing to risk everything he owned to be with the woman he loved.

★　★　★

After leaving the theater, Atlas went over to St. Paul's to check the register. Although Cooke's claim that he'd wedded Wendy shortly before her death struck him as the truth, Atlas was keen to independently confirm the story.

He entered the stone-faced church by its main entrance, his boots clicking against the stone floor. Despite a stately exterior with grand columns and a soaring slanted roof, the inside of

St. Paul's was a rather simple affair—just a large undivided room. Atlas bade a boy who was sweeping the floor to go and fetch the rector.

The rector, a bald, full-bodied man named Gilmore, appeared shortly afterward. "Yes, it is true, I did perform the service," he said in response to Atlas's question. "But it is not widely known."

"May I see the register?"

"Certainly." The rector excused himself and returned with a weighty leather-bound book he carried with both hands. Setting it on the lectern, he leafed through the register until he came to the relevant page. "Ah, here it is."

Atlas moved closer to study the entry. There it was, proof that Simon Cooke had married Esther Gillray on the fourteenth of October, just over two weeks before Wendy was killed. Both had signed their names, and the rector's signature appeared below theirs.

"Do you recall performing the ceremony?" Atlas asked.

"Of course. It was not so long ago, and Mr. Cooke is a friend. I do not believe I have ever seen two happier people." The rector's eyes crinkled at the memory. "Neither could refrain from smiling throughout the entirety of the ceremony. The bride was beautiful, and she fairly radiated happiness."

"You thought it to be a love match then."

"They certainly seemed smitten with each other. I was saddened to hear of Mrs. Cooke's demise such a short time later. Mr. Cooke sought my counsel after his bride's death. He was inconsolable. It was a very difficult time for him."

Atlas thanked the rector for his time and turned to depart. As he neared the exit, the rector called out to him.

"Mr. Catesby."

"Yes?" he turned toward the man.

"I was summoned to the tavern after Mrs. Cooke was shot. I went immediately, of course, to provide ministry at the time of death. I did not realize it was Mrs. Cooke until much later. Her face was . . . beyond recognition. It was a terrible thing."

"Yes, it certainly was." Atlas remembered his own shock at seeing what had been left of Wendy's face.

"Mrs. Cooke was full of hope at her wedding. I do hope you find her killer."

"I will certainly do my best."

★　★　★

Nicholas picked up the chalk. "I think it can be done if you . . ." He scribbled some numbers on the chalkboard Thea used to solve her equations. "And then add this to this." He tapped the tip of the chalk against the board with a clink as he indicated the separate sets of numbers.

It might as well have been Arabic for all Atlas could understand of it, but Thea appeared completely engrossed.

"That is an intriguing possibility. May I?" She held out her hand, and Nicholas promptly deposited the chalk into his aunt's open palm. She added a few scribbles to his. "And then you can carry this and put these here."

"Lord, it is as if she has found her tribe," Charlton murmured to Atlas. "Do you suppose we will ever actually get our supper?"

Atlas lifted a shoulder and dropped it. "When my sister is in this state, engrossed in whatever it is she is doing at the moment, she most certainly will not remember to feed us. And given that her butler is a thousand years old, he is likely to forget as well."

"We are destined to starve then?"

They stood near the threshold of Thea's breakfast room, both men with their hands crossed over their chests as they observed Thea with Phoebe's son, Charlton leaning his shoulders against the wall and Atlas propping one shoulder against the door jamb.

Thea had long ago turned this chamber into her workroom. The round breakfast table was littered with books and papers, and a long black chalkboard covered in white equations dominated the compact circular room.

Thea handed the chalk back to Nicholas and propped one hand on her hip as she watched him work. She'd actually taken the time to arrange her hair and change out of her customary simple black gown in anticipation of this first meeting with her nephew. Nicholas had barely gotten past the front door before the two of them had discovered their shared love of mathematics.

Somehow Thea's hair had already returned to its usual state, an unruly mass of dark curls, and chalk marks smudged not only her hands and fingers but also her pale peach evening gown.

Atlas shook his head as he watched the two of them together. "I assumed my sister's confounding love of math was an aberration, but this eccentricity must run in the Catesby bloodline."

Charlton gave a theatrical shudder. "What a chilling thought."

"It appears as if we are on our own." Atlas straightened up. "Let us see about finding some nourishment before we starve."

Charlton peeled his shoulders off the wall. "Lead on."

Several minutes later, after pressing one of Thea's footmen into service, the two men were happily ensconced in Thea's upstairs sitting room, each with a plate of lamb sweetbreads and a glass of wine to tide them over until Thea and Nicholas emerged from their mathematical reverie.

Charlton washed down a bite with a long draught of wine. "Do you think they will even notice that we have deserted them?"

"Doubtful," Atlas responded between savory bites of lamb stomach. Thea's cook was nowhere near as talented as Somerville's, but Atlas was hungry, and the food was passably good. "So much for a getting-acquainted-with-you dinner."

"Oh, I think Thea is becoming very well acquainted with young Nicholas in the language that she knows best."

"You make a good point." Atlas gestured at Charlton with his fork. "And so few people speak Thea's language."

"Speaking of getting to know your nephew better . . . what is your impression of him?"

"He seems to be a great deal like his mother, sensitive and thoughtful. But given his obsession with numbers, he clearly possess some of his aunt's peculiarities as well."

"Do you find him to be truthful?"

"I have no cause not to." He paused. "Why do you ask?"

"Did Nicholas not say he knew nothing of his elder half brother's existence until recently?'

"That is correct." Atlas bottomed out his wine.

Charlton's expression grew somber. "There could be a perfectly reasonable explanation, but . . ."

"But?" Atlas prompted.

"I saw the two of them together well before Mrs. Pike's death. I saw Nicholas speaking with Francis Pike."

Atlas set down his fork. "Where was this?"

"At Manton's. They were target shooting, as was I. I did not think anything of it until recently, after you told me that Nicholas claimed to have no knowledge of his illegitimate half brother's existence."

"Are you certain it was Nicholas and Francis Pike that you saw together?"

"Quite certain. I recognized Nicholas and even paused to say hello. They appeared to be speaking quite amiably when I approached them. They were saying something about Pike's pistol and how well he shot it."

The lamb settled heavily in Atlas's belly. "Why would Nicholas lie about such a thing?"

Charlton waited a few beats before speaking. "Does he have an alibi for the evening of Mrs. Pike's death?"

"I have no idea," Atlas answered truthfully. "I never thought to ask."

"Do you suppose discovering that he was not his father's only son could have angered Nicholas enough to kill Mrs. Pike?"

Atlas suppressed an immediate urge to defend his nephew. "Why not kill Vessey then? That whoreson is the one who deserves to take a bullet, not the woman he debauched as a young girl who had little say in the matter."

Charlton sipped his wine. "Will you ask Nicholas about the discrepancy?"

"I suppose I shall have to." Atlas exhaled long and loud through his nostrils. "If he lied to me, it was an elaborate mistruth." He remembered how pale and shaken Nicholas had looked when he'd come to Atlas after supposedly learning of Francis Pike's existence for the first time. "People seldom lie for no reason."

"He could have a reasonable explanation."

"He could. But the truth is that I have been so busy viewing Nicholas as Phoebe's son and attributing all of her most admirable traits to him that I have not observed the boy in an impartial manner."

"I would think that is natural."

"But what if I have been blinding myself to the truth?" A sense of dread, dark and unwanted, slithered into his gut. "I have been ignoring an obvious possibility. One I prefer not to face."

"And what is that?"

"That Nicholas is also Vessey's son. And we know firsthand that the Marquess of Vessey is capable of murder." He looked into Charlton's eyes. "Who is to say the son has not taken after his father?"

CHAPTER 20

"My uncles are named Atlas, Apollo, Hermes, and Jason?" Nicholas asked. "Truly?"

"Who would lie about something so odd?" Charlton asked.

They were just finishing supper. Atlas and Charlton had dutifully consumed the lamb sweetbreads served at the dining table as though their appetites hadn't been satisfied hours ago.

"Our father, your grandfather, was a great admirer of Greek mythology," Thea explained. Her eyes lingered on Nicholas as though she couldn't quite believe he was real.

"And the names Thea and Phoebe," Nicholas said with amusement. "It all makes perfect sense."

Atlas had stared at his nephew throughout the meal as well. But unlike Thea, he could not stop seeing the similarities to Vessey. The first time he'd laid eyes on Nicholas as a young man, Atlas had been struck by his physical resemblance to Vessey. In truth, the only things Nicholas had of his mother's were her eyes and seemingly gentle demeanor.

Nicholas fairly oozed goodness. But was it genuine? Many men were adept at hiding their true nature behind a pleasant facade. Atlas's nephew could be one of them. He knew little about Nicholas's upbringing. Perhaps being raised by a monster had made him into one.

"You will meet your uncles soon enough," Thea was saying to Nicholas. "I do have a painting of the entire family upstairs in my sitting room."

"May I see it?" Nicholas asked.

"Certainly." Thea rose to her feet, and the men all stood at the same time.

"I will show it to you," Atlas said abruptly with a quick glance at the earl.

Charlton took his cue and offered his arm to Thea. "And I will escort the lovely Mrs. Palmer to the drawing room."

After flashing a curious look at Atlas, Thea took the earl's arm and allowed Charlton to usher her away. "Join us for tea afterwards," she instructed over her shoulder.

Atlas led Nicholas up to Thea's sitting room to see the painting, which Nicholas quietly studied for several minutes.

The painting showed Silas Catesby seated next to his adoring wife and surrounded by all six of their children in an outdoor setting. The rustic backdrop made it appear as if the family had been caught on canvas in the midst of picnicking in the country.

"When was this painted?" Nicholas asked in a quiet, almost reverential tone.

"Just after my father was awarded his title, when he became a baron. A few months before your mother's marriage."

Nicholas examined his mother's face on the canvas. "I have never seen her likeness before. I do not think I resemble her at all."

"You have her eyes," Atlas said. "And your mannerisms, the way you speak, are much the same as Phoebe's."

Nicholas pointed to the smiling young boy seated in the grass next to Phoebe. "Is that you?"

"Yes." He lapsed into silence, allowing the boy to take in the painting's details, to become acquainted in this small removed way with the family he'd never known.

"Thank you for showing this to me," Nicholas said after several minutes. "Perhaps Mrs. Palmer . . . Aunt Thea . . . will allow me to engage an artist to copy this rendering of my mother. I should very much like to have one."

"I am certain that can be arranged." Atlas paused, reluctant to broach the subject Charlton had raised earlier. "Nicholas, before we go down and join the others, I have a question I must ask."

Nicholas turned to him expectantly. "Yes?"

"You said you had never heard of Francis Pike until recently, five days ago to be specific, when you came to visit me and we spoke at length about your mother."

"Yes," Nicholas smiled at the memory. "I shall never forget learning about my mother for the first time from someone who loved her as deeply as you did."

"Are you certain you had never met your half brother before that day?"

"I still have not been introduced to Francis. I suppose I will want to at some point. It is no fault of his that his mother was a dishonorable woman."

"Your father was no innocent either," Atlas could not resist injecting.

"Naturally I do not excuse his behavior."

Atlas took a deep breath. "Why are you lying about meeting Francis Pike?"

Nicholas blinked. "I am not lying. Why would you think that?"

"Because Charlton saw you with your brother. He says the two of you were at Manton's together."

Nicholas shook his head. "His lordship is mistaken," he said firmly. "I have never met Francis Pike. Why would I lie about something like that?"

That was precisely what Atlas was keen to know. "Charlton says he even greeted you when you were in Pike's company. That you were discussing Pike's pistol and what an excellent shot Pike is."

Nicholas flushed. "That is not true—" And then he halted abruptly, his eyes wild. "Good lord."

"What is it?"

"That man is my brother?"

"Are you now saying that you do know him?"

"Not exactly. I was at Manton's with friends, and this man was also there and I admired his skills with a weapon. We spoke briefly. But I had no idea." He paused, and when he spoke again, there was wonderment in his voice. "So that is Francis Pike. That is my brother."

Nicholas appeared genuinely shocked. A full range of emotions flitted across the boy's face, from denial to shock, to disbelief, and then finally a dazed acceptance.

"I have not met any of them, you understand. I rather should have liked to meet my sisters." Nicholas spoke almost to himself. "I have always known about them and have often wondered what they are like."

"It is understandable that you would desire to know your relations." Atlas felt for the boy. Vessey had been cruel to both Nicholas and his mistress. From what Atlas knew of Wendy, she could have been a positive force in Nicholas's life. She might have given a motherless child some of the affection he'd undoubtedly craved.

"My father mentions Francis almost constantly now." Nicholas's face clouded. "He says Francis is very much like him, while I am more similar to my mother."

Atlas fervently hoped it was true, but he could see that the comparison hurt the boy.

Nicholas's voice wavered. "It is obvious to me that Vessey wishes Francis were his heir."

"I doubt that is true." Atlas silently cursed Vessey. "He could have married the boy's mother and ensured that any children she bore him were legitimate."

Nicholas gave him a look. "Mrs. Pike was a hatmaker's daughter. Not exactly an appropriate match for a marquess in my father's view."

"Nonetheless, he made his choice, and that is why Francis is a by-blow, and you are your father's heir."

"Of late, Father has been remarking upon how clever Francis is. I cannot help but wonder whether that woman . . . Mrs. Pike . . . attempted to negatively influence my father's opinion of me."

"Why would you think that?"

"She might have done so to boost her own son in my father's eyes. Vessey is now insisting that I depend upon Francis's counsel once I assume the title. He views my half brother as a practical man who will do what needs to be accomplished in order to ensure that the marquisate continues to flourish."

Atlas laid a comforting hand on Nicholas's shoulder. "I have no doubt that when it comes time for you to assume your duties, you will execute them admirably, with or without Francis Pike." Atlas briefly considered whether Vessey intended to sow rivalry and suspicion between his sons. "When you are the marquess, you can do as you please. You shall certainly not be bound by any strictures or guidelines your father attempts to set down while he still lives."

Nicholas smiled. "I did not intend to bore you with my troubles. Shall we go down and join the others? I should not like to keep them waiting."

"One more thing before we go down."

"Yes?"

"Do you know if your father owns a flintlock pistol, one that would have been purchased from Grierson's? It has a carved walnut stock, and the barrel is particularly memorable because it is sheathed in silver."

Nicholas shook his head. "I do not believe my father owns a pistol that fits that description, but there is a man named Jasper Balfour who does."

Atlas stilled. "How do you know that?"

"I have seen him with it. We are not close, but we have socialized on occasion. Balfour and I often run in the same circles."

"When did you see him with the pistol?"

"I cannot be certain of the exact date. A few weeks ago maybe."

"His father told me that pistol had been stolen."

"Yes. By his son. It is an open secret among the young men in our circles. Jasper is deeply in debt. He gambles heavily but does not wish for his father to know. Some of his debtors, less than savory characters, have threatened Jasper, which is why he carries the pistol everywhere he goes to protect himself."

"He no longer carries it."

"How do you know that?"

"Because the pistol is in the possession of Bow Street. It is the weapon that was used to kill Mrs. Pike."

★　★　★

It was well past ten in the evening by the time Atlas departed his sister's home, but he did not make for home to Bond Street. He had a different destination in mind.

"Why are we going to the home of Lord Balfour?" Charlton inquired after allowing Atlas to commandeer his carriage.

"Jasper Balfour was in possession of the murder weapon in the days before Mrs. Pike's murder and lied about it. He claimed it had been stolen."

"You think the whelp killed her? But why?"

Atlas tapped his foot impatiently against the carriage floor. "That is what I intend to find out."

"I would be most surprised if young Balfour resides at his father's residence," Charlton remarked. "Most young bucks about town do not live in the family home."

"To be completely honest, I have no idea where Jasper Balfour lives, but I hope his father will enlighten me."

"What if they are all asleep?"

The moment their destination came into view, it became apparent that Lord and Lady Balfour had not retired for the evening. Light burned in every front-facing window of the large stone townhome. Groups of mingling people could be seen through the windows.

"It is Wednesday," Atlas said.

"As it has been all day," Charlton replied.

"Balfour holds a salon every other Wednesday evening."

"Perhaps we should return on the morrow, when the man is not entertaining." Charlton peered out the window. "It is not as though we were invited."

"This is hardly a social call." Atlas rapped on the ceiling to signal for the coachman to stop. "You need not feel obliged to accompany me. I will see myself home."

"I most certainly am coming." Charlton followed Atlas out of the carriage. "Who knows what mischief you might get yourself into?"

By the time they reached the landing, a footman had opened the shiny black front door to admit them. Once inside, Atlas and Charlton presented their cards.

Lord Balfour appeared shortly thereafter. "Welcome gentlemen," he said warmly, hurrying toward them. "You are always welcome at our salons. Please consider this to be a standing invitation to attend at any time."

"Thank you, my lord." Atlas struggled to contain his impatience to speak to the younger Balfour. "I apologize for the intrusion, but I hoped to speak with your son. Does he reside here with you?"

"Jasper? No, he keeps rooms at the Albany. However, as fortune would have it, he is in attendance this evening."

Altas's veins pulsed with anticipation. "Do you know where I might find him?"

Concern flickered in Lord Balfour's round face. "Is something amiss?"

Atlas felt an affinity for this man who had once been his father's friend. But it was possible the elder Balfour knew the murder weapon had been in his son's possession. It would not be the first time a father lied to protect his son.

"No," Atlas said, "nothing to concern yourself over. I have a question to ask him, just to clear up a minor issue, you understand."

The older man's worried expression relaxed, and Atlas felt a twinge of guilt. "Jasper's around here somewhere with his friends." He looked into Atlas's face. "He is a good boy, my Jasper. He has gotten himself into trouble in the past, but my son has truly straightened himself out since then."

"Thank you, my lord," Atlas smiled. "I would not want to keep you from your guests."

"But you are my guests, you and Lord Charlton," Balfour protested. He clasped Atlas's shoulder with a meaty hand. "Silas's son is always welcome in my home. You so resemble your father. I will always stand ready to assist you in any way that I can."

Atlas thanked Lord Balfour before he and Charlton went off in search of the man's son.

"Well, that is deuced awkward," Charlton commented as they threaded their way through the chattering guests. "The man has practically embraced you as family, and yet before this evening is out, you might very well be accusing his son of murder."

Atlas grimaced. "Perhaps Jasper will have a reasonable explanation." In fact, Atlas hoped so. He had no desire for his father's friend to discover that his wayward son might also have murderous impulses. Lord Balfour seemed to be a decent sort.

They found Jasper in the library, enjoying cheroots and brandy among a group of young men. The room's twin French doors were open to the outside, filtering out the smoke in exchange for a cool, light autumn breeze. Jasper's library companions included Francis Pike and Harry Dean, the young man who'd dueled with Pike after insulting Wendy. Dean had said the two had made amends. Their relaxed postures in each other's company suggested Dean had not exaggerated.

"Mr. Catesby." Curiosity lit Pike's gaze. "Come to partake in the discussion and debate that are the hallmarks of a Balfour salon?"

"Not this evening, I'm afraid." He turned to Jasper. "Do you have a moment?"

"Me?" Jasper darted a look at Pike before taking a long, slow inhale of his cheroot. "As you can see, I am engaged at the moment. Would you care for a cheroot, Lord Charlton?"

"Not at the moment." Charlton moved to stand shoulder to shoulder with Atlas.

"This matter is of some urgency." Atlas's tone left no doubt that he would not be put off. "It would be best if we spoke in private."

Jasper blanched. "Whatever for?"

"Look here," Pike interjected amiably, coming to his friend's rescue, "Surely it is nothing that cannot be discussed here in the privacy of his lordship's library."

Atlas couldn't decide whether Pike was prying or whether he was simply naive about what his friend might be capable of.

Atlas stared directly into Jasper's apprehensive eyes. "I think a private discussion is in everyone's best interest, particularly yours."

"Very well." Jasper tossed a comfit into his mouth. "We can use the gallery chamber."

When Atlas stepped aside to allow Jasper to lead the way, he caught Charlton's eye.

The earl reached for a cheroot on the table. "I believe I shall have a smoke after all." Pike stepped forward to light Charlton's cheroot. "I shall be out on the terrace, enjoying my cheroot and this lovely evening."

Jasper led Atlas to a magnificent gilded chamber where priceless paintings adorned red silk walls. One long wall featured six glittering, golden-framed mirrors that began at Atlas's feet and towered over him.

Atlas closed the doors for privacy, and they were alone in the opulent chamber. Jasper shifted his weight from one foot to the other. "What is this all about?"

"Why did you say your father's gun had been stolen when you are the one who took it?"

"That is a lie!" Jasper's flushed face glistened with perspiration. "Where did you hear that?"

"I think we both know it is not a lie. You had that gun for protection because you owe people a great deal of money."

Jasper clasped his hands behind his back. "That does not mean I killed Mrs. Pike."

In the mirror's reflection, Atlas could see Jasper's fingers were so tightly interlocked that the skin on his hands had gone white. "Perhaps not. But if you did not kill her, I believe you know who did, and now is the time to tell me."

"I do not know anything about it. It is true I had the pistol, but it *was* stolen."

"Did you tell anyone that your gun had been taken? If I go down and ask your friends about it, will they say that you informed them that your gun was missing before Mrs. Pike was killed?"

Jasper rocked his upper torso back and forth. "I cannot recall."

"If you do not start telling me the truth, I shall have to summon Bow Street."

He scoffed. "As if I, the grandson of a viscount, would ever be made to answer to a runner."

"Perhaps I should inform your father that it was you who absconded with his prized pistol and, in all likelihood, used it to kill Mrs. Pike."

"No, you cannot do that." Jasper clutched Atlas's arm, his fingers digging into Atlas's skin beneath his sleeve. "I did not kill Mrs. Pike. I swear it. He wanted me to, but in the end I could not do it. She seemed like a nice enough harlot. I had no quarrel with her."

"Why would you agree to murder Mrs. Pike if you held no ill will towards her?"

"To settle a debt. I have so many of them." Jasper swiped the perspiration from his upper lip with the back of his hand. "I do not want my father to know that I have disappointed him again."

"Who had a quarrel with Mrs. Pike?" Atlas pressed. "Who asked you to kill her?"

Jasper reached into his pocket with trembling hands to withdraw a comfit. "He said all I had to do was fire one shot, and then all of my debts would be erased."

"Who said that?"

Jasper sucked on his comfit. "To my shame, I was desperate enough to briefly consider doing as he asked."

The confession poured out of the young man like water cascading from a broken dam. Atlas sensed Jasper's relief at finally unleashing all that had been bottled up inside him.

Jasper swallowed the comfit, his rapid-fire words stumbling all over one another. "But in the end, I just could not do it—it was too terrible—so he grabbed the pistol from me. He took it before I knew what was happening, and then he shot her himself when she was leaving Covent Garden."

"Who?" Atlas asked patiently, although his heart was racing. "Slow down, take a breath, and then tell me who killed Mrs. Pike."

Red-faced and perspiring, Jasper did as Atlas suggested. He managed to refrain from chattering long enough to suck in a lungful of air.

A commotion sounded out in the corridor. People's shouts. Footsteps. The sound of someone running with extreme urgency drew closer and closer until the door to the chamber burst open.

A wild-eyed footman stood in the doorway panting heavily. "Are you Mr. Catesby, sir?"

Atlas kept his gaze glued to Jasper. "I am and we do not wish to be disturbed."

"Lord Charlton insisted sir. He said it was most urgent."

"Tell the earl that, whatever it is, it will have to wait."

"I do not think it can wait sir. Someone shot his lordship."

Atlas spun to face the flushed messenger. "What?"

"Someone shot his lordship," the young man repeated.

"Who? Lord Charlton?" Atlas felt the blood rush from his face. "Are you certain?"

"Yes, sir. It is the earl." The young footman was breathless. "And he is bleeding something awful."

Chapter 21

Atlas's stomach roiled at the sight of Charlton reclining in Balfour's library, a fast-spreading crimson stain soaking his white linen shirt.

"What in Hades happened?" Atlas demanded as he pushed through a small crowd of onlookers to reach his friend.

Charlton grimaced. "A bullet flew through the air, and I managed to get in its way. I am fine, truly."

"You do not look it." The ashen hue of Charlton's face alarmed him. "How did this occur?"

"I was in the garden, smoking a cheroot, when I heard a loud pop." Perspiration added an unhealthy gleam to the earl's complexion. "And then I felt an excruciating pain in my side."

"You are bleeding." Atlas dropped to his knees beside his friend. He fought the urge to cast his accounts as the metallic scent of blood—*Charlton's blood*—filled his nostrils. "We must stop it."

"We have staunched the wound," Lord Balfour assured him. Atlas hadn't noticed his host's presence until the man spoke. "The doctor has been called for and should be here shortly."

Charlton set his head back against the sofa and closed his eyes. "Feels like he is taking a bloody long time."

"Hold on." Atlas gripped Charlton's hand. Fear rippled through him at the clammy feel of his friend's skin. "You heard his lordship. The doctor is coming. Do not fall asleep." *Or lose consciousness. Or die on me.*

"No worries." Charlton smiled weakly. "I have absolutely no intention of going anywhere."

Atlas's throat constricted. "See that you don't."

★   ★   ★

"Fortunately, the bullet passed clean through," the doctor said after examining Charlton a short while later. "His lordship should recover nicely."

"Are you certain?" Atlas pressed. "Why is he so pale?"

"No doubt from the shock of taking a ball to the gut." The doctor opened his distressed black leather bag and proceeded to set out instruments on the table next to Charlton's bed.

Once the doctor had arrived and proclaimed the earl well enough to be moved, Atlas and a Balfour footman had carried the patient to one of Lord Balfour's guest chambers, a large room bedecked in pale velvets and dark woods.

"If a man has to be shot, this would be the wound to receive," the doctor continued. "No bones were struck, and it appears that no major organs are affected."

"I believe the doctor means to say that I have perfected the art of getting shot," Charlton remarked.

"As only you could," Atlas said.

Charlton's clothes had been removed, and he was propped up in bed, with pillows supporting his back, the white bed linens pulled to his belly. Charlton's state of dishabille sent shockwaves through Atlas. The earl's pale, bare torso lent him an air of vulnerability. It was a sight so far removed from Charlton's customary bright sartorial splendor that it was rather like seeing a rainbow drained of all color.

And the bandage covering Charlton's side was a stark reminder of how close the earl had come to catastrophe. A few inches had been the difference between survival and disaster.

"I will need to properly clean and rebandage the wound," the doctor said.

"May I be of assistance?" Atlas asked.

The doctor shook his head. "I have done this sort of treatment far more often than I should like." He rolled up his sleeves. "I will just go and request that the footman bring up fresh water and clean linens."

As the doctor stepped out in the hallway, Charlton turned to Atlas. "What happened with the matter you were seeing to?"

"Oh." Atlas started. He'd forgotten all about Jasper Balfour. "I left him in the gallery."

Charlton shifted gingerly and then winced, the pain in his side laying waste to the mirth that usually lit his blue gaze. "Perhaps you should see to him."

"He can wait."

"The whelp is probably catching a coach to the farthest reaches of the kingdom. You must go and speak with him before you miss your chance."

"Jasper Balfour can wait," Atlas said firmly. "First, we need to discover why someone would shoot you."

"Perhaps the two events are related."

Atlas frowned. "How so? I am the one who is investigating Jasper's potential involvement in Mrs. Pike's death, not you."

"Just so, but it is rather too much of a coincidence for my liking." Charlton closed his eyes and appeared to breathe through the pain wracking his body. "But you will have to sort it all out. I am rather indisposed at the moment."

"Too much of a coincidence?" Atlas thought out loud. He'd learned long ago that Charlton hid a sharp mind behind his glib manner. Then the realization struck him, and it could not be more obvious. He snapped his fingers. "That's it!"

"You agree then?"

"Absolutely. I would have worked it all out much earlier had I not been distracted by the shooting." But that had been the point, had it not? To distract him, to divert him. But from what? "Bloody hell."

"What is it?"

Atlas hastened toward the door, passing the returning doctor. "It is a diversion."

"What is?" Charlton's weak voice asked after him.

But Atlas was already gone, sprinting down the corridor despite suspecting that he was already too late.

★ ★ ★

A plaintive, almost inhuman sound reached Atlas before he reached the gallery.

It was somewhere between a wail and a howl, and although Atlas had never heard anything like it before, he instantly comprehended what it portended.

He had lost his chance to learn the truth from Jasper Balfour. And Lord and Lady Balfour had lost their son.

Atlas entered the chamber to find Lord Balfour sitting on the floor, his legs splayed, the scuffed soles of his slippers facing Atlas. Tears streamed down the older man's colorless face as he rocked back and forth, hugging his son's inert form to his chest.

Several people surrounded Balfour, but at a distance, as though his grief was a contagion.

"My son, my son," he moaned. "Get the doctor."

A footman hurried from the room to do his master's bidding, but it was apparent by the bluish-purple tint of Jasper's skin that the young man was beyond help. A life had ended. Abruptly. Improbably. An hour ago, Lord Balfour had harbored hopes for his errant son's rehabilitation. Now all hope was lost.

Anger surged through Atlas's veins. This was no accident. Someone had killed Jasper. He realized Harry Dean was standing beside him, ashen-faced, with his head bowed. "What the devil happened?" he asked in a low-pitched voice.

"He is dead." Dean was perspiring and looked as if he might lose the contents of his stomach. "His mother found him. Lady Balfour was beside herself. She swooned and had to be carried away. It was"—he shivered—"beyond anything I have ever had the misfortune to witness."

Atlas was barely aware of someone hurrying into the room and coming to a stop on his other side. Together, all three men stared down at the unimaginable scene before them.

"What happened?" Francis Pike was out of breath.

"I am not certain." Atlas scanned the room. He saw no sign of blood anywhere on Jasper. No obvious evidence of injury.

The door he and Pike had just come through appeared to be the only way in or out of the gallery. "How well do you know this house?" he asked Pike.

Pike stared at his friend's still form. "Reasonably well, I suppose. Jasper and I met at Eton. I spent quite a bit of time here after that."

The doctor who'd just been tending to Charlton rushed in, his boot crunching over something on the floor—a spiky brown nut, the kind that falls from horsechestnut trees in the autumn—and immediately went to tend to the father and son on the floor.

Atlas murmured to Pike. "Would you be in a position to know if there is any other way in or out of this room?"

"I beg your pardon?"

"A secret door used by servants, for example."

"No, nothing like that. This is the only door."

Atlas stared at the scene unfolding in front of him. The doctor placed a gentle hand on Lord Balfour's shoulder before saying the words every father would dread to hear. Lord Balfour listened for a moment and shook his head, unwilling to believe the truth that filled his arms.

Atlas quietly slipped from the room.

★ ★ ★

Charlton yawned. "I appreciate the offer, Atlas, but my overnight guests are usually of the female variety and are interested in seeing to my pleasure."

"I am interested in seeing to your safety, not your pleasure." Atlas repositioned the deep chair, his uncomfortable sleeping place for the night, before the lit hearth. The doctor had advised against moving Charlton before morning.

Atlas's current position afforded him a view of Charlton, now an indistinguishable silhouette on the large four-poster bed. Shadows from the flames frolicked across the darkened walls like celebrants at a ball.

Atlas dropped his leaden body into the upholstered seat, grateful for its softness, fatigue burrowing deep under his skin. "What if the person who tried to kill you decides to return to finish the job?"

"Do you think it will come to that?"

"I have no idea." Atlas rested his head against the chair and welcomed the fire's nourishing warmth. Outside, an icy rain beat against the window. "However, I think you are correct in surmising the attacks on you and Jasper Balfour are connected."

"I was the diversion."

Atlas closed his eyes. "Which means the killer was present this evening, a guest of Lord Balfour or of his son."

"And he panicked once you took Jasper away for a private conversation. He must have been worried Jasper would reveal everything," Charlton's disembodied voice surmised from the shadows. "Does that narrow your list of suspects down to the gentlemen who were in the library and saw you take Jasper away?"

"It would seem." Exhausted and still shaken by the attack on Charlton, Atlas had difficulty sorting through the disparate facts to attempt to pull them into some semblance of order. The calculated attack on his friend had resurrected emotions he hadn't experienced since Phoebe's death—a tangle of fury, horror, and helplessness. "The footman stationed in the corridor outside the gallery swears no one entered the chamber after I left Jasper."

"How did the boy die?" Charlton asked through a yawn.

"Who knows? There were no signs of a struggle. No blood, bullet, or knife wound. He was not strangled. There was nothing obvious to suggest he was attacked."

"Maybe it wasn't murder."

Atlas made a skeptical face in the dark. "What are the chances Jasper would die on his own just as he was about to reveal the murderer's identity?"

"It is possible our killer is the luckiest bastard alive."

"I suppose. But his luck must run out at some juncture." Atlas intended to see that it did. He was no longer searching solely for Mrs. Pike's murderer. He was looking for a man who had already killed twice, and who had also shot Charlton.

"Where do you go from here?" Charlton inquired. "What happens next?"

"Now we sleep." Atlas shifted in the chair, arranging his large, long body in as comfortable a position as possible. "And tomorrow, I resume my search for a killer."

★   ★   ★

The following afternoon, Charlton's valet had barely gotten the earl comfortably situated in his bedchamber when Thea burst in, trailed by Lilliana.

"Is it true that you were shot?" Thea was flushed, and her deep brown eyes burned with concern. "What happened?"

"Mrs. Palmer." Charlton's pale face brightened. "What a delightful intrusion."

Finch, the earl's butler, appeared shocked and personally offended by the scandalous appearance of ladies in his master's bedchamber. A respectable woman did not enter a bachelor's private rooms unless she was the man's mother, sister, daughter, or wife. "Mrs. Palmer, please allow me to show you to the earl's sitting room, and then I shall inquire as to whether he is receiving."

"Of course I am receiving." Charlton had color in his cheeks for the first time since the shooting. "Go away, Finch."

The butler protested. "But my lord should rest."

Charlton kept his gaze on Thea. "Go away."

"Yes, my lord." Finch reluctantly quit the room, while Thea went straight to Charlton's bedside.

"How did this happen?"

"It is just a minor wound."

"Did you get shot or not?" she asked stridently.

Atlas interjected. "He did. Fortunately, the bullet went straight through."

"Then it was hardly a minor wound." Thea glared at Charlton. "You could have been killed."

The earl's golden brows arched. "Why, my dear Mrs. Palmer, if I did not know better, I might think you actually cared."

"What has the doctor said? Are you following his orders?"

"To the letter."

"I shall leave instructions for the cook." Thea fluffed the pillows behind Charlton's back and straightened his blankets. "You must have plain food to begin with, plenty of beef tea."

"I detest beef tea," Charlton said, only a little belligerently.

"Nonetheless you must have it. If I must, I shall come around every day to make certain you take the beef tea."

"You just might have to," Charlton said happily.

Atlas crossed the room to Lilliana, who'd shown slightly more decorum than his sister by remaining near the open door. "Who is that woman?" he asked Lilliana, jerking his head toward Thea. "Why is my sister behaving so strangely?"

"Thea cares for Charlton as a dear friend."

"She does?" Atlas's brows lowered. "Then why does she continually treat him as if he is a complete nuisance?"

A slight smile touched Lilliana's lips. "For such an intelligent man, you do miss a great deal." She said the words kindly, almost fondly.

"What does that mean?" It was not the first time Lilliana had said some such nonsense to him.

"Lady Lilliana," Charlton said from the bed, "it was good of you to come. Do forgive me, ladies, for not rising."

"I wish you a speedy recovery," Lilliana answered. "We were immensely perturbed to learn you had been hurt."

"Who is dressing your wounds?" Thea's bossy nature, which always annoyed Atlas, was in full bloom. But Charlton seemed to be basking in it. "It must be done with care."

"Charlton's doctor will come every day to check on him and to look after his wound," Atlas told her.

"But he shall not be here to ensure that I drink all of my beef tea," Charlton put in.

While Thea continued to fuss over Charlton, Atlas stood by the door with Lilliana and filled her in on what had occurred. As he spoke, he watched Thea drag a bergère chair next to Charlton's bedside.

Lilliana listened intently, and when Atlas finished, she thought for a moment. "I do not think all of your likely suspects were necessarily in the library. Did you not say the doors leading to the terrace were open?"

"Yes, they were, to let out the smoke."

"Which means it is possible that someone on the terrace could have been aware of what was occurring in the library."

He seamlessly picked up the thread of her thinking. "Someone who might have seen me arrive and greet Lord Balfour."

She nodded. "And if that someone is the killer, they might have made it their business to go out onto the terrace in order to hear what you discussed with Jasper. But then he was thwarted when you took Jasper away to a room where he could not eavesdrop, which meant he could not keep abreast of how much Jasper might tell you."

"And so the killer decides he needs to create a diversion." The thought of it made rage boil in Atlas's veins. "Which he does by putting a bullet into Charlton."

His gaze wandered back to Thea, who was seated by Charlton's bedside. The two appeared to be deep in conversation. The incongruous sight of his prickly sister in apparent harmony with Charlton was like seeing a fish walk on land.

"And while you were diverted seeing to your injured friend," Lilliana continued, "the killer slipped into the gallery and did away with Jasper."

"Except that the footman stationed in the corridor swears no one went in or out of the gallery."

"He could hardly admit to it if he deserted his post for a few minutes. Perhaps he was drawn to the commotion created by Charlton's shooting."

Atlas considered her words. "That is a possibility. But there is also the question of what killed him. I saw no signs of a struggle, no blood, no obvious wound. It could have been a natural death."

But he saw in Lilliana's eyes that she did not believe that any more than he did. "When will you speak with the coroner?"

"I will send a note around to Endicott. Perhaps he will inform me when he receives the results of the autopsy."

Across the chamber, Thea abruptly rose from her chair. "We should allow Charlton to rest now," she announced. "He is no doubt tired."

"Oh, do stay. I am not in the least bit fatigued," Charlton said. But the deep lines fanning out from his eyes and the pronounced grooves bracketing his mouth belied his protestations.

Thea ignored Charlton's assertions, a return to her customary treatment of the earl, and the two ladies said their goodbyes.

Atlas saw them to the door of the bedchamber. "I think I shall stay while he rests."

"Do not keep him talking," Thea ordered before the ladies departed.

"What the devil is the matter with her?" Atlas said as he crossed to Charlton's bedside and settled in the seat Thea had recently occupied. "I hardly recognized my own sister. Except for the managing nature, which I am all too familiar with. I mean, really, to barge into a gentleman's bedchamber in that manner and then proceed to order you about."

"Indeed." Charlton gave a contented sigh. "Once I have recovered, I must seriously consider having you shoot me again."

CHAPTER 22

That evening, Atlas dismissed Jamie and settled into his preferred stuffed chair with the nargileh to enjoy a bit of solitude.

Inhaling deeply, he blew out through his nostrils, watching the twin columns of smoke dissipate before reversing course and meandering up to the ceiling. While puzzles helped clear his mind, the water pipe was an instrument of complete relaxation. The rituals involved, the gurgle of the water, the rhythmic inhales and exhales, watching the column of smoke float out of his mouth, were all deeply soothing.

Unfortunately, the hookah was not having the desired effect on this particular evening. No number of inhales and exhales could breathe away the regrettable truth that Atlas had made a terrible tangle of things. Why had he insisted on speaking to Jasper with dozens of guests present? It was pure folly. His impatience had led to Jasper Balfour's death. And Charlton had been shot. His friend could have died.

A firm knock at the door ruptured his reverie. He glanced at the ormolu clock on the table beside him. Framed with gilded turquoise porcelain, the clock had come with the apartments, another vivid color in this already lively room of bright oranges, reds, and blue paisley chintz.

It was almost ten o'clock. Normally, Atlas would assume Charlton was calling at this hour, but then he remembered the earl was at home on Curzon Street with two holes in his side, one where the bullet entered, the other where it had exited.

The tapping on his door sounded again, more insistent this time. Whoever it was seemed determined to make a nuisance of himself. Atlas reluctantly set the hookah hose down and pushed to his feet. He gave his state of dishabille—shirtsleeves, a white linen shirt open at the neck because he'd discarded his cravat, bare feet—momentary consideration before dismissing any concerns. Whoever it was should not be calling uninvited at this time of night.

He regretted the decision not to make himself more presentable the moment he opened the dark-paneled front door to find Lilliana standing on the landing. Obviously attired for an evening out, she was swathed in golden silk showcasing a deep décolletage and the double strand of pearls that fell to her waist.

"Atlas." Her gaze took in his untidy appearance. "Forgive me for intruding."

"Not at all." He ushered her in and closed the door, smoothing his hair with the flat of his hand. "Have I forgotten an engagement? Is the opera this evening?" He'd been invited to join Lilliana and Somerville at Covent Garden the following night.

"Beg pardon?" She looked down at her finery and shook her head with a small laugh. "No, we are to attend the opera on the morrow. I was on my way to a rout this evening, but then I had a thought related to the investigation and directed the coachman to stop here for a moment."

"What is it?" Rolling down his sleeves, he looked around for his slippers and pushed his bare feet into them, haphazardly trying to make himself somewhat decent for company.

She paused uncertainly in the front hall. "But this is clearly an inconvenient time." She turned back to the door. "Perhaps you could call on me in the morning, and we can discuss it."

"Nonsense." He was reluctant to let Lilliana go. "As long as you are here, please do come in."

"If you are certain?"

"I am. Otherwise, I am destined to pass the evening flagellating myself for the mess I've made of the investigation."

"Why? What has happened?"

"Is it not obvious? Because of my recklessness and lack of discretion, a young man is dead and Charlton took a bullet."

"My goodness." She placed a hand flat against her chest. "I see you are taking the weight of the world onto your shoulders again."

"Not at all," he responded with a wry smile. "I am merely straining under the weight of my own foolish mistakes."

"It seems to me that the person who should be held accountable for Jasper's death is the man who killed him, not the man who is trying to bring the killer to justice."

"I put Jasper in danger by my actions."

"You had no way of knowing that would be the case," she said. "Whoever killed Jasper Balfour and wounded Charlton is responsible."

"In the most literal sense, perhaps," he concurred, "but if I had not made my desire to speak with Jasper known in such a theatrical manner before an audience, he might still be alive."

"Or if you had spoken to Jasper privately, he might have told a friend about the conversation, and that friend could have been the killer, or that friend could have known the killer and confided in the killer."

"I can barely follow those associations, but it is kind of you to absolve me."

"But you must promise to absolve yourself, or else I shall not tell you why I have come."

For the first time in many hours, Atlas felt the urge to smile. "If you do not tell me why you diverted your coachman, I shall be up all night contemplating the possibilities."

"Then I suppose you will just have to be more gentle in your judgment of yourself."

"Where are my manners?" He'd kept her standing in the front hall far longer than was courteous. "Please do come in."

She allowed him to escort her into the sitting room. Her attention went to the nargileh. "Oh, is that your water pipe?"

His face warmed. "I will put it out." A gentleman did not smoke in the presence of a lady.

"No, please don't." She put a light hand on his forearm to stop him. "I should like to try it. Thea says it is an interesting way of smoking."

"Do you smoke?"

Mischief lit her eyes. "I have tried cheroots before. Verity and I decided to sample them once when our husbands were away." She did not often mention her late sister-in-law, by all accounts a kind and decent woman, who'd met an agonizing end. "I did not care for cheroots, but Thea seems to have enjoyed sampling your water pipe. Will you think less of me if I try it as well?"

"Not at all." He resisted the urge to tell her that he could never think less of her. "I would not want to be the first to corrupt you, but it seems your late sister-in-law already saw fit to do that."

Once they were both seated, he handed her the hose. "Just put it between your lips and breathe in."

She brought the tip of the hose to her mouth and inhaled, gingerly at first and then with more confidence. He stole the moment to admire her in all her splendor; she rivaled a royal consort in her finery.

"How unexpected," she said. "I thought it would be far more bitter."

"The tobacco is washed repeatedly and put into the pipe bowl while it is still damp."

She examined the water pipe. "What effect does that have?"

"I believe that results in a more mild taste," he explained. "Also, the Arabs use a tobacco called *mu'assel*, which means 'honey.'"

She drew on the hookah again, more slowly this time, as if trying to identify the source of the flavor. "This contains honey?"

"I have no idea." He grinned. "I never thought to ask."

She handed him the hose. "I do not mean to deprive you of your water pipe."

"Nonsense, the hookah is meant to be shared." He gently pushed it back on her. "In Constantinople, it is common for people to sit together and pass the nargileh around when they call upon one another."

She took another puff. "Would you care to know why I have come?"

The truth was that he didn't much care; he was just happy to be in her company. It wasn't entirely respectable for Lilliana to be here alone with him, but she was a widow, and widows were accorded certain liberties. "I am eager to hear what is on your mind."

She passed the hookah to him. "In terms of suspects, instead of trying to focus on Lord Balfour's guest list, it seems you could narrow the list of potential culprits by uncovering the people to whom Jasper owed money."

"That could certainly prove useful." He inhaled, mindful of the cocoon of intimacy encasing them as they sat alone in his sitting room, sharing a nargileh. "Shortly before he died, Jasper did say the killer wanted him to shoot Mrs. Pike in order to erase a debt."

"Precisely." She shook her head when he tried to pass the hookah back, so he inhaled again himself. "And one would assume the list of people Jasper was in debt to is shorter than the guest list for Lord Balfour's salon."

"Yes, that is certainly true. I do know that Jasper was in debt to Francis Pike."

"Mrs. Pike's son?"

"Yes, I overheard them, Jasper and Pike, speaking of it at a tavern on the evening that I met both men."

"Is Francis Pike a suspect?"

"Everyone is, but the victim's son would not be at the top of my list, at least not at the moment." He turned his head as he exhaled, blowing the diaphanous column of silvery smoke away from Lilliana. "Young Pike seems to have cared a great deal for his mother and is very protective of her reputation."

"Francis Pike might know to whom else Jasper was indebted."

"True," he agreed. "I shall have to speak with him."

"What is your opinion of Mrs. Pike's son? Is he an agreeable young man?"

"I find him to be so, although I am not at all well acquainted with him. Francis seems to hold both of his parents in the highest regard. He once called out a young man who insulted Mrs. Pike."

Lilliana's head went back slightly. "Truly? And what was the outcome?"

"He shot the offender in the arm but, ever the gentleman, ensured that the bullet just skimmed the offender's arm and caused no lasting damage. And then Pike accepted the offender's apology, and the two men seem to tolerate each other's company quite well now."

Her gaze caught on the amulet that hung from a gold chain around Atlas's neck. "Oh, is that talisman meant to bring you good fortune?"

"A *hamsa*—yes." Atlas pressed a couple of fingers against the gold piece, which was warm from being against his skin. "Carthaginians believe it protects against the evil eye."

She leaned forward, studying the amulet. "It is a very interesting design."

He drew the chain off and placed it in the palm of her open hand so she could examine the talisman more closely. She ran a light finger over the hand-shaped pendant with a blue jade eye at the center of its palm. Although he rarely removed the *hamsa*, few people had glimpsed the charm because it was hidden from view under his shirt, where it rested against his skin.

"It seems to have kept you from harm thus far." Lilliana smiled as she handed the amulet back to him. "It is a beautiful piece."

"It has certainly brought me good fortune." His gaze held hers as he took it from her. "Such as the pleasure of your company."

Her cheeks colored and she dropped her gaze. If he did not know Lilliana, he'd assume her to be shy. But there was something else to her reaction. The air between them suddenly became less warm and somewhat uncomfortable.

She came to her feet. "Unfortunately, the pleasure of my company has been promised elsewhere this evening. I must go."

He rose along with her. "My loss. But I do thank you for calling. You have given me some interesting possibilities to consider."

"Thank you for corrupting me," she said as he followed her into the entry hall

"I beg your pardon?"

"By allowing me to sample your hookah," she said lightly as she went out.

He watched her descend the stairs and then removed to the window to make certain she reached her carriage in safety. He'd have preferred to escort her himself, but the sight of them exiting his apartments together would provoke the gossips.

Besides, he wasn't entirely certain Lilliana desired his escort. Her recent mood vacillations confounded him. He didn't know what to make of her occasional reticence, her outright discomfort, really, in his presence, particularly on the rare occasions when they found themselves alone together.

What added to Atlas's confusion was that the lady could easily avoid his company if she so chose. Yet Lilliana had come to him this evening completely of her own accord. At one time, not so long ago, he'd been fairly confident that the duke's sister welcomed his attentions, but perhaps he was mistaken. Lilliana might simply be interested in a friendly flirtation and nothing more.

Whatever the reason, she had recently begun to withhold a part of herself from him, and it stung. He felt the loss keenly in the deepest part of him.

CHAPTER 23

Atlas awoke the following morning with a start.

He rubbed his eyes and winced. It felt as though tiny pebbles were lodged beneath his eyelids. His dreams had been particularly jarring. He'd been in hiding after committing a terrible crime; he couldn't recall the specifics surrounding the act or the victim, but the paralyzing anxiety ballooning in his chest suggested he'd done something particularly ghastly. It had not been a restful night.

He shifted onto his back and rested his forearm against his closed eyes, trying to dull the throbbing behind them. Beyond his bedchamber door, he could hear Jamie moving around. Outside his window, rain blasted against the pane.

He contemplated the day ahead. He was scheduled to attend the opera with Lilliana and Somerville that evening. After last night, he wondered if Lilliana regretted inviting him to join them in the ducal box.

"Good morning, sir." Jamie popped his head through the door, which was slightly ajar. "Viscount Beaumont has arrived."

Atlas lifted his forearm to peer at his young valet. "Nicholas is here? Why?"

"His lordship says he has brought you something." Jamie came in with a pitcher and poured fresh water into the blue-and-white-patterned ceramic bowl on the washstand.

"Tell him I will join him shortly." Atlas heaved himself into a sitting position and swung his feet over the side of the bed, the faded carpet soft beneath his feet. "And go and get us something to eat, will you?"

"I have already brought in the coffee." A knowing smile curved Jamie's lips. "And the duke's cook sent over another basket this morning."

He straightened up. "God bless Mrs. Pitt." *And Lilliana.* Was this a peace offering of sorts after last evening's awkward parting?

Jamie's face scrunched up. "Who is Mrs. Pitt?"

"Somerville's cook."

Jamie's raised brows added to his smug expression. "I doubt it was Mrs. Pitt's idea to send over a basket."

Atlas's cheeks warmed. "Wipe that smirk off your face," he snapped at the boy. "A proper valet refrains from remarking upon his employer's private matters."

Atlas's harsh tone did not have the desired effect on the boy, who departed the chamber with a cheeky smile still firmly in place. "Yes, sir."

Atlas stalked over to the washstand to splash water on his face. He cleaned his teeth and dressed quickly before stepping out to join Nicholas in his sitting room.

The young man was smartly attired in a striped brown tailcoat. He stood with a package tucked under his arm, staring down at the half-finished puzzle. Atlas paused momentarily, soaking in the sight of Phoebe's son.

Nicholas looked up when he sensed Atlas's presence. "I do beg your pardon for calling unannounced."

"Nonsense—we are family. You will soon learn that certain members of this family think nothing of appearing unexpectedly without being invited."

"There were six of you." Nicholas's smile was wistful. "As a boy, I wondered what it would be like to grow up with siblings."

"It has its merits, I suppose, but one must also pay a severe price at times for having a large family." Atlas's attention shifted to where Jamie had set breakfast out on the low table before the sofa. His stomach growled. "Come, let us eat."

"Oh no, I do not wish to intrude upon your morning meal. I have come to give you something." He presented the flat, wrapped packet to Atlas.

Surprised, Atlas accepted the offering. "What is it?" He pulled at the string and unwrapped the brown paper, revealing a framed sketch.

Anticipation shone in Nicholas's eyes. "I discovered it among my mother's things."

Atlas stared at the image, a sweet pain burrowing deep into his chest. Etched in charcoal with self-assured strokes, the drawing captured an animated boy with intensely gray eyes and a resolute mouth curved into an almost-smile. He radiated a sense of ready confidence. "I have never seen this."

"My mother drew it." Enthusiasm filled Nicholas's voice. "I found her sketchbooks. That is you, is it not?"

"Yes." It was, but it wasn't. This was Atlas before Vessey killed Phoebe. Eager and expectant, so full of anticipation for the future. So innocent. The boy in the portrait was who Atlas had been before his boyhood became engulfed in sorrow and anguish, fury and helplessness.

Then there was the lingering guilt. Atlas had never been able to shake the belief that he should have saved Phoebe. If only he had been brave enough.

In a sense, Atlas had lost his family then as well. After Phoebe's death, they became a painful reminder of what could never be replaced, of a fissure within him that could never be mended. His family was now a reminder that something deep inside Atlas had broken and was beyond repair.

"Do you not care for it?" Nicholas's voice became more hesitant, concerned. "I thought you might like to have the sketch, but if not, I can take it back."

Atlas's throat hurt. He forced a small cough to clear it. "I would very much like to have it." He looked up at Phoebe's son and smiled. "Thank you. I shall treasure this."

"Excellent." A relieved smile broke out across Nicholas's face.

"Where did you find this?" The boy in the sketch appeared to be ten or eleven years old. Phoebe must have drawn this likeness of him shortly before her death.

"After you informed me that my mother was fond of sketching, I asked our butler what had become of my mother's things. As it happens, her possessions were packed and stored away."

"Everything?"

He nodded. "Her clothing, her personal effects. I have spent days going through it all. And then I found the sketches. When I saw that one"—he indicated the frame in Atlas's hands—"I recognized you immediately."

Atlas looked down at the portrait. "You did?" He felt a million miles away from the boy in the picture. It was as if that boy had died with Phoebe, only to be reborn into a darker, restless, far less ideal version of the youth in Phoebe's sketch.

"Absolutely. The eyes, the shape of your mouth, that slight smile, the confidence. It is all the same. I decided to take the sketch to a frame shop, and here it is."

"That was very thoughtful of you." He set the frame down on the game table chair. "And you must let me thank you by agreeing to have breakfast with me."

Nicholas's gaze went to the food laid out on the table before the sofa. "It does look quite appetizing."

Soon the two men were seated on the sofa, enjoying the considerable talents of Somerville's cook, washed down with an excellent brew Jamie had procured from a nearby coffee house.

"These are beyond compare," Nicholas said, finishing off his third bath bun.

"Agreed." Atlas reached for another queen's cake. Sweet and buttery, the confections were masterfully flavored with just the right amount of orange blossom water and chewy currants.

"You must tell me where your man purchased them." Nicholas washed the bun down with a draught of coffee. "I have a mind to purchase some for myself for later."

"While you are here, I hope you can assist me in the investigation," Atlas said. "I suppose you have heard about Jasper Balfour's killing."

Nicholas's hazel eyes opened wide. "Was it murder? I heard that he passed, but neither his family nor the papers have elaborated on how he died."

"I believe so, although I have not heard what the coroner has to say as to the cause of death."

"How do you think I can be of assistance?"

"As you are aware, Jasper was deep in debt, to the point where he'd felt threatened enough to carry a pistol for protection."

Nicholas dipped his chin. "Yes."

"Do you know to whom he owed money?"

"Jasper always seemed to be in debt to someone. Of late, I do seem to recall he owed a great sum of money to Harry Dean."

"Dean?" Atlas shuffled through what he knew about the young man from the book club. It remained both possible and plausible that, despite outward appearances, Dean continued to hold a grudge against Francis Pike for publicly humiliating him during their duel. But was it enough of a grievance for Dean to push Jasper into killing Francis Pike's mother? "What is Dean like in your estimation? What is his character?"

"He is agreeable enough until you get drink into him. Getting foxed seems to bring out the worst in the man." They talked more about Jasper's death and Harry Dean, and continued to eat until they were stuffed. After about an hour, Nicholas made ready to depart.

"I consumed entirely too many bath buns," he proclaimed. "But these are so delicious that I could not stop myself."

"I have the same problem," Atlas said as the two men stepped into the front hall and Jamie rushed to bring Nicholas's coat. "If I keep eating this way, I will weigh twenty stone before long."

Nicholas allowed Jamie to help him on with his coat. "Where did you say they came from? I think I will pick some up for later, on my way home."

"They were sent over by a friend—well, not a friend exactly." Atlas realized he was bumbling. "They were made by the Duke of Somerville's cook."

Now both young men, Nicholas and Jamie, wore identical smirks on their faces.

"Ah. Why does that not surprise me in the least?" Nicholas's eyes brimmed with amusement. "Should we expect a happy announcement in the near future?"

Atlas shook his head. "You really are a Catesby."

Pausing in the open doorway, Nicholas looked delighted. "How so?"

"You have already demonstrated quite the knack for being a prying nuisance."

Atlas headed back to his sitting room, ignoring the quiet laughter of the two young men that followed him.

★ ★ ★

Atlas found few things as riveting as watching Juliet Jennings perform.

That evening, from his perch in the Duke of Somerville's box, he focused his full attention on the songstress down below on the stage. Dressed in shimmering blue silk, Juliet sang with power and emotion, her voice weighty and full. She was mesmerizing.

Juliet was one of those rare women whose vocal talent eclipsed her considerable beauty. Indeed, it was Juliet's enrapturing performances that had prompted Atlas to pursue a liaison with her all those years ago. He'd fallen in love with her talent well before being introduced to the woman herself.

At the intermission, he turned to find Somerville watching him with an imperturbable expression on his young face. Dressed in his dark evening finery, the duke looked as flawless as ever. "Enjoying the opera?"

"Very much." Atlas scanned the vacant three rows of blue seats in the ducal box, which was lit by an overhead chandelier. But there was no sign of Lilliana.

"Where has Lady Roslyn gone?" he asked.

"While you were mesmerized by the fair Mrs. Jennings, my sister decided to take a turn with a friend."

Atlas frowned. "I could have escorted her."

"She left prior to the intermission and did not care to interrupt your very apparent enjoyment of the opera."

Atlas sprang to his feet. "I shall go and find her. If you will excuse me."

"Please do be seated." The duke gestured with one elegant, manicured hand. "There is something I should like to discuss with you before my sister returns."

"Can it not wait?" Atlas was eager to find Lilliana. It perturbed him that he had not even heard her leave the box. There were times when he became so engrossed in something that the rest of the world faded away like the murky, indistinct background of an oil painting.

"No, actually, it cannot." Somerville's voice was firm. "Please do sit."

It was more of a command than a request. Despite his youth, His Grace had the air of a man used to giving orders and having them followed without question.

Atlas chose to do as Somerville asked, not because the man was a duke, but because of the deference he deserved as Lilliana's brother. He perched on the edge of his seat. "What is it, Your Grace?"

"I should like to know what your intentions are toward my sister."

Atlas allowed his full weight to sink into the chair. "My intentions?"

"Precisely."

"I hold Lady Roslyn in the highest esteem."

The duke steepled his tapered fingers under his chin. "Go on."

Atlas resisted the urge to shift in his seat under Somerville's expectant gaze. He understood what the man was asking. "She is the sister of a duke."

"And? Her last husband was a merchant. You are a considerable improvement over Godfrey Warwick."

"Most men would be." He cleared his throat, which felt somewhat clogged. "She had little choice in the matter then. Now she can freely choose a husband."

"I fear my sister's time among the masses has diminished her sense of duty to her rank."

Atlas met Somerville's gaze. "Am I to understand that you would have no objection?"

"My sister must do as she pleases. I rather think that Roslyn has suffered enough, do you not agree?"

"I am not certain that the lady wishes to be courted by me."

The duke stared at him. "I credited you with possessing greater sense than that, Catesby."

Atlas's cheeks heated. "Although she welcomes my friendship, I cannot be certain that Lady Roslyn wishes to deepen our acquaintance any further."

Somerville scoffed. "Why do you think she rejected proposals of marriage from both the Marquess of Roxbury and the Earl of Northhampton?"

Atlas's head snapped back. "Northhampton?" He knew about Roxbury, but *Northhampton*? "Lilliana . . . er . . . Lady Roslyn . . . rebuffed an offer from Northhampton? When did this occur?"

"Quite recently."

Jealousy cut through him. "I have never seen her with Northhampton." Atlas was not acquainted with Lilliana's latest suitor, but he did know who the man was. The earl was younger than Atlas and not unhandsome.

"He has apparently admired Roslyn from afar for some time." Somerville favored Atlas with a pointed look. "It seems he held back because he assumed her interest was elsewhere."

"I see." That may have been true at one point, but Atlas now doubted Lilliana was keen to pursue a future with him.

"Northhampton has reassured Lilliana that he is a patient man. He is willing to wait until she is ready to become his wife."

Atlas stopped short of blurting out, *Like Hades he will!*

"If you do not wish to offer for Roslyn, I cannot force you," the duke continued smoothly. "However, if you do not intend to court my sister, then I must insist that you step aside and allow her to examine her many other opportunities."

Atlas's hand fisted in his lap. "I am not standing in her way."

"Your very presence in London obstructs her path to contentment. If you truly wish the best for her, you will take yourself away from town and allow Roslyn to get on with her life."

"What is it exactly that you expect from me? Surely, you are not asking me to retire to the country."

"No, indeed, although the English countryside is a place of unparalleled beauty. You are a traveler. Why not take another voyage once you have completed the investigation into Mrs. Pike's death?"

"You are asking me to go away."

"Yes, the farther the better. Roslyn mentioned that you were interested in sailing for India last summer. Perhaps you should reconsider taking that journey"

It would take at least six months to reach India, a land Atlas had always longed to visit. However, at the moment, the thought of such a voyage held about as much appeal as a toothache.

The duke seemed to take Atlas's momentary silence as acquiescence. "I would be more than happy to fund such a journey," he added, "as well as expenses for you to remain in India for at least a year, and even longer if you so wish. In the best accommodations possible, of course. Money is no object."

Atlas's temper snapped. "Do you truly believe I would take money from you?" He all but snarled the question.

"No." Somerville seemed oddly gratified by Atlas's show of open hostility. "I did not."

"Then why did you offer it?"

Somerville gave an eloquent shrug. "Is it not obvious?"

"Is what not obvious?" Lilliana had reappeared, but she was not alone. The friend who'd taken her for a turn about the theater stood at her side. Atlas and Somerville rose to their feet.

"Welcome back, my dear sister." Somerville turned to Atlas and gestured to the man by Lilliana's side. "Catesby, have you met the Earl of Northhampton?"

CHAPTER 24

Atlas somehow managed to make it through the remainder of Juliet's performance without punching either North-hampton or Somerville in the mouth.

Northhampton had promptly accepted Somerville's invitation to join them in the ducal box and settled himself in the front row on Lilliana's right side, with Atlas sitting to her left. Lilliana and the earl chatted quietly while Atlas remained silent, his rigid arms crossed tight over his chest. Although his eyes were trained on Juliet, Atlas saw nothing but his own fury. His insides broiled as Lilliana entertained her latest suitor.

The earl excused himself as soon as the show ended to return to his own box, where his mother entertained some of her friends. Somerville offered his arm to Lilliana, and Atlas followed as they strolled down the stone-paved corridor. When the duke paused to greet some acquaintances, Lilliana turned to Atlas.

"I see you have a new suitor," he said before she could speak.

"Yes. *You* certainly seemed captivated by Mrs. Jennings." She delivered the words in the frosty tone she normally reserved for distant acquaintances.

"By her performance, yes. I would have thought Roxbury is the better match for you, considering that he is a marquess. Northhampton is merely an earl."

"Still making assumptions about my suitors? I would have thought you'd learned to refrain from presuming anything concerning my future."

The word *suitors* raked across his nerves. Before he could cobble together a suitable response, Somerville's acquaintances took their leave, and the duke turned to his sister. "Shall we?"

Lilliana took her brother's arm. "Yes, let's."

Beyond Somerville, a familiar face separated from the crowd. Francis Pike. The young man's entourage included Vessey, and then Atlas's surprised gaze landed on a somber, pale-faced Nicholas trailing his father and half brother. It seemed Vessey had finally seen fit to introduce his two sons to each other. An urgent instinct to protect Phoebe's son overcame him.

"Coming Catesby?" Somerville called over his elegant shoulder.

"Do excuse me. I see a friend." Atlas bowed, his attention still on Nicholas. "I shall take my leave of you here, if I may."

"Good night then." Lilliana dismissed him in an icy tone that could freeze the Thames in July.

The duke dipped his chin. "Good evening." Somerville's knowing expression suggested he assumed Atlas intended to quit the field of suitors eager to court Lilliana. Atlas left them to make his way toward Nicholas.

"Atlas!" a familiar male voice called out. Atlas ignored the summons as he battled his way through the crush toward his nephew. "I say, Atlas"—the voice was much closer now—"where are you off to in such a hurry?"

Atlas halted, allowing Jason, the eldest of the Catesby off-spring, and the brother who had inherited their late father's title, to catch up with him.

"There you are." Jason raised a gold-and-diamond-encrusted lorgnette to peer at his younger brother. "I thought that was you in the Duke of Somerville's box with Lady Roslyn."

Atlas looked beyond Jason, searching the crush of people for a glimpse of Nicholas. "I am rather in a hurry."

"The gossips say you are courting the lady." Nothing would please Jason more than an alliance with one of England's finest families. He'd taken his elevation to baron very seriously and felt it his duty to raise the standing of the Catesby name. "It would be a most agreeable connection for our family. Would Somerville allow such a match?"

Atlas suppressed a groan. "I must go."

"Wait," Jason said before Atlas could escape. "Do you know how Charlton is getting on? I heard he was shot. Terrible thing that!"

Surveying the scene ahead of him, Atlas couldn't see Nicholas. "Charlton is recovering."

"Are you still rather well acquainted with the earl? That is a friendship you should continue to cultivate."

Atlas resisted the urge to snatch Jason's lorgnette out of his hands and grind it under his heel. "I am leaving now." He turned to go.

"I comprehend that you think I am ridiculous, but I am looking out for future generations of Catesbys." Jason walked in lockstep with Atlas. "Whom exactly are you looking out for?"

Supremely uninterested in pursuing this conversation with his brother, Atlas murmured his farewell and quickened his pace, rapidly losing Jason in the crush. He trotted down the grand staircase and out onto the piazza in search of his nephew. However, the only familiar face he found in the crush belonged to Francis Pike.

"Mr. Catesby," Pike said. "Did you enjoy the performance?"

"Very much, thank you. Did I see Nicholas with you?"

"Yes, but he's gone on ahead with some of his friends. I am awaiting our father, who is still inside."

Atlas studied Pike's ashen face. "You do not look well."

Pike gave a wan smile. "What is a man supposed to look like after his father insists upon spending an evening at the very place where his mother was gunned down not three weeks past?"

Atlas felt a pang of disgust at Vessey's profound insensitivity. "I could not even begin to conceive it."

"Additionally, his lordship also chose this evening to officially introduce me to Nicholas."

"Why ever would he choose this time and this place for such an encounter?" Atlas shook his head. "I can only imagine the strain you have been under."

"Thank you for your concern." Pike's shoulders slumped as he surveyed the scene around him. "I think I shall follow Nicholas's example and find my own way home."

After Pike took his leave, Atlas decided to walk home to Bond Street rather than attempt to hail a hackney. Crossing the crowded piazza, he spotted the fruit vendor hawking her wares. He saw that Mary White had cornered a potential customer, a tall, well-dressed gentleman, who seemed to be listening intently as the woman shifted the weight of the oranges that she carried in the sling around her neck.

The man reached into his pocket and dropped payment into Mary's open palm. But she continued to hold her hand out until the gentleman withdrew more money and deposited it into her hand.

Atlas smiled inwardly. It seemed he wasn't alone in taking pity on Mary for the heavy burden she carried. The customer shifted, and light from the oil lamps suspended overhead cut across the older man's haggard face. To Atlas's astonishment, he saw a momentary flash of Vessey's face before the crush of theatergoers obscured his view of the man.

What was Vessey up to? The marquess was the last person in the metropolis to display any sort of altruism. Atlas had no idea what to make of what he'd witnessed. But he intended to make it his business to get to the bottom of it.

★　★　★

"Good evening, Mary," Atlas called out once he neared the fruit vendor.

"Guv!" The woman's lined face lit up. "Come ta buy something?"

"Possibly. If you have what I am looking for."

"Wut is it yer wantin' ta know now, guv?"

"That gentleman you were just speaking with, the finely dressed one who paid you handsomely."

Expectation filled every line in her face, the prospect of another sizable payday no doubt boosting her mood. "Wot about 'im?"

Atlas pulled his leather wallet from his pocket. "What did he want from you?"

"Maybe 'e wanted some oranges."

"Very well." Atlas returned his wallet to his pocket.

"Not so quick there, guv," Mary said urgently. "'E wanted me ta keep quiet."

Atlas kept his wallet within her view. "About what?"

"I seen 'is son arguin' with Mrs. Pike."

"Francis Pike? You saw Francis Pike arguing with Mrs. Pike? When was this?"

Mary shrugged. "Don't know 'is name. But I do know it were 'is lordship's heir."

Atlas stilled. "Surely not the heir."

She nodded. "The heir. Not 'is bastard. I knows the difference. I seen 'um both come and go before."

Atlas felt the blood drain from his face. "You are telling me Vessey just paid you to keep quiet about seeing his heir, Nicholas, argue with Mrs. Pike?"

"Yes, sir." She nodded and held out her open palm.

Atlas ignored it. "When did this argument occur?"

"'Bout a week before someone done 'er in."

"Could you hear what they argued about?"

"Na. I 'eard the cove scream at 'er. Said she ruined 'is life. Said 'e 'ated 'er and wished she were dead."

* * *

The following morning, fearing the worst and dreading what he might learn, Atlas sent a note around to Nicholas, requesting that he call at his earliest convenience.

"I had rather hoped Lady Roslyn had sent over another basket," his nephew remarked as the two men settled into the deep chairs in Atlas's sitting room. When Atlas did not respond, Nicholas paused to examine his uncle's face. "Are you unwell?"

"I was unable to sleep last evening." Atlas had spent a restless night contemplating the very real possibility that his nephew had murdered Wendy Pike. Nicholas had lied about never having met the woman. Who knows what other information he'd withheld.

"I am sorry to hear it," Nicholas said sympathetically.

Atlas's head throbbed. It felt like a stonemason was hammering away at his temple. "I could not rest after discovering that you have not been truthful with me."

"Is this about meeting Francis Pike? I give you my word that I did not know who he was when I admired his shooting skills at Manton's."

"You claimed you'd never met Mrs. Pike." Atlas pressed the tips of his fingers hard against his forehead. "Not only did you meet your father's companion, you argued with her in a public place."

Nicholas paled.

"Do you deny it?"

Nicholas shook his head. "I was ashamed to tell you the truth."

"Why?" Atlas forced himself to ask the question, even though he wasn't certain he wanted to know the answer. "Because you killed Mrs. Pike?"

"No!" Nicholas vaulted out of the chair. "I could never harm anyone."

"Then what?" Atlas stared up at his sister's son. "What were you ashamed to tell me?"

"How much I hated Mrs. Pike. How often I wished she were dead. If she were gone, then my father would finally choose me." Nicholas's voice caught. "Of course, I did not know about Francis then. I was not aware that my father had another son that he prefers. How was I to know that all of these years he was spending time with that woman's bastard while I was away at school?"

"You were loath to tell me you hated your father's mistress? Why hide such a thing?"

"Because it is ungentlemanly of me to condescend to despising a woman like Mrs. Pike, a demi–rep that all of society thinks is beneath my notice." Nicholas slumped back into his chair. "The family of a gentleman is meant to ignore such associations."

"Did you tell Mrs. Pike that you wished she were dead?"

"I did." Nicholas hung his head. "I know it was beneath me to behave in such a manner. To show that kind of emotion in public."

"Did you encounter Mrs. Pike at Covent Garden by chance on the day you confronted her?"

"No. I sought her out. When I came down from university, Mrs. Pike was not in residence at my father's home on Cavendish Square. I learned my father had moved her to Admiralty House. My father has apartments there due to his position."

Atlas knew that Vessey, in addition to being in the House of Lords, also held a high political position in the navy. "I am aware that there are ministerial flats there."

"I was curious to see what she looked like, to learn more about the woman who'd captivated my father for all of these years. I saw her come out of the Admiralty. My coachman confirmed who she was. I ordered him to follow her. She went to Covent Garden."

"What time of day was this?"

"Late afternoon."

"Do you know what she was doing there?" Atlas assumed Wendy had gone to visit Cooke.

Nicholas shook his head. "She was inside the theater for about an hour. I spoke to her when she came out."

"What did she say?"

"She refused to speak with me. At first she completely ignored me."

"And then what happened?"

"She finally broke her silence. But only to say that my father would be very angry with her if he knew we had spoken. I was in a state of extreme frustration. For years I had thought of what I would say when I finally met the woman who had cast such a long shadow over my life. And once the moment was finally upon us, she refused to utter a single word of any consequence. I was extraordinarily agitated, and that's when I told her that I hated her and wished she were dead."

"How did she respond?"

"She didn't. She just rushed away to her waiting carriage. And I was immediately ashamed for accosting her."

Atlas did not know what to believe. He fervently wanted to take Nicholas at his word. But the truth was that Atlas did not know Nicholas at all, despite their shared bloodline. He had no idea at all what lengths the boy would go to in order to get what he wanted.

"Did your father learn about the incident?"

"Yes, Mrs. Pike told him." Anger flashed in Nicholas's eyes. "She no doubt wanted my father to think less of me."

"I imagine Vessey spoke to you about it."

"Yes, he told me I must never accost Mrs. Pike again. That is was beneath me to give a woman of her status any notice at all."

Meanwhile Vessey could do as he pleased. The irony of that was not lost on Atlas. "Where were you the evening Jasper was killed?"

Shock flooded Nicholas's face. "Surely, you cannot think—"

The pain in Atlas's head ratcheted up. "Please just answer the question."

"On Wednesday last?" Nicholas paused to consider his answer. "I stayed at home on Cavendish Square. The servants will attest to that."

Atlas felt certain that the paid staff would confirm Nicholas's story. But could the word of servants be trusted when their livelihoods were at stake? "I see. And the evening Mrs. Pike was killed?"

"I was with Jasper. We went to a cockfight in Camden Town."

"Just you and Jasper alone?"

Nicholas nodded.

"I suppose there is no one who can confirm your story?" It was either extraordinarily bad luck or a convenient lie. "Someone, perhaps, who is still alive?"

"You must believe me." Nicholas's pleading gaze met Atlas's eyes. "I may have been jealous of the role Mrs. Pike played in my father's life, but I am not capable of murder."

★　★　★

That afternoon the sun made a rare appearance, staying in place long enough for Atlas to escort Lilliana to Hatchard's Bookshop on Piccadilly.

The previous afternoon, before their frosty parting at the opera, Atlas had sent around a note thanking Lilliana for the food basket. He'd also taken the opportunity to share what he'd learned from his nephew about Jasper Balfour's indebtedness to Harry Dean. Lilliana had promptly responded by asking Atlas to escort her to Hatchard's.

Atlas suspected the true reason she desired his escort was so that she could interrogate him in person about Balfour and the debt he owed Dean. He also welcomed the opportunity to discuss what he'd learned about Nicholas.

Somerville's coachman dropped them at the corner of Duke Street. As they strolled down Piccadilly, Atlas shared everything he'd learned. Lilliana's haughty froideur tended to thaw a bit whenever they discussed the investigation.

"Surely Nicholas is not capable of such an act," Lilliana said.

Atlas fervently hoped she was right. "There is something I cannot get out of my head."

"What is that?"

"When Vessey first saw Mrs. Pike's body, he said, 'Oh, Wendy, what has he done to you?"

"You fear he was speaking of Nicholas."

"It is possible. I haven't wanted to seriously contemplate that my own nephew could be a killer. Now I realize I must force myself to consider all possibilities, including the ones that horrify me."

"Mr. Dean appears to be as likely a suspect as Nicholas," she remarked as they walked past the Fortnum and Mason grocery shop.

"Dean is known to lose control when he drinks a great deal," he agreed. "It is entirely possible that he was foxed on the evening Mrs. Pike was killed."

"And was not in his right mind?"

"It is possible."

"That suggests that, in this altered state, Dean induced Jasper to kill Mrs. Pike in revenge against Francis Pike for humiliating him at the duel."

They came to the bookshop's dark green exterior, where the double doors were flanked by two bow windows. The scent of leather and books engulfed them as soon as they stepped inside. Books were set out on wooden tables and lined the shelf stacks, and a wide staircase led to an upper level.

Lilliana walked purposefully the back of the shop.

"Are you looking for a book in particular?" Atlas asked.

"Yes, Peter has become very fond of reading." She slowed before a book-lined wall and slowly walked alongside it, her gaze traveling up and down, perusing the titles. "He has requested the book *Robinson Crusoe*.

"Is that not a bit advanced for a boy of nine?"

"He shall be ten soon. Ah, here it is." She pulled a title from the bookcase. "Peter is very clever and excels at reading. He has asked for this particular book, so we shall see how he manages. If it proves too difficult at present, it shall not be long before he will be able to read it. Children learn so quickly."

"*Robinson Crusoe*! That is one of my favorites." Atlas turned toward the man's voice and found himself face-to-face with Harry Dean, who had a couple of books tucked under one arm.

"Mr. Dean." Atlas hid his pleasure at this very convenient chance encounter. "Allow me to present Lady Roslyn, sister of the Duke of Somerville. Lady Roslyn, this is Mr. Dean. Mr. Harry Dean."

Curiosity glimmered in Dean's gaze as he bowed. "Delighted to make your acquaintance, my lady."

"And I yours, Mr. Dean." She exchanged glances with Atlas, a speculative look in her eyes.

Dean held up the books he was holding. "I am purchasing these particular titles for my book society."

"If you gentlemen will excuse me," Lilliana said, "I shall go and purchase *Robinson Crusoe* for my son."

Dean bowed. "And I shall continue my hunt for new titles."

"Just a moment more of your time, if you please," Atlas said as the younger man turned to go.

Dean paused, his eyes wary. "Yes?"

"It's about Jasper Balfour. I understand he owed you a great deal of money."

"At one time, yes, that is true."

"At one time?"

Dean remained perfectly still. "He paid off the debt in full not too long ago."

"When exactly did Jasper clear up his debt to you?"

A few moments passed before Dean answered. "It was at the beginning of this month. If I had to wager a guess, I would say the fourth or fifth of November."

Atlas went through the calendar in his head. Jasper had given Dean the money two or three days after Mrs. Pike's murder. "Do you know where he obtained the money to pay you back?"

"I have no idea. As I said, I was quite surprised when he came to me with the means to absolve the debt."

"Do you have proof Jasper paid you?"

Dean huffed a laugh. "How could I possibly prove that? I no longer have the vowels. Naturally I returned them to Jasper once his debt was paid."

"Did anyone witness this?"

"No," Dean said guardedly, "that is not the sort of transaction one conducts in public."

"Do you happen to know whom else Jasper owed money to?"

Dean shrugged. "Everyone at some point or another. He even used to record it all in a notebook in order for him to keep track of his debts." He gave a sad smile. "Jasper was honorable. He took paying off his debts very seriously."

The two men parted ways, and Atlas rejoined Lilliana.

"Well?" she demanded. "What did Mr. Dean say?"

"That Jasper paid off his debt in full two or three days after Mrs. Pike died."

"Oh." She contemplated that bit of news. "That does not help much, does it?"

"If Dean is the killer, it is possible that he absolved Jasper of all his debts so that Jasper would not disclose that Dean killed Mrs. Pike."

"Or," Lilliana offered, "if Mr. Dean is not the culprit, the true killer paid Jasper to keep him quiet, and Jasper used that money to repay Mr. Dean what was owed to him."

"Fortunately, we are not out of clues as of yet. Jasper apparently had a habit of recording all of his debts in a notebook."

"The killer's name could be written down in it."

"It is entirely possible. The notebook might still be in Jasper's rooms at the Albany."

"Well then, there is nothing to be done for it," she said pertly. "We must search Jasper's rooms."

"We?"

"You might need someone to create a diversion while you access Jasper's rooms. I can be quite useful."

He bristled. "I cannot put you in that kind of danger."

"You speak as though I am a reticule to be placed somewhere. But I am not. I will put myself wherever I care to, and at the moment that means I am going to the Albany." Marching in the direction of the gentleman's apartments, which were located just across Piccadilly, she called back over her shoulder. "Are you coming or not?"

CHAPTER 25

"What the devil are you doing?" Atlas hissed as Lilliana climbed in through the window behind him. "You should not be in here."

"Neither should you." She accepted his proffered hand like a queen descending from her carriage, rather than an interloper breaking into Jasper Balfour's cozy set at the Albany. "That is why we are coming in through the window rather than the front door."

"You comprehend exactly what I mean." He spoke in a harsh whisper lest they be overheard by any of the building's residents. "You should have stayed in the carriage."

"That would hardly be fair. Neither of us would be in here at all had I not bribed the maid." Once she steadied herself, Lilliana straightened and surveyed their surroundings. Jasper's bedchamber appeared much as the young man had left it—the bed linens in crumpled disarray, a half-empty glass of brandy by the bedside.

Atlas became keenly aware of Lilliana's warm presence beside him in these close quarters, of the scent of jasmine and cloves intermingling with stale air and notes of shaving soap. His cheeks burned. A lady had no business in this intimate bachelor space.

But Lilliana's enterprising ways, her spotting and waylaying a maid leaving the Albany, were the reason they were here now. The servant had willingly pointed out Jasper's one-bedroom apartments in return for a monetary token of appreciation.

Atlas had waited with Lilliana in Somerville's carriage until dark before making his way toward the back of the building and along its ropewalk way until he found the correct apartments. Lilliana had followed, much to his dismay.

"I can only imagine what the duke will say if we are caught," he said in a low voice.

"Then let us make certain we are not found," she whispered brightly, turning to go through the drawers of the writing bureau. "We must make haste. I have an engagement this evening."

He scowled. "With Northampton I presume?"

"As a matter of fact, the earl *is* my escort for the evening."

He watched as she methodically went through each small wooden drawer. "What would Northampton say about your running around in this manner?"

"I have no idea." She did not look up from her task. "Feel at liberty to ask him if you would like."

He fumed a little at her easy references to Northampton. "Will you inform him that you were here? With me?"

"Will you inform Somerville that you brought me here?"

"I most certainly did not bring you here," he retorted in a loud whisper, refusing to be distracted. "Somerville says Northampton intends to marry you."

"Yes, that does seem to be his aim."

"You should inform the earl that he needs to look elsewhere."

Her head snapped up. "Is that so?" Even in the dim light, he saw the defiance that flashed in her eyes. "And why is that?"

"Because if you wed anyone, it is going to be me."

"How dare you—" she halted abruptly when the words sank in. "What?"

Beyond the bedchamber, the sound of the front door opening and then quietly clicking shut reached them. They weren't alone. Atlas and Lilliana froze. Hers eyes went wide. Atlas set his pointing finger in front of his pursed mouth, urging her to keep silent. He gestured for her to stay where she was while he silently went to investigate.

He peered around the doorframe. A man in dark clothing stood with his back to Atlas, searching the bookshelves behind the sofa. The man hadn't lit a lamp, which suggested he too was an interloper with about as much business being in Jasper's apartments as Atlas and Lilliana had. And if the intruder had come for the notebook, Atlas might well be looking at Jasper's killer, and possibly Wendy's as well.

He turned back to Lilliana, gesturing for her to hide herself, once again cursing himself for allowing the lady to place herself in danger. It was entirely possible she stood only a few feet from a murderer.

He went forward, tiptoeing into the darkened sitting room before realizing the interloper was no longer in view. He blinked, trying to adjust to the darkness when something slammed into his head.

"Oomph!" Atlas staggered from the force the blow. Dizzy, his eyes adjusted enough to steal a glimpse of his attacker, who was cloaked in shadow, his face obscured. The interloper grabbed an unlit lantern and swung it at Atlas, who ducked just in time, struggling through his dizziness to stay on his feet. The man hurled the lantern at Atlas, who bobbed out of the way.

Atlas hunched over with his head in his hands, deliberately feigning more disorientation than he actually felt. The ruse proved effective. His attacker advanced as Atlas hoped he would. When the man was within reach, Atlas made his move. He raised his right elbow and brought it down with brute force. The man jerked away just in time to save his face. But Atlas jabbed his left elbow in a rapid-fire motion. The grisly sound of cracking bone confirmed the full force of his jab had connected with the man's body.

The man moaned and dropped to his knees beneath the sitting room's open window. As Atlas moved toward him, Lilliana called out, "Have a care!"

He spun around, furious beyond belief. "What are you doing in here? I told you to stay in the other room."

She crossed her arms over her chest. "What if you had been hurt? I was standing by to render assistance as needed. But you are clearly more than capable." Admiration gleamed in her eyes. "Where did you learn to fight like that?"

The exchange took just seconds, but it proved long enough for Atlas's attacker to leap to his feet and throw himself from the window.

Atlas cursed and dashed after him. He reached the window in time to see the man sprinting away, disappearing into the shadows.

Lilliana appeared at the window beside him. She peered into the darkness. "Will you go after him?"

"How do you propose I do that? The entire building is full of young bachelors, and I was not able to get a good look at my attacker. He has likely already blended in with the residents." *Hellfire and damnation.* Despite his frustration, Atlas felt a frisson of relief that the attacker was gone. He didn't want the man anywhere near Lilliana.

He blew out his cheeks. "The man was probably here for the same reason we are. He came for the notebook and might well have absconded with it."

"If he was here for the notebook, that would make him the—" She paused as the implications sank in.

"Murderer," he said, finishing the statement for her. "Precisely. In all likelihood, we have just met the man who murdered both Mrs. Pike and Jasper Balfour."

She glanced around the room. "I think we should continue looking for the notebook. The intruder was not here for very long. What is the likelihood that he was able to locate it in such a short time?"

He thought about it. "He most likely did not have time to find it. Unless he knew exactly where Jasper kept it."

They resumed their search, Lilliana at a chest of drawers by the front entrance while Atlas searched the shelves behind the sofa as the intruder had done. Music, high-pitched voices, and laughter filtered in from the unit next door.

Atlas looked in the direction of the noise. "It appears Jasper's neighbor is having a party."

"It is rather convenient, would you not say?"

"Quite. They certainly won't hear us over their noise."

She paused listening to the laughter and teasing. "I can hear women's voices. I thought ladies were not allowed at the Albany."

"*Ladies* are not. And that is all I will say on the matter," he said pointedly before turning back to the shelves to continue his search. They worked quietly for almost an hour, searching everywhere they could think of, but the notebook was nowhere to be found.

"It is not here," Lilliana said after they had finished looking.

"No," Atlas agreed. "We have looked everywhere."

"Maybe the intruder did find it."

Laughter and a loud thump from the neighboring apartment quieted them for a moment.

"Either that or it was not here to begin with," Atlas said after a moment. "We should go before somebody finds us here."

"Atlas." Lilliana paused. "About what you said earlier."

"About wedding you?" He no longer felt nervous. Or unworthy. This moment was long overdue. He could feel the rightness of it deep into the marrow of his bones.

"Yes."

"This is hardly the ideal place for this discussion." He faced her. "I have never before wished so fervently that I had inherited just an ounce of my father's gift with words. Alas, I have not. All I can do is speak honestly from my heart."

Lilliana's face paled. Atlas wondered what that portended, but he forged ahead nonetheless. "Being with you allows my heart to breathe in a way it never has before," he began. "And it is the finest feeling I have ever known. I wonder if you would do me the great honor—"

"Stop at once!" she blurted, panic in her eyes.

"You must allow me to finish—"

"No," she said sharply. "There is something you must know about me before you say anything more."

She seemed extremely perturbed, but he couldn't imagine that she carried some terrible secret. "And what is that?"

"I might prove"—she hesitated—"disappointing."

His brows descended, hooding over his eyes. If ever there was a woman who knew her incalculably high worth, it was Lady Roslyn Lilliana Sterling. "How so?"

He couldn't help asking. He was curious to know where, and in what way, an accomplished woman such as Lilliana, with her formidable intellect, wicked sense of humor, and sharp tongue, would find herself wanting. Especially with all of those considerable charms packaged together with a face and form that left a man unable to sleep at night for thinking of her.

"I can be a cold woman."

Lilliana did possess a glacial manner and off-putting haughtiness. Off-putting to others, perhaps, that is, but not to him. Never to him. "I rather like that about you."

"You do not understand." Her eyes met his, her dark gaze steady and determined, although it was obvious that this conversation was difficult for her. "Godfrey said I was particularly cold in a certain aspect of marriage."

Now his brows went in the opposite direction, up instead of down, as confusion gave way to comprehension. This new distance she'd recently wedged between them, her palatable discomfort whenever they were alone or in private, suddenly made sense. He laughed.

She stiffened. "Are you amused?" While she possessed an excellent sense of humor, Lilliana did not care to be the subject of mockery.

"No." He forced a more conciliatory tone. "It is just that your late husband was an idiot."

"That may be so." She paused to correct herself. "That was most certainly so, but nonetheless I understand that a man such as yourself, who would be too honorable to stray, would expect to find . . . a certain warmth in the . . . er . . . marital bed in order for that aspect of marriage to be . . . satisfactory to you."

"Lily." He reached for her hand. "You are not a cold woman . . . in *any* respect."

Her composure did not falter. "That is very kind of you to say, but the truth is that you cannot know for certain, whereas Godfrey was in a position to know."

"Wrong. I am most certainly in a position to know." He stroked the back of her hand lightly with the pad of his thumb. Her skin was pale and feather soft, and he envisioned that she would be that way all over. "I *have* taken certain liberties with you."

He had held her in his arms more than once during their acquaintanceship, and she'd responded warmly, sweetly, and with delightful enthusiasm. "I have enjoyed certain intimacies with you, not as often as I would like and nowhere near as often as I plan to once you are Mrs. Atlas Catesby—"

Her lips quirked. "I presume you are trying to make some point?"

"I can assure you those intimacies were not a disappointment." When she parted her lips to speak, possibly to contradict him, he continued before she could interrupt. "The woman with whom I took those very pleasurable liberties was anything but cold. In truth, she was very, very warm."

"You are being gallant because you are a kind man."

He suppressed a snort. "You overestimate my gallantry. Above all, I am still a man. And you are correct to assume that this man hopes to find that kind of warmth in his wife. Particularly a man who intends to be faithful to her until his dying day."

Two faint lines, a tiny number eleven, appeared between her fine brows. "But what if that warmth does not extend as far as you might like?"

"Those sorts of things can be . . . practiced . . . improved upon. And I can be a very patient man, especially for something that is well worth waiting for."

"I see." She was quiet for a moment.

He reached for her other hand so that he now held both. "Godfrey was abominable. You did not care for him."

"I abhorred the man."

"Exactly. It is natural that you did not enjoy being touched by a man whose company you could barely countenance. But if you care for me just a little bit—"

"What of Mrs. Jennings?" She jutted her chin. "You certainly seemed entranced by her the other evening."

"I was—*am*—and probably always will be entranced by her considerable talent. But Juliet is the past. You are my future." He took her into his arms, and for the first time of their acquaintance, he kissed her unreservedly. She responded in kind, returning the intimacy in a heated manner, the way a man dreams of being welcomed by the woman he adores. A few minutes later, when he was out of breath, he broke the kiss and rested his forehead against hers. "Say yes. Tell me that you will be my wife."

Her radiant answering smile told him everything he wanted to know, but he still needed to hear the words. "Of course the answer is yes. I have been waiting for you to ask for more than a year."

He blinked. "Have you?"

She shook her head. "It is as Thea says. For a smart man, you can be awfully thick at times."

"How fortunate I am that, going forward, you will be by my side to keep me from acting like an imbecile." He cleared his throat in order to make her a proper proposal. "As I was saying, I do not have my father's gift for words, but the truth is that being in your presence allows my heart to breathe in a way it never has before, and it is the finest feeling I have ever known—"

"You are wrong," she interrupted.

"About what?"

"You claim not to possess your father's talent for words, but what you have just said is possibly the most poetic thing I have ever heard."

"All I know is that the very first time I saw you . . ." He paused, reluctant to bring up the abominable afternoon that had somehow brought the greatest sweetness into his life.

"You need not spare my feelings about Godfrey selling me in the market square." She shocked him by giving voice to the memory of her greatest humiliation, his beautiful Lily brought low by a bastard who hadn't been fit to kiss the bottom of her slippers. "I no longer regret that afternoon."

"How can you not?"

"Because it brought us together." Her off-kilter smile prompted an extra, out-of-rhythm beat in his chest. "Otherwise, you might have passed through the village, and I might still be wed to Godfrey."

He grimaced. "God forbid."

And to banish that awful thought from both of their minds, he gently folded Lily back into his arms and kissed her again— right there in a dead man's apartments and not caring in the least that they could be discovered at any moment.

Chapter 26

"I suppose I should speak to Somerville at the earliest opportunity," Atlas said to Lilliana after they'd made their clandestine escape from the Albany and were comfortably ensconced in Somerville's toasty carriage, with heated bricks to warm their feet.

"Surely you are not worried that he will object?" Lilliana sat across from him in the forward-facing seat, the oil lamps along the roadway occasionally spilling light into the carriage, illuminating her fine-boned features. "I do not need his consent to wed."

"I expect His Grace will look favorably upon our union. He has told me as much."

Lilliana stiffened. "Has he? When was this?"

"At the opera the other evening. He asked me what my intentions were."

"How did you respond?"

"Truthfully. I told him that I am not worthy of you."

Her lips quirked upward. "What changed your mind?"

"I realized no one is good enough for you, not the Marquess of Roxbury nor the Earl of Northampton. I guess I will just have to do."

Her expression was serious. "If you feel that my brother forced you into this betrothal, we can end it at once. No one need know."

"There is not a chance that I will cry off." Abandoning all propriety, he shifted across the carriage to sit next to her. "Unless you have changed your mind."

"Certainly not."

He reached for her gloved hand and interlaced his fingers with hers. "Shall I come in with you to speak with His Grace this evening, if, that is, he is at home to callers?"

"This evening might be inconvenient. Somerville is ordering more pieces for his wardrobe. That tailor from Pall Mall comes to him, and their fittings take hours. At times they go so late into the evening that Mr. Nash stays overnight in a guest chamber. You remember Mr. Kirby Nash, do you not?"

Atlas remembered Somerville's tailor all too well, but for reasons he suspected Lilliana knew nothing about. "I do."

"Perhaps you should wait a few days before you speak to Somerville."

"Why?" He squeezed her hand. "In case you come to your senses and realize I am far beneath your touch?"

"Because as soon as our betrothal becomes public, we shall have no peace. And that will hinder your investigation into Mrs. Pike's death."

"How do you mean?"

"There will naturally be a dinner to formally introduce you to my aunt and her five daughters and their families. And after that, we must plan the engagement party. In the meantime, we shall be invited everywhere, and although we do not have to accept all of the invitations, there will be some events that would be rude of us to decline."

"Perhaps I had better give this marriage idea further thought," he teased.

She pulled their linked hands into her lap. "Don't you dare."

He took the liberty of pressing his lips against the satiny warmth of her cheek. "Do you take me for a fool? I am never letting you go. As it is, I can barely tolerate the notion of allowing you out of my sight even for a few hours."

Her soft answering sigh stirred his blood. "Then it is settled," she murmured. "We shall remain betrothed, but it will be our secret to give you a few more weeks to focus on the investigation."

He pressed a kiss against her neck, inhaling the scent of jasmine and cloves. "What sorts of liberties do you suppose a man can take when he has entered into a secret betrothal?"

"It appears we are about to find out," she whispered.

"Indeed," he agreed just before his lips locked onto hers.

★ ★ ★

"Where did you learn to fight like that?" Thea asked her brother after Lilliana had relayed the details of the scuffle in Jasper's apartments.

They were in Charlton's upstairs sitting room, a masculine, tasteful space dominated by dark wood paneling and expensive furnishings. Atlas had asked Somerville's coachman to drop him at Charlton's once they'd departed the Albany. Lilliana had happily joined him after spotting Thea's battered old coach in front of the earl's opulent home.

"Atlas certainly did not acquire those moves at Gentleman's Jackson's," Charlton put in. "Jack would frown upon jabbing opponents with one's elbow."

Atlas held his hands before the hearth, soaking in the fire's heat. "Bokator is most definitely not taught at Jack's—or any other boxing saloon for that matter."

"What is that?" Charlton's forehead puckered. "It sounds like one of those frighteningly exotic foods of yours."

Clad in a puce floral dressing gown, the earl sat in a deep leather chair with his silk-slipper-clad feet propped up on a stool. Atlas was relieved to find Charlton recovering well from his wound. The threat of infection seemed to have passed, and color had returned to Charlton's cheeks.

Atlas drained the brandy from his glass. "Bokator is an ancient method of fighting that originated in Cambodia."

Lilliana sat up straighter. "You have been to Cambodia?"

"Where the devil is that?" Charlton asked.

"It is in Asia," Atlas answered, "and no, I have not been there as of yet."

Thea settled on the chintz sofa next to Lilliana. "Then however did you learn to fight in that manner?"

"When I was last in Lisbon, I studied with a Portuguese man who had mastered the art of Bokator."

"You have lost me." Charlton executed an exaggerated sigh. "I thought you said that sort of brawling came from that place in Asia."

"Cambodia," Atlas told him. "My instructor was born in Cambodia. His parents were missionaries from Portugal who spent most of their lives in Asia."

Lilliana's eyes sparkled. "How fascinating." Their gazes met and held, and the warmth that engulfed Atlas had nothing to do with the fire.

Charlton grimaced. "How perfectly awful to live one's life in a heathen country. It is bad enough that Atlas travels constantly, but at least he never forgets where he belongs and that his home is here in England."

"The Cambodians would likely say that we are the savages." Atlas crossed over to the sideboard to refresh his drink. "As I was saying, using your elbows to strike with maximum impact is crucial to Bokator."

"Does your elbow hurt?" Thea asked.

"A bit," he admitted. "But if you land the blow properly, the pain is minimal."

"You two have certainly had an eventful evening," Thea remarked.

A half smile curved Lilliana's beautiful lips. "You have no idea."

Charlton waggled his brows at Lilliana. "I see Atlas is leading you down a criminal path. What is to be next, I wonder. Perhaps bank robbery?"

Atlas failed to see the humor in his friend's comments. "I strongly advised Lady Lilliana to stay in the carriage."

Lilliana sipped her sherry. "What would be the fun in that?"

Thea glared at her brother. "Oh, do stop being such a fossil, Atlas. Lilliana is hardly a fragile porcelain creature who will shatter at the first sign of any excitement."

Atlas stiffened. "I never said that she was." He took a seat near Charlton. "I would simply prefer for her not to be caught stealing into bachelor rooms at the Albany."

"Think of the scandal," Charlton said, and then more quietly, for Atlas's ears only, he mumbled, "You might even be forced to wed her to save her reputation."

Suppressing a smile, Atlas looked to his sister. "What are you doing here?"

"Excellent distraction tactic," Charlton murmured under his breath.

"Is it not obvious?" Thea said. "I am here to check on Charlton. To make certain he is recovering."

"He looks fine to me," Atlas said.

Charlton beamed. "That is thanks to the good Mrs. Palmer's ministrations. Her presence somehow contrives to make even beef tea palatable."

Atlas stared at him. "Thea has somehow managed to entice you to drink beef tea?" He knew just how much Charlton detested the remedy.

Charlton smiled. "She has promised me certain favors if I am a very good boy and drink all of my beef tea."

Atlas did not care for the sound of that. He glared at his friend. "What sort of favors?"

"If the earl continues to drink his tea," Thea informed her brother, "then he will be ready for a turn about the garden by week's end."

"With Mrs. Palmer by my side of course."

Atlas stared at his friend. The man was accustomed to sexual affairs with some of London's most acclaimed beauties, from opera stars and actresses, to courtesans and widows, and yet he appeared enthused by the prospect of a turn about the garden with a very married woman. "What the devil is the matter with you?"

A dreamy expression came over Charlton's aristocratic face. "Rather than settle for a bountiful tavern meal that does nothing to satisfy my appetites, a man must content himself with table scraps from the most magnificent feast."

"What are you going on about?" Thea asked from across the room.

"Nothing of interest, my dear Mrs. Palmer." Charlton gazed adoringly at her. "Is it time for my beef tea yet?"

★ ★ ★

The following day, Atlas returned to the Albany; only this time there was no skulking about. He entered through the front door rather than a side window, and his arrival was announced by the porter.

Francis Pike lived on the second floor of the exclusive bachelor enclave, a mansion that had been divided into apartments for fashionable young gentlemen. Although Pike appeared surprised to find Atlas standing outside his shiny black lacquered front door, he was his usual courteous self.

"Mr. Catesby, please do come in." Pike's complexion had a sheen and was so pale that his skin almost matched his unusual white-blond hair. He had a thick blanket wrapped around his shoulders over his dressing gown. Perspiration dampened his hair.

"Are you unwell?" Atlas asked as he followed the young man inside. "Shall I summon a doctor?"

Pike led Atlas into an overly warm, snug sitting room. Tall, paned windows and high, elaborately molded ceilings lent a gracious feel to the small space, although the air felt stale. None of the windows were open.

"No, it is just a fever, one that will surely pass," Pike reassured him. "I believe the shock of Jasper's death, coming so soon after my own mother's, is what has truly laid me low. There is only so much one can withstand."

"I am sorry for your losses. I gather you and Jasper were particularly close."

"We met as boys at Eton." A wistful smile curved his lips. "He was the only person in our entire class who could climb a tree faster than I could."

Pike sat in a careful, deliberate manner, as if his physical self were as fragile as his current emotional state. "I just cannot begin to imagine what Lord Balfour is going through. He doted on Jasper."

"I shall not keep you long." Pike's sickly appearance alarmed Atlas. The man was usually impeccably turned out, his demeanor one of polished perfection.

"I am afraid I cannot offer you anything except brandy or port," Pike said. "My valet brings my meals from the basement kitchens, but I have given him leave to go and visit his ailing mother in Berkshire."

"Please do not concern yourself with my comfort. I have some questions, and then I shall leave you to your rest."

Pike perked up. "Is it about the investigation?" The subject of apprehending his mother's killer appeared to energize the young man despite his current lethargic state. "Have you found the person responsible for murdering my mother?"

"Not as of yet, but I am hoping to bring this matter to a resolution in the near future."

"I see." Pike relaxed back in his chair. "If there is anything I can do to help, I am, of course, at your disposal, as always."

"Do you know whom Jasper owed money to?"

His answering smile was more like a grimace. "Everyone at one time or another."

"And at the time of his death?"

"I believe he was indebted to Harry Dean."

"I have spoken to Dean. He says Jasper cleared the debt he owed him about a fortnight ago."

Pike's brows lifted. "Is that so? Then perhaps Jasper was momentarily debt-free when he perished."

Atlas didn't think so but decided not to share his opinion with Pike. "May I ask where you were when Jasper died?"

Pike's expression was like a door closing. "I was indisposed."

"How so? You seemed to have exerted yourself before you came in and saw the body."

"I was in the garden."

"Charlton was shot in the garden."

"I was in the garden after Charlton was shot and well after he'd been attended to by the doctor."

"Were you alone?"

"I was not."

"Who were you with?"

"As a gentleman, I cannot say."

"Ah." Pike had been engaged in a liaison with a woman in the garden. Or at least that is what he wanted Atlas to believe. "I see."

"Are you certain I cannot offer you some brandy?"

"Very certain." Atlas stood. "I will leave you now to get some rest."

Pike rose, with effort, to see his visitor out. Atlas paused when they reached the front door. "One more thing, if I may?"

"Yes?"

"Did you happen to meet your half brother at Manton's?"

"I am afraid you have caught me. I suppose your friend Charlton told you? I confess I was curious to meet Beaumont."

"Why?"

"He is my brother, and I have always longed for a brother." He smiled ruefully. "Doesn't every boy?"

"I cannot say. I have rather too many of them. I have never known anything but a life of being overrun by brothers."

"You are fortunate." Atlas registered the wistfulness in Francis's voice. "I have watched Nicholas from afar in the year or so since he came down from Cambridge and began moving about in society."

"Did you introduce yourself to Nicholas that day at Manton's?"

"No, I did not. I didn't care to anger our father."

Atlas exhaled, relieved that Francis's version of the encounter aligned with Nicholas's. This seemed to confirm that his nephew had not lied to him—at least not about Francis. He truly hadn't known Francis's identity when they'd met at Manton's.

"My father . . . our father . . . would not approve," Francis said. "It was up to his lordship to orchestrate my official introduction to my brother, as he did last evening at the opera."

Atlas thought about Pike's situation. Both Francis and Nicholas had suffered due to Vessey's desire to keep his heir and his bastard apart during their childhood. Wendy had endured a great deal as well, given Vessey's notions of social class and his ever-present reminders of her lowly place in his blue-blooded world.

Naturally, the marquess had held himself to no such standard. He'd indulged in all of his children as well as his long-time mistress, while they had not been free to do the same.

"I must thank you," Francis broke the momentary silence, "for looking into my mother's death. Most gentlemen would not think her worthy of the trouble."

Atlas held out his hand. "Everyone is worthy."

Pike shook Atlas's proffered hand. "I agree." He grimaced, pain glistening in his eyes. "My mother was a most worthy woman."

Atlas departed and as he went down the Albany's grand staircase, he felt a pang of empathy for Francis Pike. Even after all of these years, the immensity of Phoebe's loss could still take Atlas's breath away. He could only imagine how difficult is was for Francis Pike, who'd lost both his mother and a close friend within the space of a few weeks, to cope with so much loss.

CHAPTER 27

As he walked home, Atlas contemplated the coming changes in his life.

Lilliana was to be his wife. Becoming a surrogate father to her two young boys would be daunting, but Atlas found himself very much looking forward to the challenge. The idea of finally having a family to call his own was surprisingly pleasurable.

He was so wrapped in his thoughts as he went up the steps to his apartments, that Atlas barely noticed Jamie rushing out to the landing to greet him.

The boy peered down at him. "I thought that was you, sir."

"Were you expecting someone else?"

"Er . . ." The boy shifted his impossibly tall and gangly form from one foot to the other. "You have a visitor, sir."

Atlas reached the landing to find himself looking up at Jamie. "Are you going to tell me who it is, or am I expected to guess?"

Anxiety stretched tight across his valet's wide face. "This visitor is most unexpected."

"Well?" Atlas gestured with his hand, in small circular motions. "Let's have it. I am not keen on playing a guessing game."

"The Marquess of Vessey awaits you within."

"What the devil does he want?" Atlas resisted the urge to turn away and go right back down the stairs.

"His lordship says he has a matter of grave importance to discuss with you."

Atlas closed his eyes and pinched the bridge of his nose, his jubilant mood extinguished. "I suppose there is no sense in delaying. I might as well get this disagreeable task over with." He braced himself for the unpleasantness he was sure to encounter and then stepped past Jamie and into his apartment's front hall.

"Shall I go and get some refreshment?" Jamie asked.

"I would rather poke my own eyes out than offer Vessey any sort of hospitality. So unless you want to be permanently relieved of your duties as my valet and sent away without a letter of reference—"

"No, sir," Jamie interjected. "No refreshment it is."

Satisfied that he and the boy understood each other, Atlas strode into his sitting room to find the marquess standing by the window, near his half-finished puzzle. "What do you want?" he asked without any sort of preamble.

Vessey looked toward him, the light from the window emphasizing the deep lines and grooves in the older man's face. His lip curled. "Still as coarse as always, I see." Vessey wore his contempt for Atlas like an overcoat. "No one is ever likely to forget just how new the Catesby title is."

Atlas was in no mood to spar with the man who had killed his sister. "Why are you here?"

"I have come to confess."

"About what?"

"To the murder of Wendela Pike."

"I beg your pardon?"

"You heard me." Vessey lifted his chin and stared imperiously at Atlas. "I killed Wendy."

The words were slow to sink in. It didn't make any sense. The man had an alibi. "Is that so?" Atlas finally responded. "How exactly did you manage that when witnesses put you at a gentleman's club on St. James at the same time Mrs. Pike was killed in Covent Garden?"

"I walked. It took less than twenty minutes to reach Covent Garden. I shot Wendy in a fit of jealousy."

"What you were jealous about?"

"She was fucking that theater manager."

"So I have heard."

"She was a harlot. She dishonored me."

"I see."

Vessey regarded him quizzically. "Why are you reacting in this manner?"

"What manner is that?"

"As if you do not believe me."

"Because I don't believe you are being truthful." Atlas's scalp prickled when he considered why Vessey might lie. Or for whom.

"Why ever not?" The marquess's words were angry and impatient. "Is this not what you have always wanted? To see me brought low? Think of the scandal. All of the lurid details will be in the rag sheets."

"I would certainly enjoy that." For a moment Atlas briefly considered pretending to believe Vessey because the alternative—that the marquess might be covering for Nicholas—seemed too awful to contemplate.

The marquess remained silent for a moment, appearing at a loss for words. "This is certainly not the reaction I expected from you," he finally said.

"I am not sorry to disappoint you."

Vessey drew himself up. "Well, what you think is of no account, really. I am ready to be judged by a jury of the peers."

"Other lords such as yourself."

"Naturally. A marquess cannot be expected to face charges at Old Bailey."

"No, indeed. True justice is solely for the lowly masses."

Vessey hesitated, casting a look about the chamber. "Now that you know who killed Wendy, your investigation is at an end."

"Is it?"

"Of course," he snapped.

"When will you confess your crime in the House of Lords?"

"I must travel to the finishing academy where my young daughters are currently enrolled and explain the situation to them.

"What will you tell them? That you killed their mama because she finally came to her senses? Will you also tell them how eager she was to rid herself of the lecherous old man who corrupted her when she was about the same age as they are now?"

Anger flashed in Vessey's cold eyes. "Why do you even care what happened to Wendy? She was my mistress and slept in my bed while I was wed to Phoebe."

"That is your disgrace, not hers."

"Do not be ridiculous. Most peers keep a ladybird. Wendy was nothing to you. Why search for her killer?"

"Because if I do not, who will? I am the only person left to stand up for Wendy. Her son appears to have cared for her, but we both comprehend that Francis will always heel to you as his father."

"I am willing to pay for what I have done. The guilt has consumed me."

"Has it now?"

"Yes, it has," Vessey retorted. He reached for his hat, which sat atop Atlas's unfinished puzzle. "Why else would I confess?"

"Why else indeed? The possibilities are quite interesting." And potentially devastating.

"Go to the devil!" Vessey stormed out of the room. The front door slammed shut. Jamie ventured in, looking back over his shoulder. "He is gone."

Atlas's legs felt weak beneath him. "I gathered as much when I heard the door slam."

Jamie's forehead wrinkled. "I am confused."

"About?" Atlas shuffled over to sink into his chair before his legs gave out.

"You detest the marquess. He just confessed to murder, but you do not seem pleased."

"Because I do not believe him." Even though he very much wanted to.

Jamie gaped at his employer. "Why ever not? Only a bed-lamite would confess to a terrible crime he did not commit."

"A bedlamite"—the image of Vessey sobbing over Wendy's lifeless body on the tavern table flashed in his mind—"or a man so keen to hide the truth that he would do anything to protect his secret, including confessing to the murder of the woman he loved."

★   ★   ★

The following morning, with Vessey's confession still fresh in his mind, and consumed by Nicholas's possible involvement in

Wendy's death, Atlas went to Bow Street. He found Ambrose Endicott hurrying down the dimly lit corridor.

"I am about to meet with the other runners about a new case," the runner informed Atlas the moment he spotted him. "Perhaps we can speak later."

"I was wondering whether you could answer one question."

Endicott paused. "I suppose you want to know how Jasper Balfour died."

"Do you have the autopsy results?"

Endicott nodded, the ample folds of skin at his neck rippling as he did so. "The young man died of a massive dose of laudanum, which was likely administered all at once. Death was almost instantaneous."

"So it was murder."

Endicott shrugged. "We cannot say for certain, but there is no evidence to suggest that young Balfour was an opium eater." He stepped around Atlas to continue on his way. "Now, if you will excuse me."

"What of Samuel Brown, the clergyman?" Atlas asked. "Is he still locked up?"

"I believe that is more than one question." Endicott strode away, calling over his shoulder. "But the answer to your *third* question is yes, the clergyman is still here. He shot Simon Cooke and remains a suspect in Mrs. Pike's murder."

"My thanks," Atlas called after him.

Just as Endicott was about to round the corner and disappear out of Atlas's sight, the runner halted and reversed course, coming back to meet Atlas. "I almost forgot. There is another matter that will likely be of interest to you."

Atlas met the runner halfway. "What is it?"

"It concerns the theater manager that Brown shot."

"Simon Cooke? What of him?"

"Mr. Cooke has miraculously paid off all of the debt he incurred while rebuilding his theater after the fire."

Atlas blinked. "All of it?" Cooke had been very deep in debt. "How?"

"Do not know how, but I do know when. Cooke paid off everything he owed just a couple of days ago." The runner gave Atlas a knowing look. "Interesting development, is it not?"

Atlas nodded. "Very interesting indeed."

★   ★   ★

After leaving Bow Street, Atlas walked over to the Covent Garden theater to ask Simon Cooke how he'd suddenly managed to pay off his enormous debts.

This early in the day, the Covent Garden market was bustling, its ramshackle stalls packed with fruits, vegetables, and flowers brought in from the country. The air was thick with the stench of animal waste and unwashed bodies. Atlas did his best to skirt the edges of the market, sidestepping the donkeys and carts crowding the narrow passageways.

When he reached the theater, workers cleaning the pit directed Atlas to Cooke's office. He walked backstage, passing Juliet's dressing room. What he glimpsed as he went by prompted him to halt and double back, retracing his steps.

Juliet was nowhere to be seen, but her dressing room wasn't exactly empty. Several crates filled with costumes and clothing crowded the floor. The paintings that had adorned the threadbare walls were gone, leaving pale ghostly imprints where they'd once hung.

Where was Juliet? When he turned to leave to go and find her, he almost collided with her as she rushed in.

"Have a care." He placed both of his hands on her shoulders to steady her. "What is going on here?"

"Is it not obvious?" Juliet's tone was relaxed, but her cornflower-blue eyes were wary. "I have decided to retire from the stage."

He removed his hands from her shoulders. "This is sudden."

"It is a wonder I have managed to keep my position for this long." She moved sideways, maneuvering between Atlas and a crate. "Even you will agree that I am a bit long in the tooth to continue on stage."

He scoffed. Juliet was nearing her mid-thirties, but both her beauty and talent remained undimmed. "You are as beautiful as ever, and well you know it."

She paused long enough to flash him a grateful smile, but it was strained at the edges. "There is always someone younger and more beautiful."

"But not more talented. There is no one in London whose voice equals yours."

She dropped some items into an open crate. "Better that I should leave while people will still pay to see me sing. This will be my last week of performances."

"How can you afford to retire?" Even as he asked the question, he knew the answer. "Someone has paid you handsomely to abandon the stage. And if I hazard a guess, you will also be leaving town, will you not?"

She avoided his gaze. "Yes, some fresh air away from the metropolis will serve me well."

"I suppose that is part of the agreement. That you disappear."

"You really must excuse me." She kept her focus on her packing. "I am quite busy."

"Who paid you to leave London?"

"If you are wise, you will do the same." Her voice, usually so strong and confident, trembled. "I beg of you, stop your inquiry and quit town before anything happens to you."

A chill prickled the back of his neck. "So this is to do with Wendy's murder."

"Just leave town posthaste." She was practically pleading now. "Go to the country with your brother and his horses."

"You know I cannot allow a murderer to go free."

She shook her head, frustrated and upset. "You are so damned obstinate."

"It is obvious that you are frightened. Tell me the truth, Juliet," he gently urged. "We are old friends. I promise I will protect you."

She huffed a skeptical laugh. "We both know that is not true. There is no protection for women like Wendy and me. We are disposable."

"Leave her be," an angry male voice warned from behind Atlas.

He turned to find the theater manager scowling at him. "Mr. Cooke—just the man I was coming to see."

"Juliet does not know anything about Wendy's death, and neither do I." Cooke gestured toward the exit with a sweep of his hand. "Now please leave us. We have a show to prepare for."

"Do you?" Atlas asked. "I marvel that you are still working."

"What does that mean?"

"Only that there is no need to work so hard now that you have miraculously paid off all of the debt you incurred rebuilding this theater."

Cooke's face stiffened. "I cannot imagine where you might have heard such a thing."

"I thought you would be the last man on earth to allow your wife's killer to escape punishment." Contempt soaked Atlas's words. "But I suppose every man has his price. It appears that paying off the theater debts was yours."

"Atlas, stop," Juliet interjected. "You have no idea what Simon has been through."

Ignoring her, Atlas kept his focus on Cooke. "You are not an honorable man in any sense of the word. Any person who would take money in exchange for justice for his wife is no man at all."

Cooke flushed a deep florid red and stepped toward Atlas with his fists clenched, his entire body trembling. "I would advise you to leave while you still can."

Atlas planted his feet. "If only you had directed all of this considerable anger at your wife's killer."

"Stop this at once!" Juliet leapt between them just as Cooke lunged for Atlas. She practically hugged the theater manager to keep the two men apart. "Do not allow him to provoke you," she implored Cooke. "You know in your heart that you have done what is right."

"Have I?" Cooke stared down at her, his face a mask of misery. "Or am I trying to convince myself that it is so? I am not certain I can live with myself."

"Done what is right?" Incredulous anger flushed Atlas's body as he repeated Juliet's words. "Do you honestly believe Wendy would think what you have done is right?

All of the vigor seemed to drain from Cooke. His shoulders slumped as if the burden of pulling them upright was too much for him. His voice, when he finally spoke again, was anguished. "Yes. I do believe I am doing what Wendy would have wanted. She'd have hated for her children's names to be touched by scandal."

★ ★ ★

Setting out for home, Atlas grew contemplative, and when he reached his apartments, he settled in with coffee and his puzzle, which was nearing completion.

As he worked, he wondered how his judgment of Simon Cooke could have been so flawed. He'd believed the man cared deeply for Wendy. Did the theater owner truly believe Wendy would prefer to spare her children from further scandal rather than see her killer brought to justice?

Charlton's voice interrupted Atlas's thoughts. "Working on one of those damnable puzzles again?"

Atlas came to his feet, regarding his friend with delight. "This is a welcome surprise." Charlton had lost weight. His face was far narrower than it had been just a few weeks ago. "I did not realize you were out and about."

"This is my first outing since that most unfortunate incident at Lord Balfour's residence."

"Are you feeling much improved?"

"My side is still tender, but if I stay abed any longer, I shall expire of boredom."

"Did you see Olivia in the tobacco shop before you came up? She has asked after you practically every day. She's been terribly worried."

"Yes." Charlton hesitated. "I did speak with Mrs. Disher before I came up."

"She must have been most relieved to see you in the flesh."

"Not exactly." Charlton grimaced. "I have ended things with Mrs. Disher."

"Have you?" Charlton had been seeing Atlas's landlady exclusively for several months.

The earl nodded. "There is only one lady who holds my heart."

"My sister is wed."

"Try telling that to my heart, which, as it turns out, is not nearly as fickle as I would have thought." Charlton propped his hands on his hips and twisted, as if to stretch out his back, and immediately winced, freezing in place. "Ouch."

"Are you certain you are well enough to be going about the town?"

Charlton came over to study Atlas's puzzle. "I am still frightfully weak. It was all I could do to keep from collapsing when I hauled myself up the stairs to your apartments."

"Perhaps it is too early to tax your body in this way. You must give it time to heal."

Charlton's attention remained on the almost-completed puzzle. "Good lord, as if trying to put these tiny pieces together is not enough to drive a man to bedlam. Must you also use the most depressing painting in the metropolis?"

"It is a recreation of a *Danse Macabre*."

"*Dance of Death?*" Charlton translated. "How cheery."

"It is a sort of art that speaks to the universality of death."

"As if any of us needs to be reminded of that." He gave a dramatic shiver. "Speaking of death, have you discovered who killed the fair Mrs. Pike?"

"Vessey has confessed to the crime."

"I beg your pardon?" Shock stamped Charlton's face. "Did you just say that the Marquess of Vessey has confessed to killing Wendela Pike?"

Atlas indicated their usual chairs. "Let us sit and I will catch you up."

After listening attentively to the details of Vessey's confession, Charlton exhaled a long breath. "You do not believe he did it."

"No, I do not."

"Why not?"

"It is too neat. Why come here specifically to confess to me?"

Charlton studied his friend's serious expression. "I gather you have a theory."

"I do." He resolved to put all emotion and personal feelings aside. "But I don't want to speak out of turn before I know for certain. There is one piece of this that does not add up."

"Which piece is that?"

"Who killed Jasper Balfour? There was only one way in and one way out of the gallery where he died. No one went in or out, yet somehow Jasper consumed enough laudanum to kill him."

Charlton contemplated Atlas's words. "Maybe he did himself in. Maybe the shame and guilt of keeping the killer's secret was too much for him."

"That does not explain who shot you and why."

"You still believe someone shot me as a diversionary tactic."

Atlas nodded. "If I can solve that part of the puzzle, we will have our killer." He paused. "When you were out in the Balfour garden smoking your cheroot, did you happen to see Francis Pike in the garden? He claims he was there when Jasper was killed."

Charlton shook his head. "No, I did not see anyone."

Atlas thought about the events surrounding Jasper's death. What was the connection with Wendy's death? It came to him like the final piece of a complicated puzzle finally pressing into place, allowing Atlas to get a clear look at the entire picture. One that led him straight to the killer.

Now all he had to do was prove that he was right. No matter who might be hurt, the truth had to be told. Atlas would not allow his own desires to get in the way of justice.

He abruptly stood. "I must go."

Charlton looked up with surprise. "Where?"

"Covent Garden. I need to speak with Juliet."

Chapter 28

Atlas entered Juliet Jennings's bare dressing room to find her seated at the dressing table, a few cosmetics lined up on its scarred surface. Simon Cooke was sprawled on the tattered red velvet settee.

"Atlas." Her wary gaze met his in the mirror. "What brings you here?"

"I thought you would both be interested to know that the Marquess of Vessey has confessed to the murder of Wendela Pike."

For an instant, before the performer in her could mask her true reaction, Atlas registered Juliet's genuine shock. She quickly arranged her features into a placid expression. "I see."

He watched as she exchanged an unreadable look with Cooke, who remained expressionless.

"Is Vessey the man who paid both of you to remain quiet?" Atlas asked.

"Yes," Cooke said.

The theater manager was a far better liar than Juliet so Atlas kept his eyes trained on the opera singer as he asked the next question. "I gather that means both of you saw the marquess here backstage on the evening Wendy was slain."

He saw Juliet's throat convulse slightly as she swallowed. "Yes."

"Any more questions?" Impatience tinged Cooke's words. "Juliet does have a performance to prepare for."

"Just one last question that I doubt you will answer," Atlas said. "Why are you both lying?" He spun on his heels and left them before they could provide an answer, not that he expected one.

Juliet's voice called out after him. "Atlas, wait!"

He rounded on her. "Wait for what? More subterfuge and lies? You have been lying to me since the beginning."

She hurried to him, her open dressing gown fluttering behind her. "I beg of you to let this be. You could be in danger if you insist upon pursuing this line of inquiry."

"You know I cannot." He saw she was very afraid. He bent to kiss her forehead. "Be well, Juliet. I hope he deserves you."

"Who?"

"Cooke. You must love him very much. You and Wendy fought over him. I cannot imagine you behaving in that manner if you did not care for the man."

"Our disagreement seems so long ago." Her smile was wistful. "It was well before I realized what those two meant to each other."

"I have noted the way you have cared for and protected Cooke since Wendy died. And now he is alone again."

Hope glimmered in Juliet's jewel-toned eyes. "We shall see what the future brings."

★ ★ ★

The following morning, Atlas was at his game table, putting the final stray pieces into the puzzle.

Jamie had gone out to pick up their coffee, leaving Atlas totally engrossed in his task. With just over a dozen pieces left, these were the moments when everything came together.

By this time, he knew the puzzle and its various colors so thoroughly that it practically finished itself. Atlas methodically picked up each remaining piece and pressed it into place, his adrenaline running high. The satisfaction of taking hundreds of tiny pieces that made no sense at all and forging them into a breathtaking image with a thousand little details exhilarated him.

He heard the front door open and close before Jamie appeared bearing coffee, a basket, and a large grin. "It seems that Lady Lilliana has sent over breakfast."

Atlas's mouth watered. "That was very kind of her."

Jamie held out a note. "And this was set atop the basket."

Atlas read the missive and then sighed as he set the note down.

Jamie froze while sipping his own coffee. "Is it bad news from Lady Lilliana?"

"No." Atlas tilted a look at Jamie. "Why would you think that?"

Jamie flushed. "For no particular reason."

"What kind of bad news would you expect me to receive from the lady?"

"I do not know." The boy looked everywhere but at Atlas. "How would I know?"

"Exactly. How would you know? But clearly you think you know something. And what is that?"

"There are certain rumors," Jamie mumbled as he examined his coffee far more closely than was necessary.

"What sorts of rumors?"

"About you and Lady Lilliana." The words burst out of Jamie as if he could not bear to keep the secret inside his lanky form for even a moment longer. "That you intend to wed her."

"That development just occurred!" Atlas exclaimed. He hadn't even spoken to the duke yet. "How could you already be aware of it?"

"It *is* true then?" Jamie's eyes widened. "When will you wed? Will I still be your valet?"

Atlas held up a staying hand to stem the onslaught of questions. "It is far too early in the morning for me to even begin to contemplate the answers to any of those questions."

"But I will remain your valet, will I not?"

"Yes." He had grown accustomed to having the boy around. "You shall still be my valet."

"Where will we live?"

"I have no idea."

Atlas had not even begun to consider where his new family might take up residence. He would need to take a house spacious enough to accommodate Lilliana and the boys. Of course, any property he purchased would be nowhere near as grand as Somerville's palatial townhome on the edge of Hyde Park in fashionable Mayfair.

The tidy sum he'd inherited from a favored bachelor uncle would allow him to purchase a perfectly adequate home for his new family. And his limited annual income, primarily derived from a piece of property bequeathed to him by his father, would allow them to live comfortably enough.

He gazed up at Jamie. "Where did you hear that I had offered for Lady Lilliana?"

Jamie shrugged. "The servants in great houses know everything."

"As I am beginning to learn. I suppose I shall have to speak with Somerville posthaste."

Jamie's eyes went as wide as dinner plates. "His Grace is not aware that you plan to wed his sister?"

"Not as of yet. We had hoped to keep our betrothal quiet until after we find out who killed Mrs. Pike. But I suppose that shall not be possible now."

Atlas reached for the note Jamie had brought in and scanned its contents again. "This is from Lord Balfour. He asks that I call on him at my earliest convenience."

It was a meeting he dreaded. Lord Balfour would no doubt still be grief-stricken. Atlas had not seen Jasper's father since the evening the man had wept over his youngest son's lifeless body.

"Will you go?" Jamie asked.

"Of course. He was a particular friend of my father's, and perhaps he can shed some light on who would have wanted to kill his son." Atlas reached into the basket Jamie had set on the table. "But first, let us see what my future wife has sent for breakfast."

An insistent knock rattled the front door. Jamie went to see who it was and returned with a very ebullient Thea.

"Good morning," she chirped.

Rising to greet his sister, Atlas eyed her with suspicion. "Why are you looking so pleased with yourself?" His pragmatic sister was hardly the merry type. "Have you discovered a heretofore unknown branch of mathematics that will change the world?"

"No," she said cheerily, "but I do understand that *your* world is about to change."

"Good lord. Not you too? Was it in the broadsheets?"

"Not exactly, but secrets do not stay secret for long in Mayfair." She looked earnestly into her brother's eyes. "Do tell me the truth. Are you content?"

"Yes." A joyous feeling bubbled up in his chest. "I can honestly say that I have never been happier."

"At last!" Thea's answering smile was possibly wider than he'd ever seen. But before he had time to contemplate her emotive reaction, his sister behaved even more alarmingly by throwing herself into his arms and embracing him tightly.

Returning her hug, Atlas closed his arms around his sister and lifted her off the ground. By the time he returned Thea to her feet, they were both laughing.

★ ★ ★

Given that everyone seemed to have heard about his betrothal to Lilliana, Atlas judged it prudent to call upon Somerville before continuing on to Lord Balfour's residence.

Since the weather was fine, the duke received him in his expansive gardens. He was seated at a cloth-covered table set with expensive crystal and fine china, the luncheon foods laid out as elegantly as Atlas imagined one would find in the Prince Regent's dining room at Carlton House.

"I hear congratulations are in order."

"Yes. Lilliana and I had hoped to inform you ourselves."

"That certainly would have been nice. My tailor mentioned having heard rumors of a match between you and my sister."

"I realize it might have come as a surprise."

"Not at all," the duke returned. "However, you did take a bit longer than I anticipated to at last come up to scratch."

"But you approve?"

"Would it stop you from going forward if I did not?"

"No," Atlas answered truthfully.

"As I expected." A small smile curved the duke's lips. "I want my sister to be happy. I will naturally settle a very generous amount on her on the day of her marriage."

Atlas sat up straighter. "I am not a wealthy man, as you well know, but I can provide for my future wife and her children."

"I am not offering charity." Somerville had no patience for Atlas's protestations. "I intend to settle the same amount on Lilliana as I would have had she wed Roxbury or Northampton. I still have the marriage settlement agreements that were drawn up when it seemed certain Roxbury and Roslyn would wed. You are welcome to have a look at them."

"That will not be necessary." The last thing Atlas cared to see was an agreement that evidenced how close he'd come to losing Lilliana.

"Very well. I certainly shall not allow Lilliana to take less than she deserves. It would be a stain on my reputation if I did not settle a generous amount on her."

Atlas saw no point in arguing. He considered the money to be Lilliana's to spend as she desired. "As you wish then."

"I have also set up trusts to see to the boys' every need."

"You needn't bother. I intend to look after the boys."

The duke exhaled. "As charming as your stubborn pride can be, it is also a bit tiresome."

"Be that as it may, Peter and Robin are orphans, and I intend to raise them as my own sons."

"A commendable sentiment. However, Peter and Robin are my own flesh and blood. Also, I intend to petition to have Peter recognized as my legal heir, and as such I shall have a special and unique responsibility to him."

"You want the boy to assume your title?"

"Yes. As you are well aware, it is unlikely that I will ever marry."

"You could change your mind."

"I doubt that will happen."

"Is it even possible to have Peter declared your heir?"

"All things are possible. I have petitioned for a special remainder to make it so."

"A special remainder?"

"A royal provision that allows for a title to pass in a direction that deviates from the norm. The Crown has considerable latitude to act as it wishes in matters such as these. There are precedents. I am optimistic the Crown will confer a special remainder in favor of Peter."

Atlas exhaled. The thought of raising anyone's child as his own was daunting enough, but the idea that he might have a hand in nurturing the future Duke of Somerville was dizzying. He could only hope he wouldn't make a complete hash of things. "Is Lilliana aware of your intentions?"

"We have discussed the matter but shall not speak of it to Peter until I have succeeded in securing the boy as my heir."

"I see."

"And then there is the matter of my wedding gift to my sister."

Atlas steeled himself. He would not be surprised if Somerville intended to give Lilliana the crown jewels. "Your gifts to your sister are none of my affair."

"I am pleased you feel that way. I will be giving her the use of one of my London homes for her lifetime."

"You intend to give her a house?"

"Indeed."

"I am not taking a home from you."

"Do calm that prideful outrage of yours. It is only a loan. Mallon Place is part of the entail. Consequently, strictly speaking, Mallon Place would not be yours any more than this pile belongs to me. The ducal estate pays for the upkeep of all of my properties. Like Somerville House, Mallon Place shall pass to the next duke upon my death."

Atlas did not care to spend his life living off Somerville's largesse. He had no intention of being eternally indebted to his brother-in-law. "I plan to purchase a permanent home for my new family."

Somerville came to his feet, signaling their meeting had come to an end. "How quaint. Perhaps you should discuss matters with Roslyn."

Atlas stood, his head swimming. So many changes were ahead. "You can be sure that I intend to do just that." He bowed. "Good day."

CHAPTER 29

"Mr. Catesby, thank you for coming." Lord Balfour rose from his seat by the fireplace when Atlas entered his study.

The older man was neatly dressed, with a black band adorning one upper arm. His eyes were bleary and his cheeks flushed. Atlas shook Lord Balfour's proffered hand, a gesture normally reserved for closest male acquaintances.

"You will forgive an old man for his forwardness," Balfour said as they clasped hands. "It is just that whenever I lay my eyes upon you, I see such a strong resemblance to your father."

"Allow me to express my deepest condolences for your loss," Atlas said. "If there is any way that I can be of assistance, you have only to name it."

"Sit, sit." Balfour indicated the chair opposite his by the lit hearth. "There is actually something you can do for me."

"It would be my pleasure."

"I want you to find out who killed my Jasper."

The request was not what Atlas had expected. "You are convinced he was murdered?"

"The coroner found that Jasper died of a massive dose of laudanum. I know my son did not knowingly take laudanum."

"How can you be certain? It is not unusual for children to shield their vices from their parents."

"Because Jasper abhorred the stuff. He had a negative experience with laudanum as a boy after our doctor administered it. Jasper absolutely refused to touch it after that."

Balfour's revelations seemed to confirm Atlas's suspicions that Jasper had indeed been murdered. "I will do whatever I can to help."

"Silas did always say you were the most clever of his sons. I know, of course, that you have already undertaken to look into Mrs. Pike's death. I only hope you are not too busy to assist me in this matter."

"Not at all," Atlas answered truthfully. "It is possible the two deaths are related."

Balfour frowned. "But my son had no real connection to Mrs. Pike."

"I believe your son might have witnessed her killing."

Lord Balfour's mouth fell open. "Is that why you asked to speak with Jasper on the night of his death?"

Atlas nodded. "Yes, I believe he was about to reveal the killer when Charlton was shot."

"The earl's shooting was a distraction?"

"It appears so," Atlas said in his gentlest voice.

Balfour's eyes grew glassy. "My poor boy."

"I give you my word that I will do all I can to find Jasper's killer," Atlas reassured him. "Which means that there are questions I must ask you."

Balfour recovered himself. "Of course. Whatever you need."

"I am not certain that you are aware of this, but Jasper had tremendous debts that he was able to settle shortly after Mrs. Pike died. Did you give him the funds to pay his debts?"

"No, I did not." The lines in Balfour's forehead deepened. "Are you certain he was in debt? Several months ago I did settle Jasper's debts, but I threatened to cast him aside should he incur any future gaming debts. My son gave me his word as a gentleman that it would not happen again. Are you most certain that Jasper was in debt again?" The question was practically a plea.

As a rule, Atlas did not care for mendacity, but there were times when telling a lie was an act of kindness. Especially since Jasper was in no position to rehabilitate his image. "No, I cannot be certain." Atlas stood up, hoping to put a stop to this line of questions.

"Miller will show you out." Balfour remained seated. The older man seemed to sink deeper into his chair, exhausted, drained of whatever energy he'd managed to muster ahead of Atlas's visit.

"I will keep you informed if I learn anything more."

The butler materialized to see Atlas out, leading him down the corridor, past the gallery where Jasper had died. As they passed, the tall windows lined up against the long wall opposite the doorway caught Atlas's eye. Something was out of place. He stopped short and stared into the room, at the open windows that allowed the bracing briskness of the rare sunny day to permeate the long chamber. It took the butler a moment to realize his master's visitor was no longer following.

"Sir?" Miller halted, his voice courteous yet firm. "This way if you please." Ignoring the summons, Atlas walked into the gallery.

The butler followed. "Is something amiss, Mr. Catesby?"

Atlas strode over to one of the windows. "Where did these come from?"

Miller followed Atlas's gaze. "Are you inquiring about the windows, sir?"

"Yes, these were not here the evening Jasper Balfour died."

The butler smiled just a little. "The mirrored shutters are a source of fascination for many of Lord Balfour's visitors."

"Mirrored shutters?"

"If I may?" The butler stepped past Atlas and drew the shutters closed, sliding them like pocket doors. "This is likely what you saw on that unfortunate evening. We always close the shutters in the evening."

Atlas stared at himself in the mirrored shutters. One couldn't tell there was a window behind the gilt-framed mirrors. With the shutters closed, the room appeared windowless, almost the entire wall covered in mirrors. He stepped in front of another window and studied the tiny alcove between the closed shutter and the window leading to the outside. It was a place where a grown man could easily hide.

He turned to the butler. "I should like to see the gardens now."

The butler accompanied Atlas to the garden, a well-manicured space with an abundance of foliage. But what drew Atlas's interest were the tall, mature horsechestnut trees lined up like soldiers against the back of the house.

"Where is the gallery?" he asked Miller. "Which window is it?"

The butler raised his arm, pointing upward. "Those four, sir, in the middle." Only one of the trees stood directly by a gallery window. Atlas crossed over to it, his boots crunching on the carpet of maroon and gold fall leaves.

He ran a hand over the dark, rugged bark. The architecture of the trunk was unusual. Its double trunk looked like it had split in half after being struck by lighting. Each gnarled half rose up, providing solid anchor to the soaring tree. Atlas peered up at the myriad of thick graceful branches. Sparkles of daylight glimmered through vibrant yellow hand-shaped leaves and clusters of seedpods that were still waiting to fall so close to winter.

"It is perfect." Atlas shed his jacket and tossed it at the butler. "It is the final piece to the puzzle."

"I beg your pardon, sir?" A clearly startled Miller almost dropped the jacket.

Atlas grabbed a hold of the nearest branch and hoisted himself up, gaining a foothold where the trunk had split. Reaching for a sturdy branch above him, he heaved his body up until his belly rested on the branch and he could swing a long leg over to straddle it.

"Sir." Miller's words were ones of controlled alarm. "Sir, what are you doing? Surely, you would prefer to be down here on the ground where it is safe."

Already hoisting himself up to the next highest branch, Atlas barely heard the butler down below. Nor did he take much note of the long, loud tearing sound that followed, the rending of the fabric at the seat of his trousers. His focus remained on the gallery window and how close he was to it. When he finally reached the window, he gripped a strong branch overhead while reaching out to easily touch the frame of the open window.

He could almost walk into it. Instead, he leapt and landed inside the little alcove between the open window and the closed mirrored shutters leading to the gallery. It was an excellent space within which a man could conceal himself. Atlas reached for the shutters and slid them open to find himself staring into the opulent gallery where Jasper Balfour had died.

At that moment he knew without a doubt who had killed Wendela Pike. The same person had poisoned Jasper Balfour in this very chamber so that the young man would not live long enough to tell what he knew.

CHAPTER 30

The large hole in the seat of his trousers prevented Atlas from going directly to confront the killer, so after retrieving his tailcoat from Miller, he hailed a hackney and rushed back to his Bond Street apartments to change.

He dashed up the stairs, taking them two at a time, his blood pumping. Although he now knew who killed Wendy and Jasper, a missing piece of the puzzle still remained.

Atlas could not determine a motive. Why had the murderer wanted Wendy dead? The door to Atlas's apartments opened as soon as he reached the landing.

Jamie stepped out and pulled the door quietly closed behind him. "You have a visitor, sir."

"Who is it?" Atlas tried to maneuver past the boy, but Jamie mirrored the movement, preventing Atlas from going in.

Jamie pursed his lips as though he'd eaten something sour. "It is that opera singer. She says you are very well acquainted."

"Juliet is here?"

Jamie flushed, his expression indignant. "Yes, that is correct. Mrs. Jennings, an *opera singer*, is calling *here*, at the bachelor apartments of a *betrothed* man."

Atlas had no patience for Jamie's tantrums, particularly not when he was so close to confronting the person who had killed Wendela Pike and Jasper Balfour. "Juliet is part of the investigation. Move out of my way."

The warning tone in Atlas's voice caused Jamie to promptly step aside. Atlas pushed the door and entered his apartments.

Jamie followed, whispering furiously. "Do you think Lady Lilliana would approve?"

"Probably not."

Leaving his indignant valet behind in the front hall, Atlas found Juliet, wearing a long dark cape and hood, pacing the threadbare carpet in his sitting room. "Juliet?"

She hurried to him. "I have come to say goodbye."

"Are you truly leaving London? Did Vessey pay you that well?"

She winced. "He is a peer. I cannot fight him."

"What about Simon Cooke? I thought you had hopes in that direction."

"Perhaps I can return in a few months, once this is all over."

"Why are you really here, Juliet?" he probed gently. "I do not think it is solely to take your leave of me."

She drew a deep, wavering breath. "There is something I must tell you."

"Will you sit for a moment? It might calm your nerves."

She shook her head. "Being away from Town will settle my nerves. Vessey is aware that I know the truth. It is only a matter of time before he decides he is not safe so long as I am alive."

"What is it that you know, Juliet?"

"I did not see Vessey at the theater the evening Wendy died."

"I suspected as much. Tell me everything."

She told him.

And by the time Juliet took her leave a few minutes later, under Jamie's very disapproving gaze, Atlas had the final piece to the puzzle. He knew exactly who had killed Wendela Pike and, importantly, he now understood why.

★ ★ ★

Atlas went by Bow Street to have a word with Ambrose Endicott before turning up at the opulent home off Cavendish Square.

"Is his lordship expecting you?" the butler inquired.

"No." Atlas placed his card on the silver salver presented by the butler. "However, if you inform his lordship that Atlas Catesby is here to tell him who killed Mrs. Pike, I believe he'll see me."

The butler's eyes widened before he quickly cleared his face of all expression. "Very good, sir. If you will please wait here while I see if his lordship is at home to visitors."

Atlas waited, surrounded by painted scenes of various gods adorning the walls and frolicking high above on ornamented ceilings. A double-width staircase, its marble stairs covered in red carpet, bisected the front hall. It had been many years since he'd visited this house.

Atlas tapped the tip of his boot against white and black marble floors. The design pattern resembled a chessboard, which was rather apt because, after all these years, Atlas was finally ready to make his move.

A motion at the top of the staircase drew his attention. Francis Pike came down toward him.

"Mr. Catesby," he said pleasantly. "This is a surprise."

"Good afternoon, Francis. This is a fortunate coincidence. I was hoping to speak with you as well as with your father."

"What about?"

Atlas ignored the question. "I called at the Albany before coming here. The porter said you were away from home for a few days. I trust you are not still feeling unwell."

Francis reached out to shake Atlas's hand. "I am much improved Having a full staff to see to my comforts can have that affect."

"I can imagine." Francis's handshake was somewhat stiff and limited.

The butler returned. "Lord Vessey will see you now, Mr. Catesby.

Atlas turned to Francis. "Will you not join us? I am certain you will find what I have to say to be of great interest."

"Certainly." Francis came over to him. "It would be my pleasure."

"Uncle Atlas?" Phoebe's son entered through the front door. He wore riding clothes and smelled of exertion and the outdoors. "What are you doing here?"

The muscles in Atlas's shoulders tensed. "I have come to speak with your father and Francis."

Curiosity lit the boy's eyes. "I will join you as well, shall I?"

"Perhaps we can speak later. For now, it is best if I speak with your father and Francis alone."

Nicholas's smile was strained. "Of course. As you like."

"I shall take him in," Francis addressed the butler. And then to Atlas, "If you will follow me, Mr. Catesby?"

Vessey received him in a formal salon where crimson velvet draped both the walls and furniture. Atlas had never seen the room before. But he'd been only a boy the last time he'd visited this place, and this chamber seemed reserved for formal occasions.

"Father," Francis said as Atlas followed him in, "I've brought Mr. Catesby in."

Vessey, who stood before the lit fireplace with his arms crossed over his chest, looked right past his son to address Atlas. "What is this nonsense about knowing who killed Mrs. Pike? I have already confessed. I visited my daughters just today to tell them as much."

"I could have saved you the trip," Atlas said, "because you did not kill Mrs. Pike."

"I most certainly did. And I intend to confess to it in the House of Lords."

"Where you shall be judged by your peers. Who will most likely give you a slap on the wrist at most. They shall hardly send one of their own to the gallows for killing a woman as common as Mrs. Pike."

Francis flushed. "Now see here. Do not speak about my mother—"

"Do be silent, Francis." Vessey kept his cold stare fixed on Atlas. "I stand ready to face the judgment of my peers. After all, a peer cannot be tried in a court by people who are beneath him."

"No," Atlas acknowledged. "But a bastard can. Even if he was sired by a marquess."

Francis let out an audible sound of disbelief. "That's ridiculous. Surely you do not believe I killed my own mother."

Atlas's unwavering gaze held Francis's. "I do believe it."

Vessey laughed without amusement. "That's absurd. You are absurd."

Francis pressed the flat of one hand against his chest. "Why would I kill my own mother? I loved her."

"I believe that you did love her. That is, until you came upon her in the most intimate of situations with the manager of Covent Garden," Atlas said, revealing what Juliet had told him.

"That is an outrageous lie!" The words seemed to burst out of Francis's chest. "She was an honorable woman who was faithful to my father."

"Mrs. Pike was indeed an honorable woman," Atlas agreed. "What you saw that evening was a woman enjoying intimate marital relations with her husband."

"What the devil are you talking about?" Vessey's words were rife with anger and scorn. "You have finally gone mad, Catesby."

"Wendela Pike wed Simon Cooke a few weeks before her death." Calm certainty settled over Atlas as Vessey grew more agitated. "I saw the license and confirmed the marriage at St. Paul's where they wed. It is in the registry."

Both father and son appeared stunned by this revelation.

Atlas continued. "But Francis had no way of knowing that. All of his life he protected his mother from anyone who dared call her a whore. And he was right to do so. Wendela was not a whore. She was a young girl who was taken advantage of by a much older man. A man who took her innocence but refused to assure her future by giving her some sort of settlement."

"I took care of Wendy." Vessey strode over to the sideboard, where a drinks tray had been laid out. "She came from nothing. She was fortunate that I gave her everything."

Atlas watched Vessey pour himself a whiskey. "You gave her everything except your name and respectability. And a financial settlement that would assure her future."

"You should have given her the money, Father," Francis said shakily. "If you had, Mother would not have turned to that Covent Garden charlatan."

"Shut your mouth, Francis," Vessey warned.

Francis turned to Atlas. "You would have done the same if you had witnessed what I had the misfortune of seeing." Francis's pale complexion was mottled with patches of red, a sharp contrast against his pale-colored hair. "She was bent over the theater manager's desk with her skirts hiked up around her waist."

Vessey slammed his glass back onto the tray. "Not another word," he warned his son.

"He was swiving her like she was a common lightskirt." Francis's eyes were wild, as if he were seeing the scene all over again. "And Mother behaved like one. Crying out, urging him on. It was disgusting. Common and low."

"Hold your tongue, boy!" Vessey almost shouted.

"That is when I was forced to acknowledge the truth about myself." Bitterness twisted Francis's mouth, enhancing the sharpness of his long nose. "No matter how hard I try, no matter how flawless my manners are, or that my education was second to none. None of that mattered once I saw Mother for what she truly was and, consequently, myself for who I truly am. Which is nothing but the ill-begotten son of a whore."

"Silence!" Vessey roared. "You are the son of the Marquess of Vessey."

"I am a man without my father's name," Francis said wearily.

"Is that why you killed Jasper?" Atlas asked. "Is it because he saw your mother in that situation?"

Francis shook his head. "I did not kill Jasper. He was my friend."

"He may have been your friend," Atlas acknowledged, "but you did kill him."

"Stop talking this instant!" Vessey commanded his son. He lodged himself between Atlas and Francis, as if blocking Atlas's view of Francis would also shield the young man from the truth. Vessey glared at Atlas. "I insist that you leave."

"No, *I* will leave," Francis interjected. He started for the door in an almost dreamlike state. "My father wishes for me to go abroad."

"I am certain that he does. I expect he believes you shall escape justice by doing so." Atlas strolled over to the door, reaching it before Francis, and blocked the exit with his imposing frame. "I know you killed Jasper."

"You cannot know that," Francis said. "Only a monster would kill two people as you have said."

"You wanted Jasper to kill your mother after you saw her with Simon Cooke. When Jasper refused, you took his gun, the one he carried for protection against those to whom he was indebted, and killed her yourself."

Francis tilted his head as he considered Atlas. "Not true. And even if it were true, you could not prove it."

"Then you paid off all of Jasper's debts almost immediately afterwards to keep him quiet. And when you worried Jasper was about to reveal the truth to me, you poisoned him."

"Rubbish. I was out in the garden."

"Yes, you were in the garden," Atlas said. "But not with any lady. You told me yourself that you and Jasper used to love to climb trees."

"That hardly proves that I killed anyone."

"You lied the evening Jasper died. You told me there was no way in or out of the gallery except through the door. You neglected to mention that the mirrors were, in fact, hidden window shutters."

"Why would any of that nonsense be of interest to me or my son?" Vessey interjected.

"Because that is how Francis was in a position to kill Jasper. He made certain I was distracted by shooting the Earl of

Charlton." Fury flared in Atlas's gut at the memory of his friend lying pale and bloodied in Balfour's library. "And then he climbed the horsechestnut tree outside the gallery and accessed the gallery without anyone seeing him."

"That is an interesting story," Francis said, "but that is all that it is. Just a story and nothing more."

"The doctor who came to attend to Jasper stepped on a conker. One I believe fell from your clothes that evening," Atlas reminded him, recalling the spiny-cased seeds that horsechestnut trees shed in the autumn. "From climbing up the tree."

"Let us assume, just for a moment, that what you say is true." Francis regarded Atlas with what almost seemed like grudging admiration. "That I killed my mother when Jasper refused to do the deed for me, and that afterwards Jasper and I reached an agreement that I would consider his debt settled if he held his tongue about what he witnessed the evening my mother died. Would anyone blame me for acting as I did when I realized Jasper was about to betray me by telling you what he knew? Would anyone blame me for climbing up the tree and sneaking into the gallery under the guise of calming my friend's nerves? Would anyone blame me for offering a disloyal friend one of those infernal comfits he was always chewing on?"

"Only, in this instance, the sweet treat you gave Jasper was laced with laudanum," Atlas finished the story for him. "Enough laudanum to kill a man almost immediately."

"But of course, I did not do any of that," Francis said with a cool smile. "But if I had, who would blame me? Who would blame a man who has been pushed to his limits?"

Atlas placed a heavy hand on Francis's left shoulder and let it slide down his arm. "There are many who would not blame you." He squeezed Francis's biceps. "However, I am not one of them."

Francis let out a moan and jerked away, his right arm cradling his left.

"Your arm appears to be particularly tender," Atlas noted. "Is that because I broke it the night I caught you searching Jasper's rooms at the Albany?"

"I am sure I haven't any idea of what you speak."

"I noticed you seemed to be in awful pain when I visited you in your rooms at the Albany." Atlas leaned his back against the door and crossed his arms over his chest. "And you never moved your left arm. I have come to realize that the pain you were feeling was not emotional pain at the loss of your mother and friend, as I first assumed. It was physical pain because your arm was broken, or at least severely injured when I delivered that elbow strike to it."

"You are a smart man, Mr. Catesby," Francis smirked. "It is possible that if I showed you my arm right now, you would see that you are correct in your deductions. You might see that my arm is swollen and misshapen. Alas, none of that shall do you any good because even if my father refuses to give me the protection of his name, I do believe he will protect me from the gallows."

"Go now, Francis," Vessey urged his son. "Go and make certain your valet has readied your things for your extended trip abroad. The carriage is waiting outside for you to make a rapid departure."

The marquess's gaze shifted to Atlas, his expression cold and hard. "It is time Catesby and I settled matters once and for all. This reckoning has been in the making for more than twenty years."

"On that we agree." Atlas at last saw a way to put his sister's memory to rest after all these years. "It is well past time that we have this conversation."

★ ★ ★

"What is it that you want?" Vessey asked Atlas after Francis made his exit.

"Just the truth. And for those who have transgressed to be punished for it."

"Francis shall not hang for killing a whore." Vessey went to the sideboard and poured two drinks. "Surely you comprehend that."

"Did you know all along that Francis had killed his mother?"

"No, not at first. My first instinct was to believe Nicholas had done it in a fit of anger. He argued with Wendy shortly before she was killed and that encounter was the first thing that came to my mind when I heard she'd been shot." Vessey came over and offered Atlas a whiskey. "I discovered the truth the other evening at the opera. A Covent Garden fruit vendor saw Francis at the theater the night Wendy died. She told me as much the other evening and demanded money to buy her silence."

Atlas had to admire Mary White's cleverness. Vessey had paid her to keep quiet about Francis, so she'd told Atlas about Nicholas's argument with Wendy instead. Both men had gotten what they'd paid for. Vessey got the silence he'd bought while Atlas received separate information relevant to the investigation

Vessey continued. "After paying the orange seller to keep quiet, I went inside to pay off the actress and the theater manager. Afterwards I went to see Francis at the Albany, and that is when I realized he was injured."

Atlas took a drink. "Because I had broken his arm."

A muscle spasmed in Vessey's cheek. "Francis was in terrible pain but was afraid to see a doctor. That is when he confessed the truth to me."

"I gather that is why you decided to tell me you killed Wendy."

"I knew you had a special acquaintance with the opera singer. I did purchase her silence and that of the theater manager, but I was not convinced they would hold their tongues in the long term."

"Confessing was your way of protecting Francis."

"The House of Lords will never hang one of their own for killing a strumpet. And ultimately, that is what Wendy was."

"Your devotion to Mrs. Pike is heartwarming."

"Wendy is dead," Vessey said simply. "She is beyond saving. Francis is not. He is my son, and I love him beyond measure."

The sounds of a carriage pulling away clattered by the salon window. "You are likely correct about the Lords not hanging you. But your son is another matter."

"Not entirely." Vessey turned his gaze toward the window, and Atlas saw him relax a fraction at the thought of putting his son out of harm's way. "However ill-begotten, Francis is still my son, the son of a marquess. He shall not hang."

"Normally, I suspect that would be true. However, in this case your bastard son also killed Jasper Balfour, who happened to be the *legitimate* grandson of a viscount. He also tried to kill Charlton, an earl. I doubt the by-blow of a marquess will be allowed to escape punishment for those offenses."

Vessey blanched, but his voice remained dispassionate. "You have no proof Francis did anything at all."

"I think I have more than enough to convince both Charlton and Lord Balfour to see things my way. Both men are well regarded in society. If they press for Francis to be made an example of, I do not doubt they will prevail."

"Be that as it may, Francis is already on his way to the continent. And soon shall be far beyond the reach of English law."

"Unfortunately for Francis, that is not so. Before I called here, I stopped by Bow Street and alerted them to the situation. I suspect Francis was picked up the moment the carriage left the property."

Vessey jerked as though he'd been struck. "You whoreson." He spat the venomous words. "Your pursuit of this matter has nothing whatsoever to do with Wendy."

"It has everything to do with justice, which you escaped when you murdered my sister more than twenty years ago. But your son will not escape his fate. He murdered two people and attempted to kill a third. Francis shall be made to pay for his crimes. Balfour and Charlton will see to it."

Vessey gave a close-mouthed, tight-lipped smile. "I am a marquess, and I am not without my allies."

"Perhaps, but do not forget that Mrs. Pike was not some nameless whore. You saw to that by showcasing her considerable talents at your oratorios. Because of you, Mrs. Pike was acquainted with wealthy and powerful noblemen. And they in turn were charmed by her and appalled by her violent end. Indeed, even the Duke of Somerville has expressed an interest in finding Mrs. Pike's killer. "

"Somerville, of course." Vessey gave a bitter laugh. "I have heard that you are betrothed to his sister, Lady Roslyn."

When Atlas said nothing, Vessey continued.

"You are no different than your sister, trying to wed above yourself."

"You were never fit to touch the bottoms of Phoebe's slippers. But I think anyone, including myself, would agree that Lady Roslyn is far too good for me."

Vessey shot him a venomous look. "This is your way of punishing me for your sister's death. You intend to rob me of my son because you think I took your sister from you."

"I *know* that you did."

"All these years. All these years you have waited to get your revenge." The veins in Vessey's neck throbbed. "I suppose now you think the score between us is settled."

"Not even close. My sister was an innocent. We cannot say the same for your son. Like father, like son, I suppose you could say."

Vessey stabbed a finger at Atlas. "I regret not pushing you down the stairs after your sister when I had the opportunity."

"You should have pushed me when you had the chance." Feeling strangely calm, Atlas stared down the man who had murdered his sister. "Because for all of my life since then, I have lived for this—the moment I would see you destroyed."

CHAPTER 31

Lilliana shuddered. "I cannot believe Francis Pike killed his own mother."

"Why did the opera singer not tell you the truth about seeing Francis Pike at Convent Garden earlier?" Thea asked Atlas. "She could have spared you a great deal of trouble."

"Especially considering," Lilliana interjected with a sardonic tilt of her head, "that the two of you are so well acquainted."

She looked particularly lovely that evening in a silvery evening gown that caught the light when she moved. Her dark hair was upswept, and the double strand of long pearls adorned her pale neck. His gaze lingered for a moment on the diamond and pearl earrings dangling from her delicate earlobes.

He'd chosen them with great care. The earrings were his first gift to his future wife. Earlier that evening, he'd pulled her aside and presented them to her. She'd exclaimed over the betrothal gift and then thanked him quite enthusiastically in private before they'd joined their assembling guests.

Everyone was gathered in a sumptuous drawing room at Somerville House for the celebratory supper party to mark Atlas and Lilliana's betrothal. The gathering was modest in Somerville terms, with sixty guests in attendance, including all of

Atlas's siblings except for Apollo, who remained in the country with his horses.

"Mrs. Jennings is a distant memory that I barely recall at all," Atlas informed Lilliana. Admiration sparkled in his gaze as he raised a glass to his future wife. "I am quite ready to make new memories with my bride and my two new sons."

He waited for Lilliana to blush, which she did most becomingly. He would never tire of being one of the few people who could slip past this beautiful woman's icy composure.

"Here, here," Charlton said, and their little group followed Atlas in raising their glasses to toast the future bride.

"In answer to your question," Atlas said after they'd all drunk from their glasses, "the reason Juliet did not tell me about seeing Francis Pike backstage on the evening of his mother's murder is because she was embarrassed."

"About what?" Thea asked.

"Juliet had a *tendre* for the theater manager, which is why she was spying on Simon Cooke and Mrs. Pike when she spotted Francis. Confessing that she'd seen Francis meant revealing that she had behaved badly by watching the couple in an intimate situation."

"It is difficult to believe that a young man as amiable as Francis Pike not only killed his mother but also poisoned Jasper Balfour," Charlton said. "He is bound to hang for his crimes."

"As well he should." The color was high in Thea's face. "The man is a menace. He almost killed you as well."

Charlton pressed a hand flat against his chest. "It does my heart good to know that you care, Mrs. Palmer."

But Thea ignored him, her focus on Atlas. "Why didn't the theater owner tell the truth about seeing Francis backstage. You said you believe he truly loved Mrs. Pike. They were wed after all."

"Simon Cooke says he protected Francis because he believed it was what Mrs. Pike would want. She would not want her son to hang."

Lilliana's eyes rounded. "Even though he killed her?"

Atlas shrugged. "Who knows what Mrs. Pike would have wanted? We cannot ask her, obviously. But Simon Cooke knew her to be a devoted mother who loved her children more than anything. Vessey managed to convince Cooke that Mrs. Pike would have wanted Cooke to protect her son rather than condemn him."

Before long, they excused themselves from their friends in order to mingle among their other guests.

"Did you go and see the clergyman this afternoon?" Lilliana asked as she took Atlas's arm and they strolled away. "You mentioned you might do so."

"I did but he is no longer being held. Samuel Brown has already been transported."

"That was certainly quick."

"The man admitted to the crime of stabbing Cooke. His guilt was never in question. All that remained to be seen was the severity of his punishment."

"How long is his sentence?"

"Ten years. Brown is on his way to America, where he will serve out his sentence in hard labor."

"Why did he lie about being engaged to Mrs. Pike?"

"Who knows? Perhaps he so badly wanted it to be true that he convinced himself it was so. He was clearly obsessed with the poor woman."

They paused to exchange mindless pleasantries with guests Atlas was barely acquainted with, but he made every effort to pay attention and feign interest. He could not help but be well aware of the curious gazes that followed them.

Lilliana's prediction had been correct. Their betrothal had caused a minor sensation in the society pages—the fourth son of a baron with little property winning over the sister of a duke. As they turned away from a group of Somerville's friends, the couple came to Atlas's brothers.

Hermes bowed over Lilliana's hand. "Who would have thought my somber brother would be such a sly one?" he said. "To have landed such a prize."

"I am certainly undeserving of my good fortune," Atlas acknowledged. "I am most definitely wedding above myself."

"Did you know, Lady Roslyn," Jason, Baron Catesby, interjected, "that the Catesbys can trace their blood back to the Conquerer? You can be assured any children from your union will have the purest of blood."

"We shall see you both later." Atlas steered his future bride away from his brothers. "Much later," he added under his breath.

"What is the hurry?" Lilliana asked Atlas as he led her to the opposite side of the room. "I should have liked to become better acquainted with your brothers. I have barely spoken to them."

"I prefer that you become acquainted with my brothers after we wed," he said, "when it will be too late for you to jilt me."

Her beautiful eyes twinkled. He could barely believe she had consented to wed him. "Surely they are not that disagreeable," she protested.

"The Catesbys are rather like whiskey. We take some getting used to."

Her mouth curved into that delightfully crooked smile. "An acquired taste?"

Atlas spotted Nicholas, who bowed as they approached. "May I offer my most sincere congratulations?"

"You may," Lilliana said. "How do you fare? This must be a most difficult time for your family."

Nicholas shrugged, his expression one of uncertainty. "My half brother will likely hang. I cannot say I will miss him because I never had the chance to know him."

"Perhaps that is for the best considering that Francis is a murderer," Atlas said gently.

"My father is distraught," Nicholas added. "I am doing my best to be a comfort to him."

"Lord Vessey is fortunate to have you," Lilliana said.

Nicholas turned to Atlas. "I owe you my thanks."

That took Atlas aback. He had fretted that Nicholas would blame him for the misfortune that had befallen his family. "For what?"

"I know my father confessed to you but that you did not believe him. You deserve my thanks because you persisted and found the true killer when it would have been more expedient to blame my father."

"May I interrupt?" The duke approached, looking as immaculate as always in custom black evening wear that suited his trim form. As was customary for the duke, the question was more of a command, which Nicholas instantly obeyed. After greeting His Grace with the appropriate show of deference, the young man deftly excused himself.

"Are you enjoying the party?" Somerville asked them.

"It is perfect," Lilliana assured her brother.

Somerville looked to Atlas. "I felt a more elaborate celebration was in order to be truly worthy of a duke's daughter."

Atlas surveyed the numerous vases of fresh flowers, thousands of glittering candles, and the dozens of guests. "More elaborate than this?"

"Naturally. I was prepared to host a ball for five hundred, but Roslyn would not hear of it. She insisted upon something small and private."

Atlas cast a grateful look at Lilliana. "Whatever the lady desires."

"As to the house I will be gifting you, you will require a minimum of twenty servants in order to run Mallon Place efficiently. The duchy will, of course, cover those expenses."

Atlas was about to protest, but Lilliana spoke first. "That is incredibly generous of you Matthew." She was likely the only person in London to call her brother by his Christian name. "However, Atlas and I would like to choose our own home. Perhaps something new. I have never lived in a newly constructed home."

"Something new?" Somerville's mouth twisted as though his sister had just suggested she intended to reside in a hut. "But whatever for? I have plenty of properties for you to choose from."

"I rather fancy the idea of a brand new house after living in old piles for my entire life." Lilliana's smiling gaze met Atlas's. "It would be a fresh start for us in every way."

"Whatever the lady desires," Atlas repeated. The idea of purchasing a home for his new family filled him with pleasure. At the age of three-and-thirty, he was finally putting down roots.

Excitement glittered in Lilliana's eyes. "I have seen that they are building new homes where the Duke of Bedford's mansion once stood."

"You intend to reside in Bloomsbury?" Somerville looked pained. "There is a reason Bedford relocated to the West End."

Lilliana smiled brightly. "I rather like Bloomsbury. It is less stuffy than Mayfair."

Somerville threw up his hands. "You must do as you like. I suppose I shall have to think of another wedding gift," the duke said as he wandered away.

"Are you certain that you would prefer to live in Bloomsbury?" Atlas asked after Somerville had gone. "Perhaps you would be more comfortable in Mayfair."

She took his arm. "Can you be content in Bloomsbury?"

He squeezed her hand. "I shall be happy wherever we live, so long as you and the boys are by my side. My days of traveling are over."

She looked aghast. "I certainly hope not!"

"Why is that?" Her reaction confused him. "Do you fancy having a husband who is away a great deal of the time?"

"Not at all. But I also should not like for you to give up things that are important to you."

"There is nothing more important than the family we are creating."

"Perhaps when you finally do go to India, I shall accompany you," she said.

He regarded her with surprise. "But what of the boys?"

"We could engage a tutor and take them with us."

They came to a closed door, and he realized Lilliana had been directing him to this destination. She had a glint in her eye. "I have a betrothal gift for you as well."

"That is not necessary."

"I wanted to." She pushed open the door, and they were in a room surrounded by maps and globes.

"What is this place?" he asked.

"The Map Room."

"Naturally," he remarked. "I should have assumed the duke would have a room dedicated entirely to maps."

She led him over to the table. And there, laid out before him, was a perfectly put-together puzzle of Lilliana. But it was not the usual formal portrait. The woman in the painting was smiling and unguarded, her eyes warm and open. This was the Lilliana most of the world never saw. It took his breath away.

"Matthew commissioned it months ago. However, after you and I became betrothed, I thought you might like to have it," Lilliana explained. "I took it to your mapmaker on Regent Street, and he transformed the painting into one of your puzzles to your exact specifications."

"How did you know where to take it?"

"I asked Jamie."

"I am surprised the boy managed to keep a secret from me." He admired the painting of his beloved. "It is perfect."

"Since your last puzzle was of death, I thought you might like something a little less dark."

"It is beautiful. As are you." He took her into his arms. "And I am the most fortunate of men."

Author's Note

Murder at the Opera was loosely inspired by the infamous 1779 murder of Martha Ray, a talented singer and the longtime mistress of the fourth Earl of Sandwich.

Martha and the earl lived together for sixteen years before she was murdered outside of Covent Garden by a young male admirer. Some have suggested that Martha was intimately involved with James Hackman, the soldier turned ordained minister who killed her. Unfortunately, some retellings of the crime blame the victim, casting Martha as a sinful woman who bewitched an innocent man. Other accounts suggest Ray's murderer stalked her before the killing.

I am grateful to the author Louise Allen, who was kind enough to send me a print copy of her book *Walks Through Regency London*. I followed Louise's detailed walking tours during my research trip to London in May 2018.

I love to hear from readers and am very fortunate that reader Polly Brockway knows a thing or two about plants and flowers. She—in consultation with horticultural expert Dr. Michael Dirr—helped ensure that any references to horsechestnuts, horsechestnut trees, and other plants in *Murder at the Opera* are reasonably accurate. Any errors are my own.

The unique windows with mirrored shutters in Lord Balfour's home in *Murder at the Opera* were modeled after ones found in the Waterloo Gallery at London's Apsley House, home to the first Duke of Wellington and his descendants. Once I witnessed how those shutters work, I couldn't resist featuring such a clever hiding place in *Murder at the Opera*. If you're ever in London and have an opportunity to visit Apsley House, I highly recommend that you seize the chance.

Finally, thank you as always, dear Reader and Friend, for taking the time to spend a few hours in Atlas and Lilliana's company. I hope you've enjoyed reading about their adventures as much as I've enjoyed writing them.